The S
of T

BAEN BOOKS by P.C. HODGELL

The Sea of Time

P.C. Hodgell

THE SEA OF TIME

A Baen Books Original

Baen Publishing Enterprises
P.O. Box 1403
Riverdale, NY 10471
www.baen.com

ISBN: 978-1-4767-3649-5

Cover art by Eric Williams
Maps by P.C. Hodgell

First Baen printing, June 2014

Distributed by Simon & Schuster
1230 Avenue of the Americas
New York, NY 10020

Library of Congress Cataloging-in-Publication Data

Hodgell, P. C. (Patricia C.)
 The sea of time / P. C. Hodgell.
     pages cm
 ISBN 978-1-4767-3649-5 (trade pb)
 1. Imaginary wars and battles—Fiction. I. Title.
 PS3558.O3424S43 2014
 813'.54—dc23

                                                          2014009922

10 9 8 7 6 5 4 3 2 1

Pages by Joy Freeman (www.pagesbyjoy.com)
Printed in the United States of America

In memory of
Diana Wynne Jones
1934–2011
A fantasy writer without equal

CONTENTS

THE SOUTHERN WASTES

THE DEEP GRIMLY
WEALD HOLT
HATHIR

THE EBONBANE

BASHTI

THE SILVER

THE AMAR

KARKINAROTH

KOTHIFIR
ESCARPMENT
THE TARDY

GEMMA
BETWIXT APOLLYNE
VALLEY MOUNTAINS
HURLEN

NEKRIEN

SASHWAR

URAKARN

THE TENEBRAE

URAKS

DRY SALT SEA
LANGADINE

THE WASTER HORDE

THE BARRIER

PERIMAL DARKLING

HILLS
FORESTS
MOUNTAINS
SAND DUNES
ROCKY PLAINS

0   50   100   150
MILES

P. C. HODGELL '13

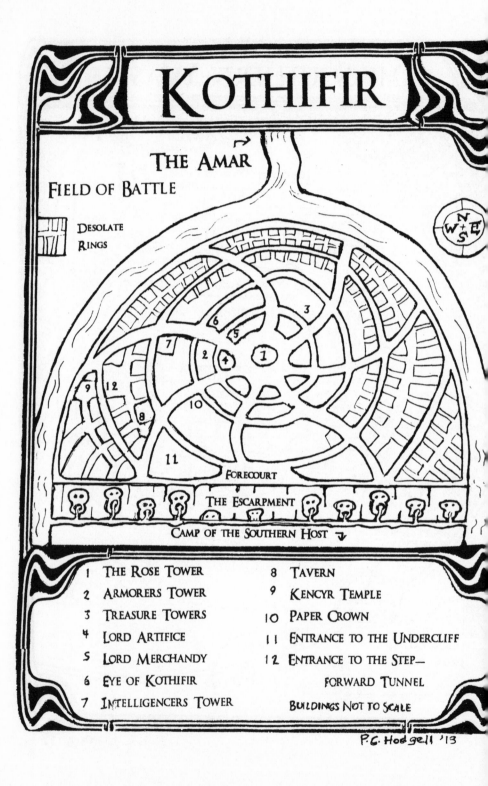

KOTHIFIR

THE AMAR

FIELD OF BATTLE

DESOLATE
RINGS

FORECOURT

THE ESCARPMENT

CAMP OF THE SOUTHERN HOST ⤓

1 THE ROSE TOWER	8 TAVERN
2 ARMORERS TOWER	9 KENCYR TEMPLE
3 TREASURE TOWERS	10 PAPER CROWN
4 LORD ARTIFICE	11 ENTRANCE TO THE UNDERCLIFF
5 LORD MERCHANDY	12 ENTRANCE TO THE STEP—
6 EYE OF KOTHIFIR	FORWARD TUNNEL
7 INTELLIGENCERS TOWER	BUILDINGS NOT TO SCALE

P.C. Hodgell '13

CAMP OF THE SOUTHERN HOST

KOTHIFIR

ESCARPMENT

LIFT CAGES

COMMANDANT'S OFFICES

INNER WARD

(MARKET)

STABLES

STABLES

CAINERON

KNORTH

BRANDAN

JARAN

ARDETH

COMAN

EDIRR

RANDIR

DANIOR

AMAR

AMAR

SOUTH GATE

TRAINING
FIELDS

BRIDGE

TRAINING
FIELDS

P.C. Hodgell '13

PROLOGUE

A Knock on the Door

Kothifir: Summer 45

"JAMETHIEL PRIEST'S-BANE."

The Knorth randon balanced the words on his tongue as if trying, dubiously, to taste them. "Queer sort of a name, don't you think?"

"Very queer," his fellow officer agreed.

"I mean, who would name a child after the Dream-weaver, given all the trouble that she caused? And why 'Priest's-bane'?"

His friend shrugged off the latter and the god that it implied. "Our priests go their way. We go ours. I hear, though, that the Highborn were marvelously put out."

They contemplated this as they leaned on the rail of a third-story balcony outside their quarters in the Knorth barracks. It was late afternoon. The smell of dinner drifted up from the kitchen and a clatter of plates rose from the mess hall. The grassy quadrangle below had fallen into shadow. Opposite them stood the limestone bulk of the barracks' south side. Beyond its ramparts, the ground dipped to reveal the red tile roofs of the Ardeth and beyond that, those of the Randir, all marching down to the South Gate which opened into the training fields and the Betwixt Valley. To the west were the Caineron, the Jaran, and the Edirr; to the east, the Brandan, Coman, and tiny Danior, tucked into an outer wall whose curve followed the eastern arm of the encircling River Amar.

This, then, was the Southern Host's garrison at the foot of the Great Escarpment, in the shadow of Kothifir, its paymaster.

1

Oddly enough, the Host persisted in calling such a substantial collection of architecture their camp, as if at any minute they might pack up and march away.

There was more than a hint of ambivalence there, thought the first officer, whose name was Spare. The Kencyrath had been given a great task by the Three-Faced God, to defeat the forces of Perimal Darkling, ancient of enemies. Instead, their deity had abandoned them and they had been forced backward down the Chain of Creation from threshold world to world, ending up here on Rathillien—for no greater purpose than to sell their swords to a local god-king?

Oh, Spare understood the necessity well enough. His people had been ceded the Riverland, far to the north, but it had proved too poor to meet their needs. And they had been on Rathillien such a long time—three thousand-odd years—that their original purpose had long since been put aside in favor of mere survival. Even Torisen Black Lord, Highlord of the Kencyrath, had had to send nearly half of his forces south to Kothifir to support his Riverland base, without which he could not maintain control over the fractious houses under his dominion.

It wasn't right that he and his fellow Knorth should be sent so far from their lord, thought Spare, not for the first time. Torisen held his followers lightly, not wanting to intrude on their lives any more than was necessary—not, of course, that any of them wished to be gripped as tightly as, say, Lord Caineron did his house. At such a distance, however, the bond sometimes trembled, giving rise to unwanted doubts. Now here was another one.

"Blackie has made this Jamethiel his heir," he said, testing the idea as he had the name, uncertain of both. "His long-lost sister, a Highborn lady—well, a girl, actually."

"I know. And he sent her to Tentir."

"Which she survived."

Both considered their own first year at the randon college, the culls, the camaraderie, the challenges. Only the best made it through.

"They say that she redeemed the Shame of Tentir by reclaiming the Whinno-hir Bel-tairi."

"How?"

"No one knows. She just showed up one day at the college with the mare under saddle, then rode off with the lost Randir

Heir, Randiroc. And she trained with Bear. And she threw Lord Caineron's uncle Corrudin out a window. And she killed a Randir tempter with a swarm of bees. And she defeated Caldane's heir, riding a rathorn. Lord Caineron can't have wanted her to graduate from the college at all. How could she with his war-leader in place as Tentir's Commandant?"

This in some ways was the biggest mystery of all. Sheth Sharptongue must have been under great pressure to fail the Knorth's unlikely heir, and from the sound of it she had given him plenty of opportunities. Yet rumor said that he had been solely responsible in the last cull for letting her pass. Sheth might be a Caineron, but his skills and integrity were legendary throughout the randon community. He would never have supported a cadet whom he believed unworthy.

"Where d'you suppose she is now?" asked Spare.

"Probably still presenting her credentials to Commandant Harn. Her contingent of second-year cadets, all eighty-odd of them, should be here any time now. In fact," he added, harkening to the sound of voices coming down the public road beyond the barrack's western wall, "that may be them now."

Movement below drew their attention as figures spilled out of the Knorth barracks into the quadrangle. Ten, twenty, thirty...

"That's the entire third-year class," said Spare's friend, leaning over the rail to look.

Thanks to the great battle at the Cataracts two years ago, an entire class of first-year cadets had either been killed or promoted on the field. Thus they had missed half of their year at the randon college, but had gained a glorious blooding against the Waster Horde. Established randon found them a bit roughedged and aggressive, but very proud of the distinction that battle had given them.

Now they rushed forward to close and lock the garrison's double gates.

"Now that..." Spare began, but halted as he sensed a presence behind him. A moment later the barracks' commander appeared at his elbow.

He and his friend made way for her at the rail, exchanging glances over her gray, short-cropped head. Ran Onyx-eyed spoke to neither of them, but she was usually silent. No one tended to remember that her given name was Marigold. Rather it was her still, dark gaze that captured attention—that, and her mask-like face. One never knew what she was thinking. It was most disconcerting.

Below, the third-year cadets were tumbling building blocks in front of the inner door. The barracks had suffered considerable decay during Ganth Gray Lord's long exile, before his son Torisen had risen to claim his place three years ago. Scaffolding rose on either side of the inner gate, bearing more stones to reinforce the southern wall.

Voices sounded out in the road:

"K-*north*! K-*north*! K-*north*!"

Was that a cheer or a jeer?

The randon above waited to see what the newcomers would do when they found themselves shut out of their new quarters. After a certain amount of confusion beyond the wall, the outer door swung slowly open.

"Maybe they forgot to lock it," said Spare's friend.

"Maybe." Spare felt a stir of excitement. "D'you remember what happened at Gothregor when the ladies tried to lock the Highlord out of the Women's Halls?"

"No. What?"

"Wait and see."

Into the expectant silence fell a sound. Someone was politely knocking on the inner door.

Its portals began to swing ponderously open. The stone blocks in the way were shoved back, digging into the grass, tumbling aside. A slim figure, hardly more than a child to Kendar eyes, stood on the threshold in the widening gap, silhouetted by lances of dying sunlight. And still the gate opened.

"'Ware the scaffolding," breathed Spare.

Wood hit wood, and the builders' framework splintered. Stones came thundering down. The third-year cadets retreated while officers burst out of the barracks to stare at the billowing dust. At last the cacophony dwindled to a trickling of sand and someone in the midst of the cloud coughing. The Highlord's sister emerged waving dust away from her face.

"Er..." she said to all the waiting faces. "Sorry."

"Huh," said Ran Onyx-eyed.

CHAPTER I
Kothifir

Summer 55

I

HALFWAY TO THE TOP, the lift cage shuddered to a stop and hung, swaying, on its ropes. Leather-winged birds flitted around it, jeering through sharp teeth. The morning sun poured between its bars like molten gold, bright and hot, and wood creaked.

The cage's sole occupant swore.

Through the slatted floor under her feet, Jame could see the garrison of the Southern Host spread out like a toy city at the foot of the cliff. There was the inner ward, there the quadrilateral, red-roofed barracks of each Kencyr house. Antlike dots moved through the streets with deceptive slowness. How high up was she? One thousand feet? Two? Kendar had warned her, with a shudder, that it was nearly three thousand to the top of the Escarpment at this point, not counting Kothifir's towering spires above that. At least she didn't suffer from the Kendars' inbred fear of heights—not that dangling here on a few strands of hemp was exactly reassuring.

Commandant Harn's headquarters were somewhere within the office block north of the inner ward. Jame remembered her reception there ten days ago, how the burly man had fidgeted around the room, bumping into furniture, avoiding her eyes.

"Ah, Jameth . . . er, Jame. So you've come at last, all the way from the Riverland. Have a nice trip?"

Such a stiff, wary greeting, as if they hadn't spent most of a year under the same roof at Tentir.

And speaking of cool receptions, what was she to make of Ran Onyx-eyed?

"Do you wish to take command of the barracks?" the woman had asked. "Such, after all, is your prerogative as the Knorth Lordan."

Did the Kendar want to shift responsibility to her, or did she resent a newcomer's claim, or was she truly as indifferent as she seemed? That smooth, bland face had given Jame no clue.

"Uh," she had said, "please continue to run the barracks for the time being."

The last thing Jame wanted was a raft of new administrative chores. Was she shirking her duty? Perhaps, as at Tentir when she had left her five-commander Brier Iron-thorn in charge of the barracks there. If so, she was worse than Timmon at sliding out of duties. There had always seemed to be more important things for her to do, though, and as the Knorth Lordan she had been allowed more freedom than most cadets.

But *"This is Kothifir, not Tentir,"* Harn had warned her. *"Watch yourself."*

Her gaze shifted to the training fields beyond the camp walls and the encircling arms of the Amar where her own ten-command was currently practicing with javelins, as she would have been too, without special permission to visit the city.

Dar, Mint, Killy, Erim, Rue, Quill, Niall, Damson, Brier...

Jame knew the names of the other second-year cadets as well, of course, and now would have to learn those of the third-years. Their leader, she gathered, was that sullen boy named Char. There were the Knorth randon officers as well. Tori knew all of them, and a thousand more besides.

Beyond the training fields was the Betwixt Valley, laced fresh green with irrigation ditches branching off from the Amar south of where its east and west branches rejoined. Beyond that rose the dusky, terraced slopes of the Apollyne mountain range. Jame wasn't high enough to see over the latter to the Wastes beyond, where the rain stopped and the true desert began. However, a glittering veil of golden dust seemed to be drawn across the southern sky behind the peaks' dark silhouettes. What lay in those desolate, wide-flung expanses? Would she be able someday to see for herself?

The cage jolted down a foot, making her stagger. Its ropes groaned.

A fine thing, Jame thought crossly, gripping the bars for balance, *to have come all this way only to be dropped on my head.*

Perhaps she should have taken one of the stairs that snaked up the limestone cliff face, carved out of it. So many steps, though, in her new dress grays with a crisp linen *cheche* wrapped about her tightly braided hair... To arrive breathless, exhausted, and sweat-soaked on her first visit Overcliff—no, thank you.

Another lift cage, this one enclosed such as the Kendar preferred, ascended smoothly beside her. Should she have taken it instead? It cost more, however, and Jame wasn't yet comfortable with having money to spend. A small portion of her new allowance hung in a pouch at her side, tapping her hip as the cage swayed. How was she to know what each coin was worth in trade? They weren't mere toys anymore for her blind hunting ounce Jorin to chase.

Ah. The cage rose again, by fits and starts.

Here caves breached the sheer cliff-face and exhaled cool air in her face through swaying vines. Faces were carved in high relief around many openings—past god-kings, perhaps, or portraits of the engineers who had designed Kothifir. Some looked proud, others merely bored. Through their yawning lips she glimpsed the jagged honeycomb of the Undercliff. Plumes of water fell from some cave mouths, also thicker jets from either end of the three-mile-wide semicircular moat that surrounded the city, bracketing it with rainbows. All were fed by the Amar, which approached Kothifir from the north. One couldn't see it from here, of course, but it was said to be the biggest river short of the Silver to feed into the southern lands.

At last here was the lip of the Escarpment. The crane swung her cage over the balustrade and it bounced to rest on Kothifir's limestone-paved forecourt. A squat, sun-darkened Kothifiran opened the gate.

"So," he said in Rendish, with a flash of crooked white teeth. "Did missy enjoy her ride? Not that such a featherweight as you is any chore, but next time, maybe the heavier lift for comfort? Yes?"

Jame glanced at the grinning winch-men. So that had been their game, angling for a higher fee. She had already paid at the cliff's foot. Fishing a small coin out of her pouch as a tip, she flipped it to the proprietor.

"For your courtesy. Have you considered installing a trap door?"

"Oh, we already have that, for those who try to shortchange us."

Looking back at the cage, Jame saw that he spoke the truth. No wonder the floor had seemed so unsteady. She extracted another coin. "On account," she said, tossing it to the winch-men, and walked off to their crack of laughter.

The city opened out to her at the foot of a broad, curving avenue. Here on the ground level, shops with brightly hued awnings lined the way, offering all kinds of food stuffs from purple eggplants to white radishes, from ruby tomatoes to sacks of golden wheat. Albino crickets sang in shaded cages. River fish gaped in tubs. Hung sheep carcasses seemed to move under a pelt of flies. Spices laced the hot morning air, their fragrance mingling with that of fresh baked bread and spilt blood. Jame breathed the mixture with delight. She had neither seen nor smelled such a wealth of Rathillien's riches since her days in Tai-tastigon.

Just as enchanting in their own way were the bustling throng of shoppers. The average Kothifiran clearly liked bright colors and wore them with abandon, in pleasing contrast to their copper skins and black hair. The natives tended to be short and squat verging on fat, but brisk and lively in their movements with sparkling dark eyes. Some were taller and fairer, though, with auburn hair, and there were even a few rare blonds. Among them passed the occasional minor noble, borne shoulder-high in a litter whose fluttering pastel curtains gave a glimpse of an unnaturally pale face peering out disdainfully.

Such arrogance was matched by the silent visages of desert dwellers come to town to tend their shabby stalls. Only their eyes showed. The rest was wreathed by the voluminous folds of indigo blue *cheches* at least twice the length of the one that Jame wore.

We know a secret, their withdrawn faces seemed to say.

Jame wondered what it was.

For all the avenue's dash and glitter, however, the eye was drawn upward toward Kothifir's famous "Painted Towers," half obscured by lines of fluttering, bright flags and, higher up, by no less colorful laundry. Jame saw now that most of these towers were actually faced with travertine, limestone, and marble ranging in color from white to tan to moss green to rose to black. Some featured solid blocks in geometric patterns. Others were faced with mosaic tiles depicting faces, animal masks, crests, and other obscure symbols. It made one's head spin to take in their lively variety even lit as they were by filtered sunshine, for wispy clouds cut off many towers some ten stories up. Rents in the cover let through shafts of light and gave filmy glimpses of the heights above, gold, bronze and verdigris copper, laced together by catwalks, bridges, and buttresses.

Odd, thought Jame, craning to look up. She had observed no such cloud cover from below; but then one couldn't see the city proper from the foot of the Escarpment.

She felt a fumbling at her side and, reaching down, grabbed the hand that was trying to loosen the strings of her purse. A small face crowned with a mop of curly chestnut hair gazed up at her reproachfully, pouting.

"You weren't supposed to catch me."

"I can see that."

"We saw it too."

The last speaker sauntered toward Jame, backed by two followers, and the shoppers parted before them, murmuring. All three wore livery composed of gilded hauberks over russet linen tunics and carried truncheons swinging from their belts. Their eyes were fixed on the boy.

"Do you know what we do to unlicensed thieves, brat? See those drain caps set in the pavement? They lift up, and underneath are dank holes in the earth, full of nasty things, all the way down to the Amar. Just last week we dropped a boy little older than you down one for stealing fruit. Shall we see if you snag on the way or if the river spits you out into the valley?"

A stout, middle-aged man bustled out of the crowd and seized the child's other hand. "Here now, Byrne, haven't I warned you not to play with strangers? Your pardon, lady. Today my grandson wants to be a pickpocket. Tomorrow it will be something else."

The leader of the men drew himself up, an ominous glitter in his eyes. "We caught him red-handed, Master Iron Gauntlet. You know the punishment."

"Now, boys, I know you too. Has service to Lord Artifice—may the Change preserve him—altered you so much that you would make sport of an infant and an old man?"

The two subordinates shifted uneasily, not meeting his reproachful gaze. In their place, Jame couldn't have either; with a few words, the elder man had reduced the younger to guilty children. Not so their leader.

"My Lord Artifice"—and here he defiantly touched thumb to

forehead in salute—"is not sentimental, like some. He believes in the honor of his craft, and in his men."

"As well he might, to be sure, and so do I, but since when has he taken over the judicial duties of Master Cut-Purse?"

"I wasn't robbed, you know," Jame put in mildly.

The three ignored her.

The boy, also ignored, craned to look up at her. "May I kick them in the shins?" he asked.

"Unnatural child, no. Besides, my boots are bigger than yours."

The boy's grandfather gave them both an amused glance. "Hush. Now, do you really want to seize this baby? What would all of these good people think of you if you did?"

The three looked around, suddenly aware that they were at the center of an attentive, not very friendly crowd. The leader turned on his heel and bulled his way out of the circle. The other two followed him, looking rather sheepish. With that, the spectators broke up, either to discuss what they had just seen or, for the minority, to return to their own business.

The older man turned to smile at Jame. "We haven't been introduced. I'm Gaudaric, Iron Gauntlet of the Armorers' Guild."

As his broad, calloused hand gripped her own slim, gloved one, Jame thought that despite his age he looked quite capable of such a demanding profession. If need be, those muscular arms should serve him well in any fight.

"Jame, a second-year randon cadet."

"By that white *cheche*, I judge that you're rather more than that."

"I suppose so." Jame eased the unfamiliar headgear where its tight folds pinched across her brow. He too wore white, she noted, in the form of a silk sash tied over richly dyed but practical leathers. "The Highlord of the Kencyrath is my brother. I'm his lordan. Who is this Lord Artifice and why does he hate you so much?"

Gaudaric sighed and rubbed his bald pate, ruffling its surrounding fringe of gray hair. "For no good reason, I should say. His given name is Ruso, a former pupil of mine who wanted not only my trade secrets but also my daughter, when she had chosen elsewhere. As for the title, you must be new in town."

"Very. I'm here to meet King Krothen."

"Are you?" He gave her a considering look, then began to walk, towing Byrne after him. "I'll show you the way."

"I want a sugared fig!" declared the boy, trying to free himself.

"Will you behave yourself this time? Then go."

They walked on as Byrne darted from stall to stall, circling back to beg for an orange, a date, a candied newt. Half of the time his fond grandfather indulged him.

"My only grandchild," Gaudaric said proudly, "although I hope for more. It does one good to see our city through new eyes. Beautiful, isn't it?"

Jame agreed, eyeing an intricate, tessellated mosaic that gave the illusion of looking into a stately apartment. Changing light hinted at elegant figures moving about in its depths, then at wandering beasts in a forest. How could mere stone achieve such subtlety?

"About Lord Artifice...?"

"It would help if you understood our guild structure. Know anything about guilds in general?"

"A bit," said Jame, remembering her days in Tai-tastigon as apprentice to the eccentric master thief Penari. How distant those shining nights seemed now. "Masters, journeymen, apprentices. Lots of rules and infighting," she said, remembering the vicious guild wars in which she had been involved. "One big scrappy, happy family, not very tolerant of outsiders."

"Do you know what we do to unlicensed thieves, brat?" A figure sprawling on the Mercy Seat, its skin splayed out like a heavy cloak. *"Steal a peach, steal a plum, see to what your carcass comes..."*

Gaudaric nodded. "You've got the basic flavor of it, if not all the nuances of political spice."

"Including Iron Gauntlet and Master Cut-Purse?"

"Indeed. Each guild needs a grandmaster, after all. Paper Crown, Leather Hood, Silk Purse, Intelligencer, Scalpel, Pliers... I lose track, but there must be a hundred at least, many with sub-chapters. Beyond that, all guilds are divided into crafts, merchants, and professions."

"Those who make things, those who sell them, those who profit by their individual skill. Hence Lord Artifice?"

"Yes, may the Change be kind to him. The Armorers' Guild was honored by his rise and no, I'm not the least bit jealous of it, whatever he thinks. Also there are Lord Merchandy and Lady Professionate."

"That's the second time you've mentioned some sort of Change."

Gaudaric shrugged this off. "Ah, never mind. It's ill fortune to speak of such things."

With that he started pointing out civic features as they passed them like a tour guide. Jame put aside her questions for the moment and listened. She had already noticed that the city was divided into four to five rings, crossed by the curved spokes of the avenues, further subdivided by streets and alleys. Buildings in the outer rings were quadrilateral, composed of obtuse and acute angles to fit the curve of the street, at least for those structures that still stood.

"We used to be a much larger city," said Gaudaric wistfully. "Three times as many people lived here when the Salt Sea was still fresh, before the desert came."

Jame remembered the scrollsman Index's words as reported by her cousin Kindrie. "That was during Rathillien's Fifth Age, some three thousand years ago, correct?"

"Just so. Now the outermost rings are mere ruins, their stones quarried to build up the innermost. Kothifir is a shell of what it once was."

As they approached the city's heart, the edges of buildings were rounded off more and more until the towers became ovals, their summits disappearing into the clouds. These last appeared to be privately owned, probably by rich merchants and minor nobility. Certainly, they were more ornate than their fellows. Gardens now occupied the spaces between them while vines climbed their walls and balconies blazed with flowers.

The avenue swerved again, and debouched on the edge of a central plaza filled with more stalls and teeming with shoppers. Here, all the avenues met—Jame counted seven. Over the noisy throng, in the center of the square, loomed the only round tower she had yet seen in Kothifir, although it was aggressively asymmetrical. With its recessed floors, it looked a bit like an inverted tornado ascending into the clouds, with a dizzying twist to its structure. It was made of white and pink marble. Carved roses climbed its window frames and the balusters of its circling, open spiral stair, giving it a lacy, almost insubstantial appearance.

"That's the Rose Tower," said Gaudaric proudly. "You'll find His Magnificence at the top of it."

Jame thanked him, promised to look in on his shop, and pushed through the crowd to the foot of the spiral stair.

The lower floors were occupied by servants. Jame passed doors and windows opening into domestic spaces, kitchens billowing with fragrant herbs, bedchambers mostly empty at this time of day, and watch rooms where guards sat playing at dice. Children ran up and down the stair shouting to each other, shouted at in turn by their harried mothers. Tradesmen came and went.

Her legs ached by the time she left the bustle of life behind and neared the level of the clouds. They appeared solider than they had from the ground, and darker. Soon she was enveloped in their twilight world. Thinner patches revealed other towers curiously drained of color.

Now the mist was growing lighter above her, and a moment later she emerged into dazzling sunlight beating fiercely on the fleecy backs of clouds. The latter slowly circled the Rose Tower and spread out to a hazy horizon—again, something that she had not seen from below. Here the tallest structures ended in glistening domes and spires, or in rooftop gardens.

Another turn of the stair brought Jame to two pikesmen guarding the way.

"I have an appointment with His Magnificence, King Krothen," she told them.

They looked down their noses at her. Perhaps Krothen chose his servants for their height, or for the length and hairiness of their nostrils.

After a pause and a sniff, however, they let her pass.

Here was a floor with filmy curtains blowing out the windows. Through them, Jame glimpsed an apartment of almost overwhelming elegance. Krothen's?

Another twist of the stair, and she found herself at the top of the Rose Tower, in a circular room some seventy feet wide. The floor was paved with pale green, golden veined chalcedony. Petals of pink marble carved so fine that the sun glowed through them made up the walls. A thin, hot breeze edged around the overlapping folds. It was like being in the heart of a giant, overheated rosebud sculpted out of stone.

Through this roseate light scurried servants, carrying musical instruments, bowls of flowers, and tray upon tray of delicacies. Half-naked acrobats tumbled among them, disregarded. Clowns pranced.

Others more somberly clothed stood like pillars amidst this rout, ignoring it. Some appeared to be officials; others, foreign emissaries. One was a thin, elderly man in a midnight blue robe spangled with silver stars. Jame recognized a high priest when she saw one. After all, Krothen was a god-king.

Where, however, was he? Presumably, taking a break from his duties. When he arrived, perhaps he would recline on that dais piled high with silken pillows near his high priest.

Then the mound shifted.

A head perched on top of it, wearing a snowy turban. Heavily lidded hazel eyes regarded her speculatively across the room out of rolls of fat. Beneath that, rosebud lips pursed over a fringe of ginger beard which in turn was mounted on too many chins to count. Trinity, was that all him, beneath that sprawl of white damask? He shifted again and released a muted, subterranean fart. Incense covered the smell, but not that of so much over-heated flesh.

Krothen, God-King of Kothifir, selected a candied slug from a plate held out to him by a lackey and popped it into the moist hole that was his mouth. As he chewed and swallowed, Jame saw that the dais on which he reclined hovered a foot above the floor and that the hems of his robes floated about him as if in a slow ocean current. Here was a god-king indeed.

An emissary clothed in layers of white lace stood before him, impatiently waiting to capture the monarch's wandering attention.

"Ahem," he said. "Sire, we understand that you have a complaint against our fair Rim city of Gemma."

"Yes." Krothen's voice was a surprising nasal tenor, as if all of that fat had pinched his throat into a thin pipe. "Gemman raids on our trade caravans have increased of late. We understand that your governing council now sells letters of marque to such enterprising bandits."

"They have official sanction, yes, which you refuse to recognize."

Krothen opened his eyes as wide as their surrounding rolls of fat allowed. "My dear man, we never agreed to any such code."

"You should. It would be the civilized thing to do, given that it guarantees humane treatment for any captives."

"But we never raid you. Given that, why should we consent to being robbed?"

"At least let us ransom our captive raiders."

"Ah, but Gemma has nothing that Kothifir wants."

The emissary was turning red in the face with anger and frustration. "Someday your arrogance will be your downfall."

"Perhaps. In the meantime, any raider whom I catch will be hung from the thorns of my tower to the delight of the citizenry and any passing crow."

"And that is the message I should carry back to my masters?"

Krothen selected another morsel. "Carry what you please," he said, chewing with his mouth open.

The Gemman gave a stiff bow and retreated.

Jame was the next visitor in line. She cleared her throat nervously.

"Er . . . Sire, my brother, Lord Knorth of the Kencyrath, sends his greetings."

She gave the rolled parchment that contained her credentials to the majordomo, who handed it to a servant, who passed it to another, and another, and another. The high priest fastidiously flicked back an embroidered cuff to receive the scroll and presented it to his master. Krothen passed it from one plump hand to the other without looking at it, then to a lackey and so on around the circle, left to right, end over end, hand to hand, flip, flip, flip.

Now what? Jame wondered, receiving it back, its seal unbroken.

A commotion arose on the stair behind her.

Servants and minor priests alike hastily retreated to the edges of the room. Jame also withdrew, to be on the safe side. A contingent of ladies entered, one veiled, another in servant's attire. They were led by a noblewoman so haughty in her bearing that it took a moment to realize that she was very short, almost a dwarf, mounted on very high heels. Trailing after them all came a handsome young man, heavily made up and dressed in a frilly robe.

"So, Nephew," growled the short noblewoman in a surprisingly deep voice. Jame realized that this must be the redoubtable Princess Amantine, first lady of the court. "I understand that you have refused yet another match. Your half-sister Cella is, of course, heartbroken."

The veiled lady clapped hands over her face. She might have been crying. Then her fingers slipped and a crow of shrill laughter broke through them. The servant whacked her on the back, at which she gulped and stood still, if subtly aquiver.

"Heartbroken, I say!" boomed the princess, glowering at her.

Krothen spoke behind a plump hand to the priest.

"Your Mellifluous Highness," said the latter, with a respectful bow. "My lord wonders if Lady Cella's heart was truly in this proposal. It was his understanding that she prefers to play with her ... er ... doll."

The lady in question nodded so vigorously that her veil fluttered up, revealing a middle-aged face painted white, with buck teeth, protruding eyes, and no chin to speak of.

"Then go," Krothen said to her in a nasal, not unkind voice. "Play."

She gave a hoot of glee, grabbed the handsome boy by the hand, and scrambled off down the stairs, pursued by the servant. Two flights down they collided with someone. The new arrival could be heard lumbering up the stairs in their wake.

"Well!" said Amantine, drawing herself up and swaying ominously. "You still need an heir, Nephew. What will happen to this city after you are gone?"

"Where am I going, Aunt? Perhaps, like my father, I choose to stay."

The princess stomped, and lost her balance. Servants rushed to prop her up.

"What my brother Kruin did was a disaster to his family. Need I remind you that on the male side only you and my dear son Ton are left? Here he comes now, to receive your blessing."

A figure loomed, wheezing, in the doorway. Unable to enter it head-on, he turned sideways and sidled in, disarranging a coat of bright pink satin as rich as the frosting on a cake. While nowhere nearly as gross as Krothen, the newcomer could easily have made up three men, although he was hardly more than a boy.

"Cousin," he said, still breathing hard and sounding petulant. "Why you have to live ... at the top ... of a damned tower ..."

Krothen stopped him with a raised hand. "Please," he said. "Eat."

A servant offered the boy a platter of locust drizzled with honey.

"Ton-ton, no," said his mother sharply.

He waved her off, took a dripping insect, and defiantly jammed it into his mouth. Krothen ate another candied slug. Prince Ton grabbed two locusts. Everyone watched first one and then the other as the royal cousins continued to match each other, insect against mollusk.

Ton started to turn green. Cheeks bulging, insectile legs a bristle between plump lips, he made a frantic gesture. A lackey ran up to him carrying a golden bucket into which he was copiously sick. His mother led him away with a grip on his ear that steadied her as much as it chastised him. Those above could hear her scolding her son all the way down the stairs.

Krothen sighed and flipped a fat, dismissive hand at Jame.

As he scooped up the remaining slugs and shoveled them into his mouth, she turned to go, bemused. Had the god-king of Kothifir just winked at her?

◄◊◊◊ II ◊◊◊►

SEVERAL TURNS DOWN THE STAIR, out of sight from above and below, Jame paused, thinking. Her call on Krothen had only really been an excuse to visit the Overcliff; her true mission was as yet unfulfilled. In the spring she had sent her half-breed servant Graykin south ahead of her to gather information. He should know by now that she had reached the Host's camp and have reported to her, but no sign of him had she seen. The bond between them told her that he at least wasn't in severe distress. Instead she felt echoes of anger and frustration when she thought about him. However, would anyone tell the Knorth Lordan what she needed to know? It was time for a change—one she had been looking forward to for a long time.

Jame stripped off her gray dress coat and reversed it. The tailor who had sewn it had asked why she wanted a finished black lining, but she had only smiled. It was a poor substitute for the knife-fighter's *d'hen*, still stowed in her luggage, but at least it was the right color. Unwrapping the tight *cheche* came as a relief to her burnt, flaking forehead. She considered winding the cloth around her waist, but guessed from Gaudaric's white sash that to do so would mean something unintended, so instead she rolled it up and stuffed it into her jacket. From an inside pocket came a black cap. The gloves she already wore.

A sense of relief and release swept over her, as if at the shedding of too tight a garment. As much as she enjoyed being a randon cadet, this freedom was an older love.

"Welcome back, Talisman," she breathed.

No one had yet come up or down the tower, but someone was bound to soon. Were those voices ascending? Time to be gone.

She had stopped near one of the suspension bridges leading to the nearest palace complex above the clouds. She stepped off onto it over the fleecy backs of clouds. At its lowest point, wisps curled over the steps and it swung gently underfoot. A murmur rose from the plaza far below as if from a distant sea lapping around the Rose Tower's base.

The structure she approached now was another tower topped with an oversized cupola. The sun glowed off sheets of riveted copper and flashed from large, round windows like portholes, ringed with gold. A second smaller glass cupola sat on top like a blister, no doubt giving light to the chamber below. Smoke trickled up the brazen shoulders along with the sound of hammers. Inside, someone was bellowing.

"...of all the incompetent, block-headed fools..."

Jame stepped off the bridge onto a balcony. One of the round windows fronted it, its glass disc tilted open a crack vertically. She edged inside, emerging behind a high-backed chair which in turn was drawn up to a huge desk covered with paper work. Other tables around the circular room were piled high with scraps of disjointed armor and tools.

In the center of the room, a ruddy, bearded man in burnished half-armor over a white tunic was roaring at a cringing apprentice. His voice made all the surrounding metal ring. Some of it clanged to the floor and tried to crawl away.

"You sodding idiot, couldn't you see that you had the thing on backward?"

Between the two was a large dog in fully articulated plate armor, trying wretchedly to scratch itself. Not only was steel in the way, but also its front and rear legs appeared to have been transposed.

Jame's eyebrows raised. Itchy skin be damned. How could it even survive, configured like that?

The ruddy man grabbed the 'prentice and shook him until his cap tumbled over his eyes and his teeth chattered.

"Out of my sight, you...you loose screw!"

He flung the man away, straight into a hole against the opposite wall. A complicated, diminishing clatter followed—thumps and yelps generally associated with someone falling down a long flight of stairs.

Lord Artifice, for surely it was he, turned to consider the unfortunate canine.

"Now, how am I going to sort you out?"

He picked up a tool, knelt, and started popping rivets at the shoulder and hip seams. The steel torso came free. He lifted it off its framework and reversed it. There didn't appear to be a dog inside after all, only a dog-shaped hollow.

He patted its metal back, which rang hollowly. "Better? Now what's the matter?"

The creature, whatever it was, had begun to sniff and snarl—a curiously echoing sound within its metal shell. Its head swung toward the chair behind which Jame crouched, and it lunged toward her. Jame broke cover.

Ruso straightened with a roar, his red beard again abristle, emitting random sparks. "Who are you, skulking there? An assassin? Ha! Don't you know that you can't kill a guild lord?"

Jame kicked the oncoming creature, catching it in the snout and jarring its head askew. It came at her again, slantwise, and again she struck, this time knocking the unsecured torso off its legs, which continued to scrabble blindly forward. Ruso tried to grab her. She felt the heat of his body, but slid past with a water-flowing move that raised steam between them, and rushed down the stairs. Below, on a landing, a knot of people had gathered around the fallen apprentice, helping him up. Jame swerved to a window, thrust it open, and plunged out onto a lower balcony swallowed by the clouds. Here was another catwalk. Without hesitation, she took it. The shouts died behind her as if muffled with a steaming towel.

The world turned a ghostly gray out of which walls and blank windows loomed seemingly at random. A few showed furtive signs of life, but most appeared to be abandoned. Jame thought that she was moving westward, but soon wasn't so sure. Tower succeeded tower, first ovoid, then with corners. Some she skirted, others she entered by one window only to leave by the next. Interior spaces no longer corresponded to outer dimensions. A reed-thin tower could take what felt like forever to circumnavigate while a broad edifice might take mere steps to cross. All were dark, dusty, and dank, with simmering heat pressing down from above. The going underfoot became more and more decrepit. Window sills crumbled; floors sagged; catwalks creaked and splintered underfoot.

Something tugged unpleasantly at Jame's sixth sense, like a thread snagging a broken tooth. It wasn't the trail she had hoped for, but she followed it almost perforce, as if toward the stench of home.

In a great square of a tower open to the sky, the temple rose up out of shattered floors so that only its upper reaches were visible from above. These at first looked snapped off. Then one realized that they had never been finished. The air rising from within wavered with power as if with heat, causing the hair on the back of Jame's neck to prickle. So did a low, continuous vibration that made the dust at her feet skitter across the boards. This, then, was the Kothifir temple of the Three-Faced God of her own people, although avoided by all except its priests. Jame saw none of the latter, but assumed that they must be there somewhere, perhaps below: otherwise, the temple's power would have run amuck.

She remembered her first sight of the Tai-tastigon temple in its circle of devastation, in that city teeming with godlings. The Kencyrath was monotheistic, believing only in he (or she, or it) of the three faces who had bound the Three People together and set them against Perimal Darkling on the long path of so many bitter defeats down the Chain of Creation from threshold world to world. Rathillien was the last of these in that here the mysterious temple Builders had died, leaving this, their last work, incomplete and unstable. If the Kencyrath was forced to move on again, assuming it could, it would finally place itself beyond its god. Some might say, "Good!" But even Jame, who hated her absentee divinity, felt oddly naked at the thought of losing him forever.

Tai-tastigon's New Pantheon "gods" had turned out to owe their existence to the mindless excess energy of the Kencyr temple as shaped by the faith of their worshippers. Jame wondered if there were any gods here besides Krothen, although Ancestors knew there was enough of him to soak up any amount of power. The closest thing she had seen so far other than he was Lord Artifice. There, surely, was power of some sort.

Ironic, that only the natives of Rathillien seemed to benefit from the Three-Faced God. Perhaps on other worlds his power had helped the Kencyrath, but here it existed only as a threat to them.

Yet, was that entirely true? Jame sensed the patterns in it as they plucked at her nerves, muscles, and will. She had directed them before with the Great Dance such as the priests used, causing the explosive untempling of the Tastigon gods. She could dance them now as a potential Tyr-ridan, but only as the Third Face of God, That-Which-Destroys.

And what would you destroy this time, Jamethiel Priest's-bane?
Kothifir, the Kencyrath, yourself?

A foot shuffled on the debris behind her. Jame spun around
to confront a young, blond acolyte in a brown robe.

"Who are you?" he demanded. "Why are you spying on us?"
He peered at her more closely. "Why, you're Kencyr. That half-
breed sneak we've heard about, probably."

Jame didn't like being confused with Graykin, much less the
boy's snotty manner or the way he drew back as if to avoid
contact with something unclean. Then the floor gave slightly
underfoot. It felt rotten. The temple's rogue power must be gnawing continually at it.

The boy smiled. "I should let you fall. The next floor might
stop you, or maybe not. It's a long way down."

The spar of a rafter jutted out overhead. Jame sprang and
caught it just as the floor dropped away beneath her. The beam
felt none too solid either and gave an ominous crack. The boy
laughed. Jame launched herself at the doorway where he stood
and knocked him back through it into a mural stair. The rafter
snapped and plummeted like a spear. Angry shouts below greeted
its descent.

"Get off of me, you filth!" the boy snarled, wriggling under
her and scrabbling at her jacket front. His expression changed.
"Why, you're a girl!"

Jame reared back, driving a knee into his groin in the process.
"Surprise."

He was, she supposed, a year or two younger than she, but
that didn't excuse bad manners. Speaking of which...

"I suppose I had better greet your high priest while I'm here."

Sulky and limping, he led her down the mural stair past
doorways gaping on shattered floors and the looming blackness
within. It was the third Kencyr temple that Jame had seen, and
no two of them had been alike. The mysterious Builders seemed
to enjoy variety. This one resembled a sheer, black pyramid with
its top missing. A clutch of priests had gathered, exclaiming
angrily, at its foot around the fallen beam and the mound of
debris it had brought down. At least it hadn't landed on anyone,
as far as Jame could tell.

"Grandfather." The boy tugged at a black sleeve. "We have
company."

The high priest swung around and glared in Jame's general direction. His eyes, under tangled white brows, were clouded over with milky cataracts. How odd that he hadn't consulted one of the order's many healers. Perhaps none were available this far south. "And who might that be, eh?"

Jame offered him a half-hearted salute which, in any event, he couldn't see. "The Talisman, sir."

As soon as she spoke, she knew she had made a mistake.

"What, M'lord Ishtier's foe? Oh, we've heard all about you and the trouble that you caused in Tai-tastigon. Theocide. Nemesis. Well, I won't have any of that nonsense here. Leave, before I bring the rest of the roof down on you!"

His gnarled hands rose, clenched, and drew down power along with more wreckage. The others huddled close to the temple's flanks although they didn't dare touch them. The temple itself trembled and seemed for a moment to be less substantial.

The boy plucked at her jacket. "Leave," he hissed. "Before worse happens."

Jame retreated step by step, unwilling to turn her back on that sullen edifice. What worse could it do? How unstable was it, really, and did she really want to find out? Then she was out of the tower, free of the baleful thing that it contained and its churlish priests.

❧ III ☙

ONCE AWAY, Jame tried to clear her senses in order to pick up Graykin's trail again. It came to her, faintly, and she followed it back into the forest of ghostly towers.

Finally here was one that seemed, after a fashion, to be occupied. At least it had a door and, inside, dusty tapestries hung on the walls between the arched windows. Most of the weavings depicted shadowy figures with their backs turned although a few pale, hooded visages faced the room. A thicket of pillars held up the roof. As she entered, a murmur as if of conversation died.

"Hello?"

Only silence answered her, and flickers of movement seen out of the corner of her eyes. There were definitely people in the room, standing behind the pillars, shifting as she moved to stay out of sight.

"I'm looking for a Kencyr named Graykin," she told the room at large.

"So are we," replied a husky whisper at her elbow, making her jump. One of the gray figures had joined her. She could see half of his face under the hood—a sharp nose and a narrow chin, thin lips pursed as if at the taste of something nasty.

"How long has he been missing?"

"Fourteen days. Are you one of his clients?"

How to answer that? "We have done business before. Is this the Intelligencers' Hall?"

"It is."

Belatedly, it occurred to Jame that she didn't know what Graykin's relationship was to the spies' guild. If he hadn't registered with it, they might well be hunting him.

More gray figures detached themselves from the pillars and the wall to surround her. They smelled of dust and dank, like dirty linen. Now she could see them clearly direct on, but out of the corner of her eye the room appeared to be empty.

"Who speaks for you?" she asked.

"One who is not here. I will show you where he was last seen."

That confused Jame. "Where who was?"

The thin lips twisted without mirth. "The one whom you seek."

There seemed no answer to that except to follow her gray guide out of the room and down the stair that angled around the corners of the tower. They passed a door at each level, all shut, but by the dingy underwear hanging from balcony wash lines Jame guessed that the guild occupied the entire structure. She tried to keep her focus on the spy who led her as he flickered in and out of view. Her sense was that he was playing with her. Whatever Graykin's association with the guild, hers with him had gained her little credit.

At last they reached the ground on a dirty back street many rings removed from the city's colorful center.

"There," said her guide, indicating a wide circular hole in the roadway, its cover dragged to one side.

Jame peered into the depths. "The Undercliff?"

"Yes," he said, and pushed her in.

IV

JAME FELL HEADFIRST into darkness, trapped air snatching at her clothes. Close-set walls echoed back her startled cry. Above, the circle of light receded but, twisting, she saw a dim glow below. Its ghostly light shone on the bars of a ladder flashing past beside her. She reached for it. Its rungs rapped her knuckles sharply, then she caught it. The wrench nearly dislocated both shoulders. For a second she dangled there, breathing hard and scrabbling for a foothold, then her grip weakened and she fell again, onto a sloping pile of rubble at the ladder's foot.

Sweet Trinity. She would never take the mere falling down of stairs seriously again.

When she got her breath back, Jame propped herself up and looked around. She had come to rest against the wall of a huge cave. Light filtered into it through the vines curtaining its mouth. The shadowy, stalactite-fanged roof must have been a good two hundred feet up and it was nearly as wide side to side. Its floor, while undulating, gave the impression of having been cleared of all obstacles and trampled smooth.

A number of people had turned to witness her sudden descent. Their curiosity satisfied, they went back to work. Jame saw that she had fallen into a subterranean marketplace. As above, so below? Getting shakily to her feet, she limped over to the nearest stall where the merchant in charge handed her a tin of cold water.

"Dropping in on us, eh?"

Jame gratefully drained the cup. The water tasted strongly of iron. "Am I welcome?"

"So long as you don't come to spy."

Still collecting her wits, she inspected his wares. Very dingy they seemed—scraps of thin gray cloth, a vest, a codpiece.

"Woven only of the finest spider web," he said proudly, "and you know how strong that is. One of these strips will stop an arrow."

He named a price that made Jame blink. It seemed to be her day to meet armorers.

Besides his stall, she saw others selling such basic necessities as fuel and food, the latter rather dispirited, apparent rejects from the market above. Sprinkled among them were more wares native

to the Undercliff: multicolored mushrooms, small rock formations apparently intended to be shrines, and water bottled from
various subterranean pools. There were also sizable chunks of
diamantine softly aglow, priced quite cheaply for such a valuable
substance. The Undercliff seemed in general to cater as much to
the Overcliff as to its own inhabitants.

The distorted echo of music reached them from farther back
in the cave.

"Here they come," said the dealer. "Happy Vediafest."

Girls clad in yellow and black robes danced out of the shadow
of towering stalagmites playing pipes. As they neared, Jame saw
that each one was wreathed with similarly colored snakes, their
tails knotted together behind the girls' necks. Each also carried
a long wand at the end of which, tethered with a leash, fluttered
a bat. The snakes strained to reach it, coil and strike, coil and
strike. When one succeeded, cymbals clashed and the girls cried
out in triumph. Supplicants wriggled on the ground at their
heels, apparently hoping to see their particular bat caught. Jame
saw the bright clothes of Overcliffers and the sturdy cottons of
farmers among the drab Undercliffers. Some had obvious injuries;
others wore their suffering in their expressions or in the twist
of their wasted bodies.

In their midst came a litter carried shoulder high on which sat
the statue of a matronly woman festooned with stone serpents.

"Mother Vedia!" the stall holder called out to her as she passed.
"Grant good health to me and mine!"

"I didn't see anything like this above," Jame said.

"You wouldn't, not since King Kruin drove all the Old Ones
Undercliff. Seems he didn't want any rivals to his own godhood.
Well, his loss, our gain."

A girl with a bald, tattooed head darted through the celebrants
and stopped the litter. The statue quivered. Its surface, laced with
cracks and white dust, floated down as both woman and snakes
stirred to life. She rose, knelt to listen to her petitioner, then signaled her bearers to set her down. While the dancers continued
to thread back and forth between the booths, still singing, she
and the girl hurried off. On impulse, Jame returned the tin cup
to the merchant and followed them.

They climbed a chiseled stair and ducked into a side cave full
of limestone columns with space enough between them for two

dozen child-sized sleeping mats. The children themselves were clustered around an alcove at one end of the cave. Jame came up behind them to peer over their heads. In the alcove was a bed and on it lay a restive child with a blood-stained bandage wrapped around his head, supported by a lanky, ginger-haired young man, well endowed with pimples. The bald girl hovered nearby while the matron consulted with another young female, this one plump and blond, wearing a white tunic.

"I *told* you that my powers are limited Undercliff," said the latter, with the hint of a child's pout. "If Kroaky hadn't been so insistent, I never would have come. Mother Vedia, can *you* do any good here?"

The matron rubbed a hand over her face, smearing the dust there into a network of wrinkles which the limestone had glossed over. In general, she looked older and more dumpy than she had before as a statue. The snakes slithered restlessly over her plump form, in and out of her loose clothing. Two snapped at each other until she absentmindedly slapped them apart.

"I should have been called sooner, say, when the boy first fell."

"He seemed all right then," the bald girl said truculently, revealing filed teeth as she spoke and snapping off her words. Jame recognized her accent from the Cataracts. A Waster, here? "Then he was drowsy and complained of a headache. That was a week ago. Now we can't get him to rest."

The boy struggled in the young man's arms. "It hurts!" he whined.

Jame wondered if this was the unlicensed child-thief whom the guards had thrown down the drain.

Mother Vedia rested a hand on the boy's head. Her fingers sank down through hair and skin to the bone beneath, which she felt.

"He's lucky not to have split open his skull. As it is, he's merely cracked it. Now, which one..." She fumbled among a collection of small bottles that hung clinking from her belt. The snakes selected one. "Ah, yes. I can at least make him sleep. Now, drink up, little man."

The child tried to refuse, but the youth with ginger hair held his nose and ruthlessly poured the potion down his throat. Soon his thrashing quieted. The young man settled him back on the pallet, then raised hazel eyes to regard Jame over the intervening heads.

"And now, as for you..."

Jame found herself suddenly the focus of all eyes. The children scattered as the bald girl hurtled through them. Jame countered her charge with a water-flowing move that sent her stumbling among the columns. She came back with a knife in her hand.

"Who are you? What are you doing here?"

"I'm not a spy, but I am looking for one—Graykin by name. Have you seen him?"

Ginger slipped between them. "Hush, Fang," he said, in a nasal voice that Jame almost thought she recognized from sometime earlier that day. "Not everyone from above is an enemy. What is this man to you?" he asked Jame.

"A servant. If he imposed on your hospitality, I apologize for him. He can be...overzealous."

"And who are you?"

"Many things. Call me the Talisman."

The youth smiled, baring big, white teeth. "Well, then, call me Kroaky. Fang, my dear, he's your catch. Will you surrender him?"

The Waster glowered. "Don't call me 'dear.' Anyway, should we trust an Overcliffer?"

"She apparently trusts us." He indicated the ragged band of urchins who had spread out around Jame and were watching her closely. "Will you fight these, Talisman?"

"Not willingly. They look too fierce."

The children nudged each other and giggled.

Fang reluctantly sheathed her knife. "Well, all right. He's more trouble than he's worth, anyway."

She led Jame to the back of the cave and a hole in the floor, extending down into a bottle-necked cavity. Firelight glistened on water on its floor. The pit appeared empty, until a white face turned to peer up from the depths.

"Graykin?"

"Lady?" His voice echoed hollowly. "At last! Get me out of here!"

"Are you sure you want him?" asked Kroaky.

Jame sighed. "No, but he's my responsibility."

A coiled rope lay nearby, fixed at one end to a rock formation. Kroaky kicked it down the hole. The line went taut. Scrabbling and cursing came from below, then a thin, grimy hand groped over the stone lip. Jame seized it by the wrist and helped a scruffy figure to climb out.

Graykin shook out his wet robe, looking furious. "Days I've been up to my knees in that stinking water, pelted with stale bread. Didn't you hear me yelling for you?"

"Not really," said Jame apologetically. "I gathered that you were annoyed, nothing worse."

"Huh! Why did you chuck me down there anyway?" he demanded of Kroaky.

"I didn't. Fang did. She doesn't like spies—and none of your Intelligencer's tricks: they don't work down here, as you may have realized."

"Why *did* you go Undercliff?" Jame asked as they made their way back to the ladder leading to the Overcliff.

Receiving no immediate answer, she glanced back at Graykin who trudged mulishly at her heels.

"You told me to find out all I could about Kothifir."

"Well, yes. I didn't expect you to get quite so...er...immersed, though."

He stopped and stomped. His boots squished. "No matter what I do, you only laugh at me! Well, I've found out more than you think. For example, I bet you didn't know that that girl in a white tunic was Lady Professionate."

Jame stared at him. "The blonde? Why, she couldn't be more than thirteen years old!"

Graykin smirked. "You don't know anything about the guild lords, do you? While they're in office, they don't age."

"And they can't be killed," added Jame, remembering Lord Artifice's declaration.

"Yes," Graykin admitted, a little huffily. "That too. The thing is that Lady P has made it through every Change for at least fifteen years, and Lord Merchandy for three times that at least."

"Now you interest me. What exactly is this mysterious Change?"

Graykin paused to wring out his dripping hem, over which he had been tripping, revealing a dirty white sash around his waist.

"I'm still investigating that. One happened soon after I first got here. Suddenly the guild lords and masters lost all of their powers, not to mention the king. It was crazy. People didn't know what to do. No one seemed accountable to anyone. Can you imagine what it's like in a rigidly structured society when that structure is ripped out of it? Suddenly—oh, horrors—everyone is equal. The Overcliff was like a ship without a rudder, less so the Undercliff from what I hear, which is another reason why I came down here to look around."

Jame wondered if the Kencyrath would go to pieces like that without its god. Would the Highborn have enough innate power to hold everything together? Now, there was an unsettling thought. Yet hadn't she often wished that the Kendar were free of their compulsion to be bound to the Highborn? If that ever happened, though, what would they do with themselves?

"And then?" she asked Graykin.

"People got tired of the disorder and began to reorganize. Former grandmasters and lords started politicking for supporters, but as far as I can see, that seldom works. The most unlikely people can suddenly find themselves elevated to lord- or mastership. Take Lady Professionate. She was only a doctor's servant when the white came to her, not that she hasn't learned a lot since then, never mind that she still looks like a child. And the more Changes she and Lord Merchandy survive, the more people believe in them. Lord Artifice is less secure."

So, thought Jame, they were Kothifir's equivalent of Tai-tastigon's New Pantheon gods, but less stable because the Kencyr temple that gave them power was too.

"How often do these Changes occur?"

"I'm told that they used to happen every decade or so, but recently much more frequently."

That in turn suggested that the temple was growing less stable. Perhaps that was what Torisen had meant when he had called Kothifir especially dangerous just now. While he and Jame had talked more freely in those last days at Gothregor than in the past two years, some things had remained unsaid on both sides.

She also sensed that Graykin wasn't telling her all he knew, so she didn't share her musings with him.

He looked up with a sudden glint in his eyes. "How were you received in the Host's camp?"

"Rather stiffly. I seem to make people nervous."

The spy snickered. "I'm not surprised. As Knorth Lordan you're supposed to lead the Southern Host."

"Sweet Trinity. No wonder Harn has been so on edge around me. He needn't worry, though: I'm not likely to claim the post."

"You aren't?" Clearly, Graykin had been looking forward to her ascension. As her servant, it didn't suit his pride at all that she shouldn't claim all the honors due to her. "But it's yours!"

"I'm just a second-year cadet, without the proper training. Besides, I don't want it. All that administrative work...ugh."

Still, she had to think of a way to get Harn over this awkwardness, knowing how much her brother depended on the big Kendar. As for Graykin's secrets...

"We'll talk again. Soon."

And she led the way back to the ladder.

&☙ CHAPTER II ☙&
A Willow Rampant
Summer 56

TORISEN DREAMED OF KOTHIFIR and half woke, confused, in the half light before dawn.

"So you've come at last, all the way from the Riverland. Have a nice trip?"

Harn had never said that to him. He remembered all too well his greeting to the Southern Host as a boy, especially Harn Grip-hard's stony face staring at him as the big Kendar tapped his credentials on the desk before him.

"So Lord Ardeth has sent you to me as a special aide. How kind of him."

Harn was second-in-command of the Host under the Caineron Genjar, but Adric would hardly have entrusted Ganth's heir to one of his father's archenemies... would he? Not for the first time, Torisen wondered what Lord Ardeth really had written in the letter that he had carried so far. After what the former Highlord had done to the Kencyrath, no kin of his was apt to find a welcome there.

"More likely," Harn had continued, "you're one of his bastards and a spy to boot. Ha, that raises your hackles, does it? Then prove me wrong. Know anything about soldiering?"

"No, Ran."

"Well, we'll find a place for you. Somewhere. Just stay out of my way. Dismissed."

And Torisen had walked out of headquarters into the dazzling glare of the Host's camp. He had been fifteen years old at the time.

"My lord?" It was Burr, carrying a bowl of porridge and a jug of milk, Torisen's breakfast. He must have dozed off again for now it was full morning with birds flitting past his tower windows. "You had a poor night?"

Torisen unwound the tangled blankets and sat up. The wolver pup Yce watched him, nose on paws, from the hearth where his restlessness had driven her.

"I dreamt about Kothifir when we first arrived there."

"Huh. Not exactly a warm welcome, was it? What clothes for today?"

"Something practical. I need to walk the fields and talk to the harvest master about the hay."

He ate, watching Burr lay out a shirt, plain jacket, sturdy pants, and high-topped leather boots, all black like most of his limited wardrobe. Black wore well. He liked it. He used to think that it made him inconspicuous, but now the Host knew him as Torisen Black Lord or simply as Blackie. In those early days he had thought that Burr had been sent by Adric to spy on him, and he had been right. Not until the Kendar had broken with the Ardeth and sworn to him had he really trusted the man.

He dressed and descended from his tower apartment into the great hall of the old keep where Marc worked in a blaze of sunrise glory at the shattered eastern window.

A furry form rose from the floor where it had been basking in the heat of the kiln and became the wolver Grimly.

"Good morning, Tori, and you too, your highness," Grimly added with a bow to the pup who briefly waved her tail at him in acknowledgement.

"You know," he said, "she's getting rangy enough to assume human form, at least partway. Adolescence comes to our kind at about her age."

Torisen didn't tell him that he had waked during that troubled night to see a shaggy young girl curled up on the threshold, gnawing at her nails in her sleep.

Marc wiped big, gnarled hands on a rag. He had been setting in place another pane of glass made from materials gathered from the land around Kothifir, brick red shading to green for the copper and iron there. The margins and trade routes of the Wastes were slowly filling out as agents sent back materials native to each region. The Kendar had found that if he properly matched areas and held up the new pieces between ironwood plates, they melded at the edges without extra heat, allowing him to build his map within its upright frame. Thus the map grew in place, a rainbow of color against the eastern sky that only resembled a map to those who knew what they were looking at.

"Did you dream, my lord?"

Marc had noticed that if Torisen added a drop of his blood to the mix, the resulting piece glowed with an inner light. This in turn had given him the idea that the Highlord might use these patches to scry on the corresponding areas, Kothifir in particular. Marc, like Torisen, wanted news of Jame.

To scry, to spy, Torisen thought uneasily. Harn's first assumption still stung, as did Burr's initial role. Unlike every other lord in the Riverland, he didn't use secret agents, hence his lack of information. As much as Jame had told him, though, in those last days they had been together after her graduation from Tentir, he hungered to know more, as if she were the dark side of his moon.

It was also strange that whereas he had once stayed awake for days, even weeks, to avoid certain nightmares, now he reluctantly courted them.

"Yes, I dreamed, but how much of it was true?"

"Anything about the lass?" asked Marc, sounding wistful.

Torisen tried to remember. Why was it that most dreams slipped away so quickly when he couldn't forget the worst ones at all? "I think she fell down a hole, but wasn't hurt, and there was something about kicking the head off a mechanical dog."

Grimly grinned. "That sounds like Jame. What d'you suppose Harn made of the letter you sent him along with her?"

Dear Harn, it had read. *Here is my sister. You know her propensities. Try to save as much of the Host as possible.*

"You know he isn't going to be comfortable having her there as a subordinate when she should be in command," said Grimly.

"Not Jame." Torisen was emphatic. "She doesn't know enough."

"Neither did you at first, but people reacted to you nonetheless, even Harn, for all his scorn. The Knorth blood is old and strong."

Burr returned with an armload of the morning post before Torisen could answer. He regarded his servant's burden with dismay; was he never to get to the bottom of these piles? Kirien had promised him a scrollsman scribe, an idea which he regarded with mixed feelings. Delegation of duty had never come easily to him, especially as Highlord when he no longer knew whom to trust. He drew out a parchment at random.

"Huh. Dari is still petitioning to be made lordan regent of the Ardeth."

"Is the old lord in such bad shape?" asked Grimly.

"I hope not."

But Adric *was* on the edge of going soft. If he died... no, when he died. The event was unthinkable, but inevitable.

"You confirmed young Timmon as his heir."

"So I did and so I hold, although the boy is Pereden's son. Jame sees something in him, though."

"Then you trust the lass's judgment."

"To a point. She knew him at Tentir, but what does she know about politics?"

He pulled out another message and scanned it, frowning. "Here's one from Adric himself. Huh. Still matchmaking."

I would be less than a friend if I did not warn you, the note went on to say, and this part Tori did not read aloud to his friends. *Your sister is a powerful Shanir. Others will be drawn to her, especially those Kendar whom you choose to bind so lightly, as though they would thank you for it. She may seduce them away despite themselves unless someone takes her firmly in hand. Now, my son Dari...*

Torisen put the rest of the letter aside.

"The Knorth blood is old and strong," Grimly had just said.

Did that apply to Jame too? But she was just a girl, and Adric was an old man, starting at shadows.

Still, the hair at the nape of his neck stirred.

"Father says it's dangerous to teach you anything," he had once told her. *"Will the things you learn always hurt people?"*

She had considered this. *"As long as I learn, does it matter?"*

"It does to me. I'm always the one who gets hurt. Father says you're dangerous. He says you'll destroy me."

"That's silly. I love you."

"Father says destruction begins with love."

Enough of that.

He drew out another note, broke the seal, and opened it.

"The Coman complain about the Edirr poaching on their side of the river. Sweet Trinity, can't they manage their own territory?"

Marc cleared his throat. "It's a bit more serious than that. I hear that sometimes one of the Lords Edirr leads a raid himself, for the sheer devilment of it."

Torisen looked up sharply. "That's dangerous. If Essien or Essiar should meet with an accident on Coman land, there'll be Perimal to pay."

Burr fumbled with the scrolls, then held out one. "This has the Danior seal."

Torisen took it and read. "Cousin Holly reports sighting a yackcarn. Odd, that, so out of season. Also he killed a large, white wolf."

"With blue eyes?" Grimly asked sharply.

"He doesn't say. Surely he would if that were the case. Anyway, why to the north of us rather than to the south? It's probably just a dire wolf from the hills."

"Or it could be the Gnasher."

They both looked at Yce, who was energetically scratching an ear. Grimly had come north to warn Torisen that the pup's father—the King of the Deep Weald, formerly known in Kothifir as the Gnasher—had sworn that no heir of his would live and had been hunting Yce since the previous year.

"Be careful," said Grimly. "That brute is a soul-stalker as well as hellishly strong and vicious."

"Believe me, I remember."

He took another scroll with a Jaran seal and raised an eyebrow. Usually he heard from that house through its lordan, Kirien, who in turn tended to communicate by far-writing with the Jaran Matriarch Trishien currently in residence in Gothregor's Women's Halls. He broke the seal, unrolled it, read, and laughed. "Listen to this:

"'From Jedrak, temporary lord of the Jaran, to Torisen, Lord Knorth and Highlord of the Kencyrath, greetings.

"'An event occurred recently that may amuse you. Or not. Word reached us that a certain golden willow had been sighted on the border between Falkirr and Restormir. Why it should still be rampant in midsummer, long after the season for arboreal drift, I cannot say, unless said tree has developed a taste for rambling. Willows are sometimes like that.

"'At any rate, we tracked it down and were securing it—with much risk to life and limb, I might add—when up rode a party of Caineron, also on its trail. They protested that we were on Caineron land.'"

"Another poaching story," said Grimly, "one way or the other."

"Hush. 'Luckily we had a singer with us who remembered an old song. Your revered great-grandfather once hunted this land while a guest of the Jaran. He had just killed a fat buck when up rode Caldane's grandfather to claim that his arrow had struck it first. That may well have been, but the beast died on Jaran land, or so your great-grandfather decreed, conveniently close to a certain riverside cliff that serves as a notable landmark to this day. We were currently on top of it. "The Hunting of the Many-Tined Stag" is a lengthy song, full of witty flourishes poking fun at the Caineron, and the singer insisted that everyone listen to the end, even to join in on the choruses. Meanwhile, the willow snapped our bonds, churned its way across the Silver, and disappeared into the no-man's-land on the other side between Wilden and Tentir. No one has seen it since.'"

"Good," said the wolver as Torisen let the scroll roll up. "I've gotten rather fond of that tree galumphing around the landscape."

"Not so good for the Caineron, though. Caldane is going to be furious. He already has a grudge against 'singers' fancies.'"

Grimly scratched his shaggy head. "I'm confused. For one thing, since when have Highlords been able to determine boundaries? You couldn't between the Randir and the Danior."

"I haven't the authority that my great-grandfather had. Besides, east and west, domains are established by the Silver. North and south, however, boundaries depend more on the strength of the nearest houses. As you can imagine, the Caineron tend to push."

"I think you could match any of your forebearers if you put it to the test. Anyway, how could a song stop anyone, much less a Caineron?"

"That," said Torisen, "is part of the Kencyrath's tangled legacy. I've told you how much knowledge we lost when we fled to this world. What we had left was largely oral, preserved by singers, with a few rare exceptions such as Anthrobar's Scroll and Priam's Codex, both since lost. Some of that has since been written down from memory, but much still exists only in songs and stories. You see the possibility for confusion. Once, we knew what was law and what was merely custom. Now that's become muddled."

"So the Jaran used a song as a legal precedent, and made the Caineron sit through the singing of it."

"Exactly. They properly rubbed Caldane's nose in his ignorance. Things get even more confusing when you consider the singer's prerogative of the Lawful Lie. Take Ashe for example. I believe that she is true to the truth as she sees it, but how much of it is to be taken literally?"

"I see what you mean. We wolvers are singers too, and true to our songs, but one betrayed lover can speak for many, or many for one."

"Just as Ashe makes one corpse speak for a company of the slain."

"Aye, that's certain," said Marc. "That song of hers about the battle at the Cataracts...I never liked killing. Now I like it considerably less. Then too, she's a haunt, neither quite alive nor quite dead. Her point of view is probably unique in our entire history. What are the odds, though, that several generations hence what she says now will be believed implicitly, especially if someone writes it down?"

"For people compelled to tell the truth," said the wolver, "you're in a fair mess, aren't you?"

Burr gave an unexpected bark of laughter. "Tell us about it. M'lord, I haven't mentioned it yet, but you have a visitor waiting below."

"Only now you tell me?"

The Kendar shrugged. "I hoped that the Jaran scroll would explain him, but maybe there's no need. He's your new scribe, fresh from Mount Alban."

Torisen sighed. "Then I had better greet him."

He went down the northwest spiral stair, past the low-ceilinged hall that Marc now used to store coal to feed the fires of his two tower kilns. His steps slowed as he approached the ground-level death banner hall. Beyond a doubt, he needed help with his correspondences. As commander of the Southern Host he had trusted Harn Grip-hard—no, face it: hardly anyone could make out Harn's writing but him. But Harn was Harn. This would be a stranger. A possible spy. He could now see the legs of some-one wearing a blue robe, narrow back turned. The scribe was examining the death banners, specifically that of Kinzi, the last Knorth matriarch. Another step down, and Torisen saw that his hair was a wild shock of white.

The voice of his father woke in his soul-image with an out-raged snarl: *Of all insults...that Jaran bitch has sent you a filthy Shanir! Retreat now. Tell Burr to send him away.*

Too late. The other had heard his foot on the stair and turned around with a tentative smile.

It was his cousin Kindrie.

CHAPTER III
Summer Solstice

Summer 66

I

THE SUMMER SOLSTICE arrived eleven days later.

In the north among the Merikit, the Earth Wife's chosen one, Hatch, would fight to keep her favor. Jame wondered, though, if he would try very hard, given how he had avoided the role during her year at the college when she herself had held that position. She also wondered about the Merikit girl Prid, Hatch's beloved, and about the new crop of babies credited to her, Jame, from her stint as the Favorite. It was odd to think about her growing family in the hills when among the Knorth she only had her brother and cousin Kindrie as blood-kin. Here in this distant land, she missed them all.

The question remained, though: should she visit Kothifir on this of all days? Did she want to risk getting mixed up with the elemental Four again, assuming they had any role in this city at all? So far, she had only met the Old Pantheon goddess Mother Vedia and such New Pantheon deities as Krothen and Ruso. The suspicion nagged, though, that if the Kencyrath was to make a real home anywhere on Rathillien, it had to come to terms with that world's native powers, and no one but Jame seemed to be making that effort.

Anyway, she was curious.

And by good fortune, the sixty-sixth of Summer happened to fall on one of the cadets' free days.

Hence by midmorning Jame again found herself Overcliff, at the foot of the avenue that curved inward away from the Rim.

39

The street swarmed with people, mostly apprentices gay in their holiday attire, bedecked with ribbons denoting their guild alliances. The shop shutters were closed against their boisterous nature, although many had set up small stands out front to sell the holiday makers refreshments and trinkets in honor of the day. There were also many spectators, mostly pushed to the side or leaning over balconies above. From the excited overall roil, it appeared that the crowd was waiting for something.

"Come to join the run?" asked a voice in Jame's ear.

She turned to find Kroaky loitering at her elbow, festooned, it seemed, with the ribbons of every guild in the city. He grinned down at her from his lanky height.

"What run?"

"Look. Tell me what you see."

Jame scanned the mob. It was made up of young men and women but also of child apprentices in their own huddles. Now she saw that similar ribbons clustered together and that one in each group carried something golden—a glove, a carved piece of wood, a fire-iron, each apparently the emblem of their guild.

"Look," said Kroaky again, and pointed at a walkway over the street. Three figures stood there. Ruso, Lord Artifice, blazed in his red armor. Beside him stood a plump youngster in a white tunic whom Jame recognized as Lady Professionate. The tall, elderly man stooping next to her must therefore be Lord Merchandy.

The latter spoke to the crowd, but his thin voice was inaudible this far back. Kroaky grabbed Jame's wrist and tugged her toward the front of the crowd of spectators. Lord Merchandy gestured, and the child 'prentices pushed forward chattering like so many sparrows. Then a silence fell on them and they tensed. A white handkerchief fluttered down. When it hit the ground, they rushed forward, many of them carried off their feet in the crush. The crowd roared. The hurtling youngsters took a sharp left into the next side avenue, trailed by someone's crying toddler. Birds fluttered up as the runners pursued their torturous course through the canyons of the city and distant onlookers cheered their progress.

Lady Professionate spoke next. Stray words reached Jame as she neared: "... city ... guild ... honor ..."

The young women among the runners pushed to the front. Down flitted another white cloth and off they went, this time turning right onto the next side street.

Kroaky put his hands on Jame's shoulders. "Now comes the main event, a straight dash to the central plaza."

The young men jostled forward. As with the previous groups, each centered protectively about someone carrying something golden, but at the edges fights had already begun with the neighboring clusters of apprentices. This race was shaping up to be a running battle before it even started.

Ruso addressed the boys in his booming voice: "For the honor of your city, your guild, and the Great Mother whose day this is...here now, wait for it!"

One group, jumping the signal, had surged forward. It checked and drew back to jeers from the others. Ruso waited a beat longer until it was in position, and then down came his handkerchief.

Simultaneously, Jame felt Kroaky's hands tighten on her shoulders and thrust her forward into the surge.

It knocked her off her feet. Bodies tumbled over her, cursing, kicking, until she fought free and managed to scramble up. Even then, the run carried her along with it. She had surfaced between two battling guild groups. Boys on either side pummeled each other between strides, then sprinted to catch up with their standard bearers. Jame wove between their fists. Never before had she used water-flowing and wind-blowing on the run. Her main goal was to avoid being trampled, but in doing so she found herself slipping through the crowd toward the lead runners. They were nearing the plaza. Suddenly a boy in front of her tripped and his precious cargo flew out of his hands. Coming up behind, Jame caught the golden boot. Its protectors re-formed around her.

"Run, *run*, RUN!" they panted.

The plaza lay just ahead. In another moment she would burst into it.

"...the Great Mother," Ruso had said, "whose day this is..."

Oh no. Not again.

Jame thrust the gilded boot into the arms of the red-haired boy who ran next to her and tried to brake. Those following carried her forward, a pace behind the redhead. Thus they rushed into the plaza, just before the girls erupted from a street to the right and the children from one to the left.

Everyone was shouting. His friends seized the redhead and hoisted him, dazed, still clutching the golden boot, onto their shoulders. They started a boisterous procession around the Rose

Tower, followed by the other apprentices wildly waving their ribbons. The noise was an assault in itself.

Jame eased out of the crush. On its edge, a lean hand with grimy nails reached out to pull her clear. She found herself looking into Graykin's wrathful eyes.

"Just what were you trying to do?" he demanded, all but shaking her.

"Not get killed, primarily."

Kroaky shouldered his way through the crowd of cheering onlookers.

"There you are," he said with a wide grin, "and you too, Master Intelligencer."

Jame took in Graykin's dusty robe and the dirty white sash bound around his waist, this time understanding the latter's significance.

"You're the master of the Spies' Guild? How did *that* happen?"

Graykin fussed with the sash, half proud, half defiant. "I'd just arrived here and joined the guild when the last Change came. Believe me, I was more surprised than anyone to be chosen."

"It's been known to happen," said Kroaky cheerfully. "Look at Lady Professionate. Just be careful which of his questions you answer, Talisman."

"You can compel the truth now?" Jame asked.

Her servant squirmed. "As Master Intelligencer, from the unwary, yes. I swore that I would never use tricks with you and I won't. However..."

"You would really, really like to try."

"You never tell me anything!" he burst out. "For example, why did this boy just call you 'Talisman'?"

Jame almost told him, but stopped herself.

"I'll answer as I see fit, thank you. As for you," she turned on Kroaky, "why did you shove me into that maelstrom?"

The ginger-haired boy shrugged. "For fun. Why else does anyone do anything? Besides, I hear that you Knorth are remarkably hard to kill. Consider it a test." He took her arm. "Now come along if you want to see how these festivities end. But not you," he added to Graykin. "You aren't welcome where we're going."

⟨⟨⟨ **II** ⟩⟩⟩

LEAVING GRAYKIN BEHIND to melt resentfully back into the shadows, Jame let Kroaky tow her through the crowd, then shook off his hand. "Where *are* we going, and why do you keep touching me?"

"Don't you like it? Fang does."

"That's another question: what is a Waster doing here?"

"That's your fault, indirectly. She lost her family at the Cataracts. The Horde tends to eat its orphans, so she wandered westward to Kothifir in search of a new clan."

"And those are the Undercliff children?"

"Yes. Runaways and orphans, most of them. The boy with a broken head is better, by the way."

"Glad to hear it."

They were in the back alleys now, approaching a dark hole in the road.

"The Undercliff again?"

"After you."

The huge cavern below bustled with people, as crowded as the square above. Some were Overcliffers in their bright, holiday clothes. Others were Undercliffers, more subdued. Many seemed to be from outside the city, farmers and herders, perhaps, and some even from the Wastes, notable for their blue *cheches*.

"This is best seen from above," said Kroaky. He made another grab for her arm, and grinned when she evaded him. They climbed the stair to the children's sleeping cave. Fang met them, scowling, at the top.

"Why did you bring *her*?"

Kroaky attempted to put an arm around each and was rebuffed by both.

"Now, ladies."

Jame sat down on the ledge overlooking the cavern, followed by Kroaky and, reluctantly, by Fang, who placed herself on his far side.

"How far back do the caves go?" Jame asked.

"Miles and miles," said Kroaky, dreamily, "getting smaller and smaller and smaller. That's where the Old Ones live. Oh, there are wonders in the depths—draperies of stone, cascading water, lace-thin shelves, caverns that glow with even a hint of outside light, silent pools where eyeless fish swim and nameless creatures eat them. Just think of it: all that below and above, tower on tower of marble, limestone, and travertine. They say that only the god-king keeps one from collapsing into the other."

Fang snorted. "If so, he doesn't always succeed. What about those rock falls this past spring? We lost one whole branch of side caves and the river nearly broke through."

"That wasn't his fault," said Kroaky, with a rare show of defensiveness. "He was distracted during the last Change."

"He always is. And it's getting worse."

"As I understand it," said Jame, "King Kruin exiled the Old Pantheon Undercliff. Why?"

"His precious prophet didn't want any competition, did he?" said Fang. "Not when he claimed to represent the one true god."

"What prophet?"

"The leader of the Karnids, of course."

"What god?"

"As to that, all I know is that they claim this world is only a shadow of the one to come where the faithful will be rewarded and the rest of us will suffer."

Jame had heard of such beliefs before, and of other prophets, but this one somehow sounded different. Perhaps it was because of the black history that the Kencyrath shared with Urakarn.

"I take it that Kruin's son Krothen doesn't share that view," she said. "Why hasn't he welcomed the old gods back?"

"How many d'you think we need Overcliff?" Kroaky demanded. "Krothen is enough for us topside."

"And the guild lords."

"Huh. Them."

"And the grandmasters." Now Jame was goading him, but she was also unclear about the difference between the three lords and each guild's individual grandmaster.

"You call them gods?" Kroaky laughed scornfully. "All right, so they have special powers, but they aren't immortal. What's a god without that?"

"Still," said Fang, "you have to admit that the Changes have come more frequently and hit harder since the Old Pantheon gods were exiled. The king should think about inviting them back."

Jame agreed. "It isn't safe to lock up gods in your cellar, so to speak."

Kroaky harrumphed, then pointed as if glad for the interruption. "Hush. Here they come now."

Faint music sounded from the back of the cavern and the crowd stilled. It drew nearer, echoing—pipes, flutes, drums, something eldritch that might have been the wind whistling between the worlds. Figures advanced carrying torches. Their shadows preceded them, casting fantastic shapes on the cavern's fissured walls. The crowd drew back as the procession entered the body of the cave.

Jame was reminded of Mother Vedia's approach on her feast day. There, in fact, she was, again seated like a living statue on an upraised litter, again surrounded by her dancing, snake-wreathed attendants, but this time without bats or followers.

Before her went a gross figure looking like a younger version of the Earth Wife but also hugely pregnant, attended by a host of waddling women in a similar state.

After them, unaccompanied, came a skinny crone carrying a box. While people cheered the other two, they turned away from this last figure, shielding their children's eyes.

"The Great Mother in her aspects of healer, life-bearer, and hungry tomb," said Kroaky, raising his voice over the renewed clamor of the crowd as the next god emerged from the shadows.

"What's in the box?"

"Death, of course."

Jame regarded the diverse figures and remembered her conversation with Gran Cyd, queen of the Merikit. Showing her a fertility figure and an *imu*, both representing the Earth Wife, she had said, "These images were ancient long before Mother Ragga was even born," which made sense since the Four had only come into being with the activation of the Kencyr temples, some three thousand years ago.

Jame had wondered at the time if the Earth Wife and the other three of Rathillien's elemental Four, while each a distinct individual, wore different, older aspects in different cultures and were subject to older stories. Here, perhaps, was the answer.

It raised a further question, however: how had the deification of the Four affected the Old Pantheon, which preceded them?

There was the Earth Wife, at any rate, in three of her earlier native aspects.

Next came a cauldron seething with river fish. Fingerling trout crept over the edge of the pot and pulled up a figure glittering with scales. Cold round eyes regarded the crowd through a net of green hair and pouting lips parted over needle teeth in a smile meant to entice.

The Eaten One, thought Jame, or some variation of her, probably linked to the Amar. Did she also take a human lover? Where was Drie now, still blissfully in his beloved's arms or deep within her digestive tract?

The goddess of love and lost causes walked behind her, backward, gazing into a mirror whose surface rippled like water. Around her feet, threatening to trip her, swarmed a host of green and yellow frogs.

"Geep!" they chorused. "Geep, *geep*, GEEP!"

Rain pattered in their wake.

Gorgo, thought Jame, happy to see an almost familiar face, or faces. She wondered how he and his priest Loogan were doing in Tai-tastigon. Sooner or later, she would have to find out.

The last frog hopped frantically past, followed by a long, low, dark shape with a scaly tail on one end and a cruelly toothed snout on the other, waddling on the plump, pale limbs of a human baby.

More followed. Those clearly aligned with the Four seemed to fare the best. Others passed as phantoms of their former selves, and received little recognition from the crowd. Who now worshipped that dog-faced being or that drifting tatter of silk, that murky orange glow or that thing of clattering bones?

A dazzling light entered the cavern.

"Ooh!" breathed the crowd, and covered their eyes.

Jame peered through her fingers at the sun in all his glory. She could almost make out a figure at the heart of the blaze, a man in red pants stumbling forward supporting a giant, swollen phallus with both hands. It was this member from which the light emanated.

The moon circled him, her face alternately that of the maiden, the matron, and the hag, just like the pommel of the Ivory Knife. She looked up with shifting features and saluted Jame.

"Sister, join us!"

Was this also a mortal who had undergone at least a temporary apotheosis—like the guild lords above? Like Dalis-sar in

Tai-tastigon? Like she herself, eventually, if she became That-Which-Destroys?

Heat washed through the cavern, worse than when the sun had come among them, but without his dazzling light. A woman carrying a hearthside firepot, a martial figure clanking in the red-hot armor of war, and then came a stillness. Heat gave way to a sudden, mortal chill. Jame felt the sweat on her brow turn cold.

"I won't look," said Fang, and hid her face against Kroaky's shoulder.

A cloaked and hooded figure had entered the cavern. He made his way forward slowly, feeling ahead of him with an iron-shod staff. Why should he cause such dread? Perhaps it was the smoke seeping from within his garments. Perhaps it was the stench of burned flesh. Perhaps it was because he came alone, without attendants, and all turned their backs on him.

"Nemesis," said Kroaky, glaring down defiantly although his voice shook. "I had nothing to do with the old man's death. Ask Tori. He was there."

"Wha—" Jame started to ask him, but memory caught her by the throat.

My father, nailed to the keep door with three arrows through his chest, cursing my brother and me as he died....

"It wasn't our fault," she said out loud. "D'you hear me, Burnt Man? Neither one of us was there!"

Wind frisked into the cavern. It swirled around the dark figure, teasing apart his robe, releasing streamers of smoke until with a flick it twitched away the garment altogether. For a moment, a man-shaped thing of soot and ash hovered there. Then the wind scattered it.

The crowd cheered.

"They think he's gone," said Kroaky in an oddly husky voice, "but he always comes back. Like sorrow. Like guilt."

The wind remained, now tumbling about the onlookers, snatching off this man's hat, flinging up that woman's skirt. Laughter followed its antics, all the louder with relief. A figure appeared, whirling like a dervish in a storm of black feathers, long white beard wrapped around him, feet not quite touching the ground.

"Who...?" asked Jame.

"The Old Man," said Kroaky, almost reverently, holding down his ginger hair with both hands. "The Tishooo. The east wind."

"In the Riverland, we call him the south wind."

"Well, he would come at you from that direction, wouldn't he? In fact, he moves about pretty much as he pleases, the tricky old devil. Some say that he governs the flow of time itself in the Wastes, don't ask me how. Here we most often get him direct from Nekrien. He keeps away the Shuu and the Ahack from the south and west, from the Barrier across the Wastes and from Urakarn. We don't honor those here."

"What about the north wind?"

"The Anooo? That blows us the Kencyr Host and occasional weirding. Blessing or curse? You tell me. Without the east wind and the mountains, though, Kothifir, Gemma, and the other Rim cities would be buried in sand like the other ancient ruins of the Wastes."

The procession wound around the cavern until it reached its center. Here torches were set in holes drilled in the limestone floor and the avatars of the Four joined hands within the circle. They began to rotate slowly sunwise. Their worshippers formed a withershins ring around them, then another going the opposite way, and so on and on, alternating, to the edges of the cave. Jame grew dizzy watching their gyrations. Everyone was chanting, but not the same thing:

"There was an old woman..."

"There was an old man..."

"There was a maid..."

"There was a lad..."

The circle next to the gods slowed, swayed, and reversed itself. One by one, the rest corrected themselves until all were revolving the same way, those innermost going slowly, those outermost running, panting, to keep up. The world seemed to shift on its axis. Torches flared blue, casting shadows across an open space grown impossibly wide, split by fiery sigils.

They had opened Sacred Space.

Into it stepped two figures, one dressed in loose red pants, and the other in spangled green. Jame recognized the former as the engorged sun god. The latter was the redhead into whose arms she had thrust the gilded boot, the winner of the boys' run. So that was how they chose the Challenger, which she nearly had become. Again.

The boys bowed to each other, then crouched and began to

glide back and forth, sweeping alternate legs behind them. At first their movements were slow, almost ritualistic, and incredibly fluid. One swung his foot at the other, who ducked under it, then swung in his turn. Thus they pinwheeled across the open space between fiery sigils and back again. The Favorite in red aimed a leg sweep at his opponent. The Challenger in green jumped over it. In the middle of a cartwheel, the Challenger launched a roundhouse kick at the other's face. They were seriously going at it now, weaving back and forth, striking and dodging in a fury of limbs.

Jame watched intently. She had learned the basics of Kothifiran street fighting from Brier, but had never before seen two experts engaged in it. They barely used their hands at all except to block foot strikes, and their legs seemed to be everywhere in graceful, swinging arcs. Some moves were like water-flowing and some like fire-leaping, but in surprising combinations. No wonder first Brier and then Torisen had beaten her at the beginning and the end of her college career, both knocking out the same tooth now barely grown back.

The Challenger leaped and twisted. His foot, scything through the air, caught the Favorite a solid blow on the jaw that dropped him where he stood.

The crowd roared. All the women in it rushed into Sacred Space, collapsing it, converging on the new Favorite whose smug look turned to one of dawning horror. A moment later they had overwhelmed him.

"There," said Kroaky, patting Jame on the back. "Aren't you glad you didn't win the run?"

CHAPTER IV
Red Dust

Summer 100

I

THE ARCHERY BUTTS were manikins made of twisted straw, mounted on the backs of giant racing tortoises. Each tortoise had a handler and spiked collars that prevented it from drawing in its head or limbs. There were two dozen of them in all, straining with slow, ponderous strength against their leashes. Two cadet ten-commands waited on their mounts with bows strung while the handlers wrangled their unwieldy charges into a loose battle formation.

It was a hot, windless afternoon on the dusty training field south of the Host's camp, and one of many such lessons there. Jame wiped sweat off her forehead with a sleeve. Like the other cadets, she was wearing a muslin *cheche* as protection against the sun. Her burn had peeled away and a tan was starting in its place. Still, she wasn't used to the southern heat.

Timmon nudged his horse closer.

"You should be riding that precious rathorn of yours, Jamethiel, not a Whinno-hir."

Jame made a face. Timmon kept teasing her with her true name until she almost wished that she hadn't revealed it. On the other hand, while other Highborn had been horrified, Timmon seemed merely amused that she had such a dire namesake, commenting at the time, "Oh, well, that explains everything."

She stroked Bel-tairi's silken neck. "True, Bel is an easier ride, but we're supposed to perforate, not decapitate. Besides, Death's-head is off hunting."

"You did warn him about the local livestock, I hope."

"He never preyed on the herds near Tentir, and he prefers his chickens roasted, not raw."

Timmon's mount sidled and tossed its head, sensing his mood. "What's the matter?"

"Nothing. Everything. Look, they're ready."

The handlers had unleashed their charges and were backing away. Behind the ten-commands was a pile of bruised fruit. The tortoises started for it, necks outstretched, snapping at each other to gain room.

"Go!" said the sargent in charge of the exercise.

A Knorth and an Ardeth spurred forward. They wove through the oncoming mass, one shooting to the right, the other to the left. With both hands occupied, they had to steer with their knees, making this also a test of horsemanship. The Knorth, Niall, scored two hits; the Ardeth, three.

"Beginner's luck," said Jame. "Wait until Erim's turn." She glanced sideways at the Ardeth Lordan, whose horse was again fidgeting. "Are you going to tell me?"

"You'll laugh. No one here takes me seriously."

Jame thought about that. All his life, Timmon had tried to measure up to the hero that he had believed his father Pereden to be. Peri had been her brother's second-in-command and then leader of the Southern Host, but he had never been a randon. His reckless sense of entitlement had led him to march the Host into disastrous battle against the Waster Horde before he had betrayed it altogether. Timmon had only recently learned about the latter, to his chagrin. Now he was among randon who had served under his father and knew his fickle nature only too well, measured by the lives he had squandered.

Timmon hadn't helped the situation by his lackadaisical attitude at Tentir. Not that he had done badly there, but he had used his Shanir charm to slip out of any duty that didn't interest him. People had noticed.

The trick now was to hit fresh straw targets, preferably in the head or breast. The cadets were also being timed: twenty seconds to loose three arrows each. Distracted by the pound of oncoming hooves, the tortoises began to scatter. The horses swerved around them.

Jame cheered a hit on Damson's part and groaned when she missed the next two.

Damson worried her. The Kendar girl could shift things in people's heads, in one case having caused the cadet Vant to lose his balance and fall into the firepit where he had burned to death—all because he had teased her about her weight. Worse, the memory of her deed gave her pleasure. On the whole, she seemed to have no inborn sense of honor at all. If she passed her second year of randon training, she would become at least a five-commander, responsible for other lives. At the moment, she was Jame's responsibility, and Jame didn't know what to do about her.

G'ah, think of that later.

"I suppose you'll have to prove yourself," she said to Timmon, returning to his problem.

"How?"

"Take your duties seriously, for one thing. No more slithering out of things."

Timmon grimaced. The habits of a pampered lifetime were proving hard to break.

A thought struck her. "D'you know the names of all your cadets?"

"I know my own ten-command," he said defensively.

"And the rest of the second-years, not to mention the third-years and randon?"

"Now, be fair. There are over one hundred and forty second-years alone here at Kothifir."

"And only eighty Knorth," said Jame, proud that she had only lost one to the last cull compared to the Ardeth's twenty. "But I know them all, and am learning the rest. Tori remembers every Kendar sworn to our house, alive or dead."

Timmon gave her a sidelong, defiant glower. "All two thousand of them, among the living alone? I heard that he forgot some."

"Only one. A Kendar named Mullen, who killed himself to make sure that Tori would remember him forever. He hasn't forgotten anyone since." As far as she knew, and as she devoutly hoped. Kindrie's genealogical chart should come in handy on Autumn's Eve, if Tori chose to avail himself of it. "The point is, would you fight, perhaps die, for a leader who didn't know who you were?"

Timmon wriggled.

It was a telling point. Second-years faced no more official culls, which wasn't to say that a wayward cadet might not be sent home in disgrace. On the other hand, at the end of the year, each house's cadets voted on whom they would most willingly follow into battle. It would be highly embarrassing for a lordan to lose that ballot.

"For that matter," said Timmon, rallying, "consider all the time you spent away from Tentir playing with your Merikit friends. That caused talk too, and so are your little visits to Kothifir now."

Jame reflected ruefully that that was true. She had never explained her peculiar role in Merikit society as the Earth Wife's Favorite, not that most Kencyr would have understood if she had tried, except perhaps for Sheth Sharp-tongue. More than ever, she appreciated the Commandant's understanding, although she also worried about what it might have cost him to let her graduate after so many excuses not to.

And now she was slipping away to Kothifir whenever she could, drawn by the lure of the city. Just that morning she had spent an interesting hour in Gaudaric's tower workshop watching him mold boiled leather to the chest of a stoic client. Rhi-sar hide worked best for such purposes, but it was the hardest to obtain, second only to rathorn ivory. Gaudaric was a trifle vague on where it came from, except that patrols into the Wastes sometimes brought it back. Modern rhi-sar came in small skins and strips. Antique rhi-sar hides were much larger and rarer. Her brother's full suit of hardened rhi-sar leather was probably the most valuable thing he owned, next to his sword, Kin-Slayer, and the Kenthiar collar.

Meanwhile, several more pairs of archers had made their runs. An Ardeth was loudly booed for grazing a tortoise's neck. Then it was Erim's turn. The stocky Kendar rode like a sack of turnips, but he had never been known to miss his mark, nor did he this time. The Knorth cheered, then groaned as his horse tripped on its way to the finish line and he tumbled off.

"Penalty, two shots," announced the sargent.

"Our turn," said Timmon, setting an arrow.

The two lordan came last. Being Highborn, they had the lightest bows but also the hardest run. By now, the tortoises had scattered all over the field, lumbering at the pace of a fast-walking man but lurching too so that the targets mounted on their backs swung wildly from side to side. Some of the manikins bristled with arrows. Jame swerved to the left after one so far unscathed, and nearly fell off as Bel stopped short to avoid another of the hulking behemoths. They were surrounded. Leathery heads snaked out and jaws snapped at the Whinno-hir's slender legs. Bel gathered herself and jumped neatly from a standstill over the nearest broad back, knocking off its burden.

"You're supposed to shoot it, not run over it!" shouted the sargent.

Jame tapped Bel's sides with her heels and they dashed after the farthest pair of reptiles. One arrow went through a straw chest. Set, nock, draw, release. A miss. Timmon had already shot his three bolts with two hits and was racing toward the finish line. Jame twisted around on Bel's back and shot almost at random. Her arrow passed straight through a nearby manikin and lodged in another farther off.

"No fair," said Timmon as she drew up beside him. "That's four down by my count, with three arrows."

Nonetheless, after two more matches with time out to reclaim arrows and corral tortoises, the Ardeth won over the Knorth, one hundred fifty hits to one hundred forty-three.

By now it was late afternoon, verging on supper. The sun had set beyond the mountains and farmers were coming in from the fields. The cadets were riding back to the stable when Rue reached over to touch Jame's sleeve.

"Look," she said. "A caravan,"

Jame turned to see a small procession trailing toward her across the valley floor from the shadowy feet of the mountain range. Dust rose into the fading light at their heels, lit above, dark below. They were about half a mile away. Kothifiran guards surrounded three wagons laden with treasures that glinted through their muslin coverings. There should also be at least one Kencyr ten-command, but it presumably had split off at the Mountain Station in the Apollynes and gone back on desert patrol, trusting that there would be no danger this close to the city.

"They look tired," remarked Mint.

And so the native riders and drivers did after weeks in the Wastes, in contrast to the fresh green of the cultivated fields through which they were now winding.

"But with whom do they trade?" asked Quill. "All the silk in Rathillien comes out of the desert, or so I hear. What's out there?"

"I told you back at Tentir," said Dar. "No one knows. Our guards aren't allowed to go all the way. Seekers lead out caravans of salt and trade goods that come back loaded with riches—that is, if they don't run into Waster splinter tribes, raiders out of Urakarn, bands of thieves from Kothifir or agents from other Rim cities."

Jame wondered if any of these had been kin to the merchants who had come through the Riverland peddling their unsanctioned wares the previous spring. Also, she wondered how Graykin's gorgeous robe was holding up. He would be brokenhearted if it turned to dust as all spoils of the Wastes not touched by King Krothen were said to do. For that matter, she should check on her own silk coat, although she was fairly sure that all the Kendar embroidery lavished on it would keep it intact, royal touch or no.

The grass beside the distant road moved, though no wind blew, and the captain of the approaching guard slowly toppled off his horse. The other riders drew their swords. Another fell, then another. Those who were left charged the ditches on either side. Horses squealed and thrashed in the undergrowth amid darting figures. The drivers lashed at the massive dray horses that pulled their wagons to speed them up.

Jame had risen in the stirrups for a better view. "It's an ambush," she said, sliding down again into the saddle, "and no other patrol is in sight."

The sargent shouted something as Bel sprang away.

Were the assailants trying to steal the wagons, this close to the Host's camp? Slow moving as the vehicles were, that made no sense.

Neither did riding to the rescue alone.

Jame glanced back and saw that the cadets were following her, but at a slight distance. The sargent had reminded them to restring their bows before setting off. Her own slapped uselessly against her back. She slung it around to brace the lower tip in her stirrup, only to find that the bow socket was on the wrong side. Dammit, why couldn't she be left-handed like nearly everyone else in the Kencyrath? As she fumbled with the upper tip, Bel swerved to avoid an incoming shaft. The bow slipped out of her grasp, nearly tripping the Whinno-hir as it fell and snapped between her legs. Wonderful. She was galloping into battle with only a knife in her boot and three arrows in her quiver.

At least a dozen of the enemy archers swarmed around the wagons. The driver of the first beat them off with the vigorous help of his passenger, a blond, middle-aged woman. A raider clambered up into the second cart, seized a slight, veiled figure cowering beside the driver and jumped off with her.

The second carter saw Jame as she approached. He rose, waving his arms, and shouted, "They've stolen our new seeker!"

Jame angled to follow the fleeing man and his captive. Behind her she heard the cadets clash with the remaining raiders. Ahead, the man ran into a stand of date palms and a moment later plunged out the other side mounted on a fleetfoot. Jame had seen such creatures offered for sale in Kothifir; they were like gazelles, but larger, faster, and often used for racing. Bel began to fall behind.

Jame caught a flash of white. The next moment the fleetfoot squealed and jinked sideways as Death's-head roared down on it leaving a swath of trampled grain in his wake. For a moment they ran side by side. Then the rathorn snapped at the other's throat and brought it crashing down with a broken neck. Captor and captive were thrown.

Jame leaped off Bel and hit the ground running too fast for her feet to keep pace, an arrow in her hand. The raider was scrambling up. The arrow caught him in the eye as she slammed into him. They went down together in a heap. Jame felt the shaft's nock punch her in the shoulder as her weight and momentum drove it home.

Rising from his still-twitching body, she turned to his former captive. The girl huddled on the ground, cradling her wrist. She had broken it. That she had also cut her arm seemed less serious, until Jame saw that the wound was driveling red dust. The skin around it fell away as the flesh beneath turned to powder. More and more fell, until the bone itself began to dissolve. She was crumbling in Jame's arms, her enormous hazel eyes wide and terrified above a rotting veil.

"Tell..." she whispered, and even her voice was a thinning thread, warped by an unfamiliar accent. "Tell my sisters..."

Her eyes glazed over and sank. The flesh on her face collapsed. Lips drew back over perfect white teeth, skin over the delicate bones of her face. Jame had been supporting the girl's head. Now she laid down her naked skull and stared at the web of white-gold hair caught in her fingers.

"Well," said Timmon behind her. "That was different, even for you."

"Who was she, Timmon? Where did she come from, and what happened to her?"

"I don't know, but she was obviously the reason for the raid. As soon as your man ran away with her, the others scattered and tried to escape. We caught them all, of course. Brier reckons they're from Gemma, a rival Rim city with no seekers of its own."

Jame remembered the Gemman ambassador in the Rose Tower, the first time she had sought an audience there. Krothen had threatened to hang any captured raiders.

"What will you do with them?" she asked.

"Take them to the king's guard. All seekers are his people, not to be touched by anyone else."

"Then I'd better tell Commandant Harn."

To one side, Death's-head pinned the dead fleetfoot with a dewclaw and bent to rip strips of flesh off its carcass. He was already splashed scarlet to the knees and all but purring.

"At least someone is happy," said Jame.

⬥ II ⬥

SHE FOUND JORIN waiting for her at the edge of the camp, sprawled in the meager shade of an arcanda tree whose leaves rolled up tight during the daytime to preserve moisture. The heat didn't suit the ounce any more than it did her or, for that matter, the rathorn, all three being natives of the northern climes. The blind hunting cat rose when Jame saw him, stretched, yawned, and trotted up to butt his head against her thigh. She scratched him, noting that he had begun to shed heavily, down to a sleek, pale gold coat mottled with creamy rings.

Together, they went through the camp. Jame was about to turn right into the Knorth barracks when she saw a stir ahead outside the Commandant's quarters on the far side of the inner ward— new arrivals to the Host from the Riverland. Jame glimpsed a familiar sharp, pale face to one side and advanced to greet Shade. The Randir cadet was clad in dress grays with her gilded swamp adder Addy draped around her neck like a golden torque. Both looked surprisingly cool, as if they shared the same cold blood.

"What's going on?" Jame asked.

Shade rolled her shoulders in an almost boneless shrug that made the serpent undulate. "There's been unrest in the Randir barracks over several unexplained deaths, also some disappearances. Ran Awl is here to investigate. I'm her new aide."

"Congratulations," said Jame, meaning it. She had wondered what the Randir would do with Lord Kenan's half-Kendar daughter, especially since she was sworn neither to her father nor to her grandmother, Lady Rawneth. Neither was the Randir war-leader Awl, as far as Jame knew. Politics at Wilden were notoriously complicated.

Awl appeared in the doorway, a tall, raw-boned woman with close-cropped iron-gray hair. Standing behind her, burly Harn Grip-hard overlapped her on all sides.

"Ask if you need any help," he was saying. "It's a strange, troubling business."

Then he saw Jame, and his bristly face reddened.

"So Lord Ardeth has seen fit to send you to me as a special aide. How kind of him."

No, that was from Torisen's dream. She wondered if her brother realized that he had shared it and more besides with her.

She saluted Harn. "Ran, an incoming caravan has lost their seeker to an ambush. She literally fell to pieces in my arms."

"Yes, yes," he said hastily, already turning away. "These things happen."

"What," Jame muttered at his retreating back, "all the time?"

"It seems you have a mystery of your own," remarked Shade.

"Several of them," said Jame, and sighed. Even now that she knew why her presence upset Harn, she didn't know what to do about it. Knorth Lordan or not, surely the man couldn't think that she wanted his post.

"Here's someone else who came south with us," Shade said, indicating a stolid figure as it limped up to them.

"Gorbel! How is your leg?"

The Caineron Lordan scowled at her under his beetling, sunburnt brow. "It hurts, thank you very much. You try getting smashed under a dying horse."

"Well, yes. You were trying to kill me at the time, you know."

Gorbel snorted. "Not likely to forget, am I? Father was disgusted with me for failing."

"Does that bother you?"

"Not as long as he's let me come south once the bone knit. Commandant Sheth Sharp-tongue is the one really in trouble."

Jame felt her heart sink. Ever since the Commandant of Tentir had beaten Honor's Paradox by letting her graduate from the college against his lord's wishes, she had worried about his fate. "What's happened to him?"

"On the face of it, not much. Now that his stint at the college is over, Father has him mewed up in Restormir twiddling his thumbs. Damned waste of a valuable asset, if you ask me."

Jame sighed, glad that it was no worse, given what Caineron had threatened. Still, for a man like the Commandant to waste his time playing the courtier... No doubt about it: Caldane, Lord Caineron, was a fool.

"Wait a minute," she said. "The last I heard, during the final cull you had earned one white stone for diplomacy and one black from the Falconer's class for absenteeism, canceling each other out. So why are you here?"

"Earned another white, didn't I, that last day of testing when you were off playing with your precious Merikit. For horsemanship, before you ask, little good it did me against that rathorn monster of yours."

"I see you brought your pook, Twizzle," said Shade, indicating the furry lump at Gorbel's heels. Only the lolling red tongue gave a clue as to which end was which.

"Woof," it said, and sat down to scratch what was probably an ear. Fur flew.

"I may still be lame, but I can ride. And hunt," said Gorbel. "Show me a better tracker and I'll take it with me instead."

There was a bit more to it than that, thought Jame. Gorbel had shown signs of being bound to the pook as she was to Jorin and Shade to Addy. He should have kept attending the Falconer's class to develop that link, not that it wasn't likely to grow on its own with use.

Several third-year cadets walked past, giving the newly arrived second-years sidelong looks. "Fresh meat," one said, not bothering to lower his voice. The others laughed.

Gorbel snorted. "Think they're so grand, do they, for having survived the Cataracts and been promoted there? If we had fought, we could have skipped a year's training too."

Last year, the college had had virtually no second- or third-year students thanks to that great battle where so many had died.

"Maybe so," said Jame, "but I would have hated to miss a minute of Tentir. Well, maybe a second or two."

Shade watched the older cadets go. "There are rumors," she said, "that the third-years have taken to blooding cadets who didn't serve at the Cataracts."

"Hence the deaths in your house and Ran Awl's presence here?"

Shade shrugged. "Maybe. I've heard that hazing was vicious when Genjar commanded, up to the massacre at Urakarn and his death. Torisen forbade it when he took the Highlord's seat. It still goes on, though, in some houses."

Gorbel grunted. "No harm in a little spilt blood. Are we training to be warriors or not?"

An elderly, white-haired officer walked past in the other direction, glowering at Jame.

"Do you still get much of that?" asked Shade.

"Some." Jame had hoped that she was past objections to her status as the only Highborn female in the Randon. "Fash hints to everyone who will listen that I only passed the last cull at Tentir because I'm the Highlord's heir."

Fash was one of Gorbel's ten-command, but not noticeably under his control in this matter.

"That man is and always has been a fool," said Gorbel heavily. "Tentir was a pond. The Host is an ocean. Let him flounder in it."

By now it was time for supper. The three cadets exchanged nods and retired to their respective mess halls.

CHAPTER V

An Unexpected Guest

Summer 110

I

TORISEN DREAMED that he was a boy again, struggling to make his way in the Southern Host.

"Here," said Harn Grip-hard gruffly, thrusting a paper at him. "Take this to the Jaran."

Young Tori accepted back the note which he himself had transcribed, Harn's handwriting being nearly unreadable. He had noted that early in his stay with the Southern Host, and it had suggested to him a way in which he might make himself useful. Harn had snarled at him at first, but he had persisted and by slow degrees had gained a measure of grudging acceptance.

Otherwise, he had no assigned role in the camp. That was hard, with everyone else so busy, so sure where they fitted in to the Host's complex, bustling structure. Only he was the outsider. He had begged to be sent to the randon college at Tentir, but Adric had said that that would be too dangerous, so close to his father's enemies, so here he was instead, where even the Ardeth wanted little to do with him. Maybe they shared Harn's belief that he was one of their lord's bastards, perhaps with a trace of Knorth blood to explain his distinctive looks. All in all, the only place he could call his own was the small, mean set of rooms not far from Harn's office, kept for him by Adric's spy Burr.

It was dusk when he emerged from the command block and set off south across the grassy inner ward under the flare of kindling stars.

A ten-command of second-year Edirr cadets trotted past him, skipping on alternate steps to the amusement of all whom they passed. For hazing, that was mild. The Randir and Caineron third-years had drawn blood, especially the latter, where a cadet had swallowed a live coal and died after being forced to tell a lie. The Randir were more subtle. There, two cadets had chosen the White Knife rather than live with what they had been made to do, whatever that was. It was rumored that Commandant Genjar had a taste for such games although he had never experienced them himself, not being a randon. His doting father Caldane had made the Randon Council accept him as Commandant of the Southern Host. Harn actually ran the camp. A proper nest of vipers, the Caineron, and the Randir no better.

The main street opened before him between the high walls of the barrack compounds. Lights shone in the Caineron to the west. The garrison would be sitting down to supper. The Knorth to the east remained dark and empty, a haunting emblem of Ganth Gray Lord's fall.

Someone moved in the latter's shadow.

"Please, sir, can you spare some food?"

A Kothifiran beggar, here, at this hour? If he were a thief, though—the camp did occasionally suffer from such infestations—should Tori call the guard? No. From the sound of his nasal voice, this was a boy not much older than Tori himself, and even more an alien here. On impulse he directed the stranger back to his own rooms.

"Tell Burr to feed you."

The next garrison block, across from the Caineron to the south, belonged to the Jaran. Its gate was shut for the night, but the door cracked open at his knock. A wiry woman took the note which he handed to her. Something about her looked familiar.

"Were you a Knorth?" he asked, speaking despite himself.

She hesitated. "Yes, I was. How did you know?"

"Someone pointed you out to me."

"A damn fine randon, and another bit of the Highlord's wreckage," the man had said. "All his house, scattered to the mercy of the winds. No wonder they curse him."

"Do they honor you here?" Tori asked abruptly.

Her figure was backlit, her face unreadable. She tilted her head as if in thought. "Well enough, considering. Rather, pity those who went to other houses or who became Caineron *yondri-gon* like Harn Grip-hard. Why do you ask?" She moved a step toward him, as if drawn. "Who *are* you?"

"No one." He stepped back. Dangerous, dangerous...

"Well, my name is Rowan. Remember it. Please."

"I will."

The door closed.

Tori turned back toward the inner ward, his mission complete.

But what had just happened? He had been drawn to his father's people before, as to Harn. Were they now beginning to respond? It felt like a scratching on the inside of his soul-image.

Let me out, let me out...

There was an unlocked door and behind it a faint voice. He tried not to listen, much less to answer.

Father, this is my life, such as it is. I left you, and the Haunted Lands keep where I was born, and the memory of the sister whom you drove out before me. You didn't keep faith with her. Why should I with you? Leave me alone.

Here again was the deserted Knorth barrack. On impulse, he put his hand on the locked door, and it swung open at his touch on rasping hinges. The inner courtyard was weed-choked and over-grown. Balconies rose above it, tier on tier up to the third floor, faced on the inside by closed doors like so many sealed eyes. What had happened here when his father had marched out the Northern Host to disastrous battle in the White Hills? How quickly had the Southern garrison felt his fall? At once, probably. They were bound to him. Then he had thrown down the Highlord's collar in petulant despair and gone away, leaving them to fend for themselves in a world echoing hollowly with his departure.

"Damn you, Father," Tori muttered to the emptiness. "Did you ever think of anyone but yourself, and her?"

Ganth hadn't then known Tori's mother (and Jame's too, he reminded himself), yet he had seemed drawn to her across the Ebonbane, into the Haunted Lands. There she had come to him and he had been happy, for a while. Her departure had destroyed him. Jame had told him that their mother was Jamethiel Dream-weaver, but what sense did that make? The Dream-weaver had been consort to Gerridon, the Master of Knorth, during the Fall three thousand years ago.

"Time moves slower in Perimal Darkling than in Rathillien," Jame had said.

(What? When? A dream within a dream. *I want to wake up,
but I can't, I can't, even knowing what comes next...*)

The wind combed the weeds, twining them around his legs,
whining: *never, forever, never, forever...*

The barrack's gate rasped again. He had been followed. Four
dark figures slipped through the opening, one after another, and
spread out to surround him. They wore their cadet scarves over
the lower halves of their faces, the insignia turned inward.

"You have enemies," Adric had said. Which ones were these?

One stepped forward to grab him. Tori caught his hand and
pulled him into an earth-moving throw that tumbled him into
a comrade. Another he avoided with wind-blowing. He took the
fight to them with a fire-leaping kick that made a fourth stagger
back and pause to spit out a tooth. Then they were upon him,
bearing him down. He struggled in their grip, among the tough,
clinging grass, but they were Kendar, a head taller than he, and
forty pounds heavier, each.

Someone yanked a hood over his head and tightened its draw-
string around his throat. He thrashed in their arms until one
of them bashed him over the ear. The world spun. Was he on
his feet or off? Which way was up? They were carrying him, he
thought, half dazed, but where?

Into a building, against whose walls their shuffling footsteps
echoed, up a stair—bump, bump, bump—into a noisy room.

They set him on something that tottered underfoot, a rickety
chair or stool. Hands held him upright until his head cleared
enough for him to balance, more or less. His hands were bound
behind him and a noose had been dropped over his head. While he
tipped forward, his hands were drawn up and the noose tightened.
The rope must have been passed over a rafter. He fought his way
upright and stood panting within the close confines of the hood.

People were talking, laughing, eating. He heard the rasp of
utensils on pewter plates and mugs thumping on tabletops.

Someone cleared his throat for silence and got it, except for a
nervous giggle off to one side. A chair scraped back. Footsteps
approached.

"Now then, mystery boy," said a voice he had never heard
before. "Who are you?"

Tori didn't answer. A swish, a searing pain across the back of
his legs. He barely kept himself from toppling forward.

"Even bastards have fathers. Who was yours?"

No response. Another fiery blow. It must be a switch or thin rod, Tori thought. Nothing that would do him serious damage, unless he lost his balance. But oh Trinity, the pain...

"The Ardeth sent you here, but they aren't in any hurry to claim you. Are you one of M'lord Adric's bastards, hmm? Answer!"

Another blow.

"Stubborn, aren't you? Well then, let's make you howl."

The switch hissed and cracked, again and again. Time stopped in one endless moment of agony.

"What in Perimal's name...?"

Harn's bellow nearly made Tori fall off his precarious perch. Hands grabbed him as he swayed. The noose and the rope binding his hands were removed, but not the hood.

"Steady," said Burr in his ear, helping him down.

"Commander Grip-hard." A new voice this time, languid, familiar. "To what do we owe the pleasure of your company?"

"I came looking for my clerk." Harn was trying to speak calmly, but his voice rumbled with enough anger to rattle the silverware. "Perhaps, not being a randon, you didn't know that hazing is strictly an in-house ritual. This boy is an Ardeth."

A deep sigh. "Well, then, take him if you must. He was proving poor sport anyway."

Burr hustled Tori out, not removing the hood until they were in the street outside a barracks.

"You may know," he said cryptically, "but he doesn't know that you know."

"How did *you* know where to find me?"

"That boy you sent me to feed saw you being hustled off. He's back in your rooms now, probably eating everything in them."

Harn emerged from the compound, still mountainous with rage. Tori had heard that the Kendar was a berserker, but this was the closest he had seen to a full eruption. The very stones seemed to shudder under him.

"One of these days," Harn was growling, "one of these days..."

Tori freed himself from Burr and touched the randon's arm. From the sizzle down his nerves, it felt as if he had grounded a lightning bolt. Harn shook himself. His small, bloodshot eyes blinked and focused.

"All right, boy?"

"Yes, Ran."

"You could complain about this to the Ardeth."

"No, Ran."

Tori had had time to think. However nasty the hazing, one didn't run to the authorities to cry about it. Besides, he wasn't really hurt, although his legs ached abysmally and threatened to give out under him. Most importantly, he had indeed recognized that drawling voice. The Commandant of the Southern Host, Genjar himself, had presided over his torture.

II

BURR HELPED TORI back to his quarters. Candles lit the suite of small rooms, and in the second chamber they found the Kothifiran boy busily devouring their supper. Tori sank down into the opposite chair. Burr gave him a glass of thin wine, which he drained with a shaking hand.

Dammit, pull yourself together.

The hand steadied.

Burr refilled the glass. Over its rim, Tori regarded his visitor. The latter was lanky and liberally bespeckled with pimples. A tangle of ginger curls crowned his head. While his clothes were filthy, they were also of fine fabric and an elegant cut.

"Who are you?" Tori asked.

"Do you grant guest rights?"

Tori gathered that he was being asked to extend his protection to his unlikely visitor.

"How can I do that when I don't know why you're on the run?"

"Who says that I am—running, that is."

Both Kencyr looked at him, the Highborn with a raised eyebrow.

"All right. So I am." He took another bite of bread and gazed longingly at the wine bottle. Tori nodded to Burr, who reluctantly poured the boy a glass.

"Running away from what?" Tori asked patiently.

"What can I say that you would believe? I hardly know myself, except that I'm scared."

"Of what?"

"Of a man who casts the shadow of a white wolf."

"Not good enough. Start at the beginning."

"All right." The boy took a long swig of wine as if to fortify himself, his skinny throat working. "I'm trusting you, d'you hear me? My father, King Kruin, is dying, but he won't admit it. And he hangs on, past all reason. Meanwhile, the Karnids' dark Prophet whispers in his ear and my kinsmen die, wasting away as the wolf's shadow falls over them. All of my brothers are dead. Now my uncles and cousins have started to disappear. No one will believe what I have seen, so I ran."

Tori had heard rumors of the mysterious deaths Overcliff among the royal family, not that they had had much to do with him personally. He supposed, though, that anything that affected the Host's paymaster, King Kruin, would eventually affect the Host itself.

"So you're afraid both of this wolf and of the prophet," he said. "What prophet?"

"As I said, a Karnid, out of Urakarn. They're all fanatics there, sworn to a world to come when death itself will die, or so they claim. Father is desperate; he listens to them. So do many of my family, hoping to save their skins. But I am my father's youngest, last son, too close to the Rose Throne for safety, and I don't trust any word that comes out of Urakarn."

The two Kencyr exchanged glances. The Kendar's scowl clearly said *Don't trust him.*

Tori wondered, *Should I?*

Moreover, what protection could he really offer? His stinging legs reminded him how vulnerable he himself was and, despite himself, he shivered. Still, this boy and he had much in common, both outcasts with problematic fathers.

"I can't promise you much," he said, "only a place to stay and a share in our rations which, I warn you, are meager. That said, again, what is your name?"

The boy grinned with relief, showing big, white teeth worthy of a colt. "I'll take whatever you can offer. What other choice have I? To answer your question, I am Prince Krothen, but you can call me Kroaky."

◄⎯ CHAPTER VI ⎯►
Challenges

Summer 111

I

JAME WOKE, confused, in pain. She had met both Kroaky and that great pudding, King Krothen. How could they be the same, hair and voice aside? Then again, how much could one trust in dreams?

G'ah, the lines of fire across her legs... She thought she could feel the welts, until she was fully awake.

Was Tori attempting to scry on her through Marc's growing stained glass window? Did he have any idea that some of his efforts might be flowing in reverse, if indeed that was the case? Genjar and the hazing... her own legs aching in sympathy...

For that matter, was Tori also privy to her own dreams? Sweet Trinity forefend.

She threw off the covers, to the disgust of Jorin who had been curled up under them, and rose. Her new quarters were located on the third floor of the Knorth barracks, looking north across the inner ward to the Escarpment and south toward the bulk of the camp. As with Greshan's apartment at Tentir, she understood that these rooms had stood empty during the long years between Knorth heirs. At least her uncle had never tainted it with his presence. Where had Tori lived when he had joined the Host, nameless and unwanted as he had been? A flicker of the past night's dream showed her tiny, shabby rooms in the office block near Harn, to whom Tori had been assigned as a special aide. She and her brother had talked about many things in those last days before her departure from the Riverland, but somehow little beyond the bare facts about his experiences in the south. Why was he still keeping secrets, if such they were, and what else might his dreams show her that he couldn't bear to speak about beyond the Caineron hazing?

Rue brought her a cup of pomegranate juice sweetened with honey. It took some getting used to after Tentir's inevitably tart cider.

"What's our schedule for today?" Jame asked.

"Not much. This is our day off. You're going Overcliff, aren't you?"

So her absences had been noted. Well, of course they would be. At least she had tried to limit them to times when she was free of cadet duties.

"I need to check with Graykin," she said. "Then Gaudaric's grandson Byrne has promised to show me something called the Eye of Kothifir. And you?"

Rue shrugged, turning to lay out Jame's clothes for the day including the black *d'hen*. Jame wondered if the cadet understood the significance of the latter. So far, only Sheth seemed to have recognized it as the proper garb of a Tastigon knife-fighter.

"I had hoped to go to the local market in the inner ward," said Rue. "Now, I don't know. One of our ten-commands got a note last night."

"Damn." Jame put down the cup, half-drained. "What did it say?"

"They've been ordered out on wide patrol to the foothills of the Apollynes, a full day's ride there and back. As a test, it isn't much. We've done the same on foot, with full packs. It's just the waste of a free day."

Similar challenges had been arriving for weeks, usually pushed under the door at night. They were never signed, but everyone knew that they came from the third-year randon cadets who had settled on this method to test the mettle of their juniors, either by groups or individually.

The tasks they assigned varied from house to house depending on its temper. The Caineron used physical trials. Only yesterday, Jame had seen one of Caldane's ten-commands clinging, terrified, to the outside of the open lift cage as it rose up the sheer side of the Escarpment. Anyone of them might have succumbed to the height-sickness so endemic in that house and fallen to his or her death.

She also remembered the nightmare about her brother being tortured by the Caineron Genjar. What had happened next?

Perhaps a future dream would tell her. Genjar, after all, was said to have suffered a "strange" death.

The Jaran, on the other hand, tended toward intellectual tests, the Edirr toward jokes such as ten-commands jogging naked through camp, painted blue.

No word came out of the Randir, but it was generally supposed that they were using this opportunity to test the loyalty of their cadets. Jame wondered if Ran Awl and Shade had made any progress in their investigation into the disappearances there and if any of the reported deaths had had anything to do with the third-years' challenges. If so, would anyone tell Shade, given her peculiar background, or Awl, with her war-leader's status?

For that matter, Jame had heard very little from within her own house. The third-years' demands must have been moderate so far or surely she would have heard more, unless her people were keeping things from her again. As with certain demanding duties back at Tentir—latrine patrol or trock eradication, for example—it hurt their pride to see their lordan so demeaned, whatever her wishes.

"The whole thing is so stupid," she said, pulling on her boots with brusque impatience. "What does it prove, to answer a riddle, to run a gauntlet, or to go on an unnecessary patrol? For example, you and the rest of my ten-command have proven yourselves over and over, even if most of you didn't fight at the Cataracts."

"You did," said Rue, with a stubborn tilt to her shoulders.

"I slashed my way across a battlefield—Ancestors know how clumsily—to bring my brother an accursed sword that he didn't know how to wield. Niall was there too, and Brier, after worse than either of us experienced. If the rest of you missed it, well, what about our adventures up and down the Riverland, all the way to the Southern Wastes and back? Sweet Trinity, you helped me to raid Restormir itself to free Graykin! You have nothing to prove either to me or to the Highlord who, incidentally, has forbidden all such hazing. I don't want to see any randon cadet subjected to it. Do the regular Kendar have to put up with this nonsense?"

"They have their own rites of passage, I suppose."

"More practical ones than ours, I bet. God's claws, isn't the average Kencyr's life hard enough as it is?"

To her surprise, Rue didn't agree.

"Of course I don't want to be beaten or humiliated or what-ever the third-years have in mind," said the towheaded cadet, turning stubbornly to face her. "But what other way is there? In a normal year, we would have gone through this at the randon college, but the second- and third-year cadets were all here by then. Now, how else are we supposed to prove that we belong with the Southern Host?"

"Aaiiee." Jame threw up her gloved hands in disgust. "Tradition!"

At the south gate to the Knorth compound, she encountered Brier talking to a tall young woman with the dark tan of a native born Kothifiran Kendar and cropped hair the color of wild honey. When the latter saw the Highborn, she smiled and said something to Brier that made the latter stiffen, flushing. Then, with a flipped salute, the stranger walked off.

"Who was that?" Jame asked, coming up.

"Amberley. A regular Caineron. Before I left to become a Knorth randon cadet we were...close."

"Oh," said Jame, listening as much to the other's flat, carefully neutral tone as to her words, knowing by now how to read most nuances in the other's manner. "How did she feel about your leaving?"

"Angry. We fought."

It couldn't have been easy for Brier to turn her back on all her former colleagues by changing houses, Jame thought, watch-ing the Southron stalk back into the Knorth barracks. She had thought so before. It just hadn't occurred to her that there might have been someone special.

The north gate of the Ardeth faced her across the road. She saw Timmon enter his compound's courtyard wearing what appeared to be a dirty apron and carrying a bucket of steaming slops.

"What in Perimal's name...?"

He gave her a rueful smile. "I got a note. It seems that all the scul-lery duty I slipped out of at Tentir has finally caught up with me."

"And you've consented to do it now?"

He shrugged. "You advised me to stop avoiding responsibility."

"I'm not sure this is what I meant."

"Should I let them humble me, d'you mean? I don't know. It's easier than hunting up some way of my own to prove myself, assuming that's what I'm doing. Anyway, it could be worse. Did you hear about Gorbel's challenge? What it told him to do was

anatomically impossible. He read it out loud to his house at dinner, then tore it up."

Jame laughed. "That's Gorbel. He can get away with it, too,
despite his fickle father. It must be nice to be so self-assured."

"And you aren't?"

"Sweet Trinity, no."

Yet she was more so than she had been before her graduation
from Tentir, or more specifically before she and her brother had
fought to establish her competence. She had surprised Tori there,
just as he had surprised her by resorting to Kothifiran street
fighting techniques. She needed more lessons from Brier.

When would a note arrive for her, she wondered as she bid
Timmon farewell, and what would she do about it? Ah, there
was no telling until she learned what was being asked of her.
Like Rue, she didn't care to be humiliated, nor was she sure that
was the way for a lordan to gain acceptance. Challenges. Huh.

⊰⟡⟡ II ⟡⟡⊱

THE OPEN LIFT CAGE took her smoothly up to the top of the
Escarpment where she was greeted by Kothifir's usual, lively street
scene. Her way from there led outward into less respectable streets
on the edge of the deserted towers. There she entered what on
the outside appeared to be a narrow structure but on the inside
opened out into a dingy tavern. A slatternly maid brought her a
mug of thin, sour ale. Sipping it, she let her eyes roam around
the edges of the room until a glimmer of white caught them.
Graykin emerged from the shadows as if given birth by them.

Jame signaled for another mug.

"You're getting very good at that," she said as her servant slid
into the opposite chair.

"Being Master Intelligencer has some advantages. Now everyone tells me their secrets, whether they intend to or not . . . well,
almost everyone," he added, with a sidelong look at her.

Knowledge was his coin of power, one that she hadn't always
been willing or able to pay him. Perhaps that hesitation wasn't
fair. She knew that he would keep her secrets to the point of

death as he had at Restormir while in Lord Caineron's power. Still, some secrets were hers alone.

"So," she said. "What news of the city?"

He shrugged. "There's not much to report. Prince Ton and his mother are still scheming against King Krothen, not that they have any chance while he retains his godhood."

"Which is to say as long as our temple remains stable. What?"

Graykin's eyes had flickered. "Maybe nothing, but there's word that the temple has shrunk slightly. That often happens before a Change. It's been known to dwindle down to the size of a clenched fist. The priests try not to be inside when that happens."

"I should think not."

Jame remembered the miniature temple at Karkinaroth and the priests trapped, starving, inside of it. Somehow, the inner and outer sizes of any Builders' work never quite matched.

"What about the guilds?" she asked.

"They go on much as always, depending in part on their guild masters. Some of the masters are generous with their skills, like your friend Gaudaric, and their members thrive—small thanks to his fellow armorer Lord Artifice who only thinks about his own projects, to the detriment of all the other craft guilds. He should watch out, though. His work is brilliant now, but from what I hear, thanks to his selfishness his talent may burn out when—or rather if—he loses his position. Gaudaric, on the other hand, is more likely to keep his. That's partly why Ruso is so desperate to remain Lord Artifice. He wants to be like Professionate and Merchandy, who have retained their power practically forever."

"That sounds like a cautionary tale about leadership," remarked Jame.

She wondered if Graykin had considered the personal implications. What would happen to him, come the next Change? He didn't seem to be doing anything at all for his own so oddly won guild except using the powers that it granted him.

"Anything else?" she asked.

"Not really, except that a few Karnids have crept back into the city."

Jame stared at him. "Graykin! You're talking about the people who slaughtered thousands of Kencyr before Urakarn!"

"Only because we chased them there, or rather because we chased their blessed prophet. Anyway, that's an old story," said

Graykin with a shrug, as if less than two decades rendered it inconsequential. "As I understand it, when King Kruin was dying, the Dark Prophet came to him and promised him immortality if he would buy it with the lives of his heirs."

"That must have been when Kroaky took shelter with my brother and the Host," said Jame, as more fragments of the previous night's dreams came back to her.

Graykin glared. "Who's telling this story anyway, and who's this 'Kroaky' fellow?"

"That's a very good question."

"You're laughing at me again."

"Well, maybe a little. Please continue. King Kruin was dying and . . . ?"

"For a while, he didn't. Meantime, Karnid priests were welcome here and made a lot of converts. When Kruin found out that he'd been fooled, he drove out his precious advisor. After his death, the city council sent the entire Host against Urakarn."

Including Tori, thought Jame, remembering the lacework of scars on her brother's hands, the mark of Karnid torture that had almost crippled him for life.

"I don't know much more," Graykin concluded, "not being a Karnid initiate."

"Well, see what you can find out."

Gray hadn't grown up within the Kencyrath, Jame reminded herself. For him, perhaps, one Kencyr disaster merged into another. The slaughter of the Knorth women, the debacle in the White Hills, Ganth's exile, Genjar's catastrophe before Urakarn, the Kencyr Host against the Waster Horde in the desert before the battle at the Cataracts . . . say "massacre," and which one did you mean? Looking back, it was hardly a surprise that the Southern Host was so depleted. Trinity, the entire Kencyrath had been bled white since it had first come to Rathillien, never mind what had happened before in all those other lost worlds or during the Fall itself. What was left to fight the final battle with Perimal Darkling? Perhaps only three, the Tyr-ridan, of whom she potentially was one.

G'ah. Jame shook her head. All the weight of the Kencyrath's past seemed to settle on her shoulders, for surely That-Which-Destroys would have to move before Preservation and Creation. She wondered how her brother and Kindrie were doing. If they couldn't learn to cooperate, the entire history of the Kencyrath would be for nothing.

Her cousin might have some sense of that, but her brother as yet had none. What a time to leave them alone together.

Then too, she had little trust in her own ability to fulfill her role—that is, without destroying everything in her path. Tai-tastigon in flames, Karkinaroth crumbling, Tentir rocked to its roots...past results did not bode well for the future.

Their conference done, she rose to depart. "Same place and time next week?"

"I'll send you word. Some of my guild are getting suspicious, especially Hangnail, the same who shoved you down the ladder into the Undercliff."

"Watch out for that one. He means you no good."

"I know," he said, and laughed soundlessly, dismissively, within his hood.

≪⫷ **III** ⫸≫

FROM THE DESOLATE OUTER RINGS, Jame made her way toward the central towers, one of which housed Gaudaric's work-shops. The lower three floors offered such armor as the average buyer might want, all well-crafted but nothing special, mostly made by apprentices and journeymen. The fourth floor, however, was the master's showroom. Gaudaric's basic style was supremely functional, whether in steel or leather, elegant in its simplicity. However, he also entertained himself with fancier touches. Shafts of light from arched windows illuminated contoured breastplates of shining steel, helmets fashioned to resemble the heads of lions or bears, woven strips of rhi-sar leather in all the colors of nature, and one whole suit that looked like some fantastic beast with horns everywhere. Most wondrous of all, however, was a simple scale armor vest made of rathorn ivory, worth half the guild's annual income.

"Talisman, Talisman!" Byrne rushed down the spiral stair from an upper floor. "Are we going to see the Eye of Kothifir?"

His grandfather followed him, wiping sooty hands on a leather apron.

"Is it safe?" Jame asked him.

"If you mean because of Lord Artifice, I think so. True, his boys were a trifle heavy-handed when we first met, but Ruso isn't so bad, really. For the most part, he's just obsessed with his craft."

"And you aren't?"

Gaudaric ruffled his fringe of gray hair, considering. "I'm serious about it, of course. It's my life, but so is my family. Ruso only has his mechanical toys, his bullyboys, and his ambition. To tell the truth, I feel a bit sorry for him."

Not entirely reassured, Jame let Byrne tug her out into the street, bound for the Optomancers' Tower. It was a tall, thin, crooked structure full of strange devices, eyeballs in jars, and prisms flaring rainbows against whitewashed walls, all glimpsed through windows as they climbed the outside stair. At the top, just above the cloud cover, the tower ended in a windowless dome, and out of its door popped a gangly young man wearing enormous lenses in wire frames that drooped with their weight.

"Welcome to the Eye!" he said as he bowed to them with a flourish into the darkness. "Watch your step. Oh!"

Byrne had barged into something that tinkled like glass wind chimes and broke.

"Not to worry. Not to worry. The Eye sees all regardless. Just stand still while I close the door. There."

They stood still as ordered in darkness so total that not even Jame's keen night vision helped her. Meanwhile their guide fumbled around them. More glass broke.

"Damn. Where is it? Oh, here."

A sudden, dazzling light pooled on the floor in a circle some four feet across.

It took Jame a moment to focus on what she saw. The lens pointed west, over Kothifir's walls along the edge of the Escarpment, toward Gemma, the circling clouds presenting no obstacle. Dots moved on the clifftop plain, the closer identifiable as Kencyr patrols. Jealous Gemma was always threatening raids on its wealthy sister-city, necessitating at least the Host's token presence Overcliff.

The lens rotated, grinding.

"Look!" cried Byrne in delight.

There was the Rose Tower, as clear as life. Tiny figures climbed up and down its circular stair. Merchants swarmed around its foot, one of them having his pocket picked. Jame waved her hand over the scene. It rippled across her fingers, which trailed shadows across the floor.

The focus shifted up the tower. Near the top was a ring of projecting thorns from which figures dangled, surrounded by diving birds. They must be hanging just outside the windows of the king's apartment. Krothen had made good his threat to execute the Gemman raiders captured eleven days ago. Jame had heard rumors that one of them was the son of a Gemman council member.

"Show me home!" Byrne demanded.

Above them, the optomancers' dome groaned and rotated. The city on the floor revolved, dizzyingly, until Gaudaric's tower came into sight. The armorer himself was sitting on a window ledge, buffing a helmet. Byrne waved to him.

"Hello, Grandpa!"

Beyond the tower, out of focus, was the rim of the Escarpment.

"If you can see over that," said Jame, "I'll really be impressed."

The image moved close to the rim, closer, and then the view angled sharply down toward the red tiled roofs of the camp.

"It's all done with mirrors," said the young man proudly.

Jame watched the flecks that were people swarming around the inner ward where local traders had set up the market that Rue had wanted to visit. A smaller cluster of specks was riding down the southern road, reminding Jame of the unfortunate Knorth ten-command whom that accursed note had sent forth to labor on this, their free day. She remembered the rest of her conversation with Rue, the things said, the things unsaid, and sudden unease gripped her.

"Can you show me the southern road?"

The retreating specks grew, then blurred, but not before she had counted them. There were only nine.

"Byrne, we have to go. Now."

The boy set up a howl, but she found his arm in the dark and grabbed it. Where was the damned door? The image on the floor cast some reflected light over its surroundings even while its brilliance dazzled the eye. She tripped over a stool, breaking more glass, and lunged toward a faint, rectangular outline.

"Oh, I say!" protested the young man behind her.

"Sorry, sorry..."

Then they were outside, on the stair, down in the street. Byrne hung back, wailing with disappointment.

"Look." Jame stopped short, still gripping his arm. "I apologize for dragging you away, but this is important... no, listen:

sometimes grownups have to do things that children don't under-stand. That's part of what makes them grownups."

Byrne wiped a snotty nose. "Like when Grandpa can't play with me because he has to work?"

"Yes. Now, do you want to grow up or not?"

"Y-yes..."

"Then humor me."

The child snuffled all the way back to the Armorers' Tower, but stopped dragging his feet. Jame left him there with one of his grandfather's journeymen.

"Get me down as fast as you can," she told the liftmen at the rim, and stepped into the cage.

It fell out from under her. She clung to the bars, suspended above the floor, wondering if they had simply dropped it. The camp rushed up to meet her. Finally, her feet touched the floor, and then her knees almost buckled. The cage slammed down onto its platform, raising a billow of dust and causing yelps of alarm from its toll-keepers. Jame staggered out, into the camp.

"Lost your command, have you, Jamethiel?" Fash called out to her, laughing, as she ran past the Caineron barracks.

Her sixth sense told her that Bel-tairi was with the remount herd to the west of the camp while Death's-head was ranging much farther afield. She called them both. Bel met her at the South Gate. She scrambled onto the mare's bare back and they set off at a gallop down the south road towards the shadowy Apollynes.

IV

BRIER AND THE REST of the ten-command had gotten perhaps ten miles away from Kothifir by the time that Jame caught up with them, having slowed Bel alternately to a trot and a walk so as not to overtire her. Jame rode up beside Brier Iron-thorn on her tall chestnut gelding. Bel's head barely came up to his shoulder. Neither spoke for the next mile. The others tactfully fell back to give them privacy.

"You should have told me," Jame said at last, nudging the Whinno-hir into a brief trot to catch up with the chestnut's longer stride. Trinity, no wonder people used saddles; her tailbone throbbed with every bounce.

Brier shrugged. "You had other things to do. Besides, why should you waste a day with the rest of us?"

"Because I'm your ten-commander, idiot. I assume that precious note of yours included me."

"It did. Specifically. In none too polite terms."

"Which made you all the more determined to leave me out."

Brier shrugged again. "It was a stupid order, and presumptuous, given who sent it, to demand that the Knorth Lordan do anything. To involve you in such nonsense demeans us all."

Jame sighed. "If it had only been addressed to me, I might have torn it up the way Gorbel did with his challenge. Rue had it right: this little expedition proves nothing unless we run into a raid. But I *am* your commander and therefore responsible for you. In the future, we aren't going to like many of the commands given to us, but we will still have to obey them. Do you have any spare water, by the way?"

Brier unhooked a goatskin pouch from her saddle and handed it down to her. Jame drank, then leaned forward to offer Bel a cupped handful of water. The mare's pink tongue rasped her fingers dry, once, twice, and again.

"All right," she said, straightening, a bit defensive. "I'm here without travel rations, tack, or even a weapon, discounting the knife in my boot. When I saw you heading out without me, well, I didn't stop to think."

She paused, flicked by her sixth sense. Death's-head was nearby, but so was something else.

"Horses," she said. "Strange ones."

They were finally in the foothills of the Apollynes, their view restricted by rolling hills, shrubs, and giant rocks. Their mounts stirred uneasily as hoofbeats approached both ahead of them and behind. Could it be another Gemman raid like the one that had cost the young seeker her life?

The rathorn Death's-head roared around a boulder lower down and surged up the incline toward them, his white mane roached up all down his spine and his tail flying like a battle standard.

Simultaneously, black mares erupted from the surrounding rocks with riders also in black, *cheches* concealing all but hard, bright eyes set in sun-dark faces.

"Karnids," Brier snapped. "Circle up."

The cadets backed rump to rump with Bel squeezed in the middle, in danger of being kicked by any one of them. Jame slipped off and dodged between the surrounding horses. Death's-head swerved toward her, as usual nearly running her over but allowing her to grab his mane and swing onto his back as he surged past. The rathorn pivoted to face the mares, then paused, snorting. Some of them were in season. Their scent drew off his attention as others dashed in.

Jame found herself in the center of a swirling storm of horse-flesh. Sleek black heads with red eyes snaked past. White fangs snapped at her. Hands grabbed. She drew her knife and hacked at them, all the time clinging to the rathorn's mane, forced to ride high by the roached spine. Brier's shout seemed distant. They were running away with her, the rathorn stumbling over rocky ground, striking almost at random.

Come. You know where you belong.

The image formed in her mind of a tall, black-robed figure lifting his arms to receive her. He wore a single, silver glove.

I hacked off that hand when it reached out between scarlet ribbons to claim me...

Death's-head snorted and steadied.

Not my lady.

Then he stumbled again and threw Jame over his head. She fell among rocks and lay there, dazed. All around her iron hooves struck spark from stone. A hand grabbed her arm and jerked her up across a saddle, knocking the breath out of her. The dimming sky whirled overhead. Then it went black.

V

FLAMES LEAPED IN THE DARKNESS, and black-clad figures hovered, flickering in and out of sight.

"Do you recant... do you profess... then we must convince you, for your own good."

... gloves of red-hot wire...

Oh god, my hands! Burning, burning...

⋙ VI ⋘

JAME HEARD THE FIRE CRACKLE and cringed from the memory of searing pain. *Ah, my hands...*

No. Rather, it was her head that ached. Again. She touched it gingerly and encountered a bandage wrapped around her temples.

Branches snapped like fingers in the fireplace and flames leaped. She was in her quarters at the camp and someone—Rue?—had set a blaze there. Jorin stretched out beside her, as usual complaining when her movement disturbed him, then rolling onto his back for a stomach rub. The bed was soft under her, the room warm although the late summer nights were growing cool. A large form eclipsed the fire and threw another log on it. Sparks flared up around him as he turned.

"Awake, are you?"

It was Harn Grip-hard.

"Y-yes, Ran. How long..."

"Enough for your ten-command to fight free and get you back here, plus a few hours. It's passing on toward midnight. You took quite a crack to your head."

"Those black mares...what were they?"

"The Karnids' mounts? They're called thorns. Introduce a mare in season to a rathorn stallion and, if he doesn't kill her, eleven months later you get the blackest, meanest little filly you can imagine. All they lack is their sire's armor. Now, why were the Karnids after you?"

"I didn't realize that they were. It was a confusing situation. I don't even know who grabbed me."

"That was Iron-thorn again, trying to get you out from underfoot before someone trampled you into jelly. Then your command ran for it, quite sensibly, with that bloody beast of yours mounting rear guard. What were all of you doing so far out to begin with?"

Jame told him about the challenge.

He snorted, went to the door, and spoke to someone, probably Rue.

Jame lay back, thinking. Why had she had that sudden image of the Master reaching out for her?

Come. You know where you belong.

Gerridon thought that she belonged with him, in Perimal Darkling, as the new Dream-weaver. What did the Karnids have to do with that?

Then there had been that flash of Tori at Urakarn, under the Karnid torture that had nearly crippled him and left his hands scarred for life. Had he just woken at Gothregor, that nightmare memory still seared into his mind? Once again, it seemed, their dreams had crossed.

Harn stumped back bringing a dark, sullen third-year cadet.

"Char here says that neither he nor his friends sent you any such message."

"We've been waiting to tell you, ever since we first heard," said Char, sounding exasperated. "We would never have made up such a lame-brained challenge."

Jame snorted. "As if any of them make any sense. Is this how you test your juniors, with stupid commands? We each find our own rite of passage. Do you agree?"

"Well, yes, of course, but..."

"But nothing. Let the other houses make fools of themselves if they must. Here and now, I'm enforcing my brother's order and forbidding it within the Knorth."

The cadet stiffened, at first with outrage and then as if drawn further up against his will by her sudden tone of authority. Here, after all, was not only a second-year master-ten but the putative commander of the Knorth barracks and the Highlord's heir.

"Yes...Lordan," he said, saluted, and left.

Harn drew up a chair and sat down beside the fire. Wooden legs groaned under his weight.

"So," he said heavily, looking into the flames. "We have to ask ourselves: who among the Host would want to lure you into such a trap, presumably in collusion with the Karnids?"

"If you're right."

"Accept for a moment that I am."

Jame considered her various enemies, in particular Fash, but how would a Caineron cadet newly arrived at Kothifir have connections with Urakarn? Further thought along those lines made her head ache anew.

"We'll know in time," she said, dismissing the matter.

"You mean, when he—or she—tries again."

"If it takes that. Harn, why have you been avoiding me?"

He shifted in his seat.

"It's been that noticeable, has it?"

"To anyone with half an eye. You can't think that as Knorth Lordan I want to take my brother's place as Commandant of the Host."

He snorted. "A fine mess that would be."

"Agreed. So?"

Harn fidgeted some more, making the chair's joints protest. "When Blackie first joined the Host, I didn't treat him very well. I was a fool."

"You didn't know him then. I don't think he knew himself yet. It takes fire to forge steel."

...oh God, my hands...!

He gave her a sidelong look under unkempt brows. "And what fires have you known, heh?"

"A few, if you can call them that. Not enough to be my brother's equal."

He snorted. "No doubt. I saw him tested early, before Urakarn. He was challenged too, by the Caineron. Burr warned me. We burst into Genjar's quarters to find Blackie standing, hooded, on a shaky stool with his hands tied behind him. The other end of the rope was thrown over a rafter and knotted around his neck."

"Yes, I know."

He shot her another glance. "He told you about it? That surprises me. I nearly flared."

"But you didn't."

"Around Blackie, I seldom do. That was no such fire as the one to come, but it showed his mettle, if I hadn't been too blind to see it. In those days, his strength lay in endurance. In you, now, we all feel the power building, like that poor booby of a third-year, when you let it out."

Now he had embarrassed her. "I can't help what I am, only what I may become, and maybe not even that. I'm a nemesis, Harn. Yes, potentially one of the Three. And I don't know yet what I might destroy."

The big Kendar rose and stood over her, a hulking shape edged with light.

"A nemesis, eh? That explains a lot of things. And your brother?"

"A creator, not that he knows it yet."

"Too bad there aren't three of you. Now, that would be something. Are you Blackie's destroyer?"

Jame forced herself not to shrink in his ominous shadow. They had known each other at Tentir, but here things were different, closer to the bone. His voice was mild, but his big hands unconsciously flexed. He would kill to protect Torisen. The thought wasn't foremost in his mind, but it lurked close to his berserker nature, and she had seen how suddenly that could be triggered.

She wrapped her hands around one of his (Trinity, how easily he could have crushed her fingers), and held it until its twitching stilled.

"I will never willingly harm my brother, or you, or anyone else whom I love."

He relaxed slowly and freed his hand. "Well, no. At least not intentionally. You'll care what you do and take responsibility for your actions afterward, however daft they are. I see that now. What more can one ask, eh? I'll bid you good night, then, my lady. Sleep well."

Jame did, although at one point she half-woke to hear Jorin growling. In the morning, Rue discovered that a note addressed to the lordan had been slipped under the door. Jame unfolded it and read the four-word unsigned message:

"Leave," it said, "and never return."

CHAPTER VII
Equinox

Autumn 1–36

I

SUMMER ENDED and autumn advanced. The days remained warm but lost that breathtaking blast of summer. The nights were cool enough to make a fire or extra jacket welcome. It even rained a bit, not that the irrigated Betwixt Valley needed it where the fall harvest was already under way. However, the farmers probably welcomed it in the terraced mountains, and it did help to lay the dust on the training fields south of the Host's camp.

Jame thought a lot about the senior cadets' challenge, if one could call it that. All it had needed to become a threat had been an addition of the words "or else." It was also double edged: if she ignored it, they had won. If she did as they demanded, not that she had any such intention, they still won. All in all, it was a game she refused to play.

Meanwhile, Harn kept her close to Kothifir for a time after the Karnids' attempted kidnapping, only allowing her to go out with her ten-command to practice. When the day was done, however, she slipped away to tend to Death's-head.

The black mares with their wicked fangs had savaged the rathorn badly, especially on his unarmored flanks, and the wounds had festered. Jame missed the Tentir horse-master's advice, but had secured poultices from his Kothifiran counterpart. The man was eager to apply them himself; however, Jame had put him off. She supposed it was only natural that he wanted to lay hands on such a fabulous equine as a rathorn. Whether Death's-head would have let him was another matter. Anyway, she was inclined to think that Bel-tairi's attentions to the injuries helped more than any ointment.

Thus it was that, on the twenty-ninth of Autumn, after a day of maneuvers in the eastern field, Jame set out for the distant tumble of boulders in the creek bed where the rathorn made his lair.

First, she had to cross the southern road and the western training field, no easy matter now that the latter was rapidly filling with wagons for the next caravan, which promised to be the largest in generations. At least a hundred carts had already gathered on the plain, each at the heart of its own campsite. Attendants swarmed around them while draft horses snorted on picket lines and a constant stream of couriers descended from the city bearing freshly minted trade goods. All the craft guilds were working full time, including Gaudaric's. Jame saw his son-in-law Ean directing the stowage of armor while Byrne ran about getting in everyone's way.

"Talisman, Talisman!" he cried, collaring her by the leg. "Are you coming with us?"

"I doubt it," Jame said with regret, ruffling his chestnut curls. She would have liked nothing better.

"Try to come. Try!"

"I will if I can."

"You aren't going anywhere," said Ean, detaching his son from Jame. "How often do I have to tell you?"

"Oh, but Papa...!"

Jame left them to what promised to be a long wrangle.

Beyond the field, the land roughened into dips and hollows carved out by the Amar's earlier channels before the Betwixt had been irrigated. Some still ran with the river's overflow. Jame descended into one. Rounding the creek's curve, she saw the rathorn standing like an ivory sentinel with the water curling around his legs while Bel licked the crescent-shaped scars on his flanks. Of course he had heard her coming. He brandished his horns, slashing rainbows out of the current, but an impatient snort from Bel held him in place. Jame ran a hand along his side. The infection was gone at last, the wounds scabbing over. In such a massed attack, unlike any he would face under natural circumstances, he needed a properly armed rider to protect his back. Jame resolved to pay more attention to her sword and scythe-arm practice.

She unslung her backpack. The rathorn's nose, nasal tusk and all, was in it as soon as she had loosened the straps and she braced herself as he rummaged. A snort inflated the bag like a bellows. Out came his jaws clamped around the roast chicken that she had brought. Bones were no problem, she had discovered. Death's-head could digest just about anything.

Leaving the creek bed, she returned to the camp in the descending twilight. After dinner in the Knorth barracks, she met Shade in the common canteen for a mug of thin ale.

Hazing had continued sporadically in the other houses but not in the Knorth, despite grumbles from the thirty-odd third-year cadets who were all that were left of fifty who had ridden to the Cataracts.

Meanwhile, randon kept disappearing from the Randir, but in such a trickle, attracting so little attention, that the other houses hardly noticed.

"The ominous thing," Shade said, cradling her mug, "is that so far the only Randir to vanish have been sworn to some Highborn other than Lord Kenan or Lady Rawneth."

"Is it a cull?"

"One would almost think so, but where are they going?"

"You aren't sworn to your father or to your grandmother. Neither is Ran Awl."

"But Frost, the current commander of the Host's Randir, is, and she doesn't seem to take the situation very seriously."

As they spoke, keeping their voices low in the noisy room, Addy moved restlessly around Shade's neck like a thick, molten torque. When she stretched out her triangular head, black tongue flickering, Jame reached out to her. Glittering scales flowed over her palm, soft and dry but with hard muscles rippling beneath. She and Shade played the serpent back and forth between them, over and under, each pursuing her own thought, finding no answers.

"Take care," Jame said as the other at last retrieved her pet and stood up. "Watch your back, and Ran Awl's too. We can't afford to lose either of you."

Shade nodded brusquely, turned and left.

⟨⟨⟨ **II** ⟩⟩⟩

THE AUTUMNAL EQUINOX came several days later. Although it was a workday, Jame got permission to visit Kothifir for the morning, taking Gorbel and Timmon with her. Gorbel had witnessed the Merikit festival honoring the harvest and the Great Hunt, but Timmon, new to any such native celebrations, was eager to see one. Jame herself wondered what approach the Kothifirans would take to the equinox.

The other two lordan argued all the way up the cliff about the recent hazing.

"It's traditional," Gorbel insisted yet again. "Cadets new to Kothifir are always tested."

"What, with being made to wash dishes?"

"That was a special task, just for you."

"Well, it didn't do much good. My house still doesn't take me seriously."

"They do as a scullery maid."

Gorbel's eyes were screwed shut and his squat face ran with sweat. Without thinking, Jame had led them to the open lift cage. She joined in the conversation to distract him.

"Perhaps your approach was the best, simply to ignore an inappropriate challenge. I don't know if I did my house a favor by forbidding them altogether. D'you think that's going to make my cadets anxious to prove themselves in other ways?"

Gorbel considered this. "It might, especially among those who haven't been blooded yet. Trinity!"

The cage had bounced and his eyes had involuntarily popped open. He stared, transfixed, at the abyss beneath his feet.

Jame hastily told him about Shade's observations concerning the missing Randir.

"Is it just cadets who are disappearing or established randon too?" asked Timmon.

"I think both."

"It's serious, then, although as the presumed commander of the Ardeth barracks—ha!—I haven't heard anything about it. Have you, Gorbel?"

"A word or two, yes. Obviously not enough."

"Well," said Jame, "the more who know, the sooner we may have an answer. Not all the Randir are rotten, and it seems to be the good ones who are being targeted."

The lift cage swooped over the balustrade and landed with a thump on Kothifir's forecourt. Gorbel let out his breath with a loud "Huh!" and wiped his brow.

When they stepped out, the swirling street greeted them. It was even more crowded than it had been at the solstice, apprentices, journeymen, and masters intermingling, each festooned with the bright ribbons denoting his or her individual guild. Distant horns and drums sounded. People began to move toward the noise, toward the central plaza. Bands went with them, playing different, discordant tunes while venders loudly hawked their wares from the sidelines. The three lordan bought fish strips dusted in almonds and paper twists full of garlic snails to munch on the way. Reaching the plaza, they climbed up onto a convenient balcony, not high enough to set Gorbel's nerves freshly ajangle.

From above, they watched the Kothifirans organize themselves into guilds. This time they didn't carry golden emblems, so they must have something other than races in mind. Dozens of pots hung some three stories up, suspended from catwalks invisible above the perennially circling clouds. Guilds were forming under them. The bands trailed off into expectant silence as the three guild lords appeared high on the stairs of the Rose Tower.

"Welcome to the Equinox!" Lord Merchandy called down in his reedy voice. The people below hushed each other in order to listen. "We meet here balanced between seasons, between success and potential disaster, or greater success. The fall harvest is safely in. The winter crops are yet to be planted. More important, we are about to launch the biggest trade caravan ever to enter the Wastes..."

He coughed, his voice failing. Lady Professionate took his arm to steady him. Ruso stepped forward.

"To the greater glory of Kothifir, then, and to profit!" he roared over the railing. "Ready, steady, climb!"

The plaza dissolved into chaos. Some rushed off to snatch materials from side streets. The carpenters' guide came running back with boards which they began hastily to bang into a platform. The masons hauled in stone blocks. Bricklayers slapped brick on brick. Tapestry makers wheeled in their largest upright loom and swarmed up the warp threads to the top bar. Binders stacked up books. Most of the others, who couldn't turn to their working materials, bent down and began to form human towers. The nearest rose close by the watching lordan, one tier, two... People leaned in to support the base while others climbed onto their shoulders and stood, wavering. Three, four, five...

The pots still swung high above their heads.

"I bet they don't make it," said Timmon.

Gorbel grunted. "How much?"

"A golden *arax*."

"Done."

Six, seven, eight...

"Look," said Jame, pointing.

A curious apparition had appeared at the edge of the plaza. It looked at first like ten gray-clad men standing, unsupported, on each other's shoulders, swaying forward in unison step by step. Then one saw that they were connected by two parallel ropes with loops for each one's feet and hands. The clouds thinned momentarily. On a catwalk overhead, two more men pushed one end and then the other of a beam balanced across the handrail. The upper ends of the ropes were secured to this bar. Its movement swung the attenuated tower forward like the crosspiece of a puppeteer.

Jame recognized the top man just as he spotted her. Graykin flashed her a grin that reminded her how young he actually was.

"Go, Intelligencer!" she called to him, clapping. "Rah, rah, rah!"

Timmon and Gorbel stared at her.

Below, the binders' pile of books began to slide, taking those who knelt on it with it. They spilled over into the next tower, taking it down, and so on and on in a spreading circle. The chaos lapped over the masons, who had only succeeded in raising one level of stone, and collapsed the carpenters' jury-rigged tower. Amid yells and not a few screams, the spies advanced, even after the lowest two had been knocked out of their stirrups. Graykin reached up and struck a pot. It burst, spraying him and those beneath him with honeyed milk.

"What in Perimal's name..." said Timmon.

"I think it's a fertility ritual, or a way to secure luck, or both. Do our ceremonies make any more sense?"

"Of course they do," said Gorbel, wiping splattered milk off his face. "If nothing else, none of them is this messy."

"Better spilt milk than blood."

Below, the plaza was sorting itself out with many cries that the Intelligencers' Guild had cheated. Graykin's tower clambered down and bolted for cover, leaving its leader to stand for a moment at the mouth of a side street making a rude gesture. Then he too scampered back into the shadows.

"As a portent, though," said Jame thoughtfully, "I don't much like it, assuming one believes in such things."

"Let's go see what the Undercliff has to offer," said Timmon.

"We have to report back at noon, not long from now," Jame said regretfully. "Anyway, I understand all that happens is that the old gods wage a glorified food-fight, and the Favorite has to eat everything that hits him."

With that, they turned reluctantly back to the Rim, where this time they took the enclosed cage down.

Rue was waiting for Jame at the gate to the barracks, practically hopping from foot to foot with excitement.

"They've posted who's going with the caravan to guard it, and our ten-command is on the list!"

Jame stopped short, remembering her recent restriction to the camp and its environs. "No."

"Yes! There are one hundred and fifty wagons, three hundred attendants, a thousand Kothifiran guards, and four hundred of us. The Commandant left you a message."

Jame accepted the note and unfolded it. "With such a large escort," Harn had written in his barely legible scrawl, "I dare you to get into trouble."

CHAPTER VIII
Pounding on the Door

Autumn 49

I

BANG, BANG, BANG!

Torisen couldn't sleep with that pounding inside his head.

"Be quiet!" he shouted at it.

Yce licked his chin. When had she slipped under the covers with him?

"Be strong," the wolver pup whined to him, her whiskered lips tickling his beard. "Remember, fathers may devour their young, but only if we are weak."

"Be still," whispered Jame's voice in his ear as her strong, slender arms wound around him and her body pressed against his. "He has to sleep sooner or later. Then we will have him."

How like them both to think in terms of fighting back. How alike they were, in so many ways.

And white-haired Kindrie? He stood aloof with his back turned, braced against that crack of anger, but stubborn too in his endurance. Ancestors knew, he had suffered as much as any of them.

Am I weaker than he? Torisen wondered.

But their cases were different: Kindrie had faced his demons and (presumably) won, while Torisen still had his dead father lodged like a festering splinter in his soul-image, behind a none too securely locked door.

The tapping began again, almost sly at first but getting louder and louder as Ganth raged.

Do you think you can ignore me? Stupid boy, who has brought a Shanir abomination into my house! Stupid girl, with your cursed blood!

Torisen tightened his grip on his sister in the bed where they cowered together, children again. "Mother is gone. I'll protect you."

"And Kindrie too?"

In the sodden field between Wilden and Shadow Rock, the healer had warned him barely in time about shape-shifting Kenan and arguably had saved his life. In return, he had welcomed their Shanir cousin into the Knorth's "small but interestingly inbred family." Father couldn't make him take back those words... could he?

The thought was greeted with harsh laughter. *Would you challenge me, boy?*

Jame was already drawing away, a child no longer but a supple-limbed temptress whose touch he longed to regain. "You let me go before. Will you again?"

"Never!" he cried, and cringed at the loudness of his own voice. "I love you!"

Tap, tap, boom!

He lurched awake in his tower bedroom at Gothregor. From the hearth, Yce regarded him warily.

⛧ **II** ⛧

THE JARAN MATRIARCH TRISHIEN sat by an open window in the Women's Halls, reading. A cool breeze scented with fallen leaves stirred the brightly illuminated pages of her book. Winter was coming. She could feel it in her bones. Soon she would have to spend more time in the warm common room, forfeiting her precious privacy. Time to enjoy it while she could.

A tentative knock on the door made her sigh and put aside her work. Kindrie sidled apologetically into the room, his white hair as always disordered and his pale cheeks slightly flushed from the climb to her quarters.

"Lady, I brought you the salve that Kells promised."

Trishien opened the glass jar which he proffered and sniffed.

"Almond oil and peppermint, I think, with a dash of cayenne. Ah, that scent clears the head, even if my problems lie elsewhere."

"Yes, also white willow and birch. I helped Kells mix it. If you like," he added, hesitantly, "and if the joint pain increases, I can work with your soul-image. I've had some practice in that area with Index at Mount Alban."

Trishien smiled, imagining what such sessions with the irascible old scrollsman must be like. What was Index's soul-image? Probably his precious herb shed. What was her own? Most people didn't know, but she suspected it was a library or even a single scroll. If the latter, how curious it would be to know which one, and how it ended. "Come winter, I may accept your offer. So." She regarded him from behind the flash of reading lens slotted into her matron's mask. "You are still assisting the herbalist. Nothing else?"

Kindrie looked, abashed, at his boots. "I help wherever I can, but no, Torisen hasn't let me near his papers yet."

Trishien sighed. "Stubborn, foolish boy, not to take help when he needs it. Even I have heard how his piles of correspondence grow daily and business goes untended. Why else does he think Kirien sent you to Gothregor? Do you miss her?"

"Yes, lady," said the healer, in a wistful tone that told her more than his words. "She gave me this," he added, as if in explanation, fingering his blue woolen robe.

"Of course she did," said Trishien with a half smile. "My grandniece has good taste in all matters."

"Am I disturbing you, lady?" asked a voice at the still-open door. There stood Torisen Highlord himself, looking ghastly. His face was white under his beard and his silver-gray eyes opaque with pain. He stepped into the room and stumbled against a chest. "Sorry. I have a blinding headache. Literally."

Trishien went quickly to help him settle into a chair.

Yce crouched on the threshold, wary and watchful.

Kindrie hovered, unsure whether to help or to go away.

"Stay," Trishien whispered to him. To Torisen she said, "How may I assist you, my lord?"

He laughed a bit shakily. "The last time something like this happened, talking to you helped. If I told Burr or Rowan, they would fuss me halfway to my pyre."

Trishien turned to her table, deliberately slid the lens out of her mask, and laid them carefully down.

As once before, her naked, farsighted gaze discerned the shadow that stooped over the Highlord's bent shoulders, shrouding him.

"Tell me," she said.

"Bang, bang, bang, he won't stop pounding on the door inside my soul-image. The panels are shaking. The lock is jumping half out of its socket."

Trishien felt her own heart knock against her ribs. Who was she to meddle with a problem such as this? But she must try. "It sounds to me," she said carefully, "as if your father is throwing a temper tantrum." The shadow raised an indistinct head over the Highlord's dark, bent one. "Yes, you, My Lord Ganth. What, pray tell, is the problem this time?"

Torisen lifted his own head so that the other's features overlay it like a caul; cold, silver eyes glimmering through.

"I want that stinking Shanir out of my house," he said in a harsh voice not his own. "Now. See how he lurks, spying. What is he thinking, eh?"

Kindrie flinched and again edged toward the door. Again, Trishien stopped him.

"What do you see?" he whispered.

Rising anger mastered her fear, although her voice still shook. "A sorry sight. You always did hide behind your anger, Ganth. When you couldn't have what you wanted, you tried to tear down everything, at whatever cost to anyone else. You were hurt, by your brother, by your father, by life, so you hurt others. All your son wants is to build a better world. He has the innate power to do that. Who are you to stop him?"

"My world ended in ruins. So will his. Do you think he is stronger than I am?"

"Or do you mean, than you were? Yes, when you leave him alone. Oh, Ganth." Her anger gave way to pity. "I loved you once. Perhaps I still do. Don't destroy yourself a second time in your son."

"Ah, Trish. I could never love you as you deserved, not after I saw her."

Again, that mysterious woman who had seduced the Highlord of the Kencyrath, had become his children's mother, and had destroyed him with her leaving.

"'Alas,'" Trishien murmured, "'for the greed of a man and the deceit of a woman, that we should come to this!'"

"You don't understand. What happened was fated."

"Well, it was certainly fatal. Accept that and leave this boy alone."

"Never!" His shadow spread, devouring the room. Kindrie shivered in the sudden chill as if under an eclipse, the past overarching the present. Yce tensed, snarling. "I do with my own flesh what I choose!"

Trishien gripped Torisen's head. It took all her strength to force the darkness back through his eyes into his bones. "Ganth, my love, you are dead. Go away."

Torisen swayed and nearly pitched out of the chair, but Trishien caught him by the shoulders.

"I think I understand what you did, lady," the healer said over the dark, bowed head which he dared not touch, "and I thank you for it, but we both know that he will never be whole while that presence haunts him."

Trishien sighed. "I have no power to exorcise it for more than a time. Perhaps you do."

Kindrie drew back. "Lady, to touch him is to release what lies within, whether he is ready or not."

"Perhaps, then, this is something he must do for himself. At least we have gained a respite."

Torisen caught his breath sharply and straightened, wiping a hand across his sweat-beaded face.

"What was I saying?" he asked, blinking, sounding dazed.

"Nothing to fret about, my lord." But her hands trembled as she fitted the lens back into her mask. Had she done good here, or further harm? "How do you feel now?"

"Better," he said in wonder, touching his temple. "The pounding has stopped. All that's left is a mutter and a sense of . . . pity? But that makes no sense."

Kindrie stirred.

"Oh," said Torisen, noticing him for the first time. "It's you."

"Do you want me to leave, my lord?"

"No." He shook his head gingerly as if to clear it, and winced again. "I've been in a damnable muddle about you for far too long. This is your family. I said so. You'll stay, if you please, and take up the job you came to do. Ancestors know, I need the help."

Trishien's eyes met Kindrie's over his head and she nodded. One step at a time.

CHAPTER IX
Into the Wastes

Autumn 50–Winter 12

I

THE CARAVAN was scheduled to depart on the first of Winter, ten days in the future. Meanwhile, Kothifir seethed like a kicked ants' nest, getting ready. Couriers came and went between the city and the western training field where the wagons met. Every day, more joined those already there. Many of the latter had never traveled the Wastes before and were more eager to join in the potential profit than knowledgeable about the risks.

"They say it's not only the biggest convoy ever," said Timmon, "but also possibly the last."

He, Jame, and Gorbel had met at the canteen after a day of maneuvers to share a cask of the Ardeth Lordan's private wine stock. Gorbel probably had his own. Jame didn't, not having thought to lay in such a supply. She sipped, trying not to make a face. Fine vintages were probably wasted on her anyway, if this was one of them.

Then too, her head still hammered from the previous night's dreams.

Bang, bang, bang...

"I do with my own flesh what I choose!"

Damn you, Father, and poor Tori, to have such a monster caged inside your skull.

If he didn't treat Kindrie properly, though, she would have something to say on her own, and he would damn well listen to her.

Timmon nudged her. "Are you all right?"

"Right enough." Jame rubbed her forehead and brought her mind back to the matter at hand.

A mixture of seasoned randon, third-year cadets and second-years were going on the expedition, mostly those who had never previously had the opportunity. Timmon was one of them, to his delight. Gorbel, to his disgust, was not, nor were any other Caineron: Lord Caldane had made his interest in discovering the caravan's destination entirely too obvious. Gorbel had told them about his father's private explorations into the Wastes, to the vast, glistening pan of the Great Salt Sea and beyond.

"All they found were ruins half buried in the sand," he had said in disgust. "Those, and the shell of a Kencyr temple."

That last had surprised Jame. "What, one of the missing five?"

"Kothifir, Karkinaroth, Tai-tastigon..." Timmon had counted on his fingers.

"Tai-than, perhaps." Jame wondered what Canden's expedition had found. Trinity, how long ago it seemed since she and Dally had seen their friend off from Tai-tastigon's walls.

"Kencyr prisoners at Urakarn claim to have sighted one there too," Gorbel had said.

"At *Urakarn*, in the enemy camp?" That idea had truly startled Jame.

G'ah, too many mysteries, too few answers.

She now asked, "Do they say why this might be the last caravan?"

"No," said Timmon with a grimace. "I've been among the drivers, buying them wine, listening for gossip, but they're so scared this expedition will fail that there's no loosening their tongues. King Krothen has enough wealth to last a lifetime—and to pay for his pet hobby, the Southern Host. He already has two treasure towers full of the finest trade silk. However, many merchants are gambling their fortunes and futures. It will be a hard time for Kothifir if this venture fails."

Jame wondered if that was true for Gaudaric. His principal capital lay in his talent, but the mission must be important or he wouldn't be sending his son-in-law.

Gorbel grunted. No doubt he had also tried to gather information, presumably without success. Jame could guess how hard his father must be pushing him.

"Will you take Bel-tairi with you, and that bloody rathorn?" he asked.

"I think not." Other horses still made her uneasy, but she would rather risk riding them into the desert than her own unlikely pair. "Bel is too valuable—remember, she's a Whinno-hir, hundreds if not thousands of years old—and Death's-head burns too easily."

"I had wondered," said Timmon. "With those red eyes, he's an albino, isn't he?"

"Yes. A rathorn mare's last foal often is, and an outcast too, poor boy. Others of his kind have black or gray coats, but still white manes, tails, and ivory. Speaking of which, in the desert he would not only have to carry all that weight but broil in it as well. I just hope I can get both of them to stay here."

Gorbel gave a snort of laughter. "Still can't manage the brutes, eh?"

"Bel, yes, and she's a lady, I'll thank you to remember, not a brute. Death's-head, maybe. If she stays, though, he probably will too. Jorin goes with me."

"Waugh," said the ounce from under the table, as if in agreement. Jame rubbed his back with her foot.

"Ten more days," Timmon said with a sigh, as if he were speaking of years. Jame wondered if he would be as enthusiastic deep in the desert.

As she left the canteen some time later, movement in the shadows to one side caught Jame's attention. Her hand brushed her knife's hilt, then drifted away. What should she fear here in the camp? Darkness resolved itself into Shade, muffled to the eyes in a cloak.

"Ran Awl has disappeared," she said.

Jame felt her heart skip a beat, as if at the opening move of some dire game. "You're sure?" Of course Shade was; she would have looked everywhere, questioned everyone. "What does Commander Frost say?"

"She suggests that, finding nothing wrong, Awl went home. But she wouldn't without telling her staff. Without telling me."

Jame recognized the tone. Bastard, half-Kendar daughter of a lord, shunned by most of her house, Shade had finally found someone to believe in, only to have her mentor disappear. Frost had only hinted at a cause. To be more explicit, especially if she knew better, would be the death of her honor. How much a Kencyr could get away with by simply not telling a direct lie. "It might be...perhaps...it seems..." G'ah. The bland smile, the easy evasion—was that all that honor had come to mean to her people?

Shade was watching her intently. *She wants something from me; some validation, some protection . . .*

The Randir opened her cloak at the neck. Within, golden scales shifted.

"Oh no," said Jame, stepping back. "Every time I take Addy into my care, you go off and try to get yourself killed." It suddenly occurred to her what Shade's soul-image might be. For a nascent changer, what better than a snake with its supple, ever-changing form? "Truly, protect her and she will protect you."

Shade considered this, then closed her cloak. "You understand more than I do, perhaps. So be it."

She stepped back.

"Wait! Promise me that we'll speak again before I leave."

The other nodded and faded into the shadows.

The days passed, full of exercises and bustle as the senior randon prepared their juniors for the trials to come. Jame heard much of the desert's threats and denizens, of sinksand and mirages, of hostile tribesmen and things beneath the sand, of thirst, hunger, and delirium. A lovely time they were all going to have, she thought, but still her spirits leaped at the thought.

Winter's Eve arrived. Despite the farewell festivities held throughout the camp, Jame waited in her apartment for Shade, but the Randir didn't appear.

Then it was Winter's Day.

❧❧ II ❧❧

"WHOA THERE! Wait your turn!"

The caravan ground was chaos. Drivers jockeyed into their prescribed positions, surrounded by clusters of family and well-wishers with hands outstretched as if to hold them back. Horses neighed and stomped. Oxen bellowed. Donkeys brayed. Brass bands bounced about the margin of the field, playing discordant melodies. Dogs fought. Every form of transport seemed to crowd the field from wind carts to ten-mule teams, from high-riding buggies to wagons with wheels rimmed by inflated rhi-sar intestines. Perhaps only a third had risked the Wastes before and knew what to expect there. Among the veteran traders, all drove flat-bottomed wagons with upturned prows, drawn by horse teams that would be switched to something more appropriate when they reached the desert proper.

"My place is forward," said Timmon to Jame. "See you tonight."

As he rode off with his ten-command, Char followed with his own of Knorth third-years, shooting a glower at Jame in passing. As far as she knew, all challenges had stopped in the Knorth barracks with her order, as sourly as Char had received it. Ran Onyx-eyed hadn't seemed to care one way or the other, but then how was anyone supposed to read that bland face? She was also with the caravan as second-in-command.

Jame saw Gaudaric standing by one of the flat-bottomed wagons while his daughter Evensong bade good-bye to her husband. As Ean mounted the vehicle, she retreated in tears to her father's arms.

"Byrne?" the latter called, cradling her, craning to look over the mob. "Come help with your mother. Curse it, where *is* that boy?"

Jame's ten-command took their assigned position a quarter of the way down the line of march, near Ean's wagon. Evensong greeted her with near hysteria, reaching up to clutch her hand.

"You'll take care of my beloved, won't you? Promise!"

"There now." Gaudaric patted her back. "I'm sure the lass has enough to manage already." But his eyes pleaded, for the sake of his daughter.

"I promise," said Jame, adding prudently, "to the extent that I can."

"True, you've a challenging trek ahead. I went once, when I was young. Now it's Ean's turn. Don't let the monotony of the desert seduce you into carelessness. It holds unexpected threats."

Now he tells me?

He read her expression and slapped her rawboned bay on the shoulder, making the excited gelding hop sideways, nearly stepping on Jorin. The ounce crouched, sprang up onto the wagon, and burrowed under its tarpaulin, leaving only the white tip of his tail atwitch in the open. Something there caught his attention, but Jame was too busy to notice.

"Truly," Gaudaric was saying, "I would have told you more if I could, but everything that happens in the Wastes lies under

King Krothen's oath of secrecy. I haven't even been able to tell my own son-in-law as much as I would have liked, although I've given him hints. Your seniors will have shared with you what they know. Note, though, that they are only allowed to travel with the caravan so far. If anything happens beyond that point, it's no longer under your control, and precious little will be before that."

The assistant wagon masters were shouting through trumpets, down the line. It was a big caravan—one hundred and fifty wagons carrying trade goods, water, food, fodder, and fuel. Each trader was expected to provide the latter four items for his own team and crew. The first lurched off down the southern road. Standing in her stirrups, Jame saw that it carried the middle-aged, blond seeker whom she had last seen during the raid on the small caravan during the summer. An old woman sat next to her on the high seat, rail-thin and white-haired. The other wagons followed one by one, like pulling out a skein of knobby yarn. Now Ean was maneuvering into position with many shouts at his team interspersed with farewells called to his wife.

Evensong collapsed against her father's chest.

"Byrne!" he shouted, holding her, still scanning the turbulent crowd, now in motion. "*Byrne!*"

"Good-bye! Good-bye!" people cried, drowning him out.

The travelers passed through the South Gate, out between the fields, dust roiling up under thousands of hooves and wheels. Ahead rose the dusky mountains, and beyond that, as yet unseen, the open desert.

III

THAT FIRST NIGHT, they camped halfway up the Apollynes, the terraced slopes stretching down behind them to the dark valley floor. Level with them were the distant lights of Kothifir, sparkling as if in imitation of the stars above. Some gazed longingly back. Most thought only of what lay ahead.

The next day they reached Icon Pass, with much scrambling up the steep road. This time the lights shone above them among the peaks where the fortress known as Mountain Station overlooked both flanks of the range. Snow crowned the heights and the air was frosty. Campfires blossomed beside the wagons. Jame and Timmon played a game of Gen in her tent before she turned him out, protesting, into the night.

On the third day the travelers crossed the pass. Horses leaned back on their hocks against the downward slope and the weight pressing close behind them. Stones rattled down the steep incline. Switchbacks helped for a while, then were left behind. Streams plunged past, fed by the beginning of the rainy season, and the sloping meadows were green. Goatherders watched them pass while edging their flocks out of reach, but the travelers still had plentiful supplies of their own and only laughed at such caution.

On the fourth day they continued to descend through the mountains' southern foothills, then through date palm groves fed by the Apollynes' largesse of streams. The desert itself enfolded them almost by stealth. The land flattened into a rock-studded plain with diminishing vegetation and waterways disappearing underground. The monotony Gaudaric had warned about lay on all sides, broken only by silently dancing dust devils and the occasional bush. It was much hotter by day, but when the sun set, the temperature dropped sharply. Jorin hunted by night, usually returning before daybreak with cold paws which he kneaded against Jame's stomach, claws retracted, under their shared blanket. So it went for several days as the caravan followed the ancient, subterranean stream with its occasional, increasingly gritty wells and stands of dusty palm trees.

Riding behind Ean's wagon, Jame noticed that it was dribbling water. When she called this to his attention, he untied the tarpaulin, threw it back, and discovered Byrne curled up in a snug hollow that he had made by partaking freely of their supplies. The water came from the wagon's reserve tank which the boy had tapped and insufficiently closed, with the result that a quarter of it had drained away.

Ean clutched at his curly hair. "What am I going to do with you?" he demanded, distraught, of his young son. "Your mother must be frantic, and your grandfather too!"

"I'm here, Papa," said the boy with implacable logic and a dimpled, self-satisfied smile. "Now you have to take me with you."

Indeed, Ean had no choice. He couldn't turn back himself, given what his father-in-law had staked on this expedition, and no one else would, however much he offered to pay them.

On the tenth day, they came to the last oasis, set in the dusty trading town of Sashwar on the edge of rolling sand dunes.

"How long do we stay here?" Jame asked.

"Long enough to prepare for the deep desert," said Ean.

He extracted a pot from his load, broke the seal and began to smear its contents on the sloping front of his wagon.

"What's that stuff?" asked Dar as the trader worked his way to the boards underneath. Byrne crawled after him, as usual getting in the way. Other veterans were performing similar work on their rigs, watched with amusement by the less-experienced drivers.

Ean held up a glistening glob. "I don't know exactly. Gaudaric brought it back from the heart of the Wastes years ago on his one trip there, but it feels, smells, and tastes—ugh—like congealed fish oil."

While he worked, Jame took Byrne to explore the town, such as it was. Her ten-command came too. A clutch of drivers whistled after pretty Mint, who made a flirtatious show of ignoring them.

Damson snorted.

"One of these days," Jame said, "you're going to get into trouble."

"I like trouble," said Mint, pouting, "the right sort, at least."

At a primitive inn they ate fried locust on toast and goat cheese curds, washed down with bitter tea. Jame noted the women's veils, reminiscent of the Kencyr Women's World, and the men's *cheches*, out of which tufts of hair poked like a furry fringe around their faces. She wondered if the latter were the ends of braids. Under her own head covering, her hair was also tightly woven Merikit style, those strands on the left side for men she had killed, those on the right for children she had supposedly sired as the Earth Wife's male Favorite. Did the desert tribes follow a similar code? Whom did they worship anyway? The Four or their desert equivalents? Urakarn's Dark Prophet or the Witch King of Nekrien? There were even rumors of a tribe sworn to the Three-Faced God, rather to the embarrassment of his Kencyr followers who would hardly have wished him (or her, or it) on anyone else.

After dinner, they went to inspect the extensive animal pens. The horses would be left here tomorrow, giving way to beasts better suited to the deep desert. The selection was wide, ranging from giant armadillos to hyenas the size of ponies to burly, long-legged woms to web-footed birds at least eight feet high at the shoulder.

"Which are ours?" asked Byrne, poking at the hyenas with a stick. Brier snatched him back barely before the powerful snap of jaws.

"I don't know," said Jame. "Hopefully not those."

Dawn came with a vivid smear of color across an endless horizon. To the southeast and southwest floated the mirages of distant mountains—the Tenebrae Range and the Uraks respectively.

Ean had unloaded his wagon the day before. Now the wheels and axles were removed, reducing it to a sledge. The goods were reloaded. Out of the growing light came two handlers leading a pair of huge beasts, some ten feet in length with correspondingly long legs and necks.

"Lambas," said Ean, pleased. "Gaudaric reserved a team of them for us by courier."

Jame noted their splayed, three-toed feet but even more their short, prehensile trunks. Fur-fringed, slit nostrils opened on either side of the latter, situated on the tops of their small heads. Their bodies, by contrast, seemed swollen.

"They have three stomachs," she was told. "The biggest one stores up to thirty gallons of water."

"So what do we ride?" asked Dar. "Oh no."

Brier had appeared out of the growing light, leading a flock of reddish-brown birds that towered over her.

"Moas," she said, "good to ride or to eat, if things get rough. Watch out for their teeth; they're omnivores and have a nasty bite. And make sure the girths are tight."

Each had a saddle on its back, secured around the rib cage before the long legs. Jame reached up to tug on a strap. The bird squawked in protest and snapped at her. She punched it in the beak.

"Now make them kneel."

"How?"

"Kick them in the knee, of course."

Jame gingerly nudged her bird. It folded with a glare and a whistling hiss, bringing the saddle within reach. She stepped on its leg and swung her own over its back. It rose with a forward jolt that nearly dislodged her.

"All right," she murmured as its head bobbed high above her own on its long stalk of a neck. "Your name is Lurcher, and don't you dare throw me off."

The caravan set forth. First went the sledge, formerly the wagon, that carried the seekers. It dragged roughly to begin with, but when it hit the sand it began to slide. A skin of water formed under it where the fish oil met the sand and a remnant of the old sea returned. The next sledge deepened the effect and so on. When Ean's vehicle joined the line, it skimmed forward behind the lambas who walked on either side of the shallow, watery pathway. The other traders followed, lumbering through the drifts, their laughter dying.

Riding a moas wasn't too different than riding a horse, if one discounted the loss of two feet and the distance to the ground. Lurcher had a tendency to sway, perhaps because it had drunk half its own weight at the oasis and so was a bit top-heavy. Jame surged back and forth from stirrup to stirrup, glad (not for the first time) that she didn't tend toward seasickness.

Jorin crouched and sprang up on the sledge where Byrne greeted him with a crow of delight. Trust a cat to spare its paws on the hot ground.

Soon they were deep in the rolling golden sand dunes under an achingly blue sky. For the most part, they tried to follow the dips that exposed the hard desert floor, but often they had to climb over the dunes' shoulders. The lambas plodded steadily ahead, occasionally hooting companionably from team to team:

Are you still there? Yes, I am. Are you?

Other beasts were soon struggling and falling behind. Most caught up that night, but late and exhausted. Some had already turned back.

"Bet you only the sledges make it," said Timmon. "We're down to just over one hundred travelers already."

They began to pass ruins, jutting out of the sand. Jame remembered that these worn walls were said to travel about beneath the sand, according to the wind. Some presented markets with bread that turned to dust at the touch. Others offered fruits and vegetables that looked whole but crumbled if breathed upon. The dust raised figures to wander about the stalls, in and out of sight. This must once have been a fertile realm, but its inhabitants had long since fled. Lizards watched the caravan go by from the stubs of walls, frilled collars flaring red, gold, and blue in the wind.

"Lesser rhi-sar," said one of the Kendar. "Useful, but nothing compared to their ancestors."

That night Jame walked among the tents to stretch her legs after a day of riding. Most traders had settled in the lee of dunes with a haze of sand whistling off the crests over them, but not so close as to be in danger of avalanches. The dunes, after all, were always in subtle motion, and drummed as they shifted slowly forward under the wind's whip. A storm was building. The lambas' tufted tails sparked and crackled with electricity. Moas crouched down, hiding their heads under their rudimentary wings. Neither stars nor moon shone, and in the distance thunder rumbled.

She came to a fire leaping high into the troubled night. Around it sat Kothifirans, listening to an old desert woman. Like her sisters in Sashwar, she wore a veil, but made no attempt to anchor it as the rising wind whipped it about her wizened face. When she saw Jame, she broke off her current story and gestured to her with a gap-toothed grin.

"Welcome, my friend, you who seek the truth! Sit with us and I will tell you of the desert gods."

The others readily made way. Jame sank cross-legged onto the ribbed sand and gazed across the dancing campfire at her ragged hostess.

"Once everything for days in all directions belonged to the Sea of Time. Ah, consider how much of the present floats atop the past. When the Sea died, or seemed to, so did its attendants and all that lived in it. But something that large and powerful never completely goes away. Desert sledge still calls to the memory of water, as you have learned, have you not?"

Most of the carters murmured agreement. Those without sledges looked glum.

"Beneath the Sea is Stone. Stone remembers and endures. He seldom speaks but always tells the truth, because silence is never a lie. If you can get his attention, you will learn much. Take care, however, that you can bear the force of the answer."

Someone offered her a goatskin of wine. She paused to drink, wrinkled throat bobbing. The fire flared sideways in a gust of wind, then leaped up straight again.

"On top of Stone creeps Dune. The cry of the jackal and the laugh of the hyena, the singing sand, the crash of ghostly wave on vanished shores and the rasp of Sandstorm are its voice. Dune reveals with one hand and covers with the other. It may lure you to your doom or tell you truths. Dune knows, but says both no and yes.

"And then there is Salt, the Eternal, the Spiritless, the Soulless. When the Sea died, that which could not be purified became Salt. It is a mystery even to the other Gods. It is not Earth or Air or Fire or Water. It is not That-Which-Creates or Preserves or Destroys—yes, girl, I know the attributes of your god and of the Four. The Gods of which I speak came after them but may well outlast them. Hah'rum! Salt is That-Which-Remains, the Sea Within us. That is why to this day salt merchants smuggle their wares throughout Rathillien and take their time at it. They know Salt will remain even if King Krothen will or won't.

"Where Stone is honest and Dune equivocates, Mirage always lies and lies without purpose. If you are not careful, Mirage can kill you or steal your soul. She is a dancer and a shapeshifter. Do I worship Mirage? Certainly not! My lies carry truths that fact's spindly legs cannot.

"Ah, but Sandstorm is the raging place of wind and Dune. It is destruction, but it is not always bad. It clears away and scours clean. Sometimes it buries things which should not walk on the Earth. And it smashes through Mirage's illusions in an instant."

Jame stirred. Had she thought before of That-Which-Destroys as a positive force? Well, yes, in her more defiant moments. "That which can be destroyed by the truth should be," Kirien had once said. Always? Sometimes Jame wondered.

The old woman went on to describe River, Oasis, and their child, the Pathless Tracker, who spoke to Stone and knew the rites to propitiate Sandstorm.

"When we die," she added, "he leads us across the Desert and through the Sea into the Story of Things That Were. You would not have gotten this far if your guides were not his initiates. You Kennies don't have to believe in Tracker, but you show him good manners if you know what's best for you."

"And who are you?" Jame asked.

"Me?" The old woman laughed and showed her few remaining teeth. The lower half of her face seemed to have become more skeletal as the night progressed, giving her a skull's lopsided, bony grin. "I am Storyteller, Granny Sit-by-the-Fire. Every hearth and every campfire is my shrine. I tell truth you'll remember, even if I have to lie to do it. Without me to tell you what you are, you would just be clever animals, no better than that overgrown wombat lying there farting by the sledge."

Her listeners laughed, but laughter died suddenly. Something dark stumbled toward them out of the night, whimpering. In a moment, they had scattered, and the old woman withdrew into shadows, leaving the memory of bones.

Jame thought at first that the advancing figure was a wounded animal, but then she recognized one of the drivers who had whistled at Mint. The man dragged a leg and cried as he lurched forward. Damson walked behind him, cold-eyed.

"I was on guard duty," she told Jame. "He said his friends might like a pretty face, but he preferred 'em plump and wanted to be friends. Then he grabbed me."

"You have the training to deal with him without this."

"Oh, I did that first. He's got a broken leg, when he has time to notice."

"Damson, let him go."

The cadet grimaced and did. The man collapsed.

By now people were gathering, including Jame's ten-command.

"You should have broken his neck," said Dar, furious. He and Damson might play tricks on each other all day long, but they were teammates and this was an outsider.

A wagon master approached, throwing on his clothes. "What's all this?"

"She led me on!" cried the man, groveling away from Damson. "She's a witch!"

He collapsed again and writhed at the girl's feet, frothing at the mouth.

"Stop that!" Jame grabbed Damson to shake her...

...and found herself abruptly in the soulscape, grappling with something dark and dire. Ivory armor slid over her limbs, shielding her. She lashed out.

...and Damson sprawled at her feet in the sand with a split lip.

"I said if you ever struck me, I would strike you back," Jame said, shaken. "I couldn't help it."

Damson spat blood. "Neither could I."

"They're both witches!" cried the driver, beginning to wax hysterical.

"*Now* what?" demanded the wagon master, distracted, as another man ran up to clutch his arm.

"It's Nevin," the newcomer panted. "Seized from his tent... through the floor..."

The master turned pale. "Gods help us. We've landed in a nest of snatchers. Everybody, get up! We have to move camp. *Now.*"

"A nest of what?" said Dar blankly. "Oh..."

Something green and scaly had emerged from the sand. It fumbled at his boot, gripped it with ten-inch claws, and pulled. Dar sank in up to his thigh.

"Help!"

Some of his friends grabbed him while others dug frantically. Finding his foot and the thing clutching it was no problem, but the sinewy arm, or neck, or whatever it was seemed to go down forever. Mint hacked through it. Dark blood spurted out of the hole, drenching Dar.

"Argh!" he said, trying to wipe the sticky goop off his face. "It burns!"

"Strike the tents!" the wagon master was shouting. "Move, move, move!"

One of the moas gave a squawk suddenly cut off, leaving only a puff of feathers afloat and the half-seen afterimage of a claw as broad across the palm as a man's torso.

Everywhere tents were falling and people scrambling to load their wagons. The wind was stronger now and the visibility diminished except where lit with cracks of lightning. Blue light ran hissing over the wagon frames and up the oxen's horns, crowning them like violet candle flames.

"'Ware the return stroke!" someone shouted.

As if his voice had called it forth, lightning seared down, striking dead the unfortunate oxen where they stood.

Jame was helping bundle Ean's rolled tent into his sledge when they heard a child scream. Where was Byrne? She and Ean scrambled up the nearest dune. From its crest they saw an enormous, scaly claw on a neck or arm shimmering with blue-violet fire, thrust up through the sand. The boy dangled from its fingertips, curled up like a kitten in its mother's jaws. Beneath, in a depression, smaller claws groped up like nestlings about to be fed by their parent.

A stocky figure stood at the base of the soaring arm and chopped at it with a sword as if with an axe.

The thing convulsed and dropped its captive. Jame took a running leap, caught the boy just above the groping claws, and rolled with him to safety.

Lightning clove the air, followed by a thunderous clap like the end of the world. The snatcher's stump of an arm (or neck) flailed, fountaining black blood in a stench of burnt flesh, then whipped back into the sand, followed by its offspring.

"Whee!" said Byrne, somewhat breathlessly as his father snatched him up.

Jame confronted the swordsman. "Gorbel, what are you doing here?"

"What?"

They were both shouting, still partially deafened by the blast.

"I said . . ."

"I heard you."

The Caineron Lordan leaned on his reeking blade, his face scrunched up against the sweat running down it. "Had to come, didn't I?" he said, raising his voice to a near bellow against the ringing in his ears and the howl of the wind. "Father insisted that I discover the mystery of the Wastes, so I bribed a trader to take me along incognito. The idiot insisted on a team of hyenas, which promptly ate him. So here I am, in the desert, on foot."

"You're more than welcome to ride on my sledge," said Ean, hugging his son.

"Appreciate that," said Gorbel, gruffly. "Assuming that this lady doesn't denounce me. Krothen's wagon masters have no fondness for the Caineron."

"I'm not sure I do either," said Jame, "but you're you. What quarrel do we have?"

"None that I know of, unless you count the last time at Tentir when I tried to kill you."

"Oh, we've already gotten past that."

"Then, sir, I accept your offer. Now let's get out of this demon-infested wilderness."

The caravan hastily trekked several more miles as the storm grew. The wind, whipping over dunes, covered and uncovered the bones of ancient, scattered dwellings so that sometimes they seemed to walk down dimly seen streets of the dead and sometimes through fields of petrified grain that snapped off under the lambas' feet. There were sand-clogged wells and things that bent over them until the sand came again to cover all. Sometimes vast shapes wheeled overhead only to disintegrate in the lightning strokes.

At last the wagon masters declared the ground safe. Once again all pitched camp, this time on the hard desert floor between dunes, and collapsed exhausted in their hastily erected tents.

Meanwhile, the storm built.

❧ IV ❧

"AND YOU DIDN'T DENOUNCE HIM?" demanded Timmon.

It was the next morning, and the sandstorm roared over them, blotting out the sun, turning everything a lurid yellow. No one would travel today.

"At least Ean has a fighter on his team now. You should have seen Gorbel handle that sand monster."

"Oh, he's good at killing things, no question about that. Some day, though, you'll have to face the fact that he's blood-kin to your brother's worst enemy."

"And you aren't?"

"Of course not. When has Grandfather Adric ever said 'no' to Torisen?"

"Repeatedly, starting when he didn't let Tori attend the randon college. Your grandfather wanted a puppet for Highlord. He's still coping with the fact that Torisen Black Lord doesn't dance to anyone's tune."

Timmon opened his mouth, then closed it. They were perilously close to bringing up his father Pereden, who had definitely been Torisen's enemy, and had made the entire Southern Host suffer for that enmity. Jame respected Timmon for coming to accept that, but she didn't care to rub his nose in it.

"I thought you liked Gorbel," she said.

Timmon ruffled his golden hair, perplexed. "I suppose I do, despite his rotten house. There's something dependable about him. Decent, even, to the extent that his father leaves him alone, and even then..."

Quill stuck his head into the tent. "You have company, Ten."

He opened the flap and bowed in a woman closely muffled in a cloak off of which sand cascaded. Jame and Timmon both rose.

"I bring an invitation from the seekers' tent," said the visitor with a marked accent which Jame had last heard from the lips of a dying girl. "If the Knorth Lordan would deign to join my mistresses for a dish of tea..."

Jame inclined her head. "I would be honored."

In Kens she added to Timmon, "Stay if you like, or go. I don't know how long this will take, nor what it's about."

The cloaked woman led her though the camp, both of them leaning sideways into the wind. Jame had donned a cape of her own, but sand as fine as flour still found its way into her clothes, eyes, and mouth where it ground unpleasantly between her teeth. Jorin trotted at her side. He at least could keep his eyes closed. The seekers' tent was four times the size of her own with internal compartments that baffled most of the wind, but still bulged and swayed at its onslaught. The blond, portly woman and her thin, elderly companion waited for her in the innermost chamber, sitting on rich carpets, steaming dishes set out before them. "Tea" was clearly a flexible term.

Jame bowed to her hostesses and, at their invitation, sat cross-legged opposite them. Jorin curled up beside her. His nose twitched at the smell of food.

"I am Kalan," said the younger. "This is Laurintine. Our kinswoman, whom you tried to save, was Laurintine's great-granddaughter, Lanielle."

"I'm sorry that my rescue failed. She tried to send you a message, but died first. My condolences."

Age and weight notwithstanding, Jame thought, these two ladies bore a striking resemblance to each other and to the young seeker who had so unnervingly crumbled to dust in her arms. They might almost have been the same woman at different ages.

They offered sweetened tea and small honey cakes. Everything was gritty with dust. The canvas walls flexed as the wind buffeted them and the flame in a hanging brazier danced wildly. Jame sipped, wondering what else this was all about.

The two seekers exchanged glances.

"Tell her," said the older one in a hoarse voice, as if the desert had her by the throat. "We agreed."

Kalan sighed. "Very well. You may have heard that this is a special caravan, perhaps the last of its kind. That may be. If so, someone in the Kencyr camp should know why in case anything goes wrong. King Krothen may demand secrecy, but your people have always been kind to us. For that and for Lanielle, we chose you." She sighed again. "Where to begin."

"Long, long ago..." croaked Laurintine.

"...there was a southern city named Langadine, on the edge of a great inland sea, surrounded by ancient civilizations. Of them all, though, it was the richest and the most dazzling, home to merchants, nobles, and gods. But no place is paradise to all. One day a girl fled from that fabulous city and tried to drown herself in the sea. She was with child, you see, and unwed. That was a great shame then..."

"As it is... to this day."

"Well, yes, but the water would not receive her. As she floundered in it, it turned to the salt of her tears. In the morning after a tempestuous night, she found herself lying on a dry salt plain with nothing but the bones of her city behind her.

"Wanderers found her and took her to Kothifir. There she bore her child, a girl, and there she lived for many years. Eventually, however, she grew homesick and longed to return to Langadine. The king had heard her story. Intrigued by the idea of a great city in the Wastes, where he only knew of ruins, he mounted an expedition to take her and her daughter home. Thus she became the first seeker of the Langadine line."

"Did they find the city?" asked Jame.

"They did. The northerners were amazed at its wealth, especially at a certain sheer fabric which they had never seen before."

"Silk."

"Yes. They took a bolt of it back to Kothifir led by the daughter who thus, because she had been born in Kothifir, became the first Kothifiran seeker. She had, by now, had a daughter of her own, who accompanied her. The travelers were welcome, but not by the king who had sent them. What for them had been only a few weeks' journey for Kothifir had taken years."

"So they had traveled in time as well as in space."

"Again, yes. The king sent a trade mission, but they only found ruins in the desert. Langadine was not rediscovered until one of its two daughters, the maiden, agreed to lead an expedition. And so it has gone ever since. We seekers are always female members of the same lineage, able to find the city of our birth. There are usually three of us bound to each city: the maiden, her mother, and her grandmother, sometimes with a skip in generations, but there are fewer and fewer of us. I can lead this expedition back to Kothifir, having left a recently dead husband and a baby daughter behind me in that city, but my mother is also dead and Laurintine is the last Langadine seeker now that her great-granddaughter Lanielle is also gone."

There was silence for a moment. Kalan clenched a plump fist and beat it against her thigh. Her hazel eyes were bright with unshed tears. "Ah, I should not have left my child and would not if she had not been ill. Will she live until I return? This is a hard life, always traveling to satisfy the greed of others. The lords of both cities ask too much of us. I only want a home and family of my own, before it is too late."

"As it is . . . for me?"

"Laurintine, I am sorry. Service to the caravans has worn you to a bone, and all your children are dead."

The wind soughed, the canvas boomed. All without was desolation. Here within, life was the fragrant if gritty cup of tea which the older woman poured and offered to the younger.

Jame watched them share the moment, the misery. Her own hand instinctively sought Jorin's rich coat for comfort and he nuzzled her fingers. Could she have left a child behind, a sick baby? The very thought of children was alien to her, but she was young. Perhaps someday she would fully understand Kalan's distress. She already knew what it felt like to long for a home.

"What about the time distortion?" she asked.

Kalan pulled herself together. "That," she said, "is the other great worry. It varies from trip to trip. At first time passed faster in the north than the south, the present faster than the past, but that stabilized and then reversed. Now only two things are sure. For one, seekers cannot revisit their own pasts. Our lives lead forward, at whatever pace our surroundings decree. Whatever is done to us, we cannot undo."

"And the second thing?"

"Langadine is catching up with Kothifir, or rather I should say with the Kothifir of three thousand years ago. Around that period, the southern city suddenly collapsed in some final, fatal cataclysm. We don't know what happened, except that beforehand the sea turned to salt water and began to dry up. The process had already begun the last time I was there. What has taken them centuries is only years to us."

Jame sat back on her heels, considering. "We could slip through one last time," she said, "or we could get caught on the cusp of disaster. Here and now, though, I don't know what we can do about it."

"Turn back," said Kalan.

Laurintine gripped the other's knee with a bony claw. "I want," she rasped, "to die...at home."

"And the wagon masters aren't likely to listen to me," Jame added. "Would they to you?"

The two seekers looked chagrined.

"I thought not."

An idea struck her. "The spoils of the Wastes can only survive in the present if King Krothen touches them. Lanielle hadn't met him yet. Is that why she died after she was injured?"

Kalan inclined her head without speaking.

Leaving their tent, Jame paused on its threshold to consider the situation. If she understood her people's role, they wouldn't be permitted beyond the boundary between past and present. That should put them out of the path of disaster unless, as Kalan said, something went wrong.

And it always does.

G'ah, she hated being out of control, but this situation loomed like the mountain ranges to the east and west, not to be changed by any puny effort on her part. At least the wind seemed to be abating. In another day or two, they should reach the edge of the Great Salt Sea.

CHAPTER X
The Sea of Time

Winter 13–15

I

THE NEXT DAY dawned clear and hot, revealing that the caravan had camped on the very edge of the sand dunes. Flat, rock-strewn land stretched away before them in unparalleled monotony, broken here and there by wind-tortured stone formations. Once again the wagons were unpacked, the wagon wheels restored, and their loads returned. Jame supposed that the rocks, as small as they were, would scrape on the sledge bottoms. Lambas whiffed and hooted, not eager to resume their harnesses. Over the past few days without water, their swollen bellies had shrunken noticeably and their girths needed to be tightened. Soon they would require another deep drink.

Few other beasts had made it so far except for the moas, who required copious amounts of water at least every third day. Horses, mules, and oxen had long since turned back or died in harness under the lash of desperate drivers. Some of the latter found passage on the wagons, abandoning all but the choicest of their own loads, but most shouldered what water they could carry and started the long trudge back to Kothifir. Jame wondered how many would make it.

To have come so far, to fail by so little . . .

At dusk on the thirteenth of Winter, the remaining travelers—some fifty wagons in all—arrived at the edge of the Great Salt Sea. It stretched out before them to the horizon, its surface broken by drought into octagonal plates. A failing slash of light from the west washed its white surface with pink and mauve. The east wind picked up, causing sparkling salt ghosts to drift across the empty plain in stately procession like an army on the march, until the shadows overtook them.

Tents were pitched, evening meals cooked.

When Jame rose early the next morning, she found that the trade caravan had slipped away in the night, leaving its Kencyr escort behind. Moreover, she smelled fresh water. They had set up camp at a brackish oasis which, when dug out of the sand, stank of rot. Now the camp was surrounded by grass, sedge, and tall reeds marching into a shallow sea. One could still make out the salt plates under the surface, but they hadn't yet dissolved to contaminate the rainwater swell. The face of the water reflected the glowing morning sky like a vast mirror, dazzling the eye.

"What in Perimal's name...?" said Timmon, coming up to her. "I know this is the beginning of the rainy reason, but surely it didn't pour last night. Runoff from distant mountains?"

"That might explain it, but not all of this established vegetation. What do you think, Ran?"

The senior officer stood near them, surveying the sudden sea. "I've heard of such a thing," he said, "when the Tishooo plays tricks."

"Because the Old Man controls the flow of time in the Wastes?" Jame asked, remembering what she had been told in the Undercliff.

He gave a short laugh. "So the natives say."

"That's what I was afraid of," said Jame.

Laurintine had guided the caravan back to lost Langadine, into the past. What if the Tishooo had taken them there too, for some obscure reason of its own? If so, where in the past might they be? She gathered that each caravan trip was closer to the Kothifir of three thousand years ago and to Langadine's ultimate, mysterious destruction. Perhaps the caravan had barely arrived there. Perhaps it had been in Langadine for days, or months, or years. How long could they wait for its return before their supplies ran out?

Brier also stood by the shore, gazing out at the watery expanse. Jame wondered if she had been there all night and had seen the flood rise. What must she be thinking now? Her mother Rose Iron-thorn had escaped with Tori, Harn, and Rowan from Urakarn on the edge of this same sea, if much farther to the west. It had been dry at first as they fled, and sinksand had swallowed Rose. Jame remembered Brier's voice telling her the story as Tori had told it to her, how at dusk they had come across the petrified remains of a boat and had collapsed into it.

"In the night, feverish," Brier had said, "he thought he saw the water return...all that flat sand plain changing back to the sea it had been, and the stone boat afloat on it. Under the surface, he saw Rose and reached down to her. She took his hand, pulled it down into the stinging salt water, pulled the whole boat across the sea...in a dream, he thought, born of fever; but in the morning, there they were safe on the northern shore, with nothing behind them but sand..."

"Do you think that your mother is still out there, under the sand, under the water?" she asked Brier.

The Southron shrugged, malachite green eyes still sweeping the sea. "Did she come back at all or did the Highlord only dream it? Did you?"

"For your brother's sake..."

Cold words, cold hands, thrusting Jame back to the surface when the returning sea had swallowed her outside Mount Alban after the weirdingstrom had swept it into the Southern Wastes. She had no doubt, herself, what she had experienced.

Brier shrugged. "Her bones at least still lie under the sand. Who knows?"

The laughter and catcalls of Char's third-year cadets sounded behind them. They turned to see Gorbel trudging toward them from Ean's abandoned tent, stripping off ropes and spitting out a gag.

"One of the wagon masters recognized me," he said with disgust. "Our friend swore that I was his assistant, but they dragged me off anyway and tied me up to keep me from following. Is that them?" He peered at vague, wavering forms on the horizon.

"It could just be a mirage," said Timmon.

"Or the spires of a city," Jame said, staring hard.

An uproar burst out near the shore where the moas had gathered to drink. Something huge lunged out of the reeds and chomped down on the nearest bird. The rest flopped down flat and froze like so many brown lumps, some with their heads inadvertently underwater.

"Ancestors preserve us," said the senior randon. "A rhi-sar."

The beast stood on the shore, ignoring the motionless birds. The long legs of its prey dangled out of its toothy jaws, twitching slightly. It threw back its massive head and bolted them down. A second giant reptile emerged from the reeds. Both stood on their powerful hind legs, smaller forearms tucked almost delicately against their armored chests. The first was blue and mottled green, its scales edged with gold. The second was orange shading to the dark red of dried blood. Their lashing, scaly tails made up nearly half of their thirty-foot lengths.

The reeds parted and a third, smaller reptile joined them, this one creamy white with watery blue eyes.

I should have brought Death's-head, thought Jame. As she had foreseen, however, he had stayed behind with Bel.

"Stand still," said the randon. "They react to motion."

Too late: Char broke ranks and dashed to grab a spear.

The two rhi-sar bellowed and charged the camp.

Yells sounded as the cadets scrambled for weapons and into formation. The blue brute lunged at one such group, catching a spear and jerking its wielder out of place. Its red mate snapped sideways, catching the cadet and folding him double backward before bolting him down. The senior randon plunged to the rescue, only to get caught between the two.

"No!" Jame cried, but already they had grabbed him, one on each side, and between them had ripped him apart. Blood sprayed the sedge. The water tinged pink.

Both rhi-sar spread their frilled collars and trilled their triumph.

Jame turned to watch the white rhi-sar. It had held back so far but not, she thought, out of fear or weakness. Its small eyes switched from reptile to reptile like a general directing troops. One of them lumbered back to it and vomited mixed body parts, steaming with acid and already half-digested, at its feet. An offering.

Someone handed her a spear. She balanced it, advanced, and threw it at the white beast. More by luck than skill, she caught the creature in one eye. It reared back, bellowing, and clawed at the shaft, snapping it off in its eye socket. The other blue eye focused on her. How well could it see? Well enough to chase her if she moved.

The other two rhi-sar seemed confused, snapping at random as cadets ran past them. Damson stood before one of them, holding it in her baleful gaze. It lunged at the air on either side of her as if unable to bring her into focus. The other rhi-sar stumbled into it and they fell, tearing at each other.

But the white one wasn't confused. It thundered straight at Jame, jaws agape. She turned and ran, trying to draw it away from the other cadets, but they in turn were running toward her. Char thrust a spear between its hind legs, tripping it. It turned its fall into a lunge at Jame, missing by inches when she dodged to its blind side. Before it could recover, she threw herself on its head and clasped its jaws shut with her arms and legs, half expecting them to be ripped off. But she had guessed right: the muscles that opened that fearful maw were weaker than those that closed it. The brute reared up, trying to shake her off, scraping futilely at her with its foreclaws.

Cadets darted in and stabbed at its exposed belly. It was armored as thoroughly as a rathorn, but there were wrinkled gaps of bare skin under the forearms. Gorbel's spear found its mark and bit deep. The creature toppled over backward, pinning Jame under its massive muzzle, knocking the wind out of her. She thought at first that she was dead, but then hands pulled her free.

The other two rhi-sar retreated to the water and reeds. The white one lay on its back, thick crimson blood sluggishly crawling down over its plated stomach. It scrabbled feebly at the sky, then fell limp, its armored jaw harmlessly agape.

Timmon pulled Jame to her feet and she clung to him, gasping. "Did I really...just do that?"

"You certainly did, and scared the spit out of me."

Gorbel braced a foot against the creature, wrenched free his spear, and limped up to them. "I could claim the kill, but it only happened because of your insanity. Besides, I've already got a rhi-sar suit. I'd say that you've just earned your own armor, Lordan of Ivory."

II

THEY GATHERED the dismembered limbs of their dead, such as they could retrieve, and gave them to the pyre. Char scowled at Jame over the flames.

I had as much to do with this kill as you did, he seemed to be thinking, and that was probably true, given that she couldn't have pinned the brute if Char hadn't tripped it first.

On the bright side, only two Kencyr had been killed, thanks mostly to Damson.

"Good work," Jame told her.

The plump cadet nodded. She looked thoughtful, not smug, as Jame might have expected.

"I asked myself what you would do, Ten, if you could do what I can. Not run."

"I did, though."

"To draw off that white monster. I saw. Then you turned on it. I know I don't think or feel the way that other people do. Something is... missing. But I can imitate you."

Jame stared at her. "Trinity, Damson, you'd do better to take someone else as a model. Why not Brier?"

The cadet shook her head. "I can see that Five is a good randon. Someday she may even become a great one. But she isn't like me. Not a bit. You are."

Jame considered that as she watched the cadets start to skin the white rhi-sar—no easy task given the toughness of its hide. When properly tanned, it would be nearly as impenetrable as rathorn ivory, which itself was the second hardest substance on Rathillien after diamantine. Brier cut free the skull and they began the messy job of hollowing it out, leaving the fearsome, hinged jaws. Others worked on the feet, flaying them but retaining the claws.

All her life, Jame had turned to the Kendar as guides, primarily to Marc, whose moral sense she trusted far more than her own. To have one of them return the favor was... unnerving. But Damson was right: as a destructive Shanir, she and Jame had a lot more in common than either did with Brier Iron-thorn.

Meanwhile, Gorbel was arguing with the senior surviving officer, Onyx-eyed. The Caineron Lordan wanted to pursue the caravan.

"That would violate our standing orders," said the randon.

"Yours. Not mine. My father told me to follow them. Anyway, as lordan I'm the highest ranking Caineron here."

"You're the only Caineron here."

"Fine. I'll go by myself."

Jame peered at the black line of the distant horizon, all that separated sky from reflecting sea. The slight, wavering distortion was still there on the edge of sight.

"How far away is it?" she asked. "Three miles? If that's a mirage, most of what casts it could be below our line of sight, if there's anything there at all. Still..."

The randon looked at her, as blank of expression as ever. "So you want to go too."

"And me," said Timmon, coming up.

"You're asking me to risk the heirs of three houses."

"We aren't asking anything," said Gorbel, his jaw thrust stubbornly forward. As a cadet, he took orders; as a lordan, he gave them. They could all feel the authority radiating off him like heat off a sun-baked stone, and like that stone his will was no easy thing to break.

Onyx-eyed blinked. "Take an escort with you, then," she said mildly, "and turn back if you lose the tracks."

"You stay here," Jame told Jorin. "What, d'you want to wade all the way to the horizon?"

She, the other two lordan, and her ten-command saddled up their moas. They could see the scrapes where the reverted sledges had entered the shallow water to become boats, and beyond that, salt plates on the bottom were broken by the lambas' hooves. The moas dithered on the shore until encouraged in with whip and spur. The water came halfway up to their knees. They lifted their three-toed, webbed feet high, almost daintily, with every step.

Jorin paced the shore behind them, crying. Jame thought of Kalan and the baby that she had left behind. Would she ever see the ounce again? How did one make clear to a cat or to an infant that it wasn't being willfully abandoned?

"I should explain some things to you," she said to her fellow lordan, and told them about Langadine. "Time is fluid here," she concluded. "Granny Sit-by-the-Fire called this the Sea of Time. The camp might be stranded on the shore forever if our seeker doesn't return, and we may find ourselves too deep in the past to return even that far."

Timmon was aghast. "Now you tell us?"

Gorbel only shook his heavy head. "It doesn't matter. Once we came to the edge of the sea, wet or dry, we had to follow the caravan. The only way back leads though this mysterious city of yours, if we can find it."

They waded slowly on. Clouds came up from the south, mirrored under their feet by the water so that one felt almost as if one could walk on either. The sun disappeared. The horizon circled them in a thin, dark band. Without the broken salt plates leading straight ahead, they would quickly have lost all sense of direction.

"How far have we come?" asked Timmon, breaking a long silence.

Gorbel grunted. "At this pace? Hard to tell. More than three miles. Out here, distance plays tricks as well as time."

The reflected sky made the lambas' trail harder and harder to follow, and the water was now up to the moas' knees, over three feet deep. They had started in midmorning. It now appeared to be midafternoon, but who could say? Had they been walking hours, or days, or years?

The suspense seemed to unnerve Timmon. "What will your father do if he learns the way to Langadine?" he asked.

"Whatever he can to get a trade mission there, or a raiding party, but from what you say"—with a nod to Jame—"he will need a seeker, and those are dying out."

"What about Kalan's daughter in Kothifir?"

"She can only find her way back to her birth city. If Laurintine is the last of her line, no one will ever find the city again, at least until after its destruction."

"And what do you make of that?"

"What can I? Something happened some three thousand years ago that shattered Langadine."

"That would be more or less when the Kencyrath arrived on Rathillien," said Jame.

Timmon scratched a peeling nose, dubious. "Coincidence?"

"I doubt it. Anyway, our appearance here and Perimal Darkling moving one world closer seem to have shaken up all sorts of things."

She was thinking about the sudden manifestation of the Four and about Langadine's climate changing, along with that of the Southern Wastes, although that seemed to have started before the Kencyrath had arrived.

Was the water getting deeper? Yes, to mid-thigh on the moas, who no longer tried to lift their feet free with each stride. The fluffy feathers on their bellies were soaked and matted. She raised her boots to keep them from getting wet.

Brier nudged her bird up level with the three lordan. "I can't see the trail anymore," she said.

Jame peered down. The moas' progress had stirred up the bottom somewhat, and further distortion made the salt plates dance. Were they broken, or simply smaller than they had been before? At what point would the lambas have started to swim, pulling their barges behind them?

All the birds had stopped and were honking uneasily to each other. The riders sat, surrounded by a seemingly infinite, trackless expanse. The sun was going down.

"Now what?" Timmon asked.

"Forward," said Gorbel, and kicked his moas into reluctant motion.

"I don't think these birds can swim," Jame said, but she followed the Caineron, her ten-command trailing after her.

The sun dipped below the clouds and set them on fire. Orange, red, and yellow ribbons streamed across the sky, perfectly mirrored in the waters below. It was like wading through the heart of a silent inferno. Then the sun's fiery disk sank into its own reflection, going, going, gone. Color died out of the sky and stars winked between sable clouds. It was hours yet before the moon would rise, if it ever did.

They splashed on into the deepening night, drawn by Gorbel's will. Water edged up to the moas' breasts.

"He's going to drown all of us," Timmon said to Jame in an undertone.

"Maybe. Turn around, if you choose."

Timmon rose in the saddle to look back the way they had come, past the following cadets. Nothing remained to mark their passage, and clouds were beginning to extinguish whatever stars might have guided them.

"Huh," he said.

They continued. The water rose until they were sitting in it as much as in the saddle, and yet it crept higher.

"Look," said Quill, pointing ahead.

A faint light shone there, perhaps a star near the now invisible horizon. Soon, however, it twinned, one above and one below.

More dim lights came out as they advanced, a cluster low in the sky, reflecting off the water.

The moas were mostly underwater now, their small heads rising on serpentine necks. A new determination animated them, a straining forward as if toward the scent of land.

Jame slipped out of the stirrups and rose to swim beside her bird's head. The others did too, except for Brier and Damson. Jame cursed herself for forgetting that neither cadet could swim. Mint supported the five-commander while Dar grabbed Damson. The lights loomed over them now, above and below, faintly defining high walls and candlelit windows.

Gorbel sank. Timmon and Jame dove, seized his arms, and pulled him up. Trinity, when had the man grown so heavy?

They were coming in between high marble wharfs topped with torches. Jame's moa found its footing and surged upward. A moment later her feet also hit a flight of marble stairs rising out of the water. The birds lurched up them, their riders staggering beside them.

Timmon and Jame dragged Gorbel to the summit and dropped him.

"Well," he gasped, rolling over, leaking water from every fold. "Here...we are."

CHAPTER XI
Night in a Lost City

Winter 14–15

I

THE NEAREST BUILDING showed lights at every window and echoed like a seashell with voices. After Tai-tastigon, Jame knew the sight, sound, and smell of an inn, wherever its location. The cordial commotion within stopped as she opened the door and stepped inside, followed by her dripping retinue. A tubby, bald man, clearly the host, approached them, drying his hands on his apron, and asked a question in a language that none of them knew.

"We seek shelter," said Jame in Kothifiran Rendish. "For myself, my friends, and our mounts."

The man brightened. "Ah! Our kin from over the sea. At last! Welcome!"

The weary, bedraggled moas were led around to the stable where the local horses could be heard protesting at their alien smell. Meanwhile, their riders were given quarters, towels, and food—a fish stew, crusty bread, and coarse, red wine—while their clothes dried before the fire. The relief, after hours of uncertainty, was profound, and perhaps premature.

"How are we going to pay for all of this?" Jame asked, dipping her bread into the stew broth. Both were delicious, although something in the stew ate most of the bread before she could.

Timmon looked blank, as if he had never been asked to account for anything in his life, which was probably true.

Gorbel, however, opened his jacket and unhitched a heavy belt. Unfolded, it spilled a cascade of thick, golden *arax* onto the table.

"No wonder you sank," said Timmon, enlightened.

The Caineron gave the snort that, for him, passed as a laugh. "This may yet turn into a trade mission, or into headlong flight. Either way, should I have come with empty hands?"

A knock sounded on the door. Gorbel scooped the coins out of sight as Jame bade their host enter.

"The company would be glad to hear your story," said the man, beaming. No wonder he was pleased: from the growing noise below, their arrival had greatly increased the inn's business for the night.

Jame stopped Gorbel from snarling a refusal. They had already argued about letting their presence be known in the city. While it carried some risks, Jame had pointed out that the alternative was that the twelve of them skulk in the shadows all night, wet, hungry and, worse, unable to learn anything useful, nor was the next day apt to produce anything better. The sea front was the place most likely to supply someone who spoke their own language or at least that of Kothifir, and so it had proved.

"I'll go down," she now said. "The rest of you, get some rest."

"I'm going too," said Gorbel with a stubborn set to his jaw. What, did he think she would conclude some bargain behind his back?

"And me," Timmon chimed in, running fingers through his drying hair. Some of the tavern maids had been pretty.

Brier and Damson both rose, looking stubborn.

"Oh, all right," said Jame.

The five descended into the common room, a whitewashed rectangle with a geometric frieze around the top in shades of blue and green. Substantial tables were centered under many-candled chandeliers, and fireplaces flanked either end of the chamber, unlit on this mild night. The room was full of dark-skinned, bright-eyed customers whose glances darted back and forth among the three lordan as they came down.

The host escorted them to a central table, which its occupants quickly surrendered. "If it please you, lady and lords, from where do you come?"

"Kothifir," said Gorbel.

"Ahh...!" breathed his audience, recognizing the name at least.

"It has been a long time since anyone came by that route," the host said.

The Iordan exchanged uneasy glances. "How long?" asked Jame.

"Some fifteen years," the host replied, turning to his customers for confirmation. "Is that not so? Yes. The last caravan arrived in a terrible storm. Our sea is changeable: these days sometimes fresh, sometimes salt; sometimes calm and shallow like tonight, sometimes as high as mountains and as deep. That night, it raged. Bodies were cast on the shore for days, men and beasts alike, also much treasure. Most drowned, except for the seekers and a few others who swam to safety."

Oh Ean, oh Byrne, thought Jame, briefly closing her eyes. *What will I tell Gaudaric?*

"One of the survivors has a stall in the night market," said a man wearing a blue, fish-stained tunic, speaking passable Rendish. "He sells armor."

The door was flung open. An old man stood dramatically on the threshold. His robe, dyed saffron with a deep hem embroidered with copper thread, swirled around him in a wind unfelt by those within. His white hair and beard flailed upward serpentlike in shaggy braids threaded with gold. He looked vaguely familiar.

"Travelers!" he cried. The others good-naturedly made way for him as he plunged into the room. "What news have you from my fellow gods to the north?"

"Er . . ." said Jame, staring.

"The end is coming, you know," he said with a broad smile, seeming to relish his news. He turned to take in his audience with a sweeping gesture that overturned tankards as far back as the corners of the room. "All of you have felt the earth shake," he proclaimed over cries of protest at the spilt beer. "The sea changes its nature more and more often. Year by year, the climate grows drier and hotter. Clearly, a great change is coming. But this world is only an illusion. Are you ready to fly away with me to the true one that lies beyond?"

"Enough of such desert talk," someone called from his audience. "Next, you'll claim to be the Karnids' long-lost prophet, returned again. Show us a trick, old man!"

"Well, now, what would you like?"

"More beer!" shouted back a chorus of voices.

"Hmm. Will this do? Landlord, a round of drinks on me!"

Tavern maids ran about with ewers, pouring amid the cheers of the patrons. Jame had a feeling that the old man had performed this "trick" before, and was all the more welcome here because of it. Her sense was that she and her comrades didn't really interest him. Rather, he had detected a center of attention and had rushed to usurp it. Timmon looked miffed and Gorbel bored, but she didn't mind: the more other people talked, the more she might learn.

The tremor started with a faint rumble like a heavy cart approaching over cobblestones. The wine in her cup rippled in concentric circles. The candle flames wavered. No one seemed to pay much attention except the old man in the saffron robe who turned suddenly pale and clutched the back of a chair. Slowly, without any fanfare, his feet left the floor. Jame grabbed his arm...

...and was falling.

They seemed to be the only two steady people in that whole jiggling room, and yet the pit of her stomach plummeted sickeningly as if the bottom had dropped out of the world. A look of wonder crossed the other's face as his braids flew upward. He let go of the chair, experimentally. Jame clung to him with both hands, hardly sure which of them she was anchoring. Then the rumble receded and his feet descended gently to the floor.

"I flew," he said in astonishment, eyes as wide as a child's. "I flew! You saw me, didn't you? *Didn't you?*"

"I saw you fall," said Jame, shaken.

No one else apparently had noticed anything, nor did they seem to take the quake very seriously except to clutch their brimming cups against another upset.

"Here he is! Here! Master!"

In rushed a crowd wearing yellow tunics. They seized the old man and dragged him with them out the door.

"I flew!" he exclaimed in protest to them as he went. "I really flew!"

"Yes, yes," they assured him. "Soon the entire city will know!"

The landlord shook his bald head as he shut the door behind them. "These uncertain days have bred many strange prophets and the rumor of gods, old and new. Sometimes I think the desert dwellers are right: our new king should never have buried the black temple."

"The what?" demanded Gorbel.

"Ah, I keep forgetting that you are strangers here. The black rock is as old as the city..."

"Older!" called someone.

"Indeed. Langadine was built around it, although I only guess to call it a temple: it appears to be a huge, black square of granite without seam or opening. The desert folk claim that, according to their prophet, it is the gateway to another world and they make pilgrimage to it, or did until King Lainoscopes came to power and quickly grew tired of their frenzied worship. A stickler for order, he, not lenient like his father, the gods give him rest. At any rate, Lainoscopes tried to break up the rock. Failing that, he built it into the foundation of a new tower."

The lordan exchanged looks.

"You said that your father's expedition found the ruins of a Kencyr temple," said Timmon in Kens. "Could it have been here? In which case at some point *something* destroyed it, and the city too."

The host was still apparently thinking about his late guest. "Prophets and gods, forsooth. Foolish fellow, to have made such a claim. Now, I suppose, that pack of madmen in yellow will put him to the test. He has finally found his true believers, and they are apt to kill him. Poor Tishooo."

Jame had chosen wine over beer. Now she choked on it.

"*That* was the Tishooo?"

"The Old Man, yes. Why?"

"I knew I had seen him before, but never clearly. This is serious," she said to the others in Kens. "'There was an old man, oh, so clever, so ambitious that he claimed to be a god. To prove it, his followers threw him from a high tower.' You remember, Gorbel: it's part of one of those Merikit rites you used to spy on."

"Oh. That Tishooo. The so-called Falling Man. But what is he doing here if he belongs to the hill tribes?"

"He belongs to Rathillien. So do the Earth Wife—your Wood Witch, Gorbel—the Burnt Man, and the Eaten One. Remember her, Timmon? She ate your half-brother Drie. Wherever they originally came from, all of them were mortal once, I think, until our temples turned them into the Four, the elemental forces that personify this world."

"You know the oddest people," remarked Timmon. "Then again, since I met you, so do I. That peculiar old man is destined to become the manifestation of air? When?"

"Potentially, any minute now."

Scowling, Gorbel planted his elbows on the table in a puddle of spilt beer. "Look here: we're back in time now, or so you tell me, before our people even landed on this accursed world."

"No one knows when the Builders constructed the temples," said Jame, "but the structures preceded us here and apparently fired up just before we arrived."

"So," Timmon said, "if that old man is about to become the Tishooo, the black rock—pardon, temple—is about to come to life. That means that, even now, Jamethiel Dream-weaver may be dancing out the souls of the Kencyr Host. The Fall is happening, the greatest disaster in our history, and here we sit, its unfortunate heirs, warm and dry, drinking in a tavern in a lost city."

Gorbel grunted. "Lost. Destroyed. How long have we got?"

"How long before the Tishooo's worshippers find a high enough tower and get him up it? He may come to his senses and resist, but still... My guess? Sometime tonight."

Timmon ticked off the events on his fingertips. "The Fall occurs, the temples activate, the Four are created, the Kencyrath flees to this world, the temple destroys Langadine, something destroys the temple, and you're assuming that all of this happens more or less simultaneously. But in our time it's actually three thousand and twenty-eight years after the Fall, if you believe our scrollsmen. Langadine could have decades yet to live. It all may not fall out exactly so pat."

Jame shrugged. "Yes, I'm making several assumptions. Do you want to take the chance, though?"

Timmon sighed and scanned the room. "Should we warn them?"

"Would they listen?" said Gorbel. "You've convinced me, girl. We need to finish our business here and get out as fast as possible." He stood up. "Ahoy! Who wants to sell us a boat? We can pay well."

"You manage that and get my ten-command on board," Jame said to him under cover of a sudden stir of interest. "I have errands to run in town."

⟨⟨⟨ **II** ⟩⟩⟩

LANGADINE SPRAWLED across several foothills in the shadow
of the Tenebrae mountain range. The highest hill was crowned by
a white, shining structure that must be King Lainoscopes' palace.
Walled terraces descended from it, curving to fit the contours of
the land. The streets on each level thus whorled like the ridges of
a massive fingerprint. Whitewashed houses lined them, presenting a solid face to the pavement. Most were two stories high at
most, given the illusion of greater height by the rolling ground
on which they were set. Jame saw, as she climbed higher, that
each building had a small, walled garden behind it like a green
jewel set in stone.

A gibbous moon lit all with a glowing, nacreous light, nearly
as bright as day to Kencyr eyes. It was a beautiful city, far more
orderly and lovingly kept than any Jame had yet seen. Was it
really to die tonight? She hoped not. While not fond of her
god—no Kencyr was—could he (or she, or it) really be so cruel
as to smash so much grace and innocence?

Brier and Damson walked behind her. The former had insisted
on coming, she said, to make sure that her lord's heir came to no
harm. The latter had simply followed, discovered too late to turn
her back. Jame wished that both of them had stayed behind. This
was a mission where the Talisman's skills might serve her best.
Brier didn't know about that aspect of her life and was unlikely
to approve of it. Damson, on the other hand, might see entirely
too much, if she was still set on imitating Jame.

Most of the city was dark, its daytime residents gone to bed,
but there were occasional clusters of lights. Jame headed toward
the brightest of these constellations.

The night market swarmed with life, as active as any of its
peers in Tai-tastigon, if cleaner. Stallkeepers hawked wares from
finger food to erotic spices, from tin trinkets to heavy goldware.
Bolts of silk dominated many a stall. Jame wondered what defect
the dark was supposed to cover, unless Langadine was so rich
that even these night offerings were of prime quality as their
merchants proclaimed.

"Talisman!"

Jame started as big hands grabbed and spun her around. A young man with curly chestnut hair stared down at her with disbelief and dawning delight.

"It is you, isn't it?" He shook her until her teeth rattled. "I always knew that you would come!"

"Byrne?" She waved back Brier, who had stepped forward and loomed over them both as if set to protect her. "It's really you?"

He was at least her age now and much taller, but he still had that small boy's mischievous grin.

"I'll take you to my father. After all these years, he won't believe this!"

Ean's quarters were a block from the market in a shabby, second-story apartment, half workshop, half sparse but well-kept living space. He started up in alarm from his bed as they entered. "Has something happened in the market? Who is tending the stall? Byrne! Night rent may cost less than day, but it's all we can afford." Then he noticed his visitors and his agitation grew. "Who are these people?"

Jame observed that his hair was now streaked with white, his face creased with wrinkles, and he was missing several teeth. The intervening years had not been kind to him.

"Ean," she said, "we came as quickly as we could, starting out the day after you left the oasis. Nonetheless, I'm sorry we arrived so late."

Like his son, Ean grabbed her; unlike Byrne, he burst into tears. "I'd given up hope. Evensong, Gaudaric, are they well?"

"As much so as when you left, if a few days older. Why didn't you return? What kept you here all this time?"

He backed away, wiping his face, then turned as if without thinking to scrounge for the makings of tea. "I tried," he said, over his shoulder. "The Kothifiran seeker, Lady Kalan, survived the storm, but in all these years the king hasn't let me see her."

"It sounds," said Jame, "as if I should pay her a visit."

Ean turned around, an empty teapot forgotten in his hand. "You can try, but she lives in the new palace tower, well guarded."

"I can show you the way," Byrne said eagerly.

"No!" Ean dropped the pot, which shattered unnoticed at his feet. "It's too dangerous! Remember how they beat me, the last time I tried?"

"How close can you safely get us?" Jame asked Byrne.

The boy pouted. "To the palace gate, anyway. Anyone could do that."

"Ean?"

"That far and no farther."

"Accepted. Then you both need to get to the harbor and take ship there. When we left, Gorbel was negotiating for a boat. The whole city may be destroyed before dawn."

"You would do that?" Ean looked aghast. "These are good people, for the most part. They don't deserve such a fate!"

"Why does everyone always blame me? Now go, and you, Byrne, lead on."

The boy escorted them up the hill past more terraced dwellings toward the palace. True enough, guards paced back and forth before its western gate, more than Jame had expected.

"That's the new tower just within the walls, the tallest in the city," Byrne said, whispering conspiratorially although no enemy was close enough to hear. "King Lainoscopes is afraid that the desert tribesmen will storm it to regain their precious black rock."

"Led by their prophet?"

"Oh, he died a long time ago. They've waited for his return ever since."

Jame considered the situation. There were too many guards to fight without raising the alarm. Somehow, the Talisman would have found a way in. Was the Knorth Lordan so much less talented?

The nearest guard stopped, yawned hugely with cracking jaws, and leaned on his spear. The next moment, he had toppled over, sound asleep. Others started toward him, stumbled, and also fell until all were down, snoring.

Damson shrugged. "Would you rather that I gave them terminal diarrhea?"

Brier looked down at her, frowning. "If you ever try that with me, brat, I'll kill you."

They entered the gate. The new tower rose out of a small courtyard, marble-faced, three stories high. There seemed to be no way into the first level, but an external stair led them up to the second.

Jame cautiously opened the door into what appeared to be a wide, square, low-ceilinged hall. Thick columns around the edges supported the floor above. Once away from the circling walk of white marble, nothing else broke that sable expanse except for rectangles of moonlight streaming in through open windows.

Could this be the top of the black rock? If so, it was embedded in the tower as well as buried under it, neither of which seemed particularly safe. Against her better judgment, Jame stepped out onto it. She had never encountered an inactive temple before. It was like setting foot on the back of an inert monster disguised as a black dance floor.

"Even now," Timmon had said, *"Jamethiel Dream-weaver may be dancing out the souls of the Kencyr Host."*

She remembered that dark pavement shot with veins of luminous green in the great hall of the Master's House. A delicate, bare foot touched it, and the veins began to throb. Glide, dip, turn, star-spangled gown aswirl and power swirled with it. She danced to her own hummed tune, smiling, and the watchers swayed forward entranced, seduced. Such beauty, such power, such innocence servant to such evil...

Strong arms grabbed Jame and flung her off the black rock into the wall. Marble shuddered against her back as the tower swayed, grinding against the temple's sullen, immobile flanks.

"The Fall is happening, even now," she said, blinked, and focused on Brier's face above her. "Sorry."

The Kendar let her go. "Sometimes," she said, "you frighten me."

"Do as I say," Jame snapped at Damson, who was watching her with raised eyebrows. "Not as I do."

"No chance of that, Ten," said the cadet. "You teach me my limits."

Some of the columns had cracked and fallen. Most, however, still stood, supporting the upper floor.

But the rock didn't move, thought Jame.

It was like a square peg rammed into this world's living flesh. It also felt solid, unlike other temples she had encountered. How would the priests control it when they arrived if they couldn't enter it? Were they even meant to? Nascent power was already stirring in it, and Langadine writhed. Were all temples like this, capable of shaking their hosts to pieces? Did the Builders, those small, gray, innocent folk, know what destruction their work could produce? Rather, she blamed the Kencyrath's Three-Faced God, who used the materials at hand so ruthlessly in its seemingly endless battle against Perimal Darkling.

The three Kencyr retreated to the outside stair and mounted it gingerly. Everything tilted, as if only the black rock below prevented the entire structure from falling over. There was no outer guardrail. One felt as if at any minute one might tip off into space.

Guards sprawled at the third-story entrance, asleep. One of them might have been dead. Damson shrugged. Accidents happen.

Jame knocked on the door. It opened a crack, then slammed shut, but the lock failed to catch. They entered.

"Hello?"

No one answered.

Within, the floor was strewn with damask pillows and shards of porcelain vases jolted off high shelves. Murals covered the freshly cracked lower walls, depicting meadowlands and forests in jewel colors. Silken veils separated interior spaces. Some were ripped. All wavering in an errant breeze. Everything spoke of a comfortable, sheltered life, rudely disrupted. A woman crouched in the far corner, clutching a bright-eyed, five-year-old child.

"Crash!" he said, with evident glee, reminding Jame of the younger Byrne. "Do it again!"

"Lady Kalan?" Jame advanced slowly so as not to frighten the woman more. Glass crunched under her boots. The marbles of some board game rolled.

The seeker looked much as she remembered, if older, her blond hair tarnished to silver gray, and thinner, with flesh beginning to sag on the bone. She blinked at Jame in surprised recognition.

"Lordan? What are you doing here?"

"Looking for you. Why didn't you come back?"

"Back?" Kalan rose, still shaken. For her, after all, it had happened more than a decade ago. She spread her hands.

"Behold my cage, the latest of many. Before, I lived in the palace, first with Laurintine to nurse after that terrible storm. Then, when she died, the old king demanded that I stay, marry one of his cousins, and start a new line of Langadine seekers."

"I'm sorry."

"You needn't be. I loved my husband, but I bore him only sons, five in all. This is Lanek, the youngest, a late blessing."

"Hello!" The boy waved.

"Hello," Jame replied gravely.

She remembered how desperately Kalan had wanted a family. After losing her first in Kothifir, here, it seemed, she had found another. "Where is your husband?"

"Dead these eight months, killed on the same fatal hunt that claimed the old king's life. Now Lainoscopes has built me this new prison. He wants me to remarry and try again for a daughter, but I am too old. Besides, two husbands are enough."

"You already have an infant girl, left behind in Kothifir."

Kalan wrung her hands. "I have thought about her every day, these past fifteen years. She was so ill when I left, and my first husband so recently dead. I always hoped that I would go back to her in the end, please the gods, to find her alive, still a baby, still waiting for me."

"You can do that now, and rescue your Kencyr escort on the way."

The seeker looked bewildered. "What, they didn't return to Kothifir? I thought they would, after they had waited long enough. Surely their scouts could have led them there from the oasis."

"From the oasis in the future, yes, but something did go wrong, as you and Laurintine foresaw. After the caravan left, the wind swept the rest of us back into the past too, although we arrived long after you did."

"This is making my head ache," Damson said to Brier. "Besides, aren't we in a hurry?"

"Quiet."

"Mother?" called a voice from outside. "What's happened to your guards? Mother!"

A well-dressed boy rushed into the apartment. He had Kalan's blond hair and a rangy build that probably reflected that of his late father. Jame guessed that he was in his early teens.

"My second oldest, Lathen," said Kalan, confirming her suspicion.

"Who are these people?" the boy demanded. "Does Cousin Lainoscopes know that you have visitors?"

Kalan drew herself up with an effort. She looked terrified. "Dear, this is an old friend. She's come to take me home."

The boy paled. "What do you mean? This is your home!"

"You know that I came here from over the sea, from a future when Langadine no longer exists. A daughter waits for me there. Don't you remember? I used to sing to you about her, your little half-sister. She's still only a baby and she needs me. Now I am going back to her."

The boy shook his head, distraught. "No, no, no. Those were only foolish stories, and you're deluding yourself now. I told my brothers that the king was pushing you too hard, but no one listens to me, not the way they did to Father. You can't leave! What about us?"

"Lanek will go with me. You and the rest are old enough to look after yourselves, unlike your sister. Please, dear..."

"The king won't allow it. You'll see." His voice broke. "Let go of me!"

Brier had taken his arm. He twisted futilely in her iron grip, simultaneously terrified and outraged that she could overpower him so easily.

"You can come with us," said Jame.

"Where? Into some fantasy of future days? This is my time. I belong here."

"Yes. I suppose you do."

At a nod from her, Brier released the boy and he darted out the door, bound, no doubt, to inform the king of their imminent escape.

"I don't understand," said Damson in Kens as they descended the outside stair, Jame supporting the seeker, Brier carrying a delighted Lanek. "If he finds any guards still awake—and he probably will: I couldn't put them all to sleep—they'll be after us. So why let him go?"

Jame sighed. "He was right: this is his time, even if it kills him. Brier could have knocked him unconscious, I suppose. That would have been more sensible. But it just didn't seem fair. He's terrified of losing his mother. Why take away his self-respect on top of everything else?"

"Why? To get us safely out of here. Ten, sometimes you think too much."

They had reached the courtyard. A cluster of men advanced on them—guards, Jame thought; Damson was right—but then she saw that they were all clad in yellow and that they escorted an old man who held back, talking fast:

"...you see, it wasn't as if I actually flew. Think more metaphysically. You know that my intellect far exceeds your own..."

"Yes, Master, of course, Master," they soothed him.

The Tishooo spotted Jame. "You were there! You said that I fell!"

"So I did. So you will. But it won't hurt you."

He looked up at the tower, his head tipping further and further back. For only three stories, it was remarkably high, "the tallest in the city," Byrne had proudly claimed.

"Don't tell me what will or won't hurt!"

"Just keep talking!" she called after him as he was hustled past. "Stall!"

They went as quickly as they could down through a city shaken awake by the latest tremor. Some dwellings had collapsed while others were on fire. Many had left their inhabitants huddled outside in the street in their nightgowns while their neighbors tried to comfort them, meanwhile keeping a wary eye on their own shaken houses. The night market was a kicked ant's nest full of merchants scrambling to save their wares. Jame hoped that Ean had taken her seriously concerning the need for haste.

At the waterfront she found not only Ean and Byrne but her own command, moas and all, piled into a sturdy fishing boat.

"Get aboard!" Gorbel shouted from the prow.

There was no wind to speak of, so the oars were out and manned by the cadets. The former owner stood on the marble wharf, his pockets bulging with golden coins, some of which he fingered, as if unable to believe either his luck or the foolish extravagance of some people.

"Are you sure you don't want to hire a crew?" he called to the newcomers as they rushed past him. "Then at least remember to cast off!"

Gorbel threw off the front hawser, Brier the stern. The boat rocked away from its mooring and began to drift sideways. The moas swayed, squawking.

"Pull, damn you!" roared the Caineron Lordan.

Some oars crashed in midair like inept duelists while others splashed into the water. The cadets hadn't had any practice rowing since their flight from Restormir in Caldane's barge more than a year ago. The Silver didn't promote such sport.

"All right, all right, calm down and start over. Up, down... pull!"

The boat backed away from the wharf, stern first. How did one turn the thing around? No matter, as long as they were making progress.

Jame stood on the prow, watching Langadine recede ever so slowly. From here, she could see several broken terraces with shattered houses spilling down through the gaps, also flames reflected on whitewashed walls. People shouted. Dogs barked. Perhaps nothing else would happen, tonight at least. Oh, to get away while that doomed, many-tiered city still stood...

Whoomp!

The palace folded in on itself in a billow of dust, then the hill on which it stood. Not so the black temple. As the built-up ground fell away, more and more of it was revealed, still square and immobile but looming higher and higher. At first it wore the tilted remains of the tower like a hat, until Kalan's former quarters fell apart and away, with the hint of a figure in gold flung from its ramparts even as it crumpled.

"Fly," Jame whispered. "Fly!" But she knew that even now the Old Man had begun his endless fall.

The collapse spread, terrace by terrace, flattening the city as if a great weight had been laid on it. More dust rose, obscuring details, muffling screams cut short.

"What's happening?" asked Timmon, wide-eyed, standing beside her.

"The temple has come to life and our people are about to arrive on Rathillien," said Jame. The weight of history bore down on her and the ancient words rose in her throat as harsh as vomit:

"'Two-thirds of the People fell that night, Highborn and Kendar. "Rise up, Highlord of the Kencyrath," said the Arrin-ken to Glendar. "Your brother has forfeited all. Flee, man, flee, and we will follow." And so he fled, Cloak, Knife and Book abandoning, into the new world. Barriers he raised, and his people consecrated them. "A watch we will keep," they said, "and our honor someday avenge. Alas for the greed of a man and the deceit of a woman, that we should come to this!"'

"Don't you see? It's all happening *now*. We are fallen, and in flight."

Oh Dream-weaver, oh Mother. Do you see, will you ever see, what you have done?

"Fallen or not, we aren't fleeing fast enough," said Gorbel, coming up to stand between them. "Are we going to be squashed flat, too?"

"Maybe, maybe not. Everyone, clear the foredeck."

While the others retreated to the waist (Timmon, reluctantly), Jame ransacked her memory for master runes. *The Book Bound in Pale Leather* was out of her hands, still hidden in the cave behind Mount Alban where the thing that was once Bane sat guard over it. In her mind, however, she flipped over its pages, quickly so as to recognize but not accidentally animate any of its dire sigils.

Nothing, nothing, nothing...

Then it came to her: the Great Dance, which even now her mother had perverted, the one intended to direct the power of the temples, of their god itself. Trinity, how long it had been since she had first learned that fearsome variant of the Senetha in Perimal Darkling, taught by golden-eyed shadows. More recently, she had danced in the Tastigon temple after its priest Ishtier had lost control of it.

Child, you have perverted the Great Dance as your namesake did before you, the Arrin-ken Immilai had said in the Ebonbane afterward, passing judgment on her. *You have also usurped a priest's authority and misused a master rune. We conclude that you are indeed a darkling, in training if not in blood. On the whole, your intentions have been good, but your behavior has been reckless to the point of madness and your nascent powers barely under control.*

Three days before, she had nearly destroyed Tai-tastigon.

Then there was Karkinaroth crumpling behind her, but that had been Tirandys' fault for sealing its temple's priests in until they died.

Darkling... No one had called her that in a long time. Tentir had almost made her forget. Nonetheless, she still was one, as the Arrin-ken had said, in training if not in blood.

The dust billowed closer. Lightning flashed within it from cloud to cloud and blue fire crept, crackling, up the boat's rigging. Jame snapped her fingers, and smiled ruefully at the resulting spark.

Tai-tastigon had survived her.

Karkinaroth hadn't been her fault.

"Your friend Marc warned me that I would probably find the Riverland reduced to rubble and you in the midst of it, looking apologetic."

Tentir had only been slightly damaged.

Langadine was dying anyway. No one could blame her for that—could they?

G'ah, don't think of it.

She might be both a darkling and a potential nemesis, but destruction had its role to play too, as Granny Sit-by-the-Fire had said. Her duty now lay with those still alive.

She could feel the power looming over her. Rather than the fierce torrent that she had experienced with other temples, it was thick and clogged with the debris that made it visible, as if the newly awakened edifice were expelling its own afterbirth. The moon and stars dimmed, then disappeared. Jame saluted the on-rolling darkness, turning the gesture into one of defiance. Time to dance.

Glide, dip, turn...

Each move summoned power and expelled it. Violet flames ran down her limbs and crackled at her fingertips. Freed of its cap, her braided hair cracked like whips as she spun. Blue lightning snapped from the ship's rigging to be met by a blinding return stroke from the roiling clouds. As one, the moas flopped over to hide heads under wings. Jame barely noticed. Darkness arched over the boat and pressed down. The mast groaned, but the light flaring at its tip held the shadows at bay. Her dance was creating a space within the clouds, a partial haven from their crushing weight.

An oar shattered. Cadets hastily withdrew and shipped the rest, then went back to holding their ears against the relentless pressure.

Whomp!

Suddenly they were falling, but only a few feet. The sea had been driven back, leaving their keel on its salty bottom among flopping fish.

Just as abruptly, the weight lifted. Jame fell to her knees on the prow. Dark stars splashed between her shaking gloved hands: her nose and ears were bleeding.

"Mommy, is it over?" asked Lanek in a piping voice through a mask of tears and snot.

"Not quite," said Gorbel, looking out to sea. "Hold on. Here it comes!"

The sea was returning in a towering wave, flinging whitecaps and fish off of its crest as it came. It rolled under the boat's stern, pitching it upward and nearly flinging out its passengers. The moas screamed. So did Lady Kalan.

The wave rolled on, driving the clouds before it up through the broken tiers of the city. Then back it came, dragging the dead with it. Jame clung to the rail staring down into all of those blank, smashed faces. The ship bobbed in a sea of corpses. Over all, power still roiling about its base, loomed the black temple crowned by the gibbous moon.

The wind returned in a swirl of tattered gold, not quite landing on the deck beside her.

"You were right," said the Old Man in a tone of wonder. "It didn't hurt at all."

"You think not? Look."

The Tishooo stared down, his seamed face going slack with shock, then taut with outrage. "Oh, my poor people, my poor city! Who has done this terrible thing?"

That, thought Jame, was a good question. Hers was supposedly a sentient god, yet his actions seemed mindless. All of this destruction—to what end? A temple had come to life, and in the process had slaughtered an innocent population. Where was the justice in that? Never mind that he might be said to have saved his own people through her actions. But honor didn't only apply within the Kencyrath, whatever some Kencyr like Caldane believed—did it? Not to her understanding. Was such an action any worse than what Perimal Darkling had done to the previous world, through the agency of the Master and the Dream-weaver? Were they also only tools, and if so, of whom? What difference was there, after all, between the Shadows and the Three-Faced God? Did her own people also worship a monster?

"There," she said, dragging herself upright and pointing at the tower.

The Tishooo breathed deep, and the air flexed with him, in and out of her own lungs until her head spun.

Then he was gone.

Jame couldn't see his progress directly, but the clouds around the base of the tower recoiled. Something buffeted them, then drove them back round and around the temple's black shaft, higher and higher. The embedded dead seemed to rise with the blast as if they were storming their destroyer. The wind drew tighter and grew faster, dispersing the clouds of god-power. The tower cracked. Massive shards toppled off of it, plummeting into the chaos below. Then it shattered and fell.

"Good," said Jame, and collapsed.

JAME WOKE to a still night, broken only by the dip and splash of oars. She still lay on the foredeck, but now under an assortment of cadet jackets with one rolled up under her head. Trinity, how long had she been asleep? The moon had set and the stars were obscured by haze. Glassy water stretched out on all sides of the boat to a featureless horizon.

Brier stood nearby, at the prow. At least they had managed to turn the vessel around. The Kendar gave her a stiff nod as Jame joined her, clutching a coat around her shoulders. It wasn't cold, but she couldn't stop shivering.

"Where are we?" she asked.

"Somewhere in the Great Salt Sea, north of Langadine."

"Oh. Helpful. Where's our seeker?"

Brier glanced toward the waist. Kalan huddled at the mast's foot between the rowers with Lanek clutched in her arms, having at last cried herself to sleep over her four lost sons.

"Don't worry," said Brier. "We're on course."

Following her gaze, Jame peered down into the water before the prow. Something pale swam there, the barest glimmer under the smooth water.

"Is that..."

"I think so."

The boat's side rose too far above the water to reach down into it, as Tori had done.

"Will you join her?"

"Should I leave you? Besides, you know that I can't swim. Go back to sleep. You need it."

Jame yawned, wide enough to hear her jaws crack. "You're right. Wake me when we get there."

"Yes, lady."

Back in her nest of jackets, still shivering, she burrowed down to the wooden deck. Oars splashed. The boat glided forward. In the morning, she would think about what she had done, or not. Whatever.

It seemed that all but Brier eventually slept, even the cadets at their oars. At dawn, laughter woke them. The child Lanek capered about the deck, stomping on it, but it gave back no more echo than a stone, for stone it had become. They were on the petrified remains of a boat in the middle of a dry salt waste.

"Is this what Tori saw, after Rose drew him to the far shore?" Jame asked Brier.

"Probably."

The Kendar's eyes were bloodshot from her sleepless watch, her movements stiff as she turned to stare back at what had been a sea and the memory of what it might have held.

"I'm sorry," said Jame.

Brier shrugged, dismissing old grief. "My mother died a long time ago. Now, where are we?"

Kalan hobbled up onto the foredeck, cramped from her night's sleep on hard planks and still red-eyed with weeping.

"Kothifir lies that way," she said, pointing north-northwest, "and your camp there." Her finger swung straight ahead, in line with the prow. Wherever she had come from, wherever she had gone, Rose Iron-thorn had aimed them true.

They unloaded the sleepy moas and set out, four birds short. Kalan and Lanek led the procession, the little boy in high glee, his mother rigid in the saddle as if sure that at any minute her feathered mount would bolt. This, of course, made it more likely to do so, until Brier took its reins in a firm hand and led it. The rest followed, trading off who walked and who rode to accommodate Ean and Byrne.

At first they saw nothing, and wondered how far from the ancient shore they were. Gorbel had had the foresight to bring sacks of fresh water, but not enough for a long trek. Hours passed. It was so hot that sweat dried on the brow and gave no relief. The sun rose, beat blindingly down against the white salt plain, then tilted toward the horizon. In its wavering glare, the mirage of mountains appeared to the northeast and to the west—hopefully the curving Tenebrae and Urak ranges. A dot appeared on the horizon ahead. Bit by bit, it grew into the single, bedraggled palm that overlooked the tiny oasis.

"We wondered if we would ever see you again," said Onyx-eyed as they limped into camp at dusk.

Jame kicked her bird's shoulder, obliging it to kneel. "How long were we gone?" she asked, swinging stiffly down.

"Only two days, as it turns out. I see that you found the seeker."

"Yes, and she found you. I'm afraid she and these other two are all that's left of the caravan. The rest drowned. Also, Langadine has been destroyed."

The randon eyed her askance. "You've been busy."

"It wasn't my fault, dammit—or at least not most of it. Anyway, that establishes where we are now. As to when . . ."

"Back in our own present, I assume. The east wind blew through last night, and this morning the sea was gone again. We'll only know for sure when we return to Kothifir. In the meantime, eat. Sleep. Tomorrow—if we're still here—we have a long trek home."

CHAPTER XII
A Season of Discontent

Winter 16–65

I

THE TRIP BACK TO KOTHIFIR proved blessedly uneventful if strenuous. All the lambas had gone with the caravan and subsequently had drowned, so the moas were pressed into service as draft animals, to their loud disgust. Rations consisted largely of rhi-sar meat preserved in salt and water from the ancient sea while it had remained fresh. Since both flesh and fluid came from the past, there was no telling how long either would stay in the present. It was a gamble whether they would be consumed before they disappeared, and what that disappearance would do to the host bodies.

The white rhi-sar hide was hitched raw side down to a team of protesting birds to serve as a sledge, onto which more provisions were piled.

"A good scrape will start the tanning process," Gorbel told Jame. "One thing about rhi-sar leather: it doesn't stain. White is an unlikely color for armor only because it's so rare. You'll need to get King Krothen's blessing on it, though, before it's worked."

At Sashwar they exchanged the moas for their horses and Gorbel parted, grumbling, with more golden coins to pay for the lost lambas.

Nine days later they came to the Apollynes and climbed them. The Mountain Station sent ahead a heliograph message to announce their return as they passed. Thus they found a considerable crowd waiting on the training field outside the camp to greet them. Jame had been dreading this sparse homecoming.

No one would believe at first that they were all that remained of that huge caravan sent out thirty days before with such high hopes. Then the wailing began, but not from all.

Kalan cuddled the baby daughter whom she had left behind so long ago as the child cooed with delight.

"Oh, my dear, my precious, I thought that I had lost you forever, but here you are barely a month older. Oh, look at those tiny hands, those tiny feet. This is your half-sister!" she said, presenting the infant to her wide-eyed young son. "No, Lanek, you are too young to hold her." She turned to the nearest Kendar, who happened to be Brier, and slid the infant into her arms. "Support her head just so."

"But...but..."

"Only for a moment. Here comes my late husband's brother, Qrink, Master Paper Crown."

As Kalan rushed to meet a tall, bald man, the rest of the ten-command laughed at Brier's expression and at the ginger way she held her sudden charge, as if afraid that it would break. The child grabbed a hanging lock of her dark red hair and pulled it, crowing with glee.

The Langadine boy would also need King Krothen's blessing, Jame reminded herself. Soon. Or risk at the first scratch crumbling to red dust as his cousin Lanielle had.

Evensong pushed her way through the crowd followed by Gaudaric, anxiously searching for her husband and son. She didn't recognize the former at first with his white-streaked hair and lined face, then gasped and threw herself into his arms. Byrne looked doubtfully down at Gaudaric.

"Grandpa? Oh, I have so much to tell you!"

"I'm sorry," Jame murmured under the young man's bubbling spate of news. "I got to them as quickly as I could, but time moves strangely in the Wastes."

Gaudaric sighed. "His first lesson at the shop, his first guild run at the summer solstice, his first apprentice piece...I have lost his childhood. Thanks to you, though, I have him back, and my daughter has Ean. Never think I'm not grateful for that."

His gaze fell on the rhi-sar hide rolled up in a wagon obtained at Sashwar.

"Is that...it is! An Old One, and in prime condition too. I've never seen an entire cape before, much less complete with head

and feet. Look at those teeth, those claws! Oh, what fun I could
have with those! You'll let me work it for you, won't you?"

Jame grinned. "I was afraid to ask."

❦ II ❦

TWO DAYS LATER Jame was requested to attend King Krothen's
court. This was quick for a royal summons, making her suspect that
the king wanted to hear about the failed trade mission firsthand.
She went, taking Kalan and her son Lanek. Her ten-command also
came with her to carry the rhi-sar hide. It required six Kendar to
bear its weight, much of it located in the skull with its fearsome
array of teeth. The other Kendar carried the four feet, spreading
them from side to side of the street. Awed Kothifirans made way
for them as if for a parade. While the small lizards that constituted
modern rhi-sar were common, the hide of an ancient one hadn't
been seen in many years.

They climbed the Rose Tower and muscled their way into the
uppermost chamber, jostling the back ranks of those already there.
Krothen was having another shouting match with his aunt, the
princess Amantine, or rather she was booming at him and he
was listening with raised eyebrows.

"This is serious, dammit! Do you know how many people have
been ruined by this lost mission? What's more, they tell me that
there will be no more in future. And whom do they blame? You
and Lord Merchandy, that's who!"

"We regret the city's misfortune," the king said in his nasal
voice. "True, Mercer and I promoted the venture, but we also
warned our traders not to be overwhelmed with greed."

"P'ah. No one remembers that now. They see their losses, and
they want someone to blame."

"What, then, would you advise?"

"You have towers full of treasure. Distribute them to the people."

Krothen pursed his rosebud lips. "So your son has proposed.
To everyone, though, or only to those whose avarice brought
about this catastrophe? What, then, would be left to pay the
Southern Host for its protection? In future days we will need

that, as never before, now that Kothifir has been so weakened. Gemma and the other Rim cities are already licking their lips. Perhaps I shouldn't have hanged those Gemman raiders, even if they did kill a seeker."

Jame thought that that last was probably true. Killing people in ambiguous circumstances rarely did any good.

As for the Host, it was preparing for what might come. That morning the camp had been shaken out of bed early by the blare of the alarm horn. Everyone had rushed to the inner ward, to be told that it was only a drill, but they had still been too slow.

Amantine stomped, regaining Jame's attention. "Oh, you and your precious toy soldiers! Prince Ton promises to raise a militia that will do every bit as well."

"Does he propose to lead it himself? Riding what two draft horses, or shall we find him an elephant? Speaking of which, what have we here?"

He had spotted the rhi-sar's fearsome head bobbing behind and above the last rank of his attendants. Courtiers turned to stare, then to back away, some in fright, some holding their noses. The great beast smelled worse dead than alive. The Kendar bore it forward and let its hide sprawl at Krothen's feet as if in obeisance. He clapped his pudgy, beringed hands in admiration.

"Your Magnificence," said Jame, bowing. "Would you deign to preserve our prize with your touch?"

Brier lifted one of the flayed forearms and extended a talon as if it were reaching out to the king. He dabbed at it, then paused thoughtfully, twiddling his sausagelike fingers. Jame could see that he was tempted to claim the entire hide as royal booty.

"Don't you dare," she said, to a gasp from the courtiers.

Krothen pursed his lips with a moue of petulance, but withdrew his hand. "Should I rob so bold a hunter of such a trophy? Take it, with my blessing. Now, who have we here?"

Kalan nudged her son forward. The Langadine boy stared up at the mountainous figure before him, wide-eyed with wonder.

"Why are you so big?" he asked.

Krothen made a subterranean sound that emerged as a fat chuckle. "Why are you so small? Here. Have a candied centipede."

The Kendar bundled up their prize and retreated, leaving Lanek perched on what was presumably the royal knee, dubiously regarding his still twitching many-legged treat.

⟨⟨≋⟩⟩ **III** ⟨⟨≋⟩⟩

WHILE THE TEN-COMMAND departed to deliver the rhi-sar hide to Gaudaric, Jame went in search of Graykin. She found him at the shabby tavern most commonly frequented by the Intelligencers' Guild, holding court among his dingy followers, none of whom looked pleased to see her.

"What do they have against me?" she asked when Graykin left them to join her at her table.

The spy shrugged. "You set me to look for Ran Awl and Night-shade, not to mention the other missing Randir. I recruited the entire guild to help me."

"Without pay, I take it."

"They should be glad to do their guildmaster's biding."

"Huh." Jame took out a golden *arax* and rapped on the table with it. "Drinks on me for the house, until this runs out," she told the slovenly maid who came to take her order.

"You didn't need to do that," Graykin grumbled.

"It can't hurt. Now tell me: have you discovered anything about Shade and Ran Awl?"

"Not so much as a tinker's fart, and we looked everywhere."

"Undercliff too?"

He gave a moue of discontent. "You know we aren't welcome below."

"All right. As it happens, I've made my own arrangements there. And don't look so sour. I remember your reception at Fang's hands the last time."

She surveyed the room, noting many sharp noses buried deep in refilled mugs but also many glittering eyes watching her and Graykin askance. Only Hangnail stared at them openly with hooded eyes, his drink untouched before him.

"Walk wary, Graykin," she said softly. "Come the next Change, you could be in trouble."

The spy shrugged. "That may not be for years. Anyway, what-ever happens, I'm still your sneak, aren't I?"

"I wish you wouldn't call yourself that. I bound you, more or less by accident, and I'm responsible for you. Nothing will change that."

Graykin let out a breath he seemed unaware that he had been holding. "That's all right, then."

Undercliff, Jame sought out the Waster Fang, who gave her a similar report.

"I can't swear that my gang of urchins has searched every single cave—remember, they go back for miles—but we would have heard something if there were prisoners here below."

Jame sighed and counted out a handful of coins. "For your efforts, nonetheless," she said. "See that the children get some fresh fruit and vegetables. Where's Kroaky?"

Fang glowered. "Here and there, as usual."

"I ask for no secrets, mind you, but what is his connection to that great lump, Krothen? Surely you've noticed the resemblance."

"No, I have not," snapped the Waster. "What, d'you think I sit in the king's pocket? I've never even seen the man."

With that, Jame had to be satisfied.

IV

WINTER PROGRESSED without a sign of the missing Randir but with growing unrest in the city. Merchants and craftsmen began to feel the pinch of their lost ventures and, as the princess had foretold, they were quick to blame Krothen and Lord Merchandy. Some also looked to Lord Artifice, but it was well known that he had risked as much of his wares as any two merchants, enough seriously to compromise him. Of the three guild lords, only Lady Professionate escaped criticism on that count, although she found her hands full dealing with the newly stressed, combative populace.

No one wanted to admit that Kothifir's days of glory might be over.

"Not that we can't survive on our own talents," said Gaudaric, sketching a shoulder plate in blue chalk on the creamy rhi-sar leather. He picked up a toothed file and began to saw. "I've said before that we have plenty of skilled craftsmen here, at least as many as the other Rim cities. True, some guilds will suffer more than others—the silk and spice merchants especially. Others shouldn't have sent more wares than they could afford to lose. My own losses will sting for a while, but they won't ruin me."

Jame perched on a stool, feeling stifled. Gaudaric had bound plates of wet, boiled leather around her torso and there she would have to remain until they took her form.

"Sit up straight," he told her, "and remember to breathe."

"You really think that the city will recover?"

"My guess is that it will never be what it was, but if everyone is sensible, yes. Mind you, not everyone will be. People have grown used to the fat times and they will resent losing them. I credit that for this cry to distribute the king's riches. Then there are the opportunists. Merchant Needham, now, there's a fellow determined to turn things to his advantage at whatever cost to others."

Jame had heard that the merchant, Master Silk Purse, was haranguing his guild about Kothifir's need for new rulers. Lord Merchandy was his prime target, although there were whispers that he also spoke in private against the king. It was unclear to Jame if he wanted a civil uprising or a Change—surely not the latter since that would put his own position as a guild master at risk as well, unless he was so arrogant that he considered himself unassailable. Then again, what did he think he could do to restore the city's now dwindling wealth?

She could only imagine how Kothifirans would react if they ever learned that a Kencyr temple coming to life in the past had caused their current distress. The sea awash with the dead at Langadine still haunted her. Damn her god anyway for his unthinking cruelty, much more to Langadine than to Kothifir. That in turn reminded her of Kothifir's temple, which she hadn't visited since her arrival in the city.

Consequently, when Gaudaric finally released her from leather bondage, she made her way toward the ruined outer ring of the city.

This time she entered the topless tower from the ground level. The temple still loomed up through the broken floors like a dormant volcano, making her wonder anew why anyone had built it there to begin with. Perhaps it had been small at first and the structure had been built around it to hide its existence. However, it wasn't quite as tall as it had been the last time she had seen it. Graykin had been right: it had shrunken, not disastrously but noticeably. Black-robed priests and brown-clad acolytes still bustled in and out of its only door. The whole structure vibrated with power, but with a catch to it, like a top beginning to falter in its spin.

"You again."

Jame turned to find the blond acolyte of her previous visit standing behind her, looking sour. She indicated the diminished temple.

"How long has it been like this?"

"Since Winter's Eve, if you must know. Every day it shrinks a little more, on the outside at least. Inside it stays the same. One of us always remains outside, just in case."

"When is it likely to trigger a Change?"

He laughed, without humor. "Grandfather would give a lot to know that. As many Changes as he's lived through, they still tend to catch him by surprise. We could go on like this for another year, or a sudden fluctuation in the weather might tip the balance overnight."

Jame regarded him curiously. The last time they had met, he had been willing to see her plunge to her death. Now he looked harried and preoccupied, not entirely focused on her presence. "I don't know much about the inner workings of the priesthood," she said. "How did you come to be here?"

"Because of Grandfather, of course. I belong to a hieratic family and trained in the Priests' College at Wilden, as my father did before me. He died at the Cataracts. He was a horse healer. Of course, no one gave him credit for that."

"I expect the horses did," said Jame.

Her own attitude toward the priesthood had changed somewhat since she had come to know Kindrie Soul-walker. She still didn't trust most of them, but she was now aware that the Priests' College was a dumping ground for unwanted Shanir children, resulting in a disproportionate number of healers and others of singular power. She wondered what talent this boy wielded, if any.

"Who are you?" she asked.

He drew himself up. "Dorin, son of Denek, son of Dinnit Dun-eyed, son of..."

"Enough."

"You asked, I answered—and I know now who you are too. You may call yourself the Talisman, but you're also the Highlord's unnatural heir, Jamethiel Priest's-bane. Did you think we wouldn't find out?"

Jame had hoped that they wouldn't, but her reputation had apparently preceded her, at least among the priesthood.

"How is M'lord Ishtier anyway?" she asked. "The last time I saw him, he was trying to gnaw off his own fingers."

Dorin glared at her. "Not well, thanks to you, but he gave us warning."

"I can imagine. Did he also tell you that he tried to create a rival deity to the Three-Faced God?"

The boy's face reddened. "Lies!"

"Truth, I'm afraid, and a word of warning: never call me a liar. 'All the beings we know to be divine are in fact but the shadows of some greater power that regards them not.' That's the Anti-God Heresy of Tai-tastigon. Ishtier used a Kencyr soul to create a demon, and believed that he had created a god, but Tastigon 'gods' spring from the power that spills over from our own temple and are shaped by the beliefs of their followers. Here in Kothifir, that gives you the guild lords, the god-king Krothen, and, to a lesser degree, the guild masters."

"What about the Old Pantheon godlings of the Undercliff?"

"Their source of power is different, bound to this world specifically through the Four, not to us."

He shook his head as if plagued with bees. "What Four? No, don't tell me: I don't believe any of it anyway. You Highborn will say anything to keep us powerless, we, who control the greatest power in the Chain of Creation through his temples."

"You keep the temples from exploding. What else you do with them, I don't know. Their power certainly doesn't help the rest of the Kencyrath. And you must be part Highborn yourself if you're a Shanir priestling."

"Lies," he said, backing away. "Lies. Who is our lord? No one. Whom do we serve? The high priests. Who is our family? Each other. On whom do we spit? Our cruel god, who has forsaken us. The temples are ours, I tell you! No one else serves or deserves them."

Jame watched him go, almost running. It seemed to her that she had let an unwelcome light into his world, or maybe she only hoped that she had.

Priests, she thought in disgust.

⋘⚬⚬ **V** ⚬⚬⋙

MIDWINTER CAME with a spate of rain, drumming on the baked ground. The Amar ran swift between its banks around the city and in channels through the Undercliff, fed by mountains to the north. Winter crops in the Betwixt Valley neared harvest.

At Tentir, the Winter War was being waged between the new first-year cadets and those who had returned for a second year.

In two three-hundred-yard pitches established in the training fields south of Kothifir, randon officers and cadets competed against regular Kendar in an all-barracks match that took three days to complete.

Thus late on Midwinter's afternoon, Jame found herself and her ten-command waiting to face their regular counterparts in the east field, surrounded by thousands of noisy spectators who had already played their own sets.

The game was called *kouri*, a native favorite usually conducted on fleetfoots with a headless goat carcass. The Kencyrath, however, preferred horses and a sheepskin ball. The object was to carry said ball between the opponent's goalposts. There were few other rules and many casualties, for it was a rough sport.

Timmon rode up, his horse lathered and his jacket stained with sweat.

"Whew," he said, wiping his brow with his sleeve. "Those regulars take this seriously, and they've had a lot more practice than we Riverlanders."

"I suppose this is their chance to show that they're our equals or better in something," said Jame. "What's the score?"

Timmon glanced toward the western field where dust rose like smoke and the crowd roared. "Counting senior matches, two hundred thirty to two hundred ten in their favor." He stood up in his stirrups to survey the opposite side of the pitch. "It looks as if you're going to be matched against a Caineron ten-command. Who's that blond Kendar? She looks formidable."

"That's Amberley," said Brier on Jame's other side. "And she's carrying a crook-whip. Watch out for her."

Jame eyed that instrument. It was exactly what its name implied, a short length of springy wood with a metal hook bound at one end and a cluster of braided leather thongs at the other.

"That hook can be used to trip mounts as well as to pull down riders," Brier said, addressing the rest of the ten-command over her shoulder. "Look to your horses."

Jame patted Bel-tairi's neck. She wished she were mounted on Death's-head instead, but the rathorn had seemed rather much for what she had assumed would be a friendly match. Bel might be more nimble, but she was also the smallest, lightest equine on the field. Trinity, what had she been thinking of to risk a priceless Whinno-hir in such a game?

The set before hers was about to conclude, the judge trotting on the sidelines, lips moving as he counted down. Ten skirmishers seethed close to the randons' goal where a cadet guarded the set of posts and four of his peers ranged back and forth waiting to intercept, intercepted in turn by four regular rangers who sought to block them. A cadet had the ball and was trying to break free while his teammates attempted simultaneously to shield him from the regulars and to open a way to the rival goalpost. He saw his chance and plunged out of the scrimmage, closely pursued. One of the regular rangers lunged for him. They ran several paces side by side before the regular wrestled away the ball, unseating the cadet who held on a moment too long and so lost both stirrups and seat. Jame winced as he fell under pounding hooves. The regular threw the shaggy ball to one of his mates, and he to another who dodged the goalkeeper and cantered between the randon posts with it held high. Watching cadets groaned and regulars cheered as the judge brought down his baton to signal the end of the set.

"Another loss for our side," said Timmon. "Watch yourself out there."

At the judge's signal, they trotted out onto the pitch and lined up opposite their opponents. Amberley absentmindedly tapped her crook-whip against her boot as she waited for the baton to drop. Jame was aware of Brier Iron-thorn on her right, riding her tall chestnut gelding. Her former friend was the ten-commander of her troop while Brier was only five-commander under Jame, although for this match Jame had designated Brier as the captain of the team, given her knowledge of the game. Regarding the two Kendar, Jame wondered again about their past relationship, how close they had been, how potentially bitter their estrangement.

Tap, tap, tap went Amberley's whip.

A passing spate of raindrops pattered against the earth, helping to lay the dust.

Brier edged her gelding closer to Bel-tairi.

The judge dropped the sheepskin ball between the two lines and retreated. Down came his baton.

Two riders wheeled to protect their respective goals while four on each team spread out to cover the middle field as rangers. The remaining ten skirmishers charged each other.

Dar swung down from the saddle to grab the ball by its long fleece, but jerked back and swerved as a regular thundered down on him, cutting him off. The other team had the ball. Cadets pressed in to prevent it from being thrown to an enemy ranger. Horses clashed, squealing. Amberley slashed at Brier's face with her whip, again and again, until the Kendar reached up and wrenched it out of her grip. Jame saw the white, furry ball pass from rider to rider under the confusion.

Suddenly it flew free.

Mint and a regular raced down on it. The Knorth got it, but the other horse crashed into her own and she dropped it. Now the regular was coming straight at Jame, the ball under his arm. No fool, Bel jumped out of the way, to a groan from the onlookers. The regular pelted on toward the goalposts and tried to throw the ball between them; but Killy, the cadet guard, caught it and threw it back into play. Now the field was thundering back toward Jame.

"Here!"

Ranger Quill tossed her the ball, which nearly knocked her out of the saddle. Trinity, but the thing was heavy. What did they stuff it with anyway? Bel wheeled and sprinted toward the opposite goal, but regulars intercepted and shoved her nearly into the crowd of onlookers. Faces flashed past, split open with shouts. Bel shied, uneasy at so many people on her blind side. Jame tried to pass the ball to ranger Erim, but it was caught by a Caineron skirmisher. The regulars formed a flying wedge around him. They swept aside Killy and plunged across the cadets' goal to a roar from the crowd.

Both sides huddled to plan their next assault.

"I'm no good at this," Jame said. "I only weaken the team."

"Too late to replace you," said Brier, speaking with the ruthless preoccupation of the team's captain. A welt ran down her face where Amberley had struck it and one eye was turning black. "Stay on the edge of the action. The rest of you, pass to her only if no one else is in the clear."

Chagrined, Jame retreated to her post as a ranger.

Again the horses clashed, but this time Niall and Mint were brought down. Amberley wasn't the only one carrying a crook-whip. One of the horses scrambled to its feet or rather to three of them as the fourth dangled useless with a shattered canon bone.

Too rough, Jame thought. *Too rough. What do they want—blood?*

Damson rode up next to her. "Ten, they aren't playing fair. What should I do?"

"The judge determines fairness."

"In case you hadn't noticed, he's Caineron."

The field seemed to shift before Jame's eyes, not cadet against regular but Knorth against Caineron, with her five-commander caught in the middle.

"Watch out for Brier," she told Damson.

The ball dropped back into play and the horses charged it. Damson rode to Brier's right, gashing her mount's sides to keep up. Crook-whips flailed and Brier's horse screamed, floundering. Then confusion seized the combatants as they found themselves inexplicably beating each other. Brier's chestnut recovered and surged out of the confining circle.

The ball, meanwhile, had fallen into cadet hands. Jame paced Quill as he charged down the field toward the Caineron goal. Bel startled the goalkeeper by streaking under his nose, and Quill broke through to score.

One to one.

"So far, so good," panted Dar as they huddled again, "except that Niall is out with a downed horse. We have time for one more win before our set is over."

Or for one more loss, thought Jame.

Brier's chestnut was bleeding at the shoulders and flanks from whip blows, likewise his rider across the brow where bright blood matted her dark red hair and dripped in her eyes.

"I'll take the ball this time," she said, impatiently wiping her face. "Cover me."

Jame withdrew, apprehensive, to her ranger's position.

The horses rushed together a third time. Brier swooped down from the saddle to snatch the ball out from under Amberley's nose. The Caineron wheeled in pursuit. She surged up on Brier's left side and bent low to swing a borrowed crook. It caught the chestnut's hock. The horse stumbled and fell. Brier rolled clear clutching the ball. She threw it to Damson, who swept past toward the goal. Instead of following, Amberley rounded on Brier as she rose, intent, it seemed, on riding her down. Brier dodged and back the Caineron came, whipping her horse's flank.

Jame cut between them.

"Up!" she cried, and Brier, grabbing her hand, swung onto Bel's back. The Whinno-hir staggered under their joint weight, but gamely swerved toward the boundary. People scrambled out of the way as she plowed into them. Amberley reined in just short of the crowd and spun back toward the action, but too late: shielded by cadet rangers, Damson had dodged past the goalkeeper and carried the ball between the posts for the winning score.

The judge threw down his baton. "Game!"

Jame extricated Bel from the onlookers and Brier slid to the ground.

"That wasn't necessary," she said.

"Maybe not, but it made me feel better."

≋ CHAPTER XIII ≋
Dreams and Nightmares

Autumn 50–Winter 14

I

WITH THE END of the autumn harvest, preparations for winter began in the Riverland. Barley was threshed, chimneys cleaned, meat smoked and salted. All of the outer ward garden at Gothregor had been gleaned except for the mangel-wurzel destined for fodder or, if necessary, for soup; but it needn't come to the latter. For the first time, Torisen could buy what he lacked, with enough left over for the odd luxury. However, as with many a man suddenly come into wealth, he hesitated to spend any more than was absolutely required. Aerulan's dowry arrived in regular installments, most of which went into an iron box shoved into a corner.

"You really could afford to buy more clothes," Kindrie said, eyeing his lord's meager winter wardrobe. "Most of these coats have darns on top of darns."

"And all the warmer they are for it." Which was true: Kendar work tended to be eerily efficient. "Besides," he added, "Burr enjoys a bit of needlework on a cold winter's night."

Burr made a face, but didn't contradict.

The two cousins were getting along reasonably well, if with some wariness on both sides.

Walking on eggshells, Torisen thought, not that he really doubted Kindrie's competence or loyalty, nor had he for some time. Rather, he was afraid of waking the wrathful voice of his father deep in his soul-image and the spates of irrationality to which it gave rise. It occurred to him from time to time that he really had to get

Ganth out of there, but how? Kindrie was a soul-walker. Perhaps he would know. However, Torisen hesitated to put it to the test, and felt all the more weakened by that hesitation.

Luckily, Riverland politics were currently quiet, although rumors came from Restormir that Lord Caineron still fretted over the loss of the golden willow long after any sensible man would have let it go. Certainly, his ire over the singers' Lawful Lies had been inflamed. Word came from Mount Alban that he was withdrawing his scrollsmen one by one and questioning them—about what, exactly, they refused to say, but they didn't look happy.

Meanwhile, Torisen continued to dream, sometimes in a confused fashion about Jame, but more often about his own past with the Southern Host. He caught fitful glimpses of his sister's journey into the Wastes, though—snatchers groping out of the sand, a rhi-sar charge, a long ride out into the waters of a vanished sea, and then a wailing, desolate cry:

"Langadine has fallen!"

"My sons," someone was weeping. "Oh, my children!"

Jame stood on the deck of a ship, looking back into nightmare, her face implacable. The slaughter of an innocent population—

"Do we also worship a monster?"

"There," she said, pointing, and the wind did her bidding. A sea of corpses rose up to storm a black tower and everything fell.

I am falling too, Torisen thought. *Away from my sister and the present, into the past...*

Harn looked up from a note on thick cream paper which he had just received.

"King Kruin wants to see you," he said.

The boy Tori was startled. "How is he even aware that I exist?"

"Ancestors know. You keep quiet enough, all things considered. D'you suppose it has something to do with your new friend?"

Of course Harn had discovered Kroaky's presence in Tori's quarters, given that the latter were only feet from his office and that the Kothifiran prince insisted on roaming about after dark. He was a restless houseguest, and a voracious one. Tori had never seen anyone eat so much while remaining so thin.

After Torisen's hazing in the Caineron barracks, Harn Griphard looked at him as if vaguely puzzled. If Tori caught his eye at such a moment, the big Kendar cleared his throat and became even gruffer; however, he also had stopped insulting his self-appointed clerk.

Tori would have liked to think that it was because he had refused to complain about his ill-treatment at Genjar's hands. However, he wondered if Harn, a former Knorth, was beginning to sense his bloodlines as Rowan apparently had.

If so, that made life easier, but also more dangerous and problematic.

While no one had dared to claim the Highlord's seat—much less that potentially lethal collar, the Kenthiar—since Ganth's exile, the Caineron, for one, would never permit the son of their former master to live if they could help it. Look how they had dealt with a senior randon like Harn, only a threshold dweller after all these years. Blood wasn't enough to protect Ganth's son. He also needed respect and power. The thought made Tori grimace. How was he to gain either, situated as he was? Nothing would be handed to him as it had been to his ancestors, never mind that they went back to the creation of the Kencyrath. Whatever he gained would be on his own.

For that matter, did he even want his father's place, supposing that it was in fact vacant? Perhaps he belonged somewhere else within the Kencyrath, gained on his own merit. If only Adric had allowed him to attend Tentir...

Harn folded the summons and handed it to him. "Whatever the reason, you'll have to go. Now. And walk wary: the Overcliff has been unsettled since the king's illness."

Tori paused in his quarters to change into the cleaner of his two jackets. Kroaky lounged discontentedly on Burr's narrow bed.

"You might find some way or someone to amuse me," he said, pouting.

"Not today. Your father wants to see me."

The lanky prince sat up, alarmed. "Will you tell him that I'm here?"

"Of course not, but Commandant Harn knows. I take it that you ran into him on one of your evening strolls."

"Can he be trusted?"

"To the death, unless someone asks him a direct question."

Kroaky settled back, marginally reassured. "You Kencyr. Inexplicable."

Torisen rode the open lift cage up to Kothifir.

The first thing he noticed on arrival was that the swirling cloud cover had dispersed. In its absence, the summer sun beat down mercilessly on the clifftop city, washing out its usually vibrant colors and glazing everything with a layer of dust. It hadn't rained since spring. The Amar ran shallow and bitter, poisoning its fish and withering crops in the field. A few residents moved languidly from shop to shop, where they found little to buy. Some gathered on street corners listening to men muffled in black robes and *cheches*—Karnids from Urakarn, Tori thought, preaching their obscure message of doom and rebirth. The Kencyrath had little to do with them. Given their own bitter experience with the Three-Faced God, most Kencyr wondered why anyone would willingly embrace any religion, much less one that made such dire promises.

"This world is but a shadow of the one to come!" cried a speaker as Torisen passed. "You, boy, stay and listen to the holy words of our Prophet!"

Here at last was the Rose Tower and the long climb up its spiral stair under the beating sun. Without the clouds, the sparsely occupied mid-towers showed up as clearly as a ring of blight. Some had broken off and fallen into the streets below. One wondered how the rest could support the gilded upper stories where the guild lords lived, although even these looked brassy and cheap in the sun's glare.

Some claimed that it was all because the Kencyr temple was currently abandoned by its priests. The guild lords also seemed to have lost their power. Tori himself didn't see the connection.

What he did see were carrion crows circling overhead. Something about the Rose Tower seemed to attract them.

No one guarded the king's audience chamber at the top. Tori stopped at the threshold on the edge of the pale green, golden veined chalcedony floor, wondering if he should announce himself. No: the wide, circular room brimmed with noblewomen, all in white-faced makeup as befitted their rank. Most wore rich but somber gowns, although a few flashed almost defiantly with brilliant color. The king himself reclined on a lofty dais wearing black in regal imitation of a Karnid's robe. He was a big man, famous for his hunting prowess. Now, however, his flesh drooped like soft wax and the color on his haggard face came out of a rouge box.

"You ask me where your fathers, and sons, and husbands are," he said, then paused to draw in a ragged breath. His eyes glittered with feverish, defiant life in their deep sockets. *I will not die,* they seemed to say, *oh no, not me*; but he stank as if already dead in that hot, rose-tinted chamber.

"My kinsmen serve me as my sons already have, all but that runagate coward Krothen whom I will find soon enough. That is all you need to know."

"My lord brother, I disagree."

The voice boomed from the front of the crowd, but Tori couldn't see who spoke. He started to edge toward the right, then froze. Genjar lounged against the wall in a turquoise court coat trimmed with blue pearls and whirls of silver thread, watching the drama play out before him with the thin-lipped smile of a connoisseur in pain. Tori moved left. He and the Caineron would settle their score, but not today and certainly not here. Now he could see the front rank of the ladies and their spokeswoman. No wonder he had overlooked the latter: she was very short and, from the width of her, very pregnant. This must be Princess Amantine, the king's sister.

"My child needs his father," she said, glowering.

"This city needs its king. Debate that with the towers themselves."

Someone tapped Torisen on the shoulder. Suppressing a start, he turned to see the shadow of a black-gloved hand withdrawing, gesturing him to follow. The marble walls of the chamber were carved as thin as rose petals and separated so that one could slip out between them. Tori did so, onto an outer walkway that circled the tower. It had no rail. Birds swooped dizzyingly through the void beyond.

"Come here, boy."

He followed the voice.

"Stop."

The other stood just beyond the curve of the thin wall, his distorted shadow falling through it.

"I was summoned by the king," said Tori, keeping his voice down, unsure if he was defending his presence in the royal hall or protesting his absence from it.

"Summoned at my request. So. You are Ganth Grayling's son."

Tori felt the flesh jump on his bones, but he held himself still. Then he remembered to breathe.

The other laughed, his voice a soft rumble. "I didn't mean to alarm you, only it surprised me to learn that you were here. Did your father really let you leave that pest hole in the Haunted Lands, or did you run away?"

"Who *are* you?" Tori demanded, taking a step forward.

A raised hand stopped him, as if he had run into a wall. "Why, child, who should I be but your true lord and master?"

That made no sense. Ganth was Highlord if he still lived, and Tori felt instinctively that he did, never mind that he had thrown away his power as petulantly as a child might a broken toy. Highlord or not, though, what right did such a man have to claim anyone's loyalty? His own Kendar had united to free his son from his unworthy tyranny.

Choose your own lord, said the mocking rumble under the stranger's voice. *Have you not earned the right, boy? Did your father keep faith with you, with anyone? Honor is a failed concept. Only strength matters. Choose me.*

Tori shook his head to clear it.

"What have you done to King Kruin?" he demanded.

The other sighed. "Nothing. He is not a young man, and has lived a profligate life. Nonetheless, he wants to live forever. I suggested that he might, if he made a few sacrifices. Look below."

Tori had been avoiding that, not because he was afraid of heights (although the Rose Tower was very high), but because the carrion birds squabbling below unnerved him. Now he looked. A ring of iron thorns circled the edifice. Many of them were tipped with round shapes from which loose hair blew in the wind.

"A lord's followers serve their master, in life, in death, don't you agree, little lordling? A variant on that ancient belief has worked for me—so far. But the Gnasher is no Dream-weaver. She reaped; he rends. The latter may not succeed for our dear Kruin."

"Death and rebirth," said Tori. Much that the other said confused him, but one thing was suddenly clear. "You are the Karnids' Prophet."

"Oh, he died millennia ago. The Karnids say that I am he, returned. It amuses me to play that role." The other's purr sank into a half-snarl. "Anyway, why should I submit to death at all? Let other fools die for me, as they were born to do."

Raised voices sounded within the chamber.

"You would not dare," Princess Amantine said, and this time her tone shook with more than anger.

"Would I not?" Kruin was panting now. He sounded ghastly. "If your child is a son... what are heirs for... if not to prolong... the life of their king? If I must take him as he is... I shall. So the Karnid Prophet has taught me. Now, come here."

Someone screamed.

Tori slipped back into the chamber to witness panicked ladies surge for the door. Caught up in the rush, Genjar stumbled and disappeared beneath billowing black skirts. Meanwhile, the cause of it all, Kruin, had risen and was lurching toward his sister, a hunting knife in his hand.

"I will gut you where you stand... you fat, little pig," he wheezed. "Give me your unborn child!"

Without thinking, Tori stepped between them. Kruin loomed over him, the king's stinking breath in his face. He tried to brush the Kencyr aside, but Tori caught him in a wristlock that brought him crashing to his knees. The knife skittered away across the chalcedony floor. Kruin tried to rise, but his legs folded under him. A look of astonishment crossed his wasted face.

"Why, I'm dying. But I can't be. You promised!"

His eyes rolled toward the stranger who stood by the dais, half in shadows. He wore a Karnid's black robe and *cheche*, the tail end of the latter wrapped around his face. A veil beneath concealed all but the silver-gray glint of his eyes.

"Too bad," he said in that deep but wryly dismissive tone. "It was an interesting experiment."

"Betrayed!" Kruin's voice cracked into a howl. "I gave you access to my city! I gave you control of my court! At your suggestion, I have slaughtered most of my heirs! And now all you can say... is 'Too bad'?"

The Prophet shrugged. "Some few merit immortality. Most do not. Yours, I fear, is the common lot."

"I am not common!"

"So every man tells himself."

Kruin's eyes desperately swept the room. "I will be avenged. You!" He had spotted Genjar near the door, unsteadily regaining his feet, his gorgeous coat torn, dripping pearls, one of his eyes blackened. "Seize this charlatan!"

Crows edged, jeering, around the stone petals and stormed the chamber in a fury of black wings. Sharp beaks stabbed everywhere. Jet eyes glittered. Genjar flailed as the birds dived at him. The princess shielded her brother while Tori stood over them both, trying to protect her.

"We will meet again, I think," said the Prophet in Tori's ear. Then he and the birds were gone, except for an eddy of black feathers spinning to the pale green floor.

Genjar lowered his arms cautiously. Finding himself more or less intact, he limped over to Tori and slapped him across the face.

"You let that monster escape!"

"No, Commandant. You did." The princess released her brother's slack body and rose, arms wrapped around her swollen belly. "The king is dead, but his last order still binds you. Here are witnesses to that effect, this boy and myself. Honor demands that you seek that false prophet throughout Kothifir, even to the gates of Urakarn if necessary. Go alone or take the entire Host with you if that gives you comfort."

A spasm of pain crossed her face.

"Now, if you will excuse me, my time has come."

⟨⟨⟨ II ⟩⟩⟩

IT TOOK NEARLY THIRTY DAYS to erect King Kruin's funeral pyre in the central plaza next to the Rose Tower.

First came the spice-wood scaffold reaching almost up to the now returned, low-hanging screen of clouds. Then the framework was stuffed with dry oil-bush from the Wastes. Finally, every guild in the city contributed to its facings. Empty suits of armor stood guard at the base. Above them fluttered choice silks, then gilded mirrors reflecting the sky, then illuminated pages, then shining boots, all toes pointing crisply out, and so on and on, guild by guild, up to vast murals depicting the late king's greatest hunts. Above that, just under the platform to which his body would be lowered, were the spoils of his famous trophy wall. The heads of yackcarn, cave bear, wild cat, and rathorn leered from the heights. Kruin had successfully hunted every creature on Rathillien worth the effort except the wolvers, rhi-sar and—to the relief of his Kencyr troops—the Arrin-ken.

Meanwhile, Kruin's body lay in a chilly Undercliff cave especially noted for its preservative qualities. As the days passed, some joked, quietly, that he would have to be broken out of a stalagmite when his obsequies finally came due.

At last, the day had arrived.

Tori looked around the plaza as he waited for the rites to begin. Despite the returned cloud cover, or perhaps because of it, the city sparkled. Recent rain had washed away the dust and fresh (if limited) produce was again offered in the food stalls lining the main boulevard. The waiting citizens struck a solemn note in their mourning garb, but under that one glimpsed more festive attire. As soon as the old king was reduced to ashes, the new one would be crowned.

Some Kencyr claimed that everything had improved as soon as their temple had come back to life, just after Kruin's death. Tori wasn't sure what he thought about that.

With Kruin's demise and the Prophet's disappearance, the king's surviving heirs had come out of hiding. Despite his blood-claims, it had taken them this long to agree on young Krothen as the new king, but only after saddling him with a council of his elders. Tori had heard his former houseguest complain long and bitterly about his lack both of power and freedom, although he still managed to slip off to the Host's camp for the occasional visit. Although his former experience there had been necessarily limited, he seemed to have developed an admiration for Kencyr life. Certainly, his gratitude to Tori for giving him shelter remained fresh. Although Tori had never spoken his full mind to his awkward guest, he wondered if Kroaky had anyone left besides himself to whom he felt he could speak freely.

Tori wished the attendants would hurry up. Something about the coming transfer of authority bothered him. As a Kencyr, he was sensitive to power—who had it, who didn't—and Kroaky still felt entirely too like, well, Kroaky. Of course, that was all he still was until his crowning, but if anyone had asked him, Tori would have said without thinking that Kruin was still alive, still king. Which was ridiculous.

One of his command, Cully, edged through the crowd to his side. "They say that the princess's husband, Prince Near, is ailing," he said, keeping his voice low.

Tori swore, also softly. The dying hadn't stopped with Kruin. One by one, his heirs were still falling ill and wasting away. Some blamed it on a parting curse attributed to the Prophet. More accused the Prophet himself, who had not been captured despite Genjar's best efforts to seal the city after Kruin's death. True, he had seized some of the street-preachers, but most of the Karnids, with their master, had simply slipped away. Genjar was not said to be pleased, nor was the Council with his efforts, and the commoners simply jeered at him whenever he appeared in public.

No one but Krothen believed in the existence of the mysterious assassin who cast the shadow of a wolf. Tori wasn't sure he did either, except for the Prophet's mysterious reference to someone (or something) called the Gnasher. Nonetheless, the new king-to-be had insisted that he, Torisen, investigate. To do so, he needed help. Harn had assigned him eleven Kendar. Most of them, like Rowan, his second-in-command, were former Knorth, but some came from other houses. Tori suspected that one, Rose Iron-thorn, a Caineron *yondri-gon*, was Genjar's spy, but like the others she had served as a guard in Kothifir during times such as the recent unrest and so had special knowledge of the city. The irony was that if Harn had stopped one short, Tori would have been assigned as a mere ten-commander. Instead, Genjar had been forced to give him the commission of a one-hundred-commander even though it was understood to be provisional and probably temporary.

On the other hand, Harn hadn't seemed displeased, almost as if he had assigned the extra Kendar to bring about exactly this result.

Tori couldn't make out what his small, new command thought about this arrangement. He knew that they called him "Blackie," mostly behind his back, but to his face they were always respectful, following his orders without question. It helped that they found the assignment interesting, even if it might end up leading nowhere.

Cully loomed over him—all the Kendar did. He and they were also at least ten years Tori's senior. If the Knorth had still been in power, Cully might have been a randon sargent in their house. And Rowan had been a randon officer, for Trinity's sake, now reduced to the standing of a common Kendar. Damn Father anyway, for setting such people adrift.

"I asked the usual questions," Cully was saying. "Had they seen anyone strange lingering nearby, or any peculiar shadows? They hadn't. It apparently isn't poison: like most of the Council these days, the prince has a taster. I didn't see him myself, but according to the servants he's wasting away. The princess is beside herself."

"I bet she is," Tori muttered. Motherhood hadn't softened Amantine's militant nature. If her husband died, she was apt to declare war on Urakarn unilaterally.

The crowd stirred and pointed. A temporary catwalk had been built over the pyre and Kruin's body was being lowered from it through the clouds. Belatedly, with a nervous rattle, the drums began to roll. Jarred awake, one of the attendants darted forward with a torch and thrust it into the kindling.

"Too soon!" said Cully.

Indeed, before the corpse had touched the bier balanced on the top, the bottom of the pyre was ablaze as the oil-bush roared to life. Flames leaped upward, outlining the guild offerings and erupting out of the top of the pyre like a volcano. Figures on the catwalk floundered about, burning. Kruin's stiff body swayed, then tumbled down the face of the pyre, trailing flames. It hit the ground hard, and shattered. Everyone had drawn back except Tori. Throwing up an arm to protect his face, he darted to where Kruin's head rolled about the pavement. For a moment he held it, looking down into painted blue eyes already peeling in the heat, then he dropped the head and kicked it back into the blaze before he retreated. His fingers were scorched by the heat, and his sleeves smoldered. Cully beat out the incipient flames.

"You don't take proper care of yourself," he fussed. "Truly, the old bastard isn't worth your hands."

"Nor anyone's," said Tori, shakily brushing off soot. "Did you see, Cully? I could almost believe that the caves petrified his bones, and I never had much respect for his brains even when he was alive, but that head was wood, through and through."

⊰⊱ III ⊰⊱

PRINCE NEAR LINGERED ON, and now the princess' twin cousins were ailing as well.

"They say that patches of their hair are falling out down to the skull, likewise odd chunks of flesh off of their bones," Rowan remarked, washing down a chunk of bread and cheese with a gulp from a flask of watered wine. "It sounds almost like the result of a soul injury—you know, like a Bashtiri shadow assassin."

Kencyr believed that the soul cast the shadow rather than the body. So did the Bashtiri guild, with lethal effect.

"King Krothen says he saw a man with the shadow of a wolf," said Rose. "A white wolf, at that, with a white shadow."

"That's just it: if a wolf is somehow involved, you'd expect blood and broken bones, not a wasting illness."

"Are you saying that the king is wrong?"

"Not necessarily, just that this isn't anything straightforward."

That, thought Tori, was an understatement. He tried to remember if Kruin's shadow had been intact. Yes. In memory's eye, he saw the king plunge to meet it on the chalcedony floor. The Prophet had claimed that he was dying of natural causes but might gain immortality if his male heirs were sacrificed. The Gnasher, plainly, was the assassin, but no Dream-weaver. The Master's consort had reaped souls. What was this man with the shadow of a wolf doing and why, now that Kruin was dead? Around and around Tori's mind went. No wonder he hadn't been able to sleep. Besides asking questions, his little command had taken to patrolling Kothifir after dark. Tonight, rather than spend another sleepless night, Tori had joined Rowan and Rose Iron-thorn on this second-story balcony overlooking the central plaza.

Laughter and music floated down from the brightly lit uppermost chamber of the Rose Tower. Krothen held a jolly court, to which entertainers and artists swarmed from all corners of Rathillien. No one ever seemed to sleep. Tori wondered if the new king just didn't want to be alone. The sense lingered that, although crowned, Kroaky hadn't yet found his feet. It was rumored that he had tried to bless a caravan of spoils from the Wastes and had failed. Merchants throughout the city had been heard to curse his name when their precious wares crumbled into dust.

Kruin, alive . . . but how could that be?

"Look," said Rowan.

A figure had descended the stair and was lurching across the moon-washed plaza, preceded by a canine shadow.

"Is that a dog?" asked Rose.

"No." Tori leaned forward, listening intently. "It's singing . . . I think."

What he heard sounded more like a modulated howl, but there were words mixed up in the cacophony, and some of them rhymed.

Rose stiffened. A child had emerged from the shadows below and was approaching the raucous singer. Before Tori or Rowan could stop her, she had swung to the ground and was racing forward to tackle the latter, who went down with a startled yelp.

Tori sprinted to the rescue. "Rose, stop! I know this fellow. He clowns for the king."

"I do not!" howled the Kendar's prey, curled up in a furry puddle on the pavement, tail tight between his legs. "I'm a court poet! *Hic.*"

The child regarded him solemnly. "Is the puppy sick?"

"No, dear," said Rose. "The puppy is drunk. Why did you attack my daughter?"

"Attack her? I didn't even *see* her!"

Tori regarded the girl. She was only five or six, as far as he could tell, crowned with a helmet of dark red hair. Even in the moonlight, her eyes were a startling shade of green, her gaze solemn and unflinching. "What are you doing in the city at night?" he asked her. "The lift cages don't even run after midnight."

"I climbed." She handed Rose a packet. "You forgot your dinner."

"Oh, Brier. How often do I have to tell you not to follow me?"

Tori nudged the crumpled figure with a toe. "You can get up now. Sorry about that."

"'Sorry.' Who apologizes to a poor wolver so far from home?"

"Ah." Now Tori understood the other's shadow as it untangled four lanky legs while its owner rose on two shaggy, shaky ones. Other than fur and a disheveled garland of flowers, he was quite naked. "That never occurred to me. Do all wolvers cast the shadow of a wolf?"

"It depends on the phase of the moon."

"Which tonight is full." On the chance, Tori had to ask: "Do you know a wolver called the Gnasher?"

"Oh, him. Steer clear... *hic*... that's my advice. I'm from the Grimly Holt, but he's from the Deep Weald. 'Nother kind of beastie altogether. What?"

He looked up, perplexed, at three intent faces.

"When did you last see him?"

"Why, tonight. He's up there, entertaining the king. Juggles lights, doesn't he? Shining Glory, they call him. He's performed for all the best families."

"Damn," said Tori. "Rose, stay with your daughter. Rowan, come on."

"Don't you want to hear one of my poems?" the wolver Grimly cried after them. "Oh, never mind."

Tori and Rowan pounded up the stairs of the Rose Tower. Both were breathless by the time they reached the chamber door where a guard tried to stop them, apparently taking them for performers.

"Here, now, what's your act?"

"We save the king's life...I hope."

The crowd within had drawn back to the edges of the room to give Shining Glory room. Tori edged between courtiers with Rowan on his heels. Lights flashed ahead, a rotating circle of spheres flying now low, now high.

"Oh! Ah..." murmured the onlookers, except for those that turned to glare as the intruders elbowed past.

The performer was a tall, white-haired man with piercing blue eyes, clad in creamy leathers. Soft explosions of light burst from his hands as he increased the number of spheres that he juggled. In their glow he cast no shadow at all, unlike the spectators whose shades whirled against the rose walls as the balls of light circulated. Kroaky sat on the dais in magnificent sky blue robes, entranced, his shadow swaying behind him.

Each ball of light encapsulated the form of a wolf caught at a different moment. Together, they blurred into a leaping figure.

"He's juggling his soul," Tori breathed.

The performer flicked one of the spheres toward a courtier. The man staggered in the splash of light, then recovered himself and applauded with the rest, although shakily. Behind him, his shadow wavered in pieces on the floor.

Another flicked sphere, aimed this time at the young king. Surging free of the crowd, Tori threw himself between it and Krothen. The ball hit him in the chest...

...and he was falling over backward grappling with a big white wolf. The floor slammed into him, tables and benches tumbling out of the way. Around him rose the stark walls of the Haunted Lands' keep that was his soul-image. Jaws snapped at his face. Blue eyes glared down at him.

"Who stands between the Gnasher and his prey? Argh!"

Tori had grabbed a broken table leg and jammed it behind the other's back teeth. The wolver twisted its head back and forth, trying to gain a grip on the wood. Nails raked at Tori's arms and chest. Bracing his feet against the beast's stomach, he kicked him off.

Footsteps sounded on the floor overhead, pacing, pacing, and the boards groaned. Boy and wolver pup froze, reduced by fear to childhood like two guilty truants.

"Is that..."

"Yes. My father."

The white pup crept backward on his belly. "My father said he would eat me, so I ran."

"So did I."

"Will he come down the stairs?"

"Sooner or later."

"You wait for him, then." The pup turned and bolted...

...and they were back in the Rose Chamber. The big wolver dropped to all fours, shaking his head. Clothes fell away from gaunt flanks, from white fur marked with shadowy whorls and tangles that resembled the horror-stricken faces of his previous victims, moving as the skin moved beneath them in silent shrieks. Snarling, he leaped toward the door, toward onlookers who scrambled out of his way. Only the hapless guard stood his ground. Jaws snapped and the man fell, his cheek and half of his shadow torn away. Then the Gnasher was gone into the night.

"Blackie?" Rowan bent over him. "Are you all right?"

Tori stared down at the remnants of his jacket, at the gouged and bleeding skin beneath. "Well enough," he said hoarsely. "The king...?"

"Here, Tori." Krothen appeared over Rowan's shoulder, looking dazed. "What happened? All I saw was a blaze of light."

"That was your shadow assassin, the one responsible for all the wasting illnesses among your kin."

"What? It was? Then after him!"

The confused, surviving guards scrambled to obey, but the Gnasher had slipped away as his master had before him.

That night, Prince Near died. At Princess Amantine's insistence and on the basis of the Gnasher's attack, Kothifir declared war on Urakarn.

❧❧ **IV** ❧❧

TORI EDGED THROUGH the limestone passageway, thrusting a torch before him. The Undercliff dwellers had assured him that this was the way to the preservation chamber, not that any of them had visited it since the king's temporary entombment there. Nor had he told any of his command that he was coming here, given the uproar they would have raised. If he didn't return, they would find a note in his quarters.

Firelight sparkled on upthrust stalagmites, on the fangs of stalactites. Water dripped.

"Hello?" he called. With no chance of approaching undetected, some warning seemed due.

Light shone ahead. Tori wedged his torch into a crack and proceeded. He could smell water, and stone, and blood. Beyond a rock formation, the cave opened up, some twenty feet wide and too low for a man to stand upright. One end dipped into a still pool. The other rose to a shelf, on which lay a body. Over it crouched a shining white figure with eyes aglow and a gory muzzle. The blood was fresh. Trickles of it ran down from the ledge to the floor and across that to the pool.

"Well," said the Gnasher, adjusting his jaw for human speech. "This is unexpected."

Tori sat on his heels. The low, rocky ceiling and general lack of room to maneuver made him nervous, but there was no helping that. At least he had been right to think that no backup could help him here.

"I have to know," he said. "Are you finished with King Krothen?"

The other laughed soundlessly through sharp teeth. "And if I'm not?"

"We fight. On the level of the soulscape or hand to hand." He touched a knife at his side. "It isn't much, but I must do what I can to ensure my friend's safety before I march out with the Host to Urakarn."

"If you march out."

"If."

"You puzzle me, lordling. You beard the monster in his den, but cannot face what lies within your own soul."

"You couldn't either."

The wolver licked his lips with a long, red tongue. "I was caught unaware. Another time, a different father... But yes, I will leave Kothifir after one last gorge. This city has nothing more to offer me."

Tori nodded toward the sprawling body. "Is that Kruin? What happened to him?"

"He started screaming and wouldn't stop. Is that how you found us? No doubt the Undercliffers talked, although none of them had the nerve to investigate."

The body twitched and whined.

"I want to live, I want..."

The Gnasher's jaw extended to tear again. Wet sounds of carnage echoed off the stone walls and the trickle became a pulsing flood. Tori winced.

The Gnasher grinned over his prey, white fangs dripping red.

"You see how hard it is to kill a god-king," he said. "Not long now, though."

Tori forced himself to remain still. His instinct had been right: until Kruin died, Krothen couldn't truly become king, and after what he had done, no one wanted Kruin back.

Like your own father, eh?

Still, it was hard to watch.

The Gnasher lowered his head again and chewed. Kruin shuddered. Then his head tipped back and fell off the ledge. It rolled almost as far as Tori. For a long moment, he looked into Kruin's horrified eyes. Then, at last, they glazed.

"There." The Gnasher wiped his muzzle with a paw and spat. "Immortality is too much for the weak. Kruin wasn't quite dead when his attendants brought him here, you see. I nursed him with soul-shreds from his heirs, even provided a wooden dummy to take his place on the pyre, but something in his mind broke. Never mind. I now know what I came here to learn."

"You didn't come to serve the Prophet?"

"Oh, he put me on the track. Our purposes ran parallel for a time, but now he has fled, and so we part."

"What will you do now?"

"Why, go home, of course, and kill my father. I advise you to do the same."

Tori shook his head. "I can't."

"Then go, lordling. Test yourself against your enemies, but always remember that that which you fear most, you hold closest to your heart."

❧ V ❧

THE ONLY ARMY that Kothifir had was the Host, supplemented by a few overenthusiastic native brigades commanded by nobles set on avenging their kin. Urakarn lay some two hundred and fifty miles to the southwest over the desert, far enough to require significant logistical planning. While this was being arranged, the Host argued among itself.

"This is madness," said Harn, stumping restlessly back and forth in his cramped quarters. "Genjar thinks that a token garrison of fanatics holds Urakarn. We don't know that. Of course, we've sent out scouts, but most haven't come back, which isn't encouraging in itself. And those who do return report a proper hornet's nest. The Karnids will also know that we're coming long before we get there. They still have sympathizers in the city. Trust me, they knew about this farce of a war as soon as it was declared. What are we supposed to do, eh? Walk up and knock on the door? What does your friend Krothen say?"

"Kroaky thinks it's a bad idea, but he hasn't yet fought free of his precious Council." Tori paused to sharpen a quill pen with his knife. Genjar, as usual, had dumped all the responsibility for preparation on his second-in-command, meaning that his self-appointed clerk had to copy out every one of Harn's scrawls. The Host was growing used to accepting orders at his hands. "He will soon, though, as the new god-king. Give him time."

"That we don't have. We're due to march tomorrow, before half our preparations are complete. Genjar smells glory. It's been too long since we last proved ourselves in battle, he says. Fah."

"It *has* been a long time," said Tori thoughtfully. "There haven't been any major conflicts since the White Hills."

"That was a slaughter, Kencyr against Kencyr, all because Ganth Gray Lord chose the wrong enemy. Are we doing that again? D'you think we need a fresh blooding too?"

"I think we have a generation of young soldiers who have never gone to war. Genjar's talk is contagious. I've heard a lot of enthusiasm around the camp hearths."

Harn turned to regard him from under shaggy brows. "Don't tell me you've caught the battle bug too."

Tori considered that. On the whole, he didn't know if he was excited or scared. Uneasy, more like: the whole expedition felt rushed and haphazard, barely under control.

"I've never fought before in a general engagement," he said.

"Huh," said Harn. "Then stay close to me. Senior officers usually survive debacles. Unfortunately."

VI

THE MARCH TO URAKARN took fifteen grueling days, with Genjar pushing hard. At the end of it, he used the vanguard as bait.

Tori rode with Harn Grip-hard in the first rank, followed by five thousand mixed Kencyr and Kothifiran troops. Day by day, the range of black, smoking mountains had drawn closer on the western horizon, and the sunsets behind it had grown more lurid. Now they were among the foothills, riding on a bed of old lava amid a fall of ash as light as a dusting of snow. Stinking gas rose out of holes in the ground. Every so often, the earth quivered and the horses spooked.

"Which one is Urakarn?" asked Tori.

"There, straight ahead, with its summit blown off."

Not only was it big but wide, perhaps twenty miles from side to side. The walls towered, despite missing their heights, snow-crowned, black and forbidding below. Trickles of smoke rose from several points in the interior.

"You've been here before?"

"Once as a junior officer. Kruin wanted to set up trade connections. The Karnids led us into their stronghold blindfolded and then laughed in our faces. It must be a bleak life inside an active volcano, but it apparently suits them."

The ground became more broken and the horses began to stumble.

"This is no good," Harn grumbled, and signaled the dismount. "We'll have to leave them here or risk half going down with broken legs."

"And what about our legs?" Rowan murmured, too low for the commander to hear. She, the rest of Tori's small command, and Burr had insisted on joining the vanguard with him, although he had tried to talk them out of it, especially Rose.

"Think of your daughter," he had urged the Caineron. "This could be a suicide mission."

Iron-thorn had only shrugged.

Now they were climbing up among jagged rocks and boulders, some the size of small houses. All provided excellent cover for an ambush. Heat rose off the black rocks in waves that distorted the air and soaked the climbers with sweat. Carrion birds flew overhead. Beyond the scrape of boots and the rattling of rocks, an eerie silence lay over the hills like a thick blanket.

"Maybe no one is home," said Cully.

The next moment he fell, an arrow through his throat. Tori knelt beside him, protected by Rowan's and Rose's shields. More arrows plinked off of them. Cully scrabbled at the wooden shaft, struggling to breathe around it, then his big hands went limp. Tori closed his eyes.

"Where are they coming from?" he asked, rising and unslinging his own shield.

"Pick a rock. Any rock," said Harn. "Circle!" he bellowed at his troops.

Most one-hundred-commands already had formed knots, those innermost raising their shields to create a roof over their heads against which arrows and stones clattered down like hail. Many Kothifirans, slower to react, fell.

It wasn't clear if they had sprung the trap that the Commandant had anticipated or if the Karnids were merely playing with them. In either case, where were they to go from here? They had reached a kind of amphitheater surrounded by a circle of fanged boulders, perhaps the site of an ancient, lateral eruption. To advance, they would have to climb out over the Rim. Even then, it was unclear where they could go, except on up the steep flank of the mountain. Urakarn was indeed huge even with its truncated top, its shoulders hunched above its neighbors, snagging clouds. If it had anything resembling a front gate, it wasn't visible from where they stood.

Black-clad figures rushed out from behind boulders and threw themselves against one of the armored huddles, only to be driven back with sword and lance.

"Hold your positions!" Harn shouted. Even as he spoke, however, a Kothifiran formation broke in pursuit, disappeared among the standing rocks, and didn't return. The others shifted restlessly, as if eager to follow.

"We can't just stand here, waiting to be slaughtered," protested Duke Far. The Kothifiran's heavy face shone with sweat and his eyes reflected near panic, but he was holding himself together—barely. "We have to rejoin the main body of the Host."

"Huh," said the commander. "We can try a breakout. At any rate Genjar should be told what he's gotten us into. Blackie."

"Here, Ran."

"Take a contingent of mixed troops. Try to reconnect with the central command."

"Yes, Ran." Tori hesitated. "Are you sure?"

"Trust me. The Kencyrath will follow you."

More missiles whistled overhead. People ducked under their shields. Harn gave a grunt as if of surprise and staggered against Tori. Tori and Burr caught the big Kendar and lowered him to the ground. The right side of his broad face was a sheet of blood, his temple gashed open by a flung stone, down to the bone.

"Damn. I think his skull is cracked. Harn? Can you hear me? Harn!"

The big man said something in a slurred voice. His eyes fluttered open, then closed again.

Tori felt panic tremble like a bubble in his chest. Whatever happened, he had always counted on Harn Grip-hard being there, a wall against which disaster dashed itself in vain. What was he supposed to do now? He looked around for Harn's second-in-command, then remembered that the man had fallen in an earlier attack. Everyone was looking at him.

They will follow you.

"All right," he said, and was glad to hear that his voice didn't shake. "Harn's last order stands. I'll take five ten-commands and anyone else who wants to go."

Most of the Kothifirans quickly volunteered, which surprised no one.

They edged up the slope of the depression, shields raised, and

entered the forest of standing stones. Random arrows plucked at
them, felling a few. For the most part, however, they proceeded
unmolested, although with the sense that they were surrounded
by many hostile, watchful eyes.

Here was the place where they had left the horses. The animals
were gone and their guards sprawled on the ground, dead.

The dull roar of combat came from ahead, punctuated by
shouts, the screams of horses, and the clang of weapons. The
Kothifirans strained forward, but hesitated as they came to the
edge of another, much larger hollow, this one seething to the brim
with Kencyr troops. It appeared that Genjar had walked into the
ambush that he had intended for his advance guard. A flight of
arrows darkened the sky, whirring like enraged partridges, from
the right, then from the left, until raised shields bristled with
shafts. In their wake, riders on black thorns swept in from all
sides. Tori watched as the charge crashed into one circle, ruptur-
ing it. The thorns screamed, bit, and kicked, savaging their way
in among the Kencyr, barely under their riders' control. More
arrows flew. The Host was obviously vastly outnumbered. So
much for Genjar's belief in a sparse resistance.

How many? thought Tori, holding his own small command
in check with a raised hand. Fifty thousand? More? Double the
Host, at least.

But no one was attacking from the east, the direction from
whence they had come. The vacancy there drew the troops like
a cool draft in that scorching cauldron. Another trap, or were
they being invited to retreat? Genjar was shouting, gesticulating.
Slowly, reluctantly, his forces withdrew eastward, taking their
wounded and dead with them. He raised his glance to the west
and for a moment locked eyes with Tori up on the basin's rim.

Yes, here we are, Tori thought. *Remember us?*

But Genjar turned away and his gestures grew more frantic.
Now he was pushing through the Host, trailed by his command
staff, in flight, drawing the others reluctantly after him. They
poured out of the cauldron, the rear rank guarding against a
pursuit that did not follow.

Tori sighed. "We're on our own now," he said to his followers.

Duke Far gave him a wide-eyed stare, then bolted in pursuit
of the retreating forces. His men threw down their weapons with
a clatter and ran after him, unimpeded.

Tori stood aside for another moment, but no one else followed, nor were they hindered on the way back to the vanguard. It felt like reentering a dark, breathless room and closing the door behind them. Kneeling beside Harn, Tori brushed the bloody hair off the Kendar's forehead. Someone had bound up the loose flap of skin with a strip of cloth. Harn twitched and began the disconcerting snore of the deeply concussed.

"What now?" Tori asked him, expecting no answer, receiving none.

"Blackie. Look."

Dark-clad figures had silently emerged from around the hollow and on top of the rocks that surrounded it, more and more of them, ranks deep. It seemed as if the entire Karnid horde had followed them back, but it neither charged nor made any sound.

"I said that we would meet again."

Tori suppressed a start at that deep, rich voice, speaking so close to him, too softly for most to hear. He squinted up into the setting sun, at a figure standing silhouetted in fire on a rock behind him.

"Shall I offer you a bargain, Grayling's son? Of these all, only you interest me. Your life for theirs."

Rowan caught his sleeve. "Don't listen to him, Blackie. He's lying. We'll take our chances."

Tori indicated the silent horde surrounding them. "What chance is this?"

His heart was in his throat, threatening to choke him. Could he really walk away from his friends, into enemy hands? What would they do to him? Then again, what did it matter if he could buy his followers' freedom? He swallowed.

"Your word on it, Prophet?"

The other nodded solemnly. "My word on it."

Karnids advanced and seized his arms.

"On second thought," said the Prophet, "take a quarter of them prisoner. Kill the rest."

Tori twisted in his captors' grip, aghast. "You swore!"

"You may also remember that I said honor was a failed concept."

Karnids swarmed into the cauldron, no longer silent. The Kencyr shouted back their defiance, each in the battle cry of his house—the Brandans' deep, sure note, the Edirrs' jeering shriek, the Cainerons' bellow, the Daniors' howl, the Jarans' defiant cry in High Kens: "The shadows are burning!" and on and on, until the uproar of battle swallowed them.

Tori used water-flowing to free himself. He started back into the fight, but hands gripped him again. Then the back of his skull seemed to explode and he fell into darkness.

⋙ **VII** ⋘

THIS IS JUST A BAD DREAM, he told himself, over and over. *Wake up wake up wake up...*

His chafed wrists were chained to the wall, pinioned too low for him to stand upright, so he sat with his numb arms raised. Water trickled down his sleeves and puddled under his buttocks. His clothes rotted. Sometimes the room seemed cavernous, sometimes as small as a closet, and it stank like spoiled meat.

Voices echoed in the corridor outside. Some called back and forth to each other in Kens: words of encouragement, words of despair. Some swore, others cried. Not long ago, black-robed Karnids had passed carrying an incandescent branding iron.

"Do you recant... do you profess..." had come their murmur down the hall. "Then we must convince you, for your own good."

With that, he had heard Rowan scream.

...the dead, ripe and rotting in piles in that cauldron under the scorching sun—no, don't think of them. It does no good, no good...

Somewhere, someone breathed heavily, almost in a snore. Harn? The rasping noise stopped and Tori held his own breath.

Breathe, Harn, breathe! Oh Trinity, don't be dead...

The sound started up again. And stopped. And started, in an echo of his own anxious breath.

They were coming for him now as they had day after day, week after week, month after year. Sandaled feet shuffled on the floor. Hooded figures entered the room and stood in a crescent facing him, themselves faceless.

"Do you recant your belief in your false, triune god?" asked the leader, soft-voiced. After so many days of exhortation, he sounded almost bored.

"...recant, recant, recant..." murmured his followers.

"Do you profess the Prophet of the Shadows to be your true lord and master?"

"...profess, profess, profess..."

He could say yes. He could lie. But that would truly make him one of them.

What choice had his own Three-Faced God given him in such matters? Where was that god now, for him, for any of them?

Honor is a failed concept.

No. Whatever his god or his father had done to him, there was a core that remained his alone, and its name was Honor.

"Then we must convince you," came the relentless response, "for your own good."

The semicircle opened. Two carried a small furnace, out of which others lifted gloves of red-hot wire. They advanced on him, carrying them.

Wake up wake up wake up...

"Oh god, my hands!"

His own voice woke him, crying out in a cold tower room. Yce nudged under his arm and licked his face to reassure him, but still he held up his hands with their aching lacework of scars.

"My hands, my hands..."

~CHAPTER XIV~
Winter Solstice

Winter 65

THE WINTER SOLSTICE occurred five days later. The Kencyrath didn't pay much attention to it, trusting rather to its own imposed dates such as Midwinter, but Kothifir seethed as it prepared for the year's longest night and the turn toward spring.

Jame took a lift cage Overcliff close to midnight when the festivities were due to start. It was very dark with an overcast sky and no moon. Lightning flickered behind the mountains over the Wastes, answered by the fizz and pop of fireworks set off at random from the Overcliff.

Once there, she wandered about the main avenue, munching on a paper cone full of grilled garlic snails and observing the scurry of townsfolk. Many wore elaborate costumes and masks reminiscent of the Old Pantheon gods whom she had seen Undercliff on the summer solstice. A few had on giant heads that required support or waved oversized hands that tried to swat the children who swarmed around them, jeering. Others, all but naked, were painted red or blue or green, touched here and there with luminous dust from the caves below. Imps, she thought, most of them guild apprentices and journeymen. Did that mean that their masters were under those more elaborate costumes? Firelight washed over all, regardless of their rank, from torches and bonfires, and the windows and balconies above were full of spectators, who threw down trinkets to encourage the capering hoard below.

"Come to watch us at play?" asked a nasal voice behind Jame. She turned to find Kroaky looming over her with Fang close at his side, clinging possessively to his arm.

"Your festivals interest me," she said. "I'm puzzled, though: since when are the elder gods welcome above ground?"

Kroaky made a face. "They aren't. These are only guild mummers and this is nothing but playacting. D'you think that King Krothen needs such competition? Still, the people want their games."

And now would be a bad time to disappoint them, Jame thought, as she wished the pair a happy solstice and passed on.

Underneath all the fun ran a thickening seam of discontent. Needham, Master Silk Purse, continued to harangue his followers against Lord Merchandy while Prince Ton and his mother stirred up the nobility. Even those not directly affected by the failed trade mission felt its sting in lost jobs and diminished income. The sense lingered that Kothifir had become vulnerable to enemies within and without.

A scuffle broke out in an alley as she passed. Drawn to it, Jame found Dar sitting on one of Amberley's ten-command, pummeling her.

"Dar, stop it!"

She grabbed his fist. He almost turned on her before he caught sight of her face. The Caineron took advantage of his start to throw him off, jump up, and dart back into the crowd.

"What in Perimal's name are you doing," Jame demanded, helping him to his feet, "and what happened to your face?"

"Two of them jumped me," he said, wiping a bloody nose. "I got away, then came across this one lurking in the shadows. We heard that Amberley's command was on patrol tonight. Five told us it was a private matter, but how could we forget what they did to her during the games? All of us except Five are out tonight, hunting them, and now they're after us too."

"You should have listened to Brier. If the Caineron are on duty, they have the right to be here. Do you?"

Dar grimaced and tugged at his jacket. He wasn't in uniform. "Well, no."

Even those cadets who had formerly shunned her had been outraged by Amberley's attack on Brier Iron-thorn during the recent contests. Every time Jame saw the healing marks on her five-commander's face, she sympathized with the Southron's sudden legion of Knorth supporters. In her more cynical moments, she thought that it was the best thing that could have happened to the former Caineron in terms of gaining support with her new house.

However, Brier's battered face bothered her too. She had always considered the Kendar to be morally superior to the Highborn, yet here they were trying to bash each other to a pulp. Would they if their lords weren't also subtly at war? She didn't think so, and that thought soothed her—for a while. But she herself was one of said Highborn.

"If Amberley's people catch you here without orders, fighting, they'll put you on report," she said. "Harn will have to punish you, and I won't be able to say a word in your defense."

Dar looked suddenly sheepish. "I'd forgotten. If we get into trouble, that reflects on you, and ever since you stopped the hazing the Knorth third-year cadets have been looking for excuses to vote against you come next Summer's Eve."

Jame had also forgotten that the cadets would be picking their presumptive leader at year's end. It might only amount to a popularity contest, but still it meant something.

Leave, and never return, Char had written.

"Ah, well," she said. "Never mind that now. We have to find the rest of my command and stop this foolishness."

Horns sounded toward the city center and gilded figures turned to answer them. Jame and Dar joined the flow, looking about as they went both for their own ten-command and for Amberley's. The performers entered the plaza under arcs of flame spat by fire-eaters to a roar of greeting from the packed crowd.

Their welcome was noticeably cooler to the three guild lords who stood on the Rose Tower's stair. Jame couldn't hear a word of their address. When it was over, the crowd turned from them, roaring anew.

The guilds had built elaborate stages all around the perimeter on which the mummers would play out the evolving story in which spring defeated winter. The first stage, spangled with glittering snow, provided the setting for the Spring Maid's birth as a golden crocus. Jame wondered if Kothifir ever actually saw snow falling from the sky. These banks of it had been carted in from the upper reaches of the Apollynes under heaped hides to insulate it. From their expressions, the mummers hadn't expected to find it so cold. Other early flowers—girls in glittering costumes—broke through the crust to form Spring's court, but Winter with his charcoal smeared face and bleak robes lurked in the background. He approached Spring. She fled to the next stage and the massed audience shifted with her, slowly, sunwise. Drums beat like feverish hearts. Horns blared.

Dar nudged Jame. "There are Killy and Niall. The game is over," he told the cadets when they met, having to raise his voice almost to a shout to be heard. "Ten has ordered us back to camp."

Sensible Niall looked relieved. "I said it was a bad idea."

"Just what was this brilliant plan anyway?" Jame asked, with a sense of foreboding.

"To get 'em alone, one on one, and give 'em a taste of what they gave Five," said Dar. "But they're patrolling in pairs," he added, as if this was not playing fair.

"Not to mention that they're older than you, bigger, and more experienced."

In turn, the Spring Maid became a bird, a fish, and a blossom borne on frothy waters, trying to elude Winter. Her attendants and his changed each time they mounted a new stage as guild succeeded guild, each setting more elaborate than the last.

Black-clad torchbearers followed the principal players from station to station, stern figures at odds with the frivolous crowd. The tails of their *cheches* were wound about their faces leaving only a slit for dark, intent eyes. They looked like Karnids, thought Jame, but surely not, any more than the prancing half-naked apprentices were really the imps of Winter and Spring or the mummers with swollen heads the giants of ancient times. She began to catch glimpses, however, of Old Pantheon faces in the turn of a head, the angle of a jaw. There for a moment were Mother Vedia's plump features, there a girl with catfish whiskers. And was that really charcoal on Winter's face or charred skin?

They found Erim and Rue. Rue looked simultaneously defiant and chagrined.

"It may have been Dar's idea, but I agreed with it," she said, meeting Jame's eyes askance like a pup expecting to be scolded. "Well, dammit, we had to do something!"

Thunder rolled beyond the mountains and lightning flickered in the bellies of banked clouds. The wind had turned fitful, pushing flames this way and that. People began uneasily to glance at the sky.

Winter caught Spring on a stage set with flowers, and in turn was seized by her attendants. They held him down, ripping at his garments. Soot flew. Then he sprang free, no longer withered Winter but the Earth Wife's youthful, redheaded Favorite, raising his arms to greet the cheering crowd.

The ornate curtains behind him split. Servants rushed out, grabbed the boy, and threw him off the stage. Many hands reached to catch him, but all somehow missed, letting him sprawl facedown, dazed, on the cobblestones.

A rotund figure clad in white with red trim waddled through the drapes. He bowed to the crowd and echoed the Favorite's gesture, inviting applause, getting only a startled silence from those close enough to see what had happened.

"Why, that's Prince Ton," said Jame, staring. "Does he think he can claim the Favorite's role so easily?"

It wasn't just that, she realized. The prince was making a political statement with his white robes, proclaiming himself Krothen's heir, perhaps even his usurper. The audience shifted uneasily and thunder rolled, closer this time.

Quill pushed through the packed ranks. "The Caineron have Mint and Damson!"

He led the way down one of the avenues away from the plaza and into a back alley. Jame had the city center memorized by now and recognized their position as being near the base of Ruso's tower. They came up facing Amberley's ten on either side of a garden patch. Mint huddled against a wall between the two commands, clutching together her torn jacket. Damson stood before her, facing the blond Caineron, holding the latter at bay with her will as Amberley paced back and forth.

"She assaulted my command. She belongs to the guards."

"Your guards tried to rape her," said Damson, glowering, her blunt jaw set.

Amberley snorted contemptuously. "Nonsense. That one likes her fun rough. Ask anybody."

Brier stepped out of the shadows. "Ask me." She came to stand between Amberley and the two Knorth. "Are you all right, girl?"

Mint dashed angry tears from her eyes and nodded. Damson helped her up. Her jacket and shirt had been ripped open. Bruises darkened her ribs and small breasts.

Brier gestured at her. "Is this a story you want spread throughout the Host? Let them go."

Amberley smiled. "Make me."

They began to circle each other, as well matched as two panthers with heavy, certain treads and muscles flowing under sun-darkened skin. At that moment, the city seemed to revolve around them. Both ten-commands drew back.

"I said you would go soft. So the false Knorth have seduced you. 'Oh, good dog,' they say as they caress. 'Good bitch.'"

"I didn't mean to hurt you, Amberley."

"Who says that you did? I know where I belong. Do you?"

They glided past each other, mirroring each other's movements in the Senetha. Hands passed close, nearly touching. Lithe bodies slid apart and then turned back face-to-face.

"Whom do you love now, turn-collar? Not me. Not Lord Caineron who was so good to you. After all, what has the Highlord done except drop you into the randon college where no one wants you? Oh, we heard the stories, even here in the south. Poor Brier. What would your mother think?"

Brier flicked a slap at her which Amberley easily brushed off. "The Highlord saved Rose's life at Urakarn, and she saved his. That score is settled."

"And now you have his sister, your little lordan. Tell me, does she please you, and what have you done to please her?"

Amberley crouched and swung a leg to trip Brier. The Southron dived over it. They were fighting in earnest now, Kothifir style, with sweeping feet and acrobatic grace. Their fire-cast shadows swirled against the close-set wall of the passage, across the cadets' watching awestruck faces.

Amberley swept Brier's feet out from under her. Brier rolled over her shoulder back onto them.

"Do you remember your heritage, Iron-thorn? I think not."

This was wrong, Jame thought. Kendar shouldn't fight Kendar. She plunged between the two. "Stop it, you fools, stop it!"

Amberley snarled and struck at her. She used wind-blowing to dodge. Their feet and hands wove about her in an ever-changing maze that took all her skill to navigate. Her impression was that Brier struck as much to defend her as she did to protect herself.

"This . . . is ridiculous!" Jame gasped.

Someone—she never knew who—caught her a glancing blow to the head, and for a moment the world flickered. She was on the ground. Then strong hands lifted her.

"Enough of this foolishness," Amberley said in the background, sounding disgusted. "Back on patrol, you lot."

Jame looked up into Brier's dark, enigmatic face. "'S all right," she said, feeling her jaw. "No teeth broken this time."

The storm had drawn closer. A flash of lightning illuminated clouds swirling overhead. But, thought Jame, they always did. These, however, were angrier than usual, veined with red and purple like internal organs and looking about as solid. The roar from the plaza had changed its timber. The air was electric.

"What's going on?" Quill asked nervously.

Jame struggled to her feet. "Let's go see."

They found the plaza packed as it had been, half its attention on the bruised sky and half on the surrounding stages where the mummery continued. Spring and the new-born, solstice Sun were receiving gifts from the Old Pantheon. Vedia granted them health in a shower of limestone dust which made the prince sneeze. Her pregnant sisters and her host of priestesses blessed the pair with fertility. Ancestors please, Prince Ton didn't subsequently find himself with child, but given his girth, who could tell? Next came the fish maid, strewing the stage with her finny progeny. Ton slipped on the cascade of scales and came up slathered with slime. He had to be helped up onto the stage where fire waited in a shower of sparkling illuminations and flames that crawled about the rigging. Spring would have abandoned him here but he kept her hand prisoner in his pudgy grip. The boy had some courage, Jame thought, if not much sense.

"Ahhh...!" breathed the spectators at the display of fireworks while those nearest beat out sparks that had nested in their clothing and hair. Prince Ton's wet suit clung to him unflatteringly and sizzled. Spring slapped at her filmy garments.

"Oh!" others further back exclaimed in alarm, for among them walked other, darker figures—a crone carrying a box, a man out of whose hood smoke trickled, and something close to the ground that snapped at ankles as it waddled along on the hands and feet of a baby. Earth, fire, and water, in their darker aspects.

The prince and Spring stumbled onto the last stage, where a rising wind was beginning to swirl silken streamers.

Lightning flickered overhead, its glare and thunder muffled by the clouds.

"Eek!" said the crowd, pointing.

Backlit, roaring, a funnel of wind descended toward the stage. Before it touched down, it gathered itself into a whirling figure wrapped in a long white beard, clad in deep purple robes stitched with gold. Jame edged closer, staring. The Tishooo grinned at her over the intervening heads and winked.

He had come to gift Kothifir with his protection, with the strong east wind to blow away the taint of the Wastes. Before he could do so, however, the black-garbed torchbearers stepped forward, surrounding the stage.

Something was wrong.

Jame pushed forward. Seeing what she was about, her ten-command surged ahead to clear the way, but they were too late. Torches flew over the Tishooo's head, dragging a fine net. He burst into a fury of black feathers, but the net caught them. His capturers converged on him. Bundling him up, they hustled him off the stage and away through the crowd, disappearing down a side street.

The east wind faltered and died. In the sudden lull, the clouds began to break up—all of them, even those that habitually circled the Rose Tower. Stars winked into sight through rends in the overcast; however, there was still no moon and the sun seemed late in rising. A breeze returned, but it stank of the Wastes and what lay beyond.

"It's the Change!" someone wailed.

A kind of madness seized the crowd. Now a mob, it fought with itself, trying to escape from the open plaza where hail was beginning to fall. Stages tottered and collapsed. Mummers fled. Women and men cried out, clutching each other. Children were trampled underfoot. Caught in the madness, Jame saw no immediate way to pursue the Karnids, for surely that was who they were. If so, what in Perimal's name did they want with the Tishooo?

Glancing at the Rose Tower, she saw that Lord Merchandy had fallen prostrate on the steps and that Lady Professionate was bending over him. Lord Artifice apparently had fled.

Which way should she go, after the kidnappers or up the tower? The Karnids were gone. On the stair, the plump girl looked wildly around for help, none of which was forthcoming.

"Take the ten and try to track down the Karnids," Jame told Brier, shouting to be heard over the uproar, gripping the Kendar's collar so that they wouldn't be torn apart. "Free the Tishooo if you can."

"And you?"

"I'm needed elsewhere."

Jame used water-flowing to make her way through the seething mob to the foot of the stair. Then she bounded up the steps. Merchandy and Professionate hadn't moved. The old man lay panting and his color, from what Jame could see, wasn't good.

"Help us!" the girl gasped.

Between them, they raised and dragged him, stumbling, up the steps. Tattered clouds revealed Kothifir's ring of desolation, then the gilded heights above, already looking perilous as the glamour below them faded. A catwalk took them across the plaza, over a nightmare scene, to a white tower. All Merchandy's servants had fled. Here in an inner chamber draped with creamy silk was his bed. They laid him down on it and Professionate loosened his clothes while Jame watched, unsure what else to do.

"What's the matter with him?" she asked.

"An old illness, potentially fatal in his current state."

"He's mortal again?"

"Yes. So am I."

As Jame had guessed, the Kencyr temple had failed. The acolyte Dorin had said that a mere change in the weather might trigger its collapse, and this was so much more.

The girl sat on the edge of the bed, holding a hand like a bunch of twigs. Merchandy gasped for breath, the cords in his skinny neck standing out, his pale blue eyes glazed with effort. Given that bone structure, he must once have been a very handsome man. Now he looked like an animate corpse in need of immediate burial. Professionate brushed thin, sweat-darkened hair off his brow and looked at Jame.

"We met once before," she said, with an obvious effort to be polite. "In the Undercliff. But we weren't introduced. My name is Shandanielle. My friends call me Dani. This is Mercer." She gave an unhappy little laugh. "By name and by nature, he would say."

"I'm Jamethiel Priest's-bane. Call me Jame. Will he recover?"

"Perhaps. If he wants to." With her free hand she dipped a cloth into a bowl of lavender water and wiped his face with it.

"He has been in pain for a long time. Being immortal doesn't stop that. If anything, it makes things worse. And he has been greatly shaken by the failure of the trade mission." A note of petulance crept into her voice. "I *told* him that it wasn't his fault, that the city, that I need him, especially now; but he insists on blaming himself for our current dilemma."

Jame shifted uneasily. Had the fall of Langadine been in any way her fault or, like Mercer, had she simply grown used to taking responsibility for everything?

"How will the Change affect you?" she asked.

Dani laughed again and wiped her eyes. "Maybe this time I will outgrow these damned pimples."

Jame remembered that this girl had been mired in adolescence for nearly thirty years. What a horrible fate.

"Would you like to remain mortal?" she asked.

"Oh, I would love it, at least until I catch up with myself. It's maddening to have an adult mind in a thirteen-year-old body—if I really am an adult. How does one know when one is grown up?"

Jame took the question seriously. "From what I can tell, some people never mature, however long they live. Others are born old."

"And you?"

"A little of both. That seems to be the way with the god-touched."

"Ah, I knew it! You too. I think we could teach each other much, whether or not I regain immortality. Oh, but what if I don't? Who will be the next Lord or Lady Professionate? It could be an architect or an engineer or, heavens save us, a lawyer. I suppose each would be good for the city in a different way, but could any of them keep Mercer alive? I think we really need him now that Kothifir must alter in order to survive. Besides, all these years he has been so kind to me, as if I were the daughter that he lost as a baby, when his wife died. My own parents sold me to the physician for whom I worked before I came into the white."

"I didn't know that there were slaves in Kothifir."

"Not as such, and only among certain old sects where females are considered chattel. The guilds call them apprentices, and not all are sold or ill-treated. You don't know what it was like, though, to be the least of servants, at everyone's command. My master took advantage of that. So did his chief assistant." She shuddered. "A gross man, that. His weight nearly crushed me. Then I became a god, still as a child, and I dealt with both of them. That taught me that revenge hurts all involved in it. I have never misused my powers again, even when my parents demanded my return, saying that they had been cheated out of a valuable asset. However, Mercer refused them and King Kruin supported him. Now they are old and my younger brother is full-grown. I still get letters from them from time to time, demanding money or other favors."

The floor seemed subtly to shift, although the bed curtains didn't sway. Mercer twitched and groaned. Jame tottered, cursing. Of course, if the Kencyr temple was down, Krothen was no longer a god-king with control of his city's heights.

"How long is this apt to go on?"

Dani shrugged plump shoulders, looking helpless. "Once it lasted for half a year, or so I'm told. That was when most of the outer towers fell. But Mercer can't survive that long now. Oh, what are we going to do?"

Jame didn't know. First, she had to determine the status of the temple. With that in mind, she bade Dani good-bye and started down the stairs.

Someone was coming up them with a heavy tread.

Jame slipped into an alcove. A large man in worn worker's clothes passed her, his expression set in a determined scowl. On impulse, she followed him up to the chamber where the former Lord Merchandy lay and the former Lady Professionate tended him.

"So there you are," he said, standing framed in the doorway. "What price godhood now, uh? Come on. You belong at home."

He crossed the room and seized her arm. Dani struggled in his grip. "No! He needs me!"

"Your family needs you more."

"Then why did you sell me as a child?"

"We needed the money to buy my apprenticeship. Don't you see, you silly chit? That way, both of us were provided for."

"But you failed your tests and had to become a common laborer."

He snarled at her. "The guild master wanted a bribe. That's all. You could have provided it."

"I keep telling you: I never ask a price for my services. People donate what they can."

"The more fool you, but all of that is over now."

Jame slipped up behind him.

"Let her go."

The brother gave her a contemptuous look over his beefy shoulder. "Who are you, to interfere with family matters?"

"Some family," said Jame, and pinched the nerve in his elbow. He let his sister go as his arm went limp and turned, furious, on Jame.

"Why, you little bitch..."

"Right sex, wrong species."

He lunged at her, and she slid past him in wind-blowing, giving him a kick in the pants as he staggered past. He ran headfirst into the bedroom wall. Then back he came as furious as a dazed bull. Jame swept his feet out from under him and he plowed into the marble floor face first. Blood spread around his head as he lay there, inert, snoring.

"With luck, it's only a broken nose and a concussion," Jame told Dani, who stood by horrified, hands over her mouth. "If he thought you were vulnerable, how long before Master Needham comes looking for Lord Merchandy? I think, on the whole, that you two should go Undercliff, where Fang, Kroaky, and Mother Vedia can look after you."

"I think...on the whole...that you are right." Mercer gasped from the bed.

Dani returned hastily to his side. "But can you make the journey?"

He dragged himself upright. "With help. I must."

Dani took one arm and Jame the other. He rose between them like an injured stork and tottered, panting, out of the room.

CHAPTER XV
Winter's Tales

Winter 80

TORISEN ARRANGED THE FUR ROBE over his outstretched legs and snuggled back into its folds. A cup of hot spiced wine gave welcome warmth to his hands, assuaging the scars' ache. It was a cold night, full of drifting snow, but Marc's two glass furnaces kept the great hall at Gothregor pleasantly warm, even with wind whistling in through holes in the as yet uncompleted stained glass window. At least, it was much better here than in his tower study above.

The wolver curled up before one tower kiln, Yce before the other. Marc ground ingredients at the head of the table nearest the window which he had appropriated as his work space. To one side, Burr was teaching Kindrie how to darn his well-worn socks using a wooden egg.

"You catch up an edge of the hole, see? Then draw the thread across the bulge of the egg to the other side. Stitch into that side. Back and forth, back and forth. Then change direction. Now weave the thread over and under the original warp...good. Keep going."

Grimly stretched and yawned. Paws in the air and furry belly exposed to the furnace's heat, he shifted his mouth for human speech.

"You look as if you should be purring."

Torisen sipped his wine. "I had a good day."

Grimly wrinkled his nose. "What, helping muck out the stables?"

They had been snowed in for a fortnight and the walls were starting to clamp down on them all. With little to do except keep the fires going, eat, and sleep, tempers had grown short.

However, nothing stops a horse's digestive tract except starvation, and provisions for both man and beast were still excellent. Moreover, the entire remount herd was currently lodged in subterranean stalls, all faithfully producing manure that must be shoveled out at least once a day.

"What did your Kendar think of you lending a hand?"

"They didn't like it, of course. What, their precious Highlord to waste his time on so menial a chore? But I had to do something."

"Better than catching up with paperwork," Kindrie murmured to Burr, who snorted.

Torisen cocked an eyebrow at them. "What's more depressing than being left with the last thing that you want to do? Anyway, afterward there was the race."

Kendar had shoveled a path around the edge of the inner ward and cartloads of manure had been emptied into it to cover the ice. Every day, the horses were brought up fifty at a time and given the run of the course for exercise. Today had been Storm's turn. The black, quarter-bred Whinno-hir had burst off the ramp with head high, eyes bright, and nostrils jetting steam like a dragon. He had pawed at the snow, then looked at Torisen askance and whickered.

The invitation was clear.

Torisen hadn't ridden in what felt like forever. He grabbed Storm's mane, up he swung bareback, and off they went, thundering down the northern straightaway with snow flying from the black's hooves. Someone whooped behind them. More horses acquired riders and it became a race. Around the northwest corner, down parallel to the western walls, up the southern side... Storm's ribs heaved between Torisen's knees. A bitter wind laced with snow blew in his face while Storm's mane whipped against his hands. A crash behind them on the southeast turn: one of the horses had slipped and fallen, bringing down several in his wake. Now they were pounding home with the towers of the old keep swinging overhead. Kendar lining the way cheered. Torisen pulled Storm to a stop just short of the slippery ramp down into the stables and let out his breath: Ah...

He didn't think that the Kendar had let him win on purpose.

"How is Cron?" he now asked Kindrie.

"The fall fractured his leg, but he should be up again soon. Meanwhile, he can tend to their new baby while his mate Merry handles his chores as well as her own. That shouldn't be hard, just now. I didn't know that male Kendar could breast-feed if necessary."

"Oh, the Kendar are full of surprises. We Highborn don't take their talents half as seriously as we should."

Ever since Cron and Merry's young son had broken his neck and Torisen had administered the White Knife to him, he had been interested in the pair. Somehow, they seemed to represent the health of his Kendar garrison. A new child was good, and it had been born under his protection, guaranteed a place in the Knorth. That couldn't be said of every Kendar who wanted to join, not because Torisen didn't wish it but because he was only able to bind so many and no more without weakening his hold on all. He had learned that the hard way with the suicide of Mullen, whose death banner now hung in a place of honor in the Knorth hall. Cron had come to him at an opportune moment to request a new child. Just the same, he was sorry that the Kendar had injured his leg.

Chunks of limestone rasped in an ironwood mortar as Marc ground them into dust. To this he added dried spice-bush and sand from the Wastes. The sound and the tang of the bush reminded Torisen of the last postrider before the snows to bring news from the south and, incidentally, a score of small bags containing raw material for Marc's window.

Grimly noted his change of expression and rolled over on his side with a thump. "What?"

"You heard that Kothifir is undergoing a particularly rough Change at the moment. I was just hoping that Harn would restrict Jame to the camp for the duration."

"Did he say that he would?"

"No."

"Wise Harn. If something interesting is going on, there'll be no keeping your sister away from it."

Torisen sighed, remembering Jame's bright, curious eyes and her talent for finding herself in absurd situations. Even as a child, she had had that knack.

"True," he said.

"D'you remember the first time we met?" asked the wolver, perhaps to distract him. "That was during the big Change when King Kruin died and Krothen came to the throne."

"I remember." Torisen eased into a laugh. "It surprises me that you do, given how drunk you were at the time."

Kindrie looked up, intrigued. "What happened?"

Grimly untangled limbs grown long, lanky, and human. "If you like, I will tell you."

"From the beginning, please," Torisen said. He and Burr knew the story. The others didn't.

"Very well. One day long ago when I was just a pup, King Kruin came to the Grimly Holt to hunt wolver. We hid and watched while he set up camp in the ruined keep that was our den. A poet sang to the king in Rendish that night, but the king was too drunk to listen. I did, though, from the cover of a nearby bush. The poet saw me but said nothing. That was his revenge against his inattentive master.

"Well, come the dawn Kruin set off into the forest, but the deep wood is dangerous and the Deep Weald wolvers are ingenious. We watched Kruin's men die in clever ways all day. Finally we offered to lead him out. He wasn't exactly pleased by our assistance, but he accepted. In return, he offered a place in his court to any wolver who cared to present himself there."

"What," said Marc, with a smile through his graying beard, "on his trophy wall?"

"That was our first thought. We didn't know it then, but a Deep Weald wolver had followed us out and was also listening. He took up the king's offer first."

Yce's ears twitched. She rolled over and regarded Grimly with unblinking frost-blue eyes.

"When I came of age," he continued, "I went south and found the poet whom I had heard sing. He was old by then, out of favor and fashion, but I didn't know that. When he offered to present me at court, I was overjoyed."

Grimly paused and sighed. His joy in storytelling dimmed. "Why are the young such fools? We see the bright path before us and romp down it."

"You were neither a fool nor a cynic," Torisen said. "Then or now. In Kothifir, you were a novelty. He used you to work his way back into favor."

"Of course I know that now. Then, they laughed at me." The old hurt whined in his voice. He coughed and shook his head, but the past still had him by the throat. "All of those years learning how to compose in Rendish, waiting to perform, and they laughed. So I began to clown and to drink in order to stand myself. 'The Wildman of the Woods,' they called me. That was who Rose Iron-thorn tackled that night in the plaza: a drunken buffoon."

"Still, if you hadn't told me that the Gnasher was performing above for Krothen in the Rose Tower, we wouldn't have been in time to save him."

And if the Gnasher hadn't served Kruin before that, Torisen thought, he would never have gotten the idea that immortality lay through killing off all of one's heirs. In that case, he wouldn't be searching for Yce, his daughter, now.

"Ah well," said Grimly, giving himself a shake. "I've told my tale. Your turn, old friend."

"What d'you want to hear?"

The wolver looked at him askance, perhaps sensing that he was relaxed enough to part with some of his long-held secrets.

"Answer a question or two, then. How did you escape from Urakarn as a boy?"

Torisen considered his cup of steaming wine, now nearly empty. Burr rose without a word and refilled it. They were waiting for him to speak. Well, why not?

"You know the basic story," he said, and took a sip. Burr had chosen a heady vintage for someone more accustomed to hard cider. It laced his veins with warmth and plucked at the knots of his reticence.

"That you, Harn, Burr, Rowan, and Rose Iron-thorn fled into the Wastes, found a stone boat, and sailed it across the dry salt sea, yes," said the wolver. "That's all plain enough. But how did you get free of Urakarn in the first place?"

"That I can't tell you. I was chained in a room of changing sizes and then I wasn't. Chained, that is. They had fitted my hands with white-hot wire gloves and the burns had become infected, y'see. My mind was none too clear. Perhaps I slipped off the cuffs myself. Perhaps someone freed me."

"Who?"

"I don't know." Torisen frowned. He thought he remembered the touch of cool hands on his own burning ones. *Wake. Live,* a voice had whispered in his ear and warm lips had brushed against his cold brow. Whose, if not a fever-born dream?

"If you can't answer that riddle," said Grimly, "then here's another. I saw you just after you rejoined the Southern Host, and thought that you were a ghost. Genjar had reported the slaughter of the entire vanguard. But there you stood and told me off for still being a drunken lout, which I was. You said you were going to see Genjar. The next thing anyone heard, he was dead. What happened?"

Danger, Torisen's instinct told him. Here was a secret, deep and dark. If Caldane ever heard it... but these were his friends. Whom else could he tell?

"As you say, I went to see him in the Caineron barracks..."

And as he spoke, memory carried him back.

No one had seen him enter or climb the stair. He seemed to pass through their midst like the ghost that Grimly had believed him to be. He felt like one, hollow and still echoing with the sand's endless whisper. But his hands throbbed with infection. They had told him to go to the infirmary. Instead he had come here.

"You don't see me," he kept muttering. "You don't see me." And they didn't.

Here was Genjar's third-story suite, with voices coming from the farthest room. The door stood open. Tori stopped within its shadow. The bedchamber beyond was awash in morning light and billows of unrolled silk. Sea, sky, and earth might have roiled there, so various were the glowing, jeweled colors. Genjar stood before a mirror, holding up a length of pale lavender.

"What do you think?" he asked.

"Nice, but it clashes with your eyes."

The second languid voice was as smooth as samite drawn lightly over steel, unexpected yet familiar.

Genjar made a petulant sound, dropped the silk, and picked up a wine glass. His hand was none too steady and his eyes were bloodshot, matching none of the treasures on which he trod.

"Are you sure you don't want some?" he asked. "A good vintage, this."

"I thank you, no."

Genjar's guest lounged in one of his ornate chairs, long, black-booted legs stretched out before him, crossed at the ankles, elegant fingers steepled under a dark, sardonic face.

"Then to what do I owe the pleasure of your visit?" asked Caldane's heir, stumbling a bit over the formal phrase.

"As you know," said Caldane's war-leader, Sheth Sharp-tongue,

"I am newly come from the Riverland. On my arrival, of course I heard about your . . . er . . . exploits in the Wastes before Urakarn."

"Then you know how outnumbered we were. I did well to bring back as much of the Host as I did."

"Still," murmured the other, "not since the White Hills have we suffered such a needless defeat."

"Our paymasters ordered me to go!"

"And so you did, well enough pleased to do so by all accounts. Did no one advise you that your first duty lay in talking the Kothifirans out of such a reckless course, based on so little evidence?"

The Caineron make an impatient gesture, spilling wine. "The Host was eager enough, at least those with any spirit."

"You mean the young bloods. What of the senior randon?"

Genjar snorted. "That pack of old women."

"My dear boy," said Sheth with a flickering smile. "Never underestimate old women. And then there are your losses. One in five dead, or so I hear, not to mention the entire vanguard . . ."

"They went too far ahead, too eager to steal my glory! How was I to know that they were in trouble?"

Tori remembered how their eyes had locked across that bloody cauldron.

Yes, here we are. Remember us?

"Scouts could have informed you, as they would have of the Karnids' strength."

"They told me nothing!"

"Because you didn't wait for their reports. Harn Grip-hard has apprised me of that much at least. Due to a crack on the skull, he remembers little else, which is probably just as well. Ah, you didn't know: he and three others have rejoined the Host. Many more were taken alive at Urakarn, but only they escaped. More lives lost. More bones unclaimed."

Genjar's flushed face mottled mauve and white. "What else did they tell you? Liars and cowards, the lot of them. *I* saved the Host! Can you hold me accountable for those too weak to fight their way out?"

"Yes." The war-leader rose with leonine grace, and Genjar retreated a step from him. "I bring you a gift." He laid a white-hilted knife on the table. The Commandant of the Southern Host stared at it, then gave a shaky laugh.

"My father would never send me such a message."

"Nor did he. This comes from the randon under your command, alive and dead."

"Them! They failed *me*, d'you hear? Why, they couldn't even defeat a band of desert savages. Take back your precious gift!"

But Sheth made no move to reclaim the ritual suicide knife. "Then keep it," he said lightly, "as a memento of honor. Good day to you."

A step outside the door, he encountered Tori. For a moment he looked down at the boy, then nodded to him and left.

In a rage, Genjar stumbled across his bedchamber, kicking at drifts of silk as they caught at his feet. He poured more wine, sloshing it over his hand, drained the glass, and threw it at the wall.

"Of all the presumption...he dares to judge *me*? Father will have his scarf when I tell him. No more a high and mighty warleader, Sheth! Cut someone else with your self-righteous tongue, if you can."

Then he saw Tori standing in the doorway and stopped short, jaw agape. "You!"

"Here I am. Remember me?"

"Are all the unburnt dead coming back to haunt me? Well, I won't have it, d'you hear me? I won't!"

Genjar snatched up the knife and lunged toward Tori, but his foot snagged in a silken coil and he fell. He picked himself up gingerly with more sheer fabric festooned over him in loops. The knife was lodged in his side. He pulled it out and stared at it, then at the blood staining his now ruined coat.

"Look what you made me do, you...you bastard!"

His legs started to give way. He stumbled backward onto the balcony, into the railing which caught him at waist height. Fabric clung to his legs. He kicked petulantly to free himself, tottered, and fell over the handrail. A bolt of silk skittered across the floor, unwinding. Its board lodged between the bars and the silk went taut with a snap.

Tori picked up the knife and walked out onto the balcony. He looked down at the swinging figure, shrugged, and tossed the blade over the railing.

Shouts of alarm started as he gained the stairs and descended, again unobserved. Where had he been going? Oh, yes. To the infirmary to...to see Harn. It had nothing to do with the throbbing, infected burns that laced his hands. He shoved them into his pockets. If the surgeons saw, they might cut them off. He couldn't have that.

The great hall was silent after Torisen finished his tale. They were all staring at him.

"You mean," said Kindrie at last, "that he simply tripped and fell?"

"'Simply' rather understates the situation, don't you think?" Grimly said. "Why, one could say that his own vanity tripped him. Nonetheless, the story should never leave this room."

"But it was an accident!" Kindrie protested.

"Did I say anything else? Think how Lord Caineron would react to it, though. As it is, the only comfort he can take out of the whole debacle is that he thinks his favorite son died honorably by the White Knife, if with embellishments."

"At least you kept your hands," said Kindrie. "A healer might have prevented the scars, though."

"No!"

In that snapped word, the barrier went up again between them.

Torisen sipped his wine, cursing himself. Just when he thought he had finally overcome his loathing of the Shanir, it sprang back at him. The wine had cooled. His scarred hands hurt anew at the encroaching bite of the cold.

"Enough of that," he said. "Sing for us, Grimly. In your own language. I promise we won't laugh."

Grimly considered. "All right," he said, and his muzzle returned to its lupine form. He began to sing them a summer's night in the Holt. A long howl, fading, swelling, fading again, traced the curve of a full moon. Yce rolled upright. Her soft yips were branches etched against its disc. Grimly paused and gave her an approving look. Together they traced the black lace of twig and leaf, the strong trunks between which fireflies danced. Wind stirred the grass. Sharper notes defined the bones of the ruined keep and a burble in the throat became the stream that wound its way down the broken hall, glinting under the moon.

Yce stopped suddenly. Her growl shattered the image and her hackles rose. Grimly also stopped and leaped to his feet.

Somewhere out in the dark, snowy night, a deep-throated howl had answered them.

CHAPTER XVI
Lost Children

Winter 90

I

THE CHILD SAT IN A PUDDLE in the middle of the road and beat at it with his small fists. He had cried himself to whimpers. Still, no one had emerged from any of the towers lining the street to rescue him. The rain had ended and a wan moon shone in the sky. A lean dog slunk out of the shadows, curious or hungry, but fled as the ten-command approached.

Jame picked up the boy.

He was about three years old, wearing a torn, wet smock with a row of daisies carefully embroidered around the yoke. It seemed unlikely that anyone had abandoned him, yet here he was, a picture of misery with tears and snot running down his face. At Jame's touch, he wailed anew and beat at her chest. She held him, dripping, at arm's length.

"Somebody, come and take this child!"

The towers rang at her challenge, but all stood dark and silent, as if untenanted. However, most of their occupants were there behind locked doors and windows, praying that the wandering mobs would pass them by. One such group staggered past an intersection with a neighboring street, raucous with drink.

"Come out, come out!" they cried, and smashed empty bottles against tower walls. "Sing with us, dance with us, drink with us! Tonight no god watches, no sin counts, no crime is punished. We are free!"

"Yes, to make fools of yourselves," muttered Brier. Like most

217

Kendar, she found such civic disorder distasteful and deeply disturbing, maybe with a presentiment of what the Kencyrath might be like without the bonds that held it together. On the other hand, perhaps she was reminded of Restormir when Lord Caineron's too-tight grip had passed on his own drunkenness and subsequent hangover to his defenseless people.

A door opened a crack and scrawny, disembodied arms hung with wrinkled skin reached out from the dark interior. Jame climbed the stairs, but hesitated near their top. Was this the boy's grandmother, great-grandmother, or no relative at all?

"Do you grant this child guest rights?" she demanded.

Knobby fingers impatiently snapped and beckoned.

"Do you?"

"Of course," came the toothless grumble of an answer. "Tell 'em that Granny's got 'im."

"Tell whom?"

"'Is parents, idiot."

Forced to be content with this, Jame held out the boy. He was snatched from her hands and the door closed, stealthily, behind him.

The ten-command had been on patrol since sunset, with midnight and the end of their tour approaching. During that time, they had seen considerable havoc, not all as innocent as the roving bands of drunks. The city was every bit as unsettled as Graykin had said it had been during the last Change. Looters were abroad, and arsonists, and assassins. All over Kothifir, scores were being settled.

Raised voices sounded around the curve of the street and torchlight flared on stone walls. Jame went to investigate with her ten-command close behind her.

Quite a crowd had gathered in front of a lit tower whose door, for a change, gaped wide open. Closest to its steps stood perhaps two dozen burly men with torches, facing a smaller clutch of men, women, and children. Jame recognized the tall, bald man in charge of the latter as the former Master Paper Crown, stripped of his apprentices by the Change. What was his name? Ah. Qrink. The rest must be his family.

"What's going on?" she asked a woman intently watching the proceedings while she clutched the hand of a child. "Why, Lanek! What are you doing here?"

The Langadine boy looked up at her with solemn, frightened eyes, his thumb in his mouth. The woman stared down at him, apparently astonished that he wasn't someone else.

"Lanek? Where is your cousin? Where is my baby?"

"Is he wearing a smock embroidered with daisies?"

"Yes, yes. He's always wandering away..." She looked about frantically but, to her credit, didn't cast Lanek off.

"Granny asked me to tell you that she has him."

"Oh." The woman sagged with relief.

"It's simple enough," the leader of the torchbearers was saying to Qrink with a broad grin. "Either swear your allegiance to Prince Ton or pay us off. Preferably both."

Jame recognized the patch of rose-colored velvet on his chest as the prince's emblem. All of his followers wore it. So this was his much vaunted militia, which he had said would replace the Kencyrath as the guardians of Kothifir.

Qrink glowered. "And if I choose to do neither?"

"Then your tower burns."

The former master licked chapped lips and frowned. From what Jame could see through its windows, this was not only the family home but also the guild headquarters. Could Qrink regain his position if he let it be destroyed? On the other hand, would he if he submitted to blackmail? One consideration cancelled out the other, leaving only pride.

"I don't like bullies," he said. "We can rebuild."

The other man scowled. "So be it."

The ten-command started forward, but the militia leader had already signaled two of his men who ran up the steps with their torches. They could be glimpsed inside setting fire to stacks of paper, scrolls, and books. Some smoldered, others caught quickly, throwing orange light to dance on the whitewashed walls.

Jame had been anxiously looking over Qrink's huddled family.

"Where is your mother?" she asked Lanek.

The child took his thumb out of his mouth and pointed at the top of the tower.

"Qrink!" Jame pushed through the crowd to his side. "Your sister-in-law..."

His quick glance confirmed Kalan's absence. He grabbed the militiaman by the arm. "Stop them! There's still someone in the tower!"

The man tore his attention away from the growing blaze, but the gloating light of fire lingered in his eyes. He grinned, wet-lipped. "Too late."

Jame felt rage kindle in her. She barely noticed that her claws had extended.

"You would burn someone alive?"

He blinked and retreated a step, fire-lust giving way to uncertainty. So one might confront a small creature gone suddenly rabid. Jame stalked him.

"Call them off."

"No..."

"So you like fire." The fragment of a master rune came into her mind unbidden. "Taste it, then."

Her nails sparked together under his bulbous nose, setting its nostril hairs alit. He flailed at his face, but every move only spread the flames. They kindled his greasy hair. He backed away, wailing, into a widening void as his men retreated from him in horror. Jame slipped past, up the stairs, into the burning tower.

She was surrounded by fire. It licked at paper on all sides, orange, red, and yellow tipped with blue. Kindling inks sparkled green and gold. Pages turned in the draft, their edges blackening, their wonderful images eaten away. Charred fragments swirled past her up the interior stair as if up a chimney. The very air seemed to burn.

Dance.

She began to move in the fire-leaping and wind-blowing patterns of the Senetha, threading her way between flames. Blades of cool air from the open door gave her paths. Flares of heat warned her away from stacks of paper about to ignite. It was intoxicating. She could have played thus until the very stones exploded around her, but she had come here to do something. Oh yes. The Kothifiran seeker.

The stairs were burning, but she mounted them, barely touching their charred surfaces where paint boiled in the heat. Wind-blowing upheld her. Heat lifted her. She could almost fly.

Behind her a step cracked. Jame looked over her shoulder and saw Brier Iron-thorn at the bottom of the stair, one foot on a tread which had broken under her weight. The rushing air stirred her red hair into a fiery aureole about her face as she looked up. Her sleeve was already on fire. She couldn't live in this inferno, but she wouldn't retreat without Jame.

Jame turned back. Weight returned to her with the fading of the enchantment and steps crunched underfoot. Heat caught her by the throat. She grabbed the Southron's arm and hustled her out of the tower.

Both of them were coughing when they reached the cool evening air.

"What in Perimal's name were you playing at?" demanded Brier as Rue and Mint beat out her flaming sleeve.

"I might ask you the same."

Jame saw that the militiamen had departed, taking their singed leader with them. Ha. Cowards, the lot of them, when it came to a dose of their own fiery medicine. Meanwhile, Qrink's family still huddled together on the other side of the street, staring in dismay as their home was reduced to blackened stone and ash.

"Look!" one of them cried, pointing upward.

Near the tower's summit, a window had been thrown open. Kalan stood in it framed by fire, holding her baby daughter. She looked back at the burning room, then down at the ninety foot drop before her.

"Jump!" some of her relatives cried.

Others shouted, "Don't!"

Kalan threw her baby out the window.

Brier caught it.

The next moment flames erupted out of the tower's roof and Kalan was sucked back into their incandescent grip.

The Southron cradled the infant in her arms, staring down at it. "She said to hold its head just so..."

It looked merely asleep, warm and rosy from the heat, tiny hands only just beginning to relax, but it was dead.

Qrink eased the body away from Brier and handed it to his womenfolk.

"Brier?" said Jame.

The Kendar turned away.

"Look after her," Jame told Rue. "It must be almost midnight by now. All of you, your tour of duty is over. Go back to camp. Have a drink. Sleep."

Rue hesitated, looking dogged. "And you, Ten?"

"I still have an errand to run."

II

PAPER CROWN'S TOWER was only three blocks from Gaudaric's. Had the militia already been there?

Jame was alarmed at first to see it also blazing with lights and
people moving in front of it. Then someone emerged from the
shadows in full armor, leveling a spear at her chest.

"Stand. Who are you?" Then he relaxed. "Oh, Talisman. I didn't
recognize you in that jacket."

True, she was dressed as a cadet. It was unclear to Jame how
many Kothifirans besides the Kencyr priests knew of her dual
identity. She hadn't made a secret of it in Tai-tastigon nor had
she here, but people were still apt to see her either as the Knorth
Lordan or as the fabled Tastigon thief.

"What's happening?" she asked.

"The prince's bully boys have been to call, but we showed them
off. Before that . . . Well, you should talk to Ean."

"Not to Gaudaric?"

"He isn't here. Come on."

Following him toward the tower, Jame noted that many of
Iron Gauntlet's apprentices were in evidence standing guard,
unlike Paper Crown's. When she mentioned this to her guide,
he shrugged.

"Gaudaric opened the tower to our families when the Change
first occurred. We've taken shelter here ever since, and carried
on with our work. Who wants to sit idle?"

An island of stability in a sea of change. If Gaudaric eventually lost his position as grandmaster, it would be through no
fault of his own.

Jame wondered, not for the first time, about Graykin. Was
he still, somehow, in charge of his fractious guild or was he on
the run? If the latter, why hadn't he sought her out? When she
thought about him, an echo returned of anxiety, underlain by a
strong streak of stubbornness.

. . . whatever happens, I'm still your sneak, aren't I?

What had she done to requite such loyalty? Precious little.

Ean waited for her on the tower steps, his time-ravaged face
haggard under gray-threaded hair.

"Have you any news?" he asked anxiously.

"About what?"

"Byrne. My son. He was snatched by Ruso's agents early this evening. Ruso sent word that Father had to come to his tower, alone, and Father went. Armed."

Jame felt her heart sink. "When was this?"

"About two hours ago. The rest know that the master is gone, but not where or why, otherwise they would be storming Lord Artifice's tower and Byrne would be dead. Where are you going?"

"To Ruso, of course, but don't worry: I'll be careful."

"As you were in Langadine?"

"More careful, then."

When she reached it, the tower of Lord Artifice was dark except for its uppermost floor under the cupola dome. She climbed the stair silently. Voices floated down from above. Ever so slowly, she raised her head. Gaudaric leaned panting against a table at one side of the room and Ruso against one opposite him. The former held a sword, the latter an axe that seemed too heavy for him. Both wore full armor. Gaudaric's reflected his taste for the simple and efficient; Ruso's was more elaborate with red-trimmed scales and serrated spikes on his shoulders. Steam rose from the collars of both their gorgets and their hair hung down dank with sweat. From that and the disheveled state of the room, it appeared that they had been going at each other furiously for hours and only now had stopped for a much needed rest.

Ruso coughed and wiped his bedraggled red beard from which no sparks now flew. Without his fiery aura, he looked common enough, and quite young. "You're finished, old man," he said hoarsely. "Just let me kill you and this will all be over."

"It was your idea that we fight to the death, lad, although I keep telling you: I have no ambition to become the next Lord Artifice."

"Ha. Ambition has nothing to do with it. Gods know, I have enough for both of us. Don't you understand? When I lost the lordship, I lost my talent. D'you know how that feels?"

"I can guess," said Gaudaric, not unsympathetically. "Yet you weren't so bad before that as my apprentice."

"But not good enough to marry your daughter."

"Easily that good, except that she had chosen Ean."

"She would have taken me if you had told her to."

"Now, would I do a thing like that against her wishes?"

Ruso shook his tousled head. "You're too soft, old man. If we had joined forces...but now that withered fool Ean calls you father and what am I? Nothing."

An impatient voice sounded from the edge of the room: "Is this going to take all night?"

Although it wasn't he who had spoken, Jame could make out Byrne standing in the shadows. Behind him, a tall, thin man held a knife to his throat. Two others flanked them, one short and squat, the other as wide as a temple door. All three wore black, but their garments otherwise appeared to be threadbare street clothes, and their masks looked suspiciously like pillow cases dyed black, with eye holes cut out of them.

"Are you all right, Byrne?" asked Gaudaric.

"Yes, Grandpapa, but I'm getting tired of standing."

"Patience, boy. You know," he added, addressing the shabby, black-clad figures, "I still don't understand your place in all of this. Ruso is almost broke. What has he promised you?"

The squat leader stirred. "Recognition," he said. "For an official assassins' guild."

"Oh dear. If the gods haven't granted you a grandmaster in all of this time, what d'you think Ruso can do about it?"

"He will have power and influence when the Change ends. He told us so."

"Yes, but don't you understand? An assassins' guild would fall under the auspices of Professionate, not Artifice. If Shandanielle comes back, healer that she is, do you see her sanctioning your efforts?"

The broad would-be assassin stirred. "Here now, brother," he said in a surprisingly high-pitched voice. "Why didn't you think of that? Lady Professionate is no friend to killers. Anyway, I'm tired of standing too. What say we cut out of this?"

Gaudaric twitched at the word "cut," but the tall man lowered his knife. "Right," he said. "It seems to me that we should be approaching a professional. Any suggestions?" he asked Gaudaric.

The armorer sighed. "Maybe the former Mistress High Hat of the Philosophers' Guild. *I* don't know. This is the Change, after all."

The three trooped away down the stair. Jame flattened herself against the wall, but the first two only glanced at her as they passed. "It's your party now," said the third in disgust. Then they were gone.

Jame slipped up the steps and joined Byrne. "Are you sure you're all right?" she asked him, seeing the shallow cuts that scored his neck and drops of blood on his collar.

"Well enough," he said, fingering his throat. "Toward the end, his hand started to shake."

Gaudaric pushed himself away from the table and lowered his visor. "Well, shall we?"

Ruso threw down his axe with a clatter. "Oh, what's the use? I can't kill you. Come to that, I don't even want to. I'm a failure at everything."

One of his mechanical dogs crept out of the shadows and nuzzled him. Gaudaric stared.

"But I thought that our special powers ended when the Change began. How did you animate it?"

Ruso scratched the metal head as it nosed its way under his arm with a high-pitched whine. "I cheated. See?" He opened a panel between its shoulder blades to reveal busy wheels and cogs. "It's clockwork."

"Really?" Gaudaric dropped his sword on the table, took off his helmet, and went to crouch by his former pupil. He stared at the younger man's creation. "Why, it's wonderful! Don't you see? This is a skill that no Change can take away!"

"Let's go," Jame said to Byrne. "Your parents are worried half to death about you."

"But Grandpa..."

She laughed. "Unless I miss my guess, he and Ruso are going to be discussing nuts and bolts until dawn."

III

JAME ESCORTED BYRNE back to the Armorers' Tower, all the way listening to his enthusiastic description of the fight which she had missed. It sounded as if the two had been fairly evenly matched. However, there was little question that in Byrne's mind Gaudaric's superior armor and skills had been about to triumph over the other's youth. On the whole, he was sorry that his grandfather hadn't finished the job, but he also had to admit that the mechanical dog was something special. Maybe Grandpa would build him one.

At the Armorers' Tower, she turned the boy over to his anxious father and, as she departed, heard Byrne launch into his story again from the beginning with unabated zeal.

It was only shortly after midnight, but already it felt like a long day. Jame took the last lift cage down to the camp. As she approached her barracks, she saw more lights burning there than she would have expected at this hour.

Rue met her at the gate.

"Thank Trinity you're back. It's Brier. I think she's gone mad."

Crashes sounded inside the mess. Older randon looked in through the windows from the outer courtyard, but retreated as a harsh voice from within ordered them back.

"That's Harn Grip-hard," said Jame. "What's he doing here?"

"I sent for him," Rue said. "With you gone, someone had to do something."

Jame pushed through the crowd and stopped in the doorway. A plank, formerly part of a dinner table, hit the wall near her head and shattered, showering her with splinters. Brier upended a bench and smashed it against the fireplace. The room was littered with similar debris. Here too there had been a long battle, one woman against herself.

"Now, now . . ." rumbled Harn and caught her around the waist. When he swung her off her feet, she lashed backward at him and he dropped her with a grunt. She spun and went after him. Jame slipped between them.

"Brier, stop."

The Southron loomed over her, fists raised, then gave a half-strangled sob and lurched away.

"What in Perimal's name is going on?" Jame asked Harn, as Brier sank down on one of the few remaining benches and laid her head on the table in her hands. "Is it a berserker flare?"

"Huh. No. She's drunk."

"But Brier doesn't drink."

"She did tonight—on your orders, your cadet tells me."

"Go back to camp," she had said. *"Have a drink. Sleep."*

Jame glanced at the hovering onlookers. "Send them away," she said, "and Harn, please go with them. Thank you for your help, but I'll take care of Brier now."

He gave her a dubious look. "Sure about that, are you?"

"She's my responsibility. Somehow, I've failed her."

"Huh," he said again. "As you will."

He went to the windows and secured the shutters, then stepped outside, closing the door after him. His booming voice could be heard in the courtyard, sending everyone back to bed.

Jame sat down opposite Brier and took the Kendar's hands across the table. They were bleeding, gouged with splinters.

"Brier, what is it?"

The other's hands turned in her grasp and gripped her so hard that her bones ground together and her breath snagged in a hiss. Images flooded her mind, as sharp as knives.

—Kalan's baby plummeted downward. She reached up and caught its slight weight. Its head bent backward over the crook of her arm. There was a muffled crack as if of a dry twig breaking—

She told me how to hold it.

...dead, dead, dead...

Mother, gone into the Wastes. Days waiting. Weeks. Months. She never came back except as a pale shadow under the sand, skimming before a stone boat...

What did I do wrong? Why did she leave me?

Blackie, telling me the story; the Highlord, offering me a place.

(Oh, Amberley...)

Caineron: "Pretending to be a Knorth now, aren't you? Not easy. Not possible, I should think. On your knees. Kendar are bound by mind or by blood. Such a handsome woman as you, though, deserves to be bound more pleasurably. By the seed..."

The rustle of his breeches dropping, and then a descending blur—the Highlord's mad sister: "Boo!"

"Hic!" Now Caldane was floating, pants around his ankles, turning over in the air...

The Highlord is kind, but do I deserve kindness? Do I trust it? Rather give me strength, even if it is cruel. Oh, Trinity, am I Knorth, or still Caineron?

And the memories started again in a vicious loop: Kalan's baby falling, its neck breaking...

Brier raised her head and croaked, "More wine. More noise. Anything to stop that sound, like a dry twig snapping..."

"Stop it, Brier. It wasn't your fault. None of it was."

The Kendar's bloodshot eyes focused on her.

Torisen Black Lord was too far away, too...gentle. Jamethiel Priest's-bane was not, and she was here. Need speaks to need, as it had with Graykin in the gorge at Hurlen beside the Silver. Like Marc, Brier had the moral strength and the experience which Jame felt she lacked. Would she have survived as a cadet without the Kendar's support? How much she had come to depend on the other's solid presence behind her.

"I need you," she heard herself say through numb lips.

Brier's fragile bond to Torisen bent and broke. Another, stronger, formed in its place.

"I am yours."

Then the Southron's lids fluttered and her head dropped back to the tabletop. Jame freed her hands and leaned back, shaken, massaging her bruised wrists.

Rue emerged from the shadows. "What just happened?"

"Nothing that was intended." *Was it?* "Tell no one, Rue. This is our secret, yours, mine, and Iron-thorn's. D'you hear? Now help me get her up to bed."

Between them they urged Brier to her feet and supported her to the foot of the stairs. There she shook them off and climbed by herself, holding tight to the railing.

Perhaps she had given the Southron what she needed after all, Jame thought as she followed Brier, and had received the same in return; but oh lord, what was Tori going to say?

CHAPTER XVII

Wolver Hunt

Winter 95

I

"YOU DON'T LOOK as if you got much sleep last night," said the wolver Grimly as Torisen descended from his tower apartment into the Council chamber's early morning light.

The Highlord wore neat black hunting leathers reinforced with braided rhi-sar inserts, high boots, and gauntlets, but his hair was ruffled and his eyes deeply shadowed.

"This makes it—what? Five days in a row?"

Torisen rubbed his bearded face, feeling as if he had either slept too little or too much. Certainly, his wits felt as tarnished as old silver. In the past he had stayed awake much longer to avoid certain dreams, but this time the cause was different.

"I've been through their names over and over again," he said. "Every one of them from Harn down to Cron and Merry's new baby. Who else is bound to me that I've forgotten?"

The last time it had been the Kendar Mullen, who had flayed himself alive in the death banner hall so that he would never be forgotten again. Trinity knew, Torisen remembered the dying man's blood soaking through his clothes as he had knelt beside him.

"Mullen. Welcome home."

Five nights ago Torisen had woken with that same terrible, hollow feeling that someone was missing. Whom had he failed this time?

Can't hold them, can you? sneered his father behind the locked door in his soul-image. *I always said that you were weak.*

229

Above, Yce threw herself at his closed door, yipping with distress and agitation. Her claws raked the wood, then rudimentary fingers fumbled unsuccessfully with the lock.

"She'll tear your bedroom apart," Grimly warned.

"That can't be helped. She mustn't go with us today. Has the hunt master reported yet?"

"He's waiting for you below."

Burr appeared with a covered tray. "First, my lord, your breakfast."

"Burr, I haven't time..."

"Sit. Eat."

Torisen sank into a chair and glowered at the porridge set before him. "Well, then, send him up."

The hunt master duly appeared, a middle-aged Kendar with grizzled hair still touched with fox-red, wearing russet leathers.

"The lymers have been out since before dawn," he reported. "They haven't picked up a fresh scent yet, but we did come across some odd pawprints. The toes looked wolfish, complete with claws, but elongated."

"Like this?" Grimly stood on one hairy foot and obligingly held up the other, shaped half between lupine and human.

"Well, yes, but much larger. Whatever this beast is, it's huge."

Torisen and Grimly exchanged glances.

"That certainly sounds like the Gnasher," said the latter.

Since that howl had answered them out of the winter night, they had been on their guard, not that that had helped herdsmen out with the black, irascible cows that preferred to calve in the snow rather than sensibly in the safety of a stall. Several Kendar had been found torn literally to pieces and half devoured among their scattered charges. Torisen had felt each passing like a cold wind through his soul. At least those names he remembered. The attack against Kencyr rather than cattle seemed calculated to draw a response, as had the baleful howl that followed each kill. They hadn't really known, however, if they were dealing with some monstrous dire wolf out of the hills or with Yce's homicidal sire.

Now Torisen put down his spoon, the porridge half eaten and, in any event, untasted. "We have to assume that it's the Gnasher."

"Ancestors know," said the hunt master, resting his elbows earnestly on the table, "we've tried to pursue it as a mere wolf. The traps we've set, the woods we've baited...but it's too clever to fall for such tricks." A howl from Yce made him start and look over his shoulder.

"Perhaps we haven't offered him the right bait," said Grimly.

"Don't even think it," Torisen said.

"Well, she can't stay mewed up here for the rest of her life."

That much was true, thought Torisen, making their current hunt all the more essential. Why, though, did he feel that they were going about it all wrong—or was that just his general uncertainty this morning? He had apparently already failed one Kendar. What if he failed Yce as well? Then too, Storm had an abscess in his hoof so Torisen would be riding his secondary mount, a gray gelding named Rain. Everything seemed subtly out of kilter.

The faint sound of a horn blowing reached them.

"At last!" said the hunt master, springing to his feet.

They clattered down the spiral stair, out into the inner ward where grooms held their horses. Torisen swung up onto Rain, who danced nervously sideways under him. He set his spur to the gray's right flank to correct him and the horse lashed out at the mount behind him. Torisen had forgotten that instinctive response to a sore rib. Oh, for Storm, who had the sense not to make such a fuss. Some twenty Kencyr were riding to the hunt, not counting the dog handlers already in the field, on the scent. The horn sounded again, to the north. Direhounds were loosed, then the massive Molocar. Grimly stayed by Torisen's side although he had dropped to all fours and ran on shaggy paws. The whole party swept out the gate, down the steep incline, and through the apple orchard. Ahead loomed the forest.

It was a bright, late winter day with snow still lying in the shadows and along branches in ridges from a brief flurry the previous night. Melting, it dripped from tightly rolled buds in diamond drops as the riders plunged underneath. Torisen pulled back on Rain to keep from crowding the hunt master. The direhounds coursed ahead of him, black tails whipping, on the track of the lymers.

The whole party plunged among the trees. Few paths ran here. Close as it was to the fortress, this area was tricky. Here Ganth's hunt had gone astray, losing him and his followers, the night that the shadow assassins had come for the Knorth ladies. Some said that he had heard their screams but couldn't find his way back to them until too late.

The horses no longer ran together but swerved back and forth between thickets, stands of trees, and the occasional boulder rolled down from the heights, following the cry of the hounds. Torisen lost sight of Grimly when they split to pass on either side of a small grove. He could hear the others but caught only flickers of movement between the bare branches. There went the hunt master's russet jacket. Rain gathered himself and jumped a fallen tree, landing with a surprised snort in a tangle of brush. By the time he had fought free, the flash of red was gone although hunters' cries still filtered back through the trees. They seemed to be moving away.

Torisen slowed Rain to a trot.

Except for the distant hunt, now no more than a rumor, the wood was silent. No bird song, no wind, only the crunch of snow underfoot. The trees thinned and the land dipped toward a shallow stream running between ice-fretted banks. Flakes drifted down from the cloudless sky. It was as if he had ridden into a pocket of winter.

The low-slung sun dazzled and confused him. Had he somehow gotten turned around, heading south rather than north? The land here was fully capable of playing such a trick.

Rain hesitated on the bank, ears flicking nervously back and forth. He snorted plumes of steam and tried to back up. Torisen patted him on the neck.

"Now what, you? Go on."

Gingerly, the horse crab-stepped down into the hock-deep water, onto slick stones, then stopped again, trembling.

The opposite bank seemed to erupt.

Rain tried to spin away, but slipped. As he floundered, something huge, white, and shaggy rose over the bank's crest. A claw raked across the gray's neck, followed by a crimson spray on the snow. Rain squealed and fell. It all happened too quickly for thought. Torisen found himself in the creek bed, water rushing over his face, his left leg pinned by the horse's weight against the rocky bottom. The shock of the fall and of the cold made him gasp, then choke on icy water. He struggled up on an elbow. Rain's thick blood swirled past him, borne on the current. Although a chunk of his neck had been ripped away, the horse still struggled to rise, in the process grinding Torisen's leg against the stones. He tried to drag himself free, and almost fainted from the pain.

As he lay back in the stream, panting, something came between him and the sun.

"So," said a thick, familiar voice overhead. "We meet again, lordling."

Torisen held up a hand to shield his eyes. Below the red halo of his fingers, he saw that the Gnasher stood on the bank, his hind legs bent backward at the knees. The rest of his bulk, half lupine, half human, hunched against the sun. He was much bigger than Torisen remembered, and if his soul cast either light or shadow, it was swallowed by that greater glare.

"Where is that little bitch, my darling daughter?"

"Safe from you."

The Gnasher laughed. Even against the sun, his teeth were very white. "For how long, eh? Who will protect her once you are dead? Might she even try to avenge you? Oh, that would be perfect."

Squinting, Torisen could now make out the wolver's stomach and chest. Both were thickly matted with whorls of white fur that suggested the smashed heads of pups, silently howling. Trinity, how many litters of his progeny had he slaughtered?

"Hasn't there been blood enough?"

The Gnasher's laughter turned to a snarl. "The young always consume the old—unless the old strike first. Kruin taught me that, even if he didn't have the guts to succeed himself. How else could I have become the King of the Wood if I hadn't killed my father? No pup of mine will survive to do the same to me and so I will live forever."

Icy water found its way through the seams and inserts of Torisen's leathers. More poured down his collar. His teeth began to rattle together with the cold and shock.

Mortality, immortality . . . which was the trap? The Gnasher, King Kruin, and the Master all had traded the souls of their followers for life and yet more life, but how fulfilling had they found it? Dying was easy, to avoid such entrapment. However, Torisen's people depended on him. What, here and now, was he willing to risk against imminent death, assuming he had anything left with which to barter?

Not rocks but the wooden door in his soul-image pressed against Torisen's back. His hand fumbled behind him as if with a will of its own at the bolt that secured the door.

That's right, boy, came the hoarse, eager whisper from shriveled lips through the keyhole. *Let me out. Remember how this cur turned into a shivering pup at the mere sound of my foot upon the stair?*

So long ago, in Kothifir, before Ganth was even dead...

That last had never struck Torisen before.

Trinity, how long had his father haunted him? How had it started, and what sustained that possession now?

The image formed in Torisen's mind of a drop of blood trembling on a knife's tip, falling into a cup of wine:

Here, son. Drink to my health.

Back in the Haunted Lands keep, had his father tried to blood-bind him as Greshan had the young Ganth? Was that why he was haunted by his father now, with that drop of blood still sunk into his soul, poisoning it? But surely only a Shanir could do such a thing.

Words rose in Torisen's mind, spoken by his father through his mouth to the Jaran Matriarch, forgotten until now: *Do you wonder that I could never entirely throw Greshan off? That I should come to hate all Shanir?*

Argh. What good did it do to think of such things now?

But some day he would have to open that door. His hand was on the latch. Would it be today?

Remember, son, anger is strength.

The Gnasher stopped pacing. "What are you doing? Stop it!"

The sun had cast Torisen's shadow behind him. Now he felt the chill of it gathering around him. His voice came out rough-edged, more his father's than his own.

"Would you cross souls with me, cub-killer? Come closer, if you dare."

With a snarl, the wolver dropped to all fours and sprang into the stream. Simultaneously, Torisen drove his spur into the right flank of the dying horse. A steel-shod hoof lashed out in a rainbow of spray. The Gnasher yelped and fell with a mighty splash.

"What have you done, wretched boy?" he cried, floundering in the current. "Ah, my leg!"

The hunt sounded in the distance, drawing closer. The Gnasher must have backtracked on his own trail, but now they had turned with it and were catching up.

"Run. Hide, child-slayer. For surely we will meet again."

The wolver's bulk heaved out of the water as direhounds ran

at him, red-mouthed and baying. He batted the leader out of midair as it sprang and ripped the head off its mate. Then he was running on two forelegs and one hind as the pack streamed after him in full cry, followed by the booming Molocar.

Torisen eased himself back into the water, panting. In his soul-image, he gingerly released the bolt, amazed that he had brought himself to touch it at all, worried that in doing so he had somehow compromised himself.

Still, he thought, *Not today, Father.*

Here came Grimly, the wolver, exclaiming with distress, and Rowan, and Burr. Many hands lifted Rain's dead weight off his leg and drew him onto the bank. The air felt as cold as the water, and the sun had slid behind a cloud.

II

"NOT BROKEN. Just badly sprained and bruised."

So the herbalist Kells had said once they had cut the wet leathers away from Torisen's throbbing leg. Already the flesh was turning a mottled black and purple and the swollen knee barely bent.

Kells glanced at white-haired Kindrie who stood to one side, hands clenched behind him against his instinctive urge as a healer to help. Torisen glared at him.

Don't you dare.

Now he was back in the study of his tower apartment, having rejected all offers of help and stubbornly limped up four flights of stairs. Yce, released from the southwest bedchamber, sulked by the cold fireplace.

"We haven't heard the last of this," remarked Rowan, glancing at the wolver pup. "Her sire has escaped into the wilds."

"With a broken hind leg," muttered Burr, as if to himself, as he moved about the room straightening things that were already in their place. "With luck, unable to hunt, he'll starve to death."

"Anyway," said Rowan, "he's shown himself to be formidable but not invincible. Why didn't he attack while you were pinned under Rain?"

"Maybe he wanted to gloat," said Kindrie.

No, thought Torisen, *he was wary of my soul-image. Ganth still scares him.*

It had clearly shaken both Burr and Rowan to so nearly have lost their lord. After all, where would they be without him? The Knorth would collapse (it was foolish to think that his sister and cousin could hold it together), and the other houses would pick its bones. Thus would end the Kencyrath's divine mission, unwelcome as it had always been. In life, in death, he was responsible. As usual, the thought flicked Torisen like a fly on flayed skin. Dammit, why did everything always depend on him?

Because you are Highlord, said the voice, a snide echo in his mind. *You accepted that responsibility when you assumed that lethal collar, the Kenthiar, and it accepted you.*

"Burr, stop fidgeting. Leave me alone, all of you."

It was unlike Torisen to be short-tempered. Surely, however, he had cause enough today. The hunt had been a failure and here he was back again, mere hours later, half crippled and no closer to discovering which Kendar he had failed.

Kindrie stood in the doorway, looking poised for flight but stubborn too. "I meant to give this to you earlier, Highlord. It may help."

He held out a scroll.

Torisen unrolled it, and saw to his amazement that it listed all of the Knorth Kendar, with lines indicating the various paternal and maternal lineages.

"The first draft was illuminated," said Kindrie wistfully, "but Lady Rawneth burned it. It's taken a while to reconstruct the chart from my notes."

Traditionally, the Kencyr favored memory above writing for most things unconnected with the law. It had never occurred to Torisen that he might fall back on such an aid. Part of him wanted to snap, "D'you think I need this?" Another part grudgingly admitted that he did.

"Thank you," he said, his eyes already sweeping up and down the columns for the name that he had forgotten.

Kindrie hadn't moved. He gulped. "Er, Highlord. Has it ever occurred to you that any act of binding, blood or otherwise, might spring from a Shanir nature?"

Torisen's expression drove him back a step like a physical blow. "Get out."

Kindrie scrambled down the steps. Below, he could be heard nervously conferring with Burr and Rowan.

Alone again, Torisen leaned back in his chair, shaken by his own heartbeat. He could accept that blood-binding was a Shanir skill. Ruthless as it was, hardly anyone used it anymore...

Except your uncle Greshan and perhaps your father.

...but as for the mental bond, all lords employed that. What else, after all, held the Kencyrath together? Were they all Shanir without knowing it? Torisen wished he could talk to his mentor, Lord Ardeth, but Adric was unstable these days, sometimes coherent, sometimes trapped in the dementia of extreme old age. He might say anything.

Am I Shanir?

No, no, no...

With an effort, he put the thought out of his mind.

It did, however, suggest something. So far, he had concentrated solely on remembering the names of all the Kendar in his house. What he hadn't checked was the tie that bound them to him. With that in mind, he started over from the beginning, using Kindrie's scroll to prompt his memory. Half an hour later, his finger paused on a name that woke no answering spark:

Brier Iron-thorn.

CHAPTER XVIII
"Please"

Winter 100

I

"NOW TRY SITTING," said Gaudaric. "And remember to breathe."

Jame gingerly lowered herself onto a wooden chair, misjudged the distance, and dropped the last few inches with a thud. Every joint of the rhi-sar armor creaked in protest.

"Hmm," said the armorer, regarding her critically, stroking his chin. "Now bend forward. I thought so: the shoulder straps are too tight."

Byrne detached and lifted each shoulder guard in turn to let the strap beneath out a notch—like adjusting the girth on a horse, thought Jame, grumpily, feeling the front- and back-plates of the cuirass shift downward. Unused as she was even to shopping for clothes, the fitting sessions were beginning to try her patience. But the armor did feel better. Now she could reach down to stroke Jorin with a gauntleted hand. The ounce rolled over on his back and stretched, purring. The gloves at least were marvels. The smallest rhi-sar teeth marched down the fully articulated backs, which in turn were sewn to leather gloves with slits in the fingertips to accommodate her extended nails. She hadn't realized that the armorer had noticed them.

"It will grow more supple the more you wear it," said Gaudaric. "The trick in making it is to use as little wax and resin as possible to give it its initial shape. Too much and it becomes brittle."

"I feel like a tortoise," said Jame in a muffled voice, speaking to her knees. Their leather cops showed the pattern of fine, mottled scales, surprisingly dainty to have come from such a monster.

"You should feel like a dragon," said Gaudaric. "Stand up. Take a look at yourself."

Jame rose and stepped in front of the full-length mirror. What she saw reflected there was a fantastical creature sheathed in white leather reinforced by the ivory of tooth and claw. The armor fit together as steel plate would, but it was much lighter. Braided inserts increased its flexibility and vented body heat. Gaudaric had reinforced the helm with a ridged crest and one rhi-sar fang thrusting downward from it as a nasal guard. Two more teeth pointed upward, socketed in the cheek guards. Jame hoped that these last were as unbreakable as Gaudaric believed, given that they presented two very sharp tips just below the slit out of which she peered. Larger teeth encased her torso like an external ribcage, their points tucked under a reinforced breast- plate. Smaller ones in addition to claws marched up her arms and down her legs. It wasn't hard to imagine the white rhi-sar's mad, blue eyes glaring back at her from within that cage of ivory.

"I see what you mean," she said.

"Never think that you're invulnerable, though. A bludgeon swung with sufficient force can break ribs through the leather, and some weapons can pierce or slice through it, especially in a lateral blow falling between the ivory. Remember, the beast had to be skinned in the first place and then I had to cut out the pieces, mostly with persistent sawing. Does it pull anywhere else?"

Jame rolled her shoulders and head, then twisted her body, to the right, to the left. Presumably the leather would also creak less with use.

"Good," said Gaudaric. "We can still make minor adjustments, but that, I think, completes the final fitting. Now, let's see you get out of it."

Jame considered the arming sequence in reverse. First she removed the helmet and gauntlets; then, with Byrne's help, the shoulder cops with their toothy spikes, the arm harnesses, and the gorget. Next Byrne unstrapped the cuirass and removed both back- and frontplates. Then the thigh protectors with their knee cops were unhooked from the belt and the belt itself was unbuckled, followed by the greaves and articulated shoes. This reduced Jame to the padded underwear of a gambeson. To her amusement, both men tactfully turned their backs as she stripped and then gratefully re-dressed in her own clothing.

Gaudaric turned back. "Getting it off is always faster than putting it on, but you'll have help with that, I should think. I'll wrap it up and have it delivered to your quarters in the Host's camp." He paused, as if about to say something else, then shook his head and bent to gather up the pieces.

Jame thanked him, remarking with a shade of guilt, "So much work for a few leftover scraps."

His payment for the work was whatever was left of the rhi-sar.

Gaudaric chuckled. "They're more than that. Every bit of antique white rhi-sar leather is highly prized among the few with the rank and money to afford it."

Jame crossed over to the open window, through which the smell of dust and rot drifted. Earlier there had been a crash quite nearby, loud enough to make everyone jump. Another tower must have fallen.

"I'd forgotten that King Krothen is the only Kothifiran with the right to wear all white," she said over her shoulder, "or is it different since he lost his god status?"

"These days," said Byrne darkly, with the moral certainty of the young, "anyone can wear anything. It's disgraceful."

It was nearly half a winter's season since the Change had begun, with no sign yet of resolving itself. However, just when it had seemed that things couldn't get any worse, the city had begun to organize itself. Leaders arose. Committees formed. Neighborhoods started to protect themselves. And politicking began.

No one saw this as the new, permanent state. Never before in living memory had a Change lasted so long, but eventually it would end and new leaders, divinely chosen, would emerge. It was impossible to guarantee who they would be, but there was some evidence that those in whom others had faith had the best chance. Consequently a scramble was now on in many quarters to attract followers.

Needham, the former master of the silk merchants, clearly aimed to become the next Lord Merchandy. In this he was all the more desperate since the Wastes were the only source of silken goods and that trade had ended, probably forever. It was common knowledge that his assassins were hunting for Mercer. So far, however, the Undercliff had protected the former guild lord. Although Kroaky hadn't been seen since the Change began,

Fang and her urchins seemed to be making it a game to spot and plague these would-be killers—without endangering themselves, Jame hoped. Then again, from what she had seen of Kothifir's assassins, they were a limited threat.

Lady Professionate had fewer rivals. Most (excluding her family) saw it as a universal good that a healer should have special powers and wished her well, but she stayed in hiding to nurse her mentor.

As for Ruso, Lord Artifice, many guild masters would have contended for his position, but most of them were too busy fighting off challengers within their own houses. In the meantime, he had been seen working in Iron Gauntlet's shop on strange creations run by gears and wheels. As Gaudaric's apprentice had said, no one with a true vocation wanted to sit idle.

Jame looked out over the domed rooftops to the Rose Tower. Krothen might have his share of enemies among the ruling class, but his loss was felt in the very fabric of the city. From the start, buildings had begun to collapse in the ruinous outer rings. Now the destruction was creeping inward as the limestone that supported the Overcliff gave way here and there to the weight of its soaring towers. For that matter, several lesser towers had broken off at the decrepit level formerly obscured and supported by clouds, raining destruction on the streets below. Kothifir clearly needed its king.

But "Which king?" Prince Ton and his mother Lady Amantine asked. He too was seeking followers among the nobility, hoping that he could overthrow his uncle when the Change ended. He at least could sire an heir. Krothen, he claimed, couldn't, or at least not without crushing his would-be consort.

Gaudaric bowed her and Jorin out of his private workshop. Below, members of the Armorers' Guild pursued their craft as if everything were normal, except for their children playing at their feet.

Jame paused as usual in the display room to admire the rathorn ivory vest with its intricate scale armor and high, elegant collar. Would it jab her in the throat the way the new gorget did? Its tiny scales looked as supple as a serpent's belly. But then Gaudaric had said that the rhi-sar leather would soften with use, so she shouldn't complain.

Outside, the sun was setting in a crimson haze. Sand eddied in ripples down the street and formed mounds in corners, blown from the south now that Kothifir had lost the protection of the

Tishooo. How long before the next storm—or two, or three—buried the city altogether? Already the Host's camp in the valley below was having problems, as were the farmers with clogged irrigation ditches and wells.

Meanwhile, it still seemed odd to see not circling clouds but the tops of towers, as if heaven had been dragged down to earth, quite literally in some cases. Debris littered the street from the recent partial collapse of a neighboring spire, surely the source of the earlier crash. Like many others, it had broken off at the cloud level. Stone blocks, broken furniture, clothes and trinkets...some minor noblewoman's bedchamber spilled its treasures across the street. Urchins picked through the ruins, strips of cloth wound around their faces against a lingering cloud of dust.

One scavenger paused, listening, then another. Suddenly all were in flight.

Jame squinted into the dust cloud. Forms moved there, ghost-like, approaching. What in Perimal's name...?

Someone grabbed her arm. She spun around and nearly struck down the dingy figure that clung to her.

"Graykin! I've been looking everywhere for you."

"Save me!" her servant gasped, his grip tightening. "Here they come!"

"Who..."

But in a moment she guessed. Shabby, hooded forms emerged from the dust, a dozen, two dozen, more. She could clearly see those whom she looked directly at, but a quick turn of her head, to the left, to the right, revealed more of them hidden from her peripheral vision. The Intelligencers' Guild had come for its former master.

Hangnail stepped to the fore. "We have been watching you come and go for days, Talisman, knowing that he would reveal himself to you sooner or later. Now leave. This is no business of yours."

Graykin gulped, released his grip, and stepped away from Jame. "He's right, lady. There are too many of them."

Jame glanced at his white, set face, impressed despite herself.

"Give us the sash," said Hangnail.

The Southron's hands fluttered to his waist. The strip of silk there was now more gray than white, but he clung to it as he had these many long days, symbol that it was of the first real power he had ever possessed. "No."

"It means nothing until the crisis ends," Jame told him. "Let them have it. You can reclaim it later, perhaps."

Graykin bit his lip, then fumbled with the knot. "All right," he said, almost in tears. "Take the filthy thing."

He balled up the sash and threw it. The entire guild swayed forward, but it was Hangnail who snatched it out of the air. The spy held the silk for a moment, clutched tight to his chest, snarling at those who would have taken it from him. Then he slipped it into a pocket. His eyes rose, glittering in the shadow of his hood.

"Do you think we would risk it ever falling into your clutches again, outsider?"

His hand emerged from his cloak holding a knife. More glinted all around him. In this, at least, they were unified. *There are too many of them,* Graykin had said. He was right.

Footsteps approached and voices sounded, speaking Kens.

The Intelligencers' Guild melted away.

A ten-command appeared out of the growing gloom. Randir, Jame noted.

"Having trouble?" asked the leader, a third-year randon cadet. What was his name? Ah, Shrike.

"A bit," Jame admitted as Graykin shrank back out of sight into Gaudaric's doorway. She recognized the cadet as one bound not to Rawneth but to some other Randir Highborn. Curious, how one never met one bound to Kenan, Lord Randir, himself. "Still no word from your war-leader or Shade?"

"Ran Frost says that Shade must have followed Ran Awl back to the Riverland."

"Assuming that's where Ran Awl went."

"Yes. Assuming. But where else could she have gone?"

That indeed was the question, to which so far Jame had no answer. Would the Randir even say if Awl and Shade arrived at Wilden? That secretive house liked to conceal its comings and goings from outsiders, perhaps even from members of its own community not within the inner circle.

"We're fresh off duty guarding Krothen's treasure towers," said Shrike. "Prince Ton and Master Needham are both advocating that their wealth be distributed throughout the city—this, assuming that either the prince or Master Silk Purse can seize control of said towers. As you can imagine, their claims and promises have attracted a lot of attention."

"So I've heard."

At the moment, whoever controlled those towers controlled Kothifir. Krothen had gained vast wealth and considerable ill will over the years by claiming the best of the city's spoils, but out of them came the Host's pay. Jame could see both why the former god-king wanted his treasures protected and why the Host had a vested interest in their safety. It did seem unfair, though, if the city suffered as a result.

"The word is out to all the guards," said Shrike. "King Krothen wants to see you."

That was unexpected.

"Why?" Jame asked, adding, "Oh, never mind," when the Randir shrugged. "I'd better go. First, a favor: will you escort this man to the Knorth barracks on the way to your own?"

She reached into the shadows and drew out a reluctant Graykin. Shrike regarded him with a curled lip. "Your personal spy? Oh yes, we know who and what this fellow is."

Not entirely, thought Jame. No one knew or even suspected that Graykin was bound to her. To reveal that would be to expose a major breach of custom, never mind that Rawneth bound Kendar all the time or that Jame herself had just bound Brier Iron-thorn.

It was tempting to touch the thread of their new connection. What was Brier doing now? What was she thinking and feeling? But the Southron's habitual reticence made Jame hesitate to intrude. She only hoped that she was giving the Kendar the support that she needed, unlike her brother. Tori didn't seem to realize that some Kencyr required something to lean on. Ancestors knew, Jame herself would sometimes have liked such support. It was hard to stand alone. At least, there had been no repetition of Brier's excesses on the night that Paper Crown's tower had burned and Kalan's baby had fallen to its death.

"And why should we oblige you in this slight matter?" Shrike was saying with a smile.

Oh yes. There was also Graykin, who leaned on her all too heavily.

Behind the Randir, his ten-command stirred and chuckled.

"For the novelty of it, perhaps?" said Jame, stifling a flash of irritation. Why could one never deal freely with the Randir, except for Shade and Randiroc? "How often do you have the chance to grant a Knorth anything?"

"Say 'please.'"

"I thought that was implied. Please."

"Very well. Come along, you."

Graykin shot her a glance, then turned away, straightening. He disappeared with the Randir, a shabby, oddly dignified figure, into the falling night.

And now, thought Jame, for Krothen.

II

IN BETTER DAYS, the Rose Tower was a hive of activity. Now it drowsed, its lower rooms untenanted.

It had also suffered damage without the god-king to maintain it. For one thing, that subtle twist in its construction seemed more pronounced so that Jame, walking up the spiral stair, felt as if she was about to pitch out over the balustrade into space. For another, the stone roses that rambled around the window frames and up the balusters crumbled at her touch. At the level of the absent clouds, they had worn away altogether, leaving pocked stone, and the marble steps were hollowed out with use.

Here was the level at which guards usually stood. Not now. Above, curtains as ragged as cobwebs fumbled at the windowsills of Krothen's apartment. Inside, chaos.

However, Krothen still had servants, as Jame found when she climbed to the top.

"Welcome," said a wheezing voice.

Labored breath seemed to fill the circular room, rasping and rattling within its stone shell. It was dim and hot inside, despite a cool evening breeze edging around the marble petals, and it stank.

As her eyes adjusted, Jame made out a great mass of flesh slumped on the dais. The Krothen of old had been obese beyond reason, but he had also seemed oddly buoyant, no doubt thanks to his god-given power. Now, deserted by it, his flesh dragged him down in heavy, sagging folds as if he were a sculpture of butter left out in the sun. Servants had removed a side panel of his white brocade robe. One was struggling to hold up a pallid slab of fat while another sponged the exposed crevasse with lavender water.

"Forgive me for not rising to greet you," said the former king with a twisted smile that more closely resembled a grimace. "My skin tears if I move. Ah, mortality. It's killing me, you know."

What to say to that? Jame kept a respectful silence and waited.

"I miss my acrobats and clowns," he said peevishly, pausing between sentences to gasp. "What, am I never to have any fun again? I even miss that stodgy prick, my high priest. He's saying that I've lost the favor of the gods, you know. What gods? I was one. I will be again. That's why these few servants have stayed. They still have faith in me. Do you?"

"I do," said Jame, surprised to find that this was true. "At least as king."

He wheezed a laugh. "I forgot. You Kencyr and your one true god, whom you hate. Do the Karnids love their precious prophet or only fear him? What about the Witch King of Nekrien? No matter. Their followers believe in them, and belief is power."

That certainly was the case in Tai-tastigon, thought Jame, where gods died along with the last of their worshippers. For that matter, she suspected that even in his current state Krothen had more followers than the few in this room. After all, common folk spoke more often of his return to power than of his nephew and possible successor, Prince Ton.

"To make it worse," he continued, "Gemma is bestirring itself. They've always envied our prosperity. Now that they see us weak, how long before they rise up to strike? Ah, their emissary was right: my arrogance may yet come back to haunt my people. Hanging their raiders certainly didn't help, even if they did indirectly cause a seeker's death. And I had to endure their bodies dangling in front of my windows."

"What can I do for you, your majesty?"

"Just this: find that cursed temple of yours and start it up again."

She should have guessed that Krothen, no fool, knew the ultimate source of his power.

"When it first failed, I went to look for it," she said. "The tower built around it has collapsed. It must be buried in the ruins, perhaps shrunk too small to find."

Krothen quivered. Jame wondered if he was going to be sick. No, the entire tower was shaking. A stone rose petal split with a sharp report, then another. Cracks etched the pale green chalcedony floor. The servant lost his grip on the slippery fold of flesh which he had been supporting and it closed over his companion's hand with a smack. The trapped man stifled a cry of pain and tried to pull free, but couldn't. Krothen's eyes rolled up in his head until only the whites showed. His mouth gaped, wide, wider. Something pale emerged: fingers, prying the plump lips further open, cracking their corners. Inside, behind rows of teeth, a face appeared. Kroaky.

"I can't get out," he gasped. "I can't get out. Help us!"

Krothen shuddered again. Sweat ran down his multiple chins as if over a waterfall and his face was a patchy greenish-white. He reached up and stuffed his younger self's fingers and face back down his throat. Then, with a mighty gulp, he swallowed them.

The Rose Tower stopped swaying. The servant at last pulled free his hand and retreated, cradling broken fingers. Krothen gave a sickly smile.

"Look again," he said. "Please."

III

THE RICKETY STRUCTURE surrounding the Kencyr temple had collapsed more or less in place, filling the stump of its shell with a jumble of broken floorboards, rafters, and stones. The resulting pile was at least ninety feet across and three times Jame's height. She regarded it dubiously from across the street, Jorin huddled close at her side. Nothing had changed since she had last been here, just after the winter solstice. Then as now, her sixth sense gave her not so much as a twinge, yet the dormant temple was presumably somewhere under that mass of wreckage, perhaps reaching nearly to its top, perhaps shrunken to the size of a grain of sand at its bottom. Nothing would prove which except shifting through the entire lot.

When she had first seen the scope of destruction, she had turned her back on it. The temple was the priests' business. They had said so, emphatically. Therefore, let them deal with it. But half a season had passed since then, and they had done nothing.

Jame remembered the priests at Karkinaroth who, shut up in their temple, had died of hunger and thirst. Marc had tried to free them. Was she so much more callous than her old Kendar friend? If she hadn't freed her cousin Kindrie from their god's theocracy, he might have been in there. However reluctant she was to learn, experience was beginning to teach her that not all priests were alike.

Feet shuffled on the sandy road and Jorin growled. Jame turned quickly to confront a blond, tattered figure in the brown robe of an acolyte.

"You," she said to Dorin, son of Denek, son of Dinnit Dun-eyed. "So you're the guard they left outside the temple. Are the rest inside?"

"Yes." He sounded dazed, as if he were having trouble bringing her into focus. Whom else had he seen over the past fifty-odd days of isolation, and what had that meant to someone accustomed to the hive mentality of the priesthood? "Grandfather, all the others, trapped..."

"Do they at least have provisions sealed in with them?"

He shook himself, coming to life a little and regaining a shade of his normal haughty nature. "D'you think we're fools? The temple is unstable. This could have happened at any time, so of course they do. Some. But not enough to last all this time." Again his manner and voice cracked. "We've got to get them out!"

They couldn't help what they were, Jame thought, fashioned by a god who didn't care.

She looked up at the frail sickle of a moon declining to the west overhead. "In this light, we might easily miss them, and there are only two of us. Tomorrow morning, early, I'll bring my ten-command and heavy tackle."

"No!"

He grabbed her arm. She could feel the nervous tremor of his flesh through her own. Instinct told her to shake him off, but she restrained herself.

"You don't understand," he said. "The temple isn't here. Just after it shrank, before the tower collapsed, they came and took it."

"Who did?"

"Men in black, muffled to the eyes in black *cheches*."

Jame scrambled through images and came up, incredulously, with the memory of the Tishooo's capture during the winter solstice.

"D'you mean...Karnids?"

His eyes slid away from her own. "They might have been."

Was it possible? Both the Tishooo and the Kothifir temple? What were Urakarn and its precious prophet playing at?

Jame envisioned a map of the Wastes. "It will take...what, ten days to follow them?"

"Less. Much less," the acolyte said, an eager light kindling in his eyes. "There's a secret way under or near every temple, connecting them."

Jame cursed herself for having forgotten that. The mysterious Builders had chosen the Anarchies south of the Riverland as their base, and had linked it to each of their building sites throughout Rathillien by a series of subterranean tunnels lined with step-forward stones. She, Marc, and Jorin had traveled by them from the Anarchies to Karkinaroth in a matter of hours, although the two cities lay almost a thousand miles apart. And Gorbel had mentioned that, after the Massacre, Kencyr prisoners reported having seen a Kencyr temple at Urakarn, of all places.

Should she go, though? Right now, without telling anyone?

Dorin was tugging at her arm while Jorin continued to snarl at him, the golden fur rising down the ounce's spine. That, for so well-mannered a beast, was unusual.

Listen to Jorin, her instincts urged.

The boy is upset, said her better nature. *He has reason to be.*

"Come on, come on. They need us!"

After so much time on increasingly diminished rations, a night's delay might not matter, or it could prove fatal. Would it hurt at least to scout out the situation?

"Come on, damn you," said Dorin again, pulling harder. "Please."

⪻⪻ IV ⪼⪼

THE ENTRANCE to the step-forward tunnel was only paces away in the middle of the street, disguised as one of the many hatches leading to the Undercliff.

A tight spiral stairway led down from the surface. The narrow, triangular risers were perhaps a foot high each, but gave the sensation of much greater depth as one descended. Jame supposed that they were composed of step-downward stones—that is, of rock slabs with such an affinity for their original geological placement that they took anyone who trod on them immediately to that level. With a particularly jarring step, they bypassed the Undercliff into the solid rock of the Escarpment and so on down, presumably, to beneath the valley floor. Darkness had closed around them almost at once. The walls ran with water and the stones underfoot were slippery. With no rail to clutch, it felt as if at any moment one might step off into empty space.

Jame stumbled at the foot and fell to her knees. The impact of her hands caused the coarse moss beneath them to fluoresce, shedding a sickly green light upward between her fingers, onto her face. The acolyte's footprints led away into the darkness.

His voice floated back from ahead. "Hurry!"

"Dorin, wait!" she called after him, scrambling to her feet, receiving no answer.

She and Jorin followed his footsteps. Only a few strides took them well beyond the stair, Ancestors only knew how far into the Wastes. They were on step-forward stones now. Water dripped on their heads. Walls continued to sweat. Behind them, the light began to fade as it did ahead when they slowed. Jame stopped altogether, realizing that the ounce was no longer with her. She found him a few paces back, nosing a rock. It chittered angrily and rose on its claws, pinpoint eyes glowing like baleful green dots. Jorin dabbed at it with a paw. It snapped at him. Jame seized the ounce by his ruff and drew him away.

"Leave it alone, kitten. That's a feral trock, not like Dure's pet. Let's hope that there are no more of them."

The Builders had brought these little creatures with them to Rathillien because of their ability to digest stone, but they also liked shoes and feet and paws.

More green spots blinked in the shadows back the way that they had come, spreading across the path. The chittering grew.

Perforce, they continued, following Dorin's fading trail. Jame wondered at the boy's pace, in the dark, with no light ahead of him that she could see. Had he come this way before? If so, when and why? She began to feel uneasy and more than a bit foolish for having followed his lead so readily.

The passageway went on and on. The track ahead vanished. Their own luminous footfalls shed light in a tight sphere around them, enough to reveal the abyss along whose edge they trod. Things stirred in the depths at their passing. A misstep would be fatal.

Suddenly here was another narrow stair, this one ascending.

Jame followed Jorin up into thin moonlight and a desolate land-scape. She couldn't see much of the latter at first because of the mist rising off a nearby bubbling lake. Tendrils drifted around her, stinking of rotten eggs. The lake seemed to be at the bottom of a series of terraces, the ones higher up studded with smoking pits and boiling mud pots. Underfoot, the ground trembled con-tinually, making Jorin pick up his paws as if loath to tread on it.

Across the water stood a structure little bigger than a hut, but so black that the feeble light seemed to fall into it as if into a hole cut out of space. Its outline warped—because of the wavering air? No. Jame's sixth sense set her teeth on edge and her head began to thump in time to her heart. Despite its size, this was an active Kencyr temple, and not the one that she had come to seek.

A shrill voice was shouting something in the distance. It sounded like Dorin, but she couldn't make out the words.

More drifting steam blurred her vision. Through it, she glimpsed towering volcanic walls, now near, now far, honeycombed with holes out of which black-clad figures dropped like so many malignant ants. Dorin ran toward them, pointing back at her. This time, his words were clear:

"You see? *You see?* I said I would bring the Prophet's chosen one to you, and I have. Now give me back my grandfather!"

Jame swore under her breath. Next time, she would listen to Jorin—if there was a next time. She leaned over the mouth of the stair. At its base, darkness seethed and clattered angrily. To descend was to risk being eaten alive, but where else could they go? The landscape offered few chances for concealment or escape. Meanwhile, approaching Karnids spilled over the lips of the upper terraces and raced toward them.

The Prophet's chosen one? Be damned to that, whatever it meant.

She ran the only direction she could, around the lake toward the temple with Jorin scampering at her heels.

The structure gained little definition as she approached it. Was it without a door like its much larger counterpart in Langadine? Was it really as small as it had seemed from a distance? Her eyes told her yes, but her other senses insisted that she was approach-ing something huge.

She found the door not by its own outline but by the rattling of the bar that secured it.

"Let me out, let me out!" cried a muffled voice from within.

Jame wrestled the heavy bar out of its brackets. A blast of wind threw the door open in her face and knocked her backward. She tripped over Jorin and fell flat on her back. Black feathers streamed over her head out of the door, borne on a mighty wind. The world dissolved into roaring chaos. Jame hugged the ground with Jorin pinned under her, protesting. Then, suddenly, all was deathly still. She looked up. Walls of racing clouds surrounded her, flecked with blue lightning, studded by the dark shapes of Karnids snatched off their feet, flying. The black feathers coalesced into a figure far up, silhouetted against the crescent moon at the tornado's circular mouth, plunging down. A shriek trailed after it. It was going to land on top of her.

Jame scuttled out of the way, tensed for its impact on the stony ground. None came. Looking up, she saw that it had stopped in midair some twenty feet up, although it still gave the impression of plummeting toward the earth.

"Tishooo?"

The Falling Man flailed about with his robe inverted over his head.

"I'm blind!" he wailed.

"You're upside down."

He righted himself and clawed purple velvet away from his face. "I'm still blind! Why is it so dark?"

"It's night."

"Oh. That's a relief." He forced down his flapping robe and hooked his long white beard aside so that it flew upward behind his ear. Now he was parallel to the ground, seeming to hover over it although his clothing continued to whip upward. "You again."

Jame detached Jorin, who had been clinging to her with all his claws, and got to her feet. "Yes. Me."

"Harrumph! Is there any reason why I shouldn't rip you apart where you stand?"

Jame frowned, confused. Her past encounters with the Falling Man for the most part had been almost playful. For all his power, Old Man Tishooo had always seemed somewhat of a clown. "Er... is there any reason why you should?"

"D'you have any idea how long I've been held captive in that damned temple? Because I've lost track of time. And that smug prophet of yours—thought he'd caught some minor desert godling, Kothifir's native guardian who was best kept out of the way. Of what, though, damned if I know."

"But you do guard. The city has missed you."

"I should think so," said the Tishooo, somewhat mollified.

"Anyway, what do you mean, 'our' prophet?"

"This is a Kencyr temple, isn't it? So was the one that destroyed Langadine. And isn't the Prophet a Kencyr himself? Oh, I sniffed that out soon enough, for all his wiles. Invaders and despoilers, the lot of you. Why don't you go back to where you came from?"

"That was another world, a long time ago."

"Huh. The Earth Wife has taken an interest in you, girl. And I sense that you still carry her *imu* although you may have forgotten it. But she hasn't yet made up her mind. Neither have I. Who knows what the Eaten One and the Burnt Man think?"

Jame scrambled for the right words. If the Four didn't accept her people on Rathillien, they had nowhere else to go, nor a place to stand in the final battle with Perimal Darkling.

"I don't know who this prophet is, but if he leads the Karnids, then he's our enemy too. There's a dark force behind him, one that threatens this world as well as the Kencyrath. How much of Rathillien is left, even now? Our scrollsmen tell us that it's round, like every other threshold world we've encountered. So what's on its far side?"

The Tishooo fidgeted with his fluttering robe, looking uncomfortable. Blue sparks snapped in his flying beard, threatening to set it alight. "I can't be everywhere, can I?"

"Why not? After all, you're the elemental spirit of air, manifested as the wind. Do you even know what's happened to the Western Lands of this continent?"

"Why?" he said sharply. "What have you heard?"

"Nothing. That's the point. If Perimal Darkling has eaten them too, then most of this world has already been consumed by the shadows."

"It can't have been. I would know...wouldn't I?"

In his agitation, he began to tumble again, and the cloud wall wobbled about him. For a moment, the sky above Jame was full of flying Karnids. A brown-clad figure with storm-tossed blond hair tumbled with them, his mouth and eyes circles of terror—Dorin, thought Jame, getting what he no doubt deserved. She turned from him.

"Why don't you find out before you kill me?" she shouted up into the raging sky. "I and my people may be your last, best hope."

The Tishooo righted himself with energetic swimming motions.

"All right. I'll go look. Mind you, we aren't through with each other yet."

He whisked up into the sky, drawing the wind with him. The tornado inverted and died, leaving a faintly moonlit night. All around Jame, bodies crashed to earth or into the simmering water.

"Waugh!" said Jorin, pressing against her leg.

"Yes," she said. "Time to go."

The temple door still stood open, gaping into darkness, and power poured out of it. Jame hesitated on the threshold. To whom did she trust herself—her despised god or Urakarn?

Better the devil you know . . .

She stepped inside and the door slammed shut behind her.

CHAPTER XIX
A Walk into Shadows

Winter 100

I

NO LIGHT, NO SOUND. It was utterly dark inside the temple, like being stricken both blind and deaf. Even the flow of power had stopped as if dammed. Jame was at length aware of her breath, panting, and of Jorin standing on her foot. The blind ounce depended on her eyes to see and protested their mutual handicap in a low, fretful whine.

"Be still," she told him in a whisper. "Listen."

Silence.

It didn't surprise her to reach back and touch nothing. Gingerly, she took a step forward, then another, wobbling. It was hard to keep one's balance in such a void. Only her feet pressing against the floor gave her a sense of direction. Two more steps and she should have reached the other side of the hut, but there was still nothing. This also was not unexpected: most Kencyr temples were bigger inside than out.

Air breathed in her face.

Ahhh...

It stank of rot and of something sweet. It was also bitterly cold.

Jame followed the smell, step by step, her stomach curdling within her as if at some long suppressed memory. She *knew* that stench. It spoke to her at a level below the rational, beneath the skin, within the very bone, to the helpless child that she had once been.

Something ahead grumbled, like distant thunder, and the air vibrated. Coarse grass now wrapped, whining, around her boots.

Don't go, don't go...

A muted flash of light shone ahead. Against scuttling clouds, the front of a structure reared up before her, many roofed, where it had roofs at all, with dark windows and open doors out of which the rank wind breathed.

Hahhh, ah, ah, ah...

Darkness again, and another distant rumble, in the flesh, in the bones.

Was that thunder, or stones grinding one against another? She couldn't see it now, but for a moment it had seemed as if that massive pile were inching toward her, out of a greater darkness. Even now, it might loom over her, poised to fall...

Jame swallowed panic. She was still within the Urakarn temple... or was she? Something like this had happened to her before, at Karkinaroth, when she had plunged deep into Prince Odalian's palace only to emerge in Perimal Darkling, inside the House. If so again, another step might take her under shadows' eaves.

Don't go...

As she hesitated, Jorin stood on her toes, his shoulder pressed against her thigh, chirping in agitation. She was in danger enough; was it right to risk him too? But he was a comfort, here on the brink of madness. Moreover, it was important that she find... what? The immediate past blurred. She took another cautious step forward into darkness, onto hard pavement.

Lightning flashed again, closer, with a boom that imprinted the image on her mind of broken rafters overhead against a stricken sky. As her eyes cleared, she found that light had lingered here below. Underfoot was a floor paved with cold, dark stone, laced with veins of luminous green. Walls towered around her. On them hung the woven faces of many death banners, all of them fidgeting and grimacing in a thin wind that threatened to pry them from their perches.

Ahhh...

Her heart chilled within her. This was the dire hall where the Dream-weaver had danced and the Kencyrath had fallen.

Alas for the greed of a man and the deceit of a woman...

Here she had played as a child after her father had driven her out of the Haunted Lands keep, away from her twin brother Tori, and here the changer Keral had tormented her.

"*No mementos for you, brat. This is your home now. Shall I comfort you? No? Then I will leave it to our lord and master.*"

Then *he* had come down the stairs out of the ruined past to claim her as his own, to take her mother's place.

"*So you've lost a father, child,*" a soft voice had said. "*I will be another one to you and much, much more. Come. You know where you belong.*"

The tapestry faces seemed to lean in over her.

You fool, she thought, fighting a wave of dizziness. *You're breathing too hard.*

She crouched and gathered Jorin into a warm, furry hug, an anchor in a reeling world. The ounce licked her cheek with a rough, anxious tongue, then stuck his wet nose into her ear.

She was *not* the frightened child who had fled this hall after forcefully declining the bridal bed and hacking her way to freedom through the hand that had reached out to claim her from between fluttering red ribbons. After that had come flight from the House, leaving it in flames behind her, then nearly a year as an apprentice thief in Tai-tastigon, Karkinaroth, the battle at the Cataracts, that terrible winter in the Women's Halls at Gothregor, and finally blessèd Tentir. When she considered all that had happened since then, her childhood seemed a lifetime ago. She wasn't even the same young woman who had stumbled into this hall two years ago out of Karkinaroth. An old, defiant chant came back to her:

> *If I want, I will learn.*
> *If I want, I will fight.*
> *If I want, I will live.*
> *And I want.*
> *And I will.*

Her breath steadied. She glowered up at the banners, and realized that there were fewer of them than since her last visit here. Many now hung in tattered rags, stripped to bare warp strings that whined in the wind and tapped restlessly against cold stone. Others slumped on the floor, barely twitching.

An answer to their dilapidated state came to her out of the past: *the souls have been eaten out of them.*

Blood trapped a Kencyr's spirit in the weave of its death.

Gerridon, the Master, needed these souls, reaped for him by his sister-consort Jamethiel, in order to maintain his ill-gotten immortality. (There: she had spoken his name at last, if only to herself.) Now that the Dream-weaver was gone, he needed her, Jame, to take her mother's place. In the meantime, he had been subsisting on Highborn leftovers, as it were, but it looked as if he had nearly run out of them. What next? He could turn to the fallen Kendar and to the changers, as the latter had feared when they had started the revolt that had led to the Cataracts. He could accept what Perimal Darkling offered and become at last its creature, its Voice. Or he could try again to win her to his side, to reap new souls among the Kencyrath's Highborn of whatever house. It was no good, she told herself, turning solely on the Knorth, where only she, Tori, and Kindrie remained.

So think. This is now. You are here. What else in this seemingly ageless House has changed?

Her eyes swept the hall, flinching at half-remembered memories. There were the death banners which scrabbled fretfully against the walls, the luminous floor, the stinking wind, the cold hearth at the end of the room piled high with pelts of the Arrin-ken slain during the Fall...

But something else rested on the hearth, something small and black. Jame crossed the floor to investigate and found a tiny, obsidian pyramid nestled between a pair of flayed paws. It was all of three inches high. Well, she had said that the Kothifiran temple might be reduced to the size of a grain of sand. This was at least bigger than that. Gingerly she picked up the object, rather surprised that it didn't weigh more. If she tilted it, what would happen to the priests within? A temple inside a house inside a temple... the very thought made her head spin.

Some catch in the wind caught her attention. A dark figure stood in the middle of the silently pulsing floor, watching her. From what she could make out, it looked like a Karnid. Damnation. Had one of them followed her into the temple and from there into this hall? Now it was advancing toward her, unwrapping its *cheche* as it came. Jame slipped the miniature temple into a pocket so as to free her hands, aware as she did so that it tipped and fell on its side. Oh well. The approaching figure had bared its face—square and dark, with piglike close-set eyes, but it changed as she watched. Even before it had settled into

familiar lines, Jorin was trotting forward to greet it. Jame followed the ounce.

"Shade."

The Randir stood before her in oversized robes which nonetheless showed lengths of bare, slender ankle and wrist.

"I can change shapes, but apparently not my basic weight," she
remarked, regarding the pale gleam of her limbs with disapproval.

Jame caught her in a hug. "I looked for you everywhere!"

"Er...yes." Shade hesitated, then gingerly returned the embrace
before disengaging from it, but not before Jame had felt Addy's
warm length coiled around the other's waist within her robe
and heard the serpent's sleepy, warning hiss. "You didn't find me
because I had assumed this form and didn't dare break cover to
communicate. Do you know that Karnids are secretly gathering
in Kothifir? Well, they are. This was one of them until I took
his place." She frowned, remembering. "There was a lot of blood.
While it helped me to make the change, I find that I don't particularly like killing."

"I would worry if you did. But what are you doing here?"

Shade tugged at her sleeves as if this would lengthen them. "I'm
still looking for Ran Awl and the missing Randir, of course," she
said. "They weren't in Kothifir and no word came from Wilden
of their arrival there. Given the number of Karnids in Kothifir,
that suggested Urakarn. When a courier returned here to report
to their prophet, I followed him. That was a strange trip, underground and surprisingly fast."

"The step-forward tunnel."

"Is that what they call it? Well, I've been here for more days
than I care to count, poking around, finding nothing. Only the
temple remained to be searched. Most Karnids avoid it as a sacred
site, so when I saw you dart in..."

"You followed again."

"And found myself here, wherever this is." She caught Jame's
arm with a sudden hiss of warning. "Look."

An errant breath of wind had brought something translucent
into the hall. It drifted across the dark floor, gliding and bending with aching grace, trailed by white, floating drapery. Delicate
feet moved to an unheard melody. A pale face fragile as the new
moon turned in their direction without seeing them, locked in
dreams. Oh, how sweet its faint smile was.

"So beautiful..." breathed Shade and took an involuntary step toward it, but Jame held her back.

Then the air changed...*ahhhhh*...and the apparition was gone.

Shade turned on Jame furiously with a glint of tears in her eyes. "Why did you stop me? Who was she?"

Jame drew a ragged breath. It had taken all her own self-restraint not to rush across the floor to clutch at that diaphanous skirt like a lost child.

Mother...

"That was the Dream-weaver," she said unsteadily. "Perhaps that was how she danced the night the Kencyrath fell. Perhaps it was on some other occasion. Time moves in different currents here."

"Was she a ghost, then?"

"Not exactly. Her world is as real to her as it would be to us if we got too close to her."

Shade gave Jame a hard look. "You obviously know more about this place than I do."

"I told you once before: we're both unfallen darklings, you thanks to your changer blood inherited from your grandfather Keral, I because of where I grew up. Here, in fact."

"And where exactly are we?"

Jame told her.

"Oh."

Lightning threw the hall into sudden, stark relief, and Jorin crouched, squalling in protest. Thunder roared. Some banners lost their perilous grip on the surrounding walls and plummeted, shrieking, to the floor. A cold, hard rain began to fall through the shattered roof beams, giving way after a moment to hail. The ounce scuttled back toward the hearth, into the shelter of the partial roof. The two young women followed him, both shivering, their breath puffs of cloud.

"Now what?" Jame asked.

Shade clenched her teeth to stop them from rattling, and not only because of the cold. Like most Kencyr, she had previously thought little about Perimal Darkling as a living entity. The worst stories of her childhood were coming to life around her.

"I still need to find Ran Awl," she said with a gulp, committing herself to nightmare. "And there was something else I overheard among the Karnids—that she and the others had been taken 'where changers are made.' What?"

Jame had sworn under her breath. With the Kothifiran temple in her pocket, she had hoped that her mission here was ended. After all, what did the depths of the House offer her except bitter memories best forgotten and perhaps a very real current threat? If the Master was here, in any level of the structure's past, her presence would call to him.

"I know that place," she said reluctantly. "It lies deep within the House. You'll need help to find it."

"And you will give me that help."

Jame sighed. Shade wasn't giving her a choice. Anyway, Awl was a fellow randon and a good woman, even if she was Randir. Whatever was happening to her now, she didn't deserve it.

Jame led the way across the hall and through an archway. The House opened out around them in a seemingly endless procession of high-vaulted passageways, broad stone stairs spiraling up or down, more corridors, more halls. Everywhere lay cold stones, colder shadows, and desolation. At length they came to an open archway whose upper curve was shaped like a mouth. It had been walled up, but the massive blocks now lay tumbled about on the floor like broken teeth through which the wind blew.

"What is that smell?" Shade asked, speaking barely above a whisper.

Something dead, something alive, many things in between...

And there was a faint, sickly light within, coming from a barred window curtained with vines and white flowers shaped like swollen, pouting lips.

Jame stopped Shade from going for a closer look. "Those blossoms are vampiric," she said.

Was it her imagination, or for a moment did the wisp of a figure hang in their obscene embrace? They had caught her once and had nearly drained her dry before Tirandys and his brother Bender had come to her rescue.

Ah, Tirandys, Senethari, who taught me honor by your bitter mistakes...

Although he had died at the Cataracts, the victim of Honor's Paradox, he would be here too in some fold of the House's past, perhaps no more than a breath away. She wanted to see him, to warn him against what lay ahead.

But *"The past cannot be changed."*

Who had said that? Ah. The Master himself, explaining why

he could not reap souls in the past. What happened there happened only once.

Shade had been cautiously maneuvering to peer out the window between the bloated white flowers.

"The sky is green," she said.

"We aren't on Rathillien anymore."

The Randir gave her a blank look. "Where, then?"

"The House spans the entire Chain of Creation, from threshold world to world. Each time the Kencyrath has fled, it has walled up the older apartments behind it except when we came to Rathillien. The Fall happened too quickly; there was no time. Since then, the Master has smashed all the barriers, laying the House open from end to end."

"Has Rathillien been breached?"

"After a fashion. This sort of invasion has happened before, where this world is 'thin.'"

She was thinking of Karkinaroth, the Moon Garden where Tieri's death banner had hung, the Haunted Lands, and the White Hills. She had thought at the time that Karkinaroth was unique. Apparently not.

Shade scowled. So much new information obviously disturbed her, and she was inclined to blame Jame for enlightening her. "Then why doesn't Perimal Darkling burst into Rathillien and overwhelm it?"

Jame remembered standing in the Moon Garden before that gaping hole into the House's shadows while the threads that had been Tieri's death banner wove themselves into an obscene semblance of the dead girl. Then as now, the Master hadn't seemed ready to take advantage of this sudden breach into Rathillien, any more than she had been prepared to carry the battle to him.

Besides, Jame suspected that there had been a change in Gerridon's plans since the Fall. He still wanted immortality, but on his own terms, not as a consuming gift from the shadows. She remembered the rebel changers who had wanted to seize this world as a bastion against their former lord. Perhaps they had gotten the idea from Gerridon himself. If he was to defy Perimal Darkling, he needed a place to stand. Where else if not on Rathillien, the last threshold world to which the Kencyrath had access?

"Come on," she said to Shade, adding, when the other hesitated, "You want to find your Senethari Awl, don't you?"

They walked deeper into the House, trying to stay close to the outer wall and whatever windows it supplied. Dim light seeped from above and sometimes from below. The rooms grew progressively stranger as life and death, animate and inanimate, intermingled more and more. That was the nature of Perimal Darkling, Jame thought, sidestepping a soft, crusty spot on the floor that looked and smelled like a weeping ulcer. It had occurred to her before that the shadows weren't so much evil as antithetical to human life, so that contact with them perverted it. The Master had used them to pursue his own selfish ends and now was trying to avoid paying the price. Did that make it any less necessary to fight them? No. They were a spreading blight on reality whose triumph would change everything. She could only hope that defeating the Master would also defeat them.

Shade looked more and more nervous, and her face began to twitch. She had only started to show changer characteristics within the past year and didn't yet have full control over them. Worse, despite Jame's reassurance about unfallen darklings, she apparently thought of herself as compromised, if not tainted. Jame began to question her, as much to distract the Randir as to gain information.

"You've spent a lot of time now with the Karnids. What have you learned about them?"

Shade slipped Addy out of her robe, looped the serpent around her neck, and traced the gilded scales with nervous fingertips as the snake tasted the foul air, its black, forked tongue darting. Finally, absentmindedly, she began to talk.

Some of what she told Jame was familiar: the Karnids had originally been a nomadic desert folk who worshipped Stone, Salt, and Dune. Then a holy man had come to them preaching of a true world beyond the harsh one evident to their senses, an eternal place where death itself would die. The gateway to it, he said, was a black rock on the shore of a vast inland sea. Then he had died. His people continued to make pilgrimages to the rock for a millennium, waiting for his return, even after a trading city had grown around it.

That would have been doomed Langadine, Jame thought, remembering the metropolis's cheerful bustling, nighttime streets in contrast to the sullen black rock around which the king's palace had been built. Few had known that the rock was actually a Kencyr temple and that its activation had destroyed the city. Fewer still knew that a grief-stricken Tishooo had subsequently smashed the Langadine temple.

"The Karnids wandered for a long time after that," Shade was saying. "Eventually, they settled at what came to be known as Urakarn. Why here . . . there . . . wherever . . . I don't know."

"Probably because they found another Kencyr temple," said Jame, thinking out loud. "It may have been a lot smaller to look at than the one at Langadine, but it also seemed to be without a door, perhaps solid."

Shade turned to stare at her. "What are you talking about?"

"But it wasn't solid, because the Prophet finally emerged out of it, which was proof enough for them of his identity. How many years has he been back?"

"About fifteen, but . . ."

That would be roughly the same time that Tori joined the Southern Host and was taken prisoner at Urakarn, thought Jame.

"Let me guess," she said. "Before that the Karnids weren't particularly hostile to the Kencyrath. After it, they were. So we can pretty well guess who their reborn prophet really is."

Shade stopped. "We can? Who?"

"Gerridon, the Master."

"But why?"

"Among other things, because the Karnid temple has a link to the House."

"So was the Master the first prophet as well?" Shade asked, trying to keep her voice level.

"I don't think so. The Karnids' holy man came to them long before the Kencyrath arrived on Rathillien. Maybe he really was a prophet. Of course, the Builders were already here erecting the temples. It's a good question, anyway."

The Randir took a step away from her. Like a nervous tic, one of her eyes fluctuated between her own and the porcine orb of the Karnid whose form she had assumed. "You know too much."

"I've been asking questions for a long time, in many strange places. What's wrong?"

Shade retreated another step. "Everything is too much. The Master, the Prophet, you, me . . . is anyone what they seem to be?"

They had stopped in a room where every surface was crusted with luminous lichen. Flat leaves, scales, and hairy clumps of ochre, rust, chartreuse, and leprous white crawled around them like sluggish thoughts trapped in a bad dream.

Shade backed into a wall. When she tried to step away from it, she couldn't. Fungus crept up over her shoulders and down her arms, holding her as she strained to free herself. Jame unsheathed her claws, but hesitated to use them for fear of ripping the other's skin off. Filaments inched across Shade's startled face and took root. Addy struck at them, drawing blood, until fungus encased her too. The wall sucked both in with a dry rustle and closed over them. All that remained was a blurred image shaded with lichen, in the process of dissolving.

☜ II ☞

JAME RAKED THE WALL with her claws, calling Shade's name, answered by the flat echo of an enclosed space. Lichen flaked off under her nails. The gouges bled. A section of the wall bulged, then expelled gas between fungal leaves in a flatulent cloud. What if Shade had emerged on the other side? She darted up and down the wall's length, looking for some turn that would bring her to its far side. None appeared.

Jame stepped back, panting.

"Shade!" she cried again.

No response . . . or was there one, muffled, somewhere in the distance?

If one called here, who knew what might answer?

Fool, thought Jame. *Now it knows where you are.*

No wind blew, but the halls around her seemed to breathe.

Ahhh—a long, slow exhalation. *Ha, ha, ha, ha . . .*

In its wake came a pressure against the ears and against the heart, as if the air had thickened with a taste of corruption. With Shade beside her and the conversation between them, she hadn't felt this intolerable isolation. Trinity, to be alone in the House . . .

But Jorin was with her. She knelt and buried her face in the ounce's rich fur. Its feeling and the familiar clean smell of it anchored her.

"Oh, kitten," she whispered to him. "What have I gotten us into?"

Haaaah..., said the House, and again there was that distant echo:

...help, help, help...

Jame looked around. She had drifted away from the exterior windows into the heart of the House. What world was this on the Chain of Creation? The walls seemed to expand and contract about her like the bowels of some great creature that had swallowed her whole. Who had called?

Go to them, said one voice in her mind. *Stay away,* said another.

The House tended to take one where it chose. Jame began to drift, listening for distant voices. Shadowy arches, halls leading nowhere, great, intricately muraled domes admitting strange, filtered light...

Shadows and movement began to catch the corner of her eyes. Others walked with her or shied away as if she were the ghost. Some wore elaborate court gowns of a style millennia out of date. Others were draped in dark robes similar to those of Kencyr or Karnid priests. The latter were chanting:

"Do you recant...do you profess..."

The voices tugged at her. She followed them. Here was a corridor lined with rooms flexing like the harsh breath in her lungs.

"Do you recant your belief in your false, triune god? Do you profess the Prophet of the Shadows to be your true lord and master?"

...no, no, no...

"Then we must convince you, for your own good."

Someone screamed: "Oh god, my hands, my hands!"

They were hurting Tori. She wouldn't allow that. But her steps seemed as slow as if caught in thickened honey. Shapes passed, carrying the glow of a furnace.

"Do you recant...do you profess..."

That was Rowan, crying out as the incandescent iron seared her forehead, and beyond that, there was Harn with his cracked skull, breathing in, breathing out, as stentorious as a drunkard.

What can I do? What can I do?

She found herself on a threshold, peering into a dim room. Someone hung from the far wall, his wrists secured too low for him to stand, too high for him to sit. His hands were enflamed with suppurating burns and infection ran down his arms in red streaks. A swathe of black hair covered his bowed face. His coat gaped open over a boy's wiry chest, over the bars of unmoving ribs.

"You can save him," said a voice behind her. She knew those deep, rich tones with their underlying touch of mockery, and her very bones shook. "He is worth nothing to me, but you..."

Jame licked dry lips. She wouldn't turn to face him. She couldn't.

"Tell me, girl: for what were you bred?"

"To replace the Dream-weaver, my mother."

"Well, then. Come to me."

He was standing so close behind her that she could feel his breath stir the short hairs on the nape of her neck.

"Blackie," someone called from a neighboring room. "Blackie!"

The boy shuddered and gasped.

What if he stopped breathing again? His hands were already a frightful mess, possibly beyond the power of *dwar* sleep to heal. Could he survive without them? Would he want to?

"Decide," said the Master. "Dear child, think what I can offer you. You will never be alone again. The Shanir power that you curse will find its true use. I wait to embrace you."

For a moment she swayed. What had she ever wanted except to belong? Her god had impressed that need on all of her people, even if the way led through a different concourse than himself. Not even her father had wanted her.

However, she had won a place at Tentir, dammit. The Master was speaking to the outcast child whom she had been, not to the young woman whom she had become.

But Tori... could her sacrifice save him, or was this just another of Gerridon's tricks?

The past cannot be changed. The Master had said so himself.

Yet Tori had somehow escaped this trap and gone on to become Highlord of the Kencyrath. That was his destiny. Nothing she did now could alter that... or perhaps her next action would allow that future to exist.

"Will you let your brother die?"

Out of the corner of her eye, she saw his hand—the right, of course—glide down her arm without touching, but so close that she could feel its heat. She stepped away from it, into the room, across it, and knelt before Torisen.

When she brushed the hair aside, his face was pale with a sheen of sweat and his eyes were closed. He looked impossibly young. The gyves from which he hung were secured by threaded bolts and the bolts by pins out of his reach, but not out of hers. She drew one.

"Don't," said that voice by the door. Had it changed in timber, becoming almost petulant? As it grew fainter, it was hard to tell.

The bolt unscrewed and Tori's hand fell. She caught it, flinching at the heat of its infection, then freed the other one. He sagged into her arms. For a moment she held him, then laid him down on the floor and kissed his clammy brow.

"Wake. Live."

She wanted to tell him more: that she missed him, that she loved him, that he must trust her. His eyelids flickered, but already he was fading, the outline of the flagstones under him showing through. He was slipping back into the past. That was the way with the House, where time shifted at will. Others had escaped with him, all of those years ago. She hoped that he would regain his wits enough to free them—but then he must have, because Harn, Rowan, and the rest had survived.

Jorin crouched in the doorway, chirping anxiously.

His prints and hers marked the dust, as did a larger set of footsteps almost overlapping her own. Damnation. Gerridon, or someone, had stood that close behind her, breathing down her neck. She could see where he had turned away, the signs of his passing trailing off within a few steps. Had he also retreated into the House's past, or had he gone into its future to wait for her there? What game was he playing, anyway? As twisted as his plots had become, did he himself even know? Time would tell. With Jorin trotting at her side, she retraced their path.

Here again was the lichen-splotched suite of rooms, crawling with subdued, leprous color.

Jame stopped. She couldn't leave without Shade, but where was the Randir? Her own childhood memories of the House were incomplete, assuming she had ever come this far into it. Later, though, she had found Prince Odalian "in the place where changers are made," in the process of becoming one himself, poor boy. Was Shade there now, or trapped in the very fabric of this foul place?

"Shade," she called. Her voice came out in a croak, hesitant to be heard. No good. Try again. "Shade!"

Filaments and glowing, hairy clots of lichen humped together on the wall. At first they formed a blotch, then a small, blurred image that grew as if something were stumbling toward the wall from its far side. Mittlike appendages fumbled against the inner surface, stirring the outer fungus, leaving red stains. They found the gouges that Jame had ripped with her nails. Fingertips forced their way through, then hands. Jame grabbed them and pulled. The lichen peeled back and Shade plunged through.

Released, the Randir huddled on the floor, hiding her face. One side showed oozing punctures where Addy had missed the encroaching lichen and struck flesh—with dry bites, Jame hoped: Kencyr were hard to poison, but venom was nasty stuff. The other side which had twitched before now seemed to be racked with spasms. Blood covered her hands up to the elbows and her legs from the knees down, as if she had knelt in a pool of gore.

"Sweet Trinity, Shade. What happened?"

The Randir drew a shuddering breath. "D-dead," she stammered. "They're all dead. I-I found Ran Awl chained to the floor in a room full of crawling shadows. She told me that she and the rest were members of a secret group within the Randir loyal to its lost heir, Randiroc. The Karnids seized them in Kothifir and brought them here, apparently as a favor to Lady Rawneth."

"She's mixed up with Urakarn? How did that happen?"

"I don't know. Awl asked me as Lord Randir's daughter to grant her an honorable death. I didn't want to, but she grabbed Addy and Addy bit her. She went into convulsions. Then I saw... I saw that she was becoming a changer, against her will. So I gave her the death she wanted."

Shade's face altered as she spoke, becoming raw-boned like Awl's. Then it changed again, twitching and sagging.

"There were more Randir there, a dozen at least, chained to walls and ceilings and floors. Some were dead already. Others... they were changing too, with no control over their bodies. They begged me... they begged... Ancestors forgive me, I killed them all."

Jame held her as the faces of the slain writhed in torment over her own and her limbs twitched in sympathy with them.

"Hush. You did the honorable thing, in a monstrous situation."

"No. I'm the monster!"

"Not unless you make yourself one, and so far you haven't. Shade, trust me. I've been wrestling with situations like this longer than you have. Our darkling blood doesn't help, but it doesn't damn us outright either."

Addy slithered out of the Randir's disordered hair with a warning hiss, wicked, triangular head darting and mad, orange eyes ablaze.

"You. Behave," said Jame. "Before I tie you into a knot."

The serpent's black, forked tongue flickered near her fingertips, then she submitted sullenly to being picked up. Jame slung the molten coils around her own neck since Shade looked as if she would collapse under the weight.

"Come on. We have to get out of here."

They stumbled through seemingly endless, empty corridors, all the time feeling that they were being pursued. Dry whispers echoed in corners and debris rustled furtively. Eyes gleamed in the shadows, only to become patches of luminous mold as they passed. Jame wondered about the golden-eyed creatures who had taught her how to perform the Great Dance and about Beauty, their innocent child. Somewhere here too were Tirandys, Bender, and the Serpent-Skin Cloak, last seen slithering back into the House to avoid an earthquake in Karkinaroth, the coward.

At last they emerged in the main hall of the House. Stiffened death banners scraped against the walls with threadbare, frozen fingertips. The rain had stopped, giving way to ragged clouds skating past a gibbous moon waxing toward the full. Below, the floor was sheathed in ice over which they slipped and slid, bound for the darkness that gaped on the hall's far side, between columns.

Here Jorin paused, sniffing, then trotted into the shadows. For once the sensory link between them was acting in Jame's favor. She could feel first pavement, then clutching grass, then stone again under the cat's paws, then under her own feet as she followed, half dragging Shade with her. Would they be able to find the door? Yes. Shade hadn't entirely closed it, so it was edged with faint light.

Jame cautiously pushed it open and slipped through. The exterior bar had fallen off. She kicked it away and shouldered the door shut, so that no sign remained of it. Let the Master and the Karnids find their own way back inside, if they could.

Outside it was still dark—perhaps, judging by the stars, around three in the morning—but which night? Time moved slower in the Master's House than in Rathillien, which was how her twin brother Tori had managed to gain ten years on her. The moon had been a waning crescent when she had entered the temple. Now it was waxing gibbous, tumbling down the sky. Jame counted on her fingertips. Was it possible that she had been gone up to twenty-four days? Someone was bound to comment on that.

Of more immediate concern, where was everybody? She would have expected the Karnids to be astir, even this early. Mud pots spat. The lake seethed. Dead trees hung over it, their white branches wreathed with mist. Nothing else moved, except for something that bobbed in the water. It seemed to be wearing a black robe, but with that thatch of blond hair, Jame suspected that the garment was actually a Kencyr acolyte's brown.

"Dorin?"

She eased Shade to the ground, picked up a dead branch, and gingerly poked the floating figure. Bubbles erupted around it as it sluggishly rolled over to bare its teeth. The flesh had boiled off its face and its eyes were poached. The movement detached an arm at the shoulder, but the sleeve prevented it from drifting away. Mixed with the sulfur stench of the lake was the smell of overstewed meat, reminding Jame how long it was since she had last eaten.

Jorin chirped anxiously. A moment later, the ground began to quiver and the lake to ripple. Jame and Shade staggered as fissures opened in the valley floor. Geysers erupted. Farther away, sections of the caldera wall cracked and fell, laying bare Karnid cells.

"This is worse than the last time," said Jame. "We'd better get going."

Not far away was the opening to the step-forward tunnel. When Jame leaned over it, hot air rose in her face, lifting the wings of her hair, and a red light glowered below, but at least there was no sign of the trocks. To go underground, though, with the earth so restless... Well, what choice did they have unless they wanted a long, long walk back across the Wastes?

Jame pulled Shade to her feet and edged down the steep risers with her, clutching the rail with her free hand.

CHAPTER XX
A Season of Fog

Winter 110

I

PATCHES OF MIST snagged in the bare trees and drifted, torn, between their trunks. Leafless limbs dripped. Beside the New Road ran the Silver, a sinuous, smoking snake of a river that hid one bank from the other and chuckled slyly to itself as it went. The ground was sodden with last year's leaves and last night's rain, the undergrowth snarled with skeins of fog. It was early morning, the sun barely risen over the eastern Snowthorns in a haloed presence.

Along the road's western bank came the muffled clop of hooves. A white horse emerged from a fog bank as if taking shape out of it. Its rider, on the other hand, wore the black leathers that had given him his nickname.

Storm was still lame and Rain was dead, hence this new mount, a normally placid mare named Snow. Like Storm, Torisen continued to limp. Just as his bruised leg had begun to heal, he had tripped over Grimly lying at the top of the old keep's stairs and had fallen down a flight, wrenching it anew. It hadn't helped to be told that his sister made a habit of tumbling down stairs without harming herself.

Torisen wondered what Jame was doing now, at this very moment. He missed her more than he imagined he would, but thoughts of her also made him uneasy. She was so unpredictable, so inclined to ridiculous situations. His dreams of late had been confused, apparently relating to his own past rather than to her present, but seen from a strange angle. If Marc was right about the scrying potential of his stained glass window, he must be mistaken about how it worked.

As to more conventional means of communication, Torisen had sent a post message to Harn asking what had happened to Brier when he had realized that the Kendar cadet had slipped away. He owed such personal attention not only because of Brier's mother Rose, who had saved his life in their escape from Urakarn, but also because by all accounts Brier was shaping up into something special. In future years, she might well join the ranks of such legendary randon as Harn Grip-hard and Sheth Sharp-tongue. She already had the earned name of Iron-thorn, unusual in one so young, even if she held it in part in honor of her dead mother.

Can't hang on to your people, can you, boy? came his father's taunting voice through the locked door in his soul-image. *I lost all except those foolish enough to follow me into the Haunted Lands. Are you stronger than I was? Than your sister is? Ha. You pathetic little cripple.*

"It's only a sprain," Torisen muttered to himself. Snow's ears twitched at the sound of his voice. "I'll be well soon enough, dammit."

But part of him wondered. He had never outgrown his dread of mutilation, stemming from the time at Urakarn when he had nearly lost his burnt hands to infection. A young man might feel immortal. An older one knew that he was not. Was such knowledge good or bad? What if it was hindering him in his role as Highlord? Ardeth had warned Torisen that he held his people too lightly. To them, his consideration might feel like impotence when what they needed most in an uncertain world was a strong hand. Almost anything could be forgiven a lord but weakness.

"*I fear, however,*" Ardeth had gone on to say, apparently now addressing Torisen's dead father as, these days, he was wont to do, "*that you may have mistaken anger for strength. Use your rage as a tool, not a crutch, if you must use it at all. Never let it use you.*"

His former mentor was slipping, Torisen thought, with a shiver. As much as he had sometimes resented the old lord's high-handed manner, the decay of that formidable intelligence was a fearsome thing.

He wrenched his thoughts back to the postriders carrying his message to Harn. Ten days on the road south to Kothifir at the very least, ten north again. By that reckoning, Harn's reply was already five days late. It might arrive any time now.

Torisen reined in, listening. From uphill came the muffled thud of axes, then a warning cry and the rip of wood giving way. Branches snapped. The ground shook. He left the road and nudged his horse to climb. Soon Chantrie's ruined walls loomed over him. A pity, he thought, that no one had ever set about rebuilding it, but then Gothregor on the opposite bank had plenty of roofless, abandoned halls at its own heart. There simply weren't enough Knorth to restore the ancient fabric of either keep.

Forms moved ahead of him in the fog. One advanced and became his chief forester, Hull, a burly Kendar with a grizzled beard and a bald, lumpy head.

"How goes it?" Torisen asked him.

Hull wiped his brow which dripped with sweat, precipitation, or both. Steam rose from the collar of his open shirt as if from the withers of an overworked horse.

"We've our work cut out for us, so to speak, m'lord. Many trees fell during the recent rains when their roots couldn't hold 'em in the earth. There's thinning to do too, and pruning, and the alder coppice down by the river is ready to harvest. We'll have a nice lot of waterproof wood from that, along with seasoning for our cheese."

"By no account, forget the cheese," said Torisen dryly. "Well, watch out for pockets of weirding. You'll recognize them by their brightness." *Huh*, he thought; *as if the man didn't know that.* "Are there any signs yet of arboreal drift?"

"The sumac always begins to creep with the first thaw. So do other brush." Hull chuckled. "I had a crew caught up yesterday in a patch of crawling raspberry canes that nearly carried them away. We're anchoring the more valuable standing trees, in case they get restless. How is it downriver?"

"The water meadow dikes are rebuilt. Now they're working on the terraces."

Torisen remembered watching Kendar hoist stone blocks back into place that morning after the flood that had dislodged them the previous year. Before that, the Riverland had been wracked with earthquakes, tornadoes, and fire. Earth, air, fire, and water.

All since your sister came home.

Now, that *had* to be a coincidence... didn't it?

The water meadow itself would grow the coming year's crop of hay. Above it, tier on tier, would rise stands of oats, wheat, rye, and barley, unless another natural disaster wiped them out.

Torisen wished that he could lend a hand in the restorations, not that he actually had the strength or skill to do so. God's claws, at present he could barely dismount without help.

Cripple.

No doubt, though, his people were glad to see him keep his hands clean for once.

"We should be planting peas and beans within a few days," he said, "as long as the shwupp stay in the river bottoms."

Hull grimaced. "I hate those sneaky bastards. One wrong step and you're in a mud pot with your bones half stripped."

He started as a white shape ghosted out of the trees and trotted past him with lolling tongue and cold blue eyes. Nothing had been seen or heard of the Gnasher since Torisen's encounter with him in the woods north of Gothregor. Perhaps his broken leg had done him in, as Burr had hoped. At any rate, Yce couldn't be confined forever.

As they talked, workers passed, bound downhill. Someone below exclaimed in surprise. Foresters started to run, calling questions.

"There's something unexpected in the coppice," said Hull. "Your pardon, my lord."

He hurried off into the fog, axe in hand. Torisen followed more slowly on Snow. A babble of voices rose to meet him:

"Can you see..."

"What is it?"

"Damn this fog...watch out!"

Wood splintered and rocks churned together. Men shouted in alarm. Something huge was coming up the hill, grinding and smashing its way through the undergrowth. A shape loomed out of the mist.

Snow squealed, spun, and bolted. Before Torisen could rein her in, she cut too close to a tree and slammed his sore knee against it. Dazed with pain, he fell.

The thing was almost on top of him. Bare golden branches swayed back and forth overhead and a massive trunk seemed to reel against the sky. Long fringe roots snaked past him, each tipped with a secretion that ate into the ground and gave the tree innumerable toeholds with which to pull itself along. One nearly lanced through his thigh. The tree which he had hit began to tilt as its own roots lost their grip in the loosened soil. It crashed over, luckily away from Torisen, but the next moment he had tumbled into the cavity left by its root ball. A writhing node of rootlets passed over him like so many wooden snakes, stiff and acreak with the sap just beginning to flow through them. For a moment the tree's full weight sagged into the hole, pressing him down into the mud. Then it lifted, and the golden willow churned on its way.

People were shouting his name. "Highlord! Blackie! Where are you?"

Torisen spat out mud and croaked back, "Here. In the earth."

Yce appeared at the edge of the pit, yipping, to be shoved aside. Just as hands reached down to grab him, something under the mud caught his boot and nearly jerked him out of their grasp. Bubbles rose around him through the liquefied soil.

Bloop. Bloop, bloop.

"Shwupp," said Hull, and pulled.

They extricated Torisen hastily, with such brute force that he thought they were going to tear him in two. Once he was out of the hole, a circle of anxious faces closed around him. Without thinking, he put weight on his sore leg and pitched forward into their arms. Snow, caught, was led back to him and with difficulty he mounted.

"You *are* going back to the keep, aren't you?" Hull asked anxiously, looking up at him.

Cold and shock made Torisen's teeth clatter, and his sodden clothes dripped with mud. No clean hands this time, after all.

"I'd better, hadn't I?" he said, trying to smile.

II

LORD CAINERON and the Director of Mount Alban sat in the college's library on either side of its massive oak table. The southward-facing window was curtained with oiled cloth to keep out the fog, leaving a gloomy interior lit with candles as if it were twilight. In fact, it was morning on the last day of winter. The

Director leaned back in his chair, his blind, opaque eyes overhung by shaggy, scar-broken brows. Caldane sat opposite in hunting leathers that strained against his girth. He had just finished a late breakfast, more by fretfully scattering its remains about the table and the floor than by consuming them. He seemed simultaneously eager and on edge, although he did his best to hide it. The former randon who served as the college's current director might not have noticed, but Kirien suspected that he did: Taur was no one's fool.

Kirien herself stood behind a screen by the door.

The inhabitants of the college had kept their visitor under covert observation since his arrival the previous evening with a large hunting party that claimed to be lost in the dense fog. The Director had pointed out that Valantir across the river had better accommodations, but Caldane had insisted that he couldn't find the Jaran keep, which might have been true. On the other hand, the Caineron and the Jaran hadn't been on good terms since the previous summer. Certainly, the current if temporary lord of Valantir, Kirien's uncle, would have objected to Caldane's hunters on his land. So did Kirien, as the Jaran Lordan.

Caldane wiped his mouth on the sleeve of his gilded leathers, leaving a greasy smear.

"For this hospitality, again, much thanks," he said. "Such a fog I've never before seen, although we do get some monsters in the early spring. They can last for days."

"I trust you wouldn't be exiled from your home for that long, my lord," said Ran Taur dryly.

Caldane shot the big Kendar a suspicious look. Was he being hinted away?

Yes, thought Kirien. *Go.*

Caldane leaned back. His chair groaned as he overlapped it on all sides.

"We won't be leaving just yet," he said. "I've wanted to have a word with you for some time, Ran Taur." He gestured around him at the library's scrolls on their towering shelves under the vaulted roof. "It's about these. How many would you say came with us to Rathillien?"

"Several dozen, at least. We didn't have time to gather more."

"And the rest?"

"Scrollsmen and singers dictated them from memory."

"Ah. Singers. Now, this has always puzzled me: given their use of the Lawful Lie, how can we trust anything that they say?"

"Singers swear not to distort the basic truth in their songs."

"But they do take liberties with it."

"They may. Such songs as abuse the privilege, however, don't endure, nor do we record them."

Caldane leaned forward. "But how do you know what to write down and what to let fade? This summer, my hunters were put off the trail of a particularly valuable golden willow with some song only two generations old. I gather, after questioning my own scrollsmen, that that song endures only in memory."

"Then it isn't law. Your hunters were misled."

"Ah. I thought as much. And what about these songs of Ashe's about the battle at the Cataracts? I was *there*, man. The dead didn't speak to me. They were just that: dead."

"If you don't hear something yourself, my lord, does that make it a lie?"

"If some blasted singer says it, does that make it the truth?"

"That depends on the judgment of the scrollsmen, when it comes to recording a particular song. The two branches of the college keep each other in check. Have you discussed this matter with my lord Corrudin?"

Caldane looked huffy. "I've talked to my uncle, yes, although he tends to back into a corner whenever addressed. What that little Knorth bitch did to him at Tentir, I've yet to discover, except that it involved falling out a window. He helped me to make sense of things, although we didn't reach the same conclusions on some matters."

He made himself sit back with a creak of wood and leather. His beringed, pudgy fingers tapped nervously on the arms of his chair. "Now see here: I don't quarrel with the oldest songs, the ones composed before the Fall that come to us only through memory. After all, those can be dismissed as legends rather than laws. It's the more recent lot that worry me. For instance, those that demand individual responsibility rather than loyalty to one's lord."

"Honor's Paradox," murmured Ran Taur, "born of Gerridon's fall."

"Yes. That. A lot of romantic claptrap, if you ask me. Why, my own war-leader, Sheth Sharp-tongue, was misled by it, and the result? He released that brother of his..."

"Bear."

"...a dangerous madman, mind you, to roam the Riverland at will. Then the Highlord's hoyden sister graduated from Tentir, against my express orders."

"The randon have their own code, as you may have noticed. They are not political."

"Tell that to the Randir."

The Director sighed. "M'lady Rawneth pushes to have her own will, not unlike you, m'lord."

Caldane scowled, uncertain if he had just been handed a compliment, an insult, or simply a fact.

"You think I am wrong to want the Knorth so-called lordan returned to her proper place? What kind of a success has she been at Kothifir, pray tell? I'm told that she is often absent from her post in the camp. Will Harn punish her for that? Probably not. He has also been corrupted by such songs as Ashe sings. Huh. That woman is an abomination. She should have long since been consigned to the pyre where she belongs."

Kirien became aware of a coldness beside her, and Ashe's yellow, knobby hand touched her arm.

"Caldane's men...have sealed off the college," the haunt singer muttered in her hoarse, halting voice. "Not that the fog...hadn't already."

"But why would Caldane do such a thing?"

"I don't know...but from what I've heard...I suspect."

"Have we no way to signal Valantir for help?"

"Not...that I can see."

"Well, we still have this." Kirien extracted a tablet from her jacket and began to write on it in her rapid, spiky script.

"There are no far-writers closer than Gothregor," said Ashe. "It and the Matriarch Trishien...are a hundred miles away."

"I know Tori and Aunt Trish. They'll find some way to answer, although it may take time."

"Then there's another song of special interest to me," Caldane was saying, leaning forward again, more eagerly than before although he sought to hide it. "'Gerridon Highlord, Master of Knorth, a proud man was he. The Three People held he in his hand—Arrin-ken, Highborn, and Kendar—by right of birth and might.' D'you remember it?"

"Everyone does," said the Director. "So?"

"My own scrollsmen tell me that it was composed on this

world after the Fall and subsequently written down. Only one copy exists. Now, that I would like to see."

"Why?"

Caldane airily waved a fat, dismissive hand. "What would your scholars say? Intellectual curiosity." He looked around the library. "Is it here?"

"Possibly. Most Kencyr know that song by heart, though, passed on as it has been from mouth to mouth. No one has had to refer to the original manuscript in years. Who even knows where it is?"

"One man, I'm told," said Caldane, leaning back again with a smug smile. "A scholar named Index."

III

SOMEONE MUST HAVE RUN ON AHEAD, because Torisen and Yce were met at the gate of Gothregor by Burr, Rowan, Grimly, and a dozen other Kendar. So much for his hope to slip in unobserved.

"We've built up the mess hall fire," said Burr, steadying him as he dismounted. "You can strip and bathe in front of it."

"I thought maybe the stable would be more suitable..."

"No."

Torisen submitted. He owed them that much for having given them such a scare, and the warmth of the leaping fire would be more than welcome. His fingers shook with the cold as he fumbled at clasps and laces. The black leather was slimy with mud, and it clung. With Rowan's help, he peeled it off. Grimly hauled free a boot and regarded its ripped sole.

"Shwupp?" he asked, looking up.

"On a hillside, no less, and that damn golden willow too. It must have been hibernating under cover of the alder coppice."

They sluiced him down with warm water, leaving a muddy mess on the floor. Burr returned with clean clothes and boots. Kindrie burst into the hall on his heels.

Torisen and his cousin hadn't spoken since the latter had suggested that all binding might be a Shanir trait—something which Tori didn't wish to consider. In the meantime, Kindrie had stayed out of his way, devoting himself in his own quarters to sorting through the Highlord's long-neglected correspondence. He had a scroll in his hand now and his face was nearly as white as his hair.

Now what? Torisen wondered as he dried himself with a scrap of sheepskin.

"Speaking of the willow," he said, turning to Rowan, "it occurs to me that it only does harm when someone is chasing it. Therefore, I'm giving it the freedom of the forest, as long as it stays on my land."

"Well enough," said Rowan, with her habitual lack of expression, "but who's going to explain that restriction to a tree?"

Kindrie was virtually dancing with agitation. "Please, read this."

"You read it. My hands are wet."

Kindrie gulped and unrolled the scroll. "'From Caldane, Lord Caineron, to Torisen, Lord Knorth, greetings,'" he began in a shaky voice.

"Caldane never calls you Highlord if he can help it," remarked Rowan.

"'Last summer you may have heard of a dispute between the Caineron and the Jaran over the ownership of a particular golden willow. The Jaran sought to prove their case with a song, and while they were singing it, the tree in question escaped. As you may recall, I have never cared for singers' fancies. Consequently, I propose to visit Mount Alban near winter's end to undertake some long overdue housecleaning. If I hear nothing from you before that time, I will assume that you agree with the measures that I intend to undertake.'"

"Sweet Trinity," Torisen said, staring at his cousin. "When did this arrive?"

"A fortnight ago. He must have known that you wouldn't get to it in time."

A disturbance at the door caused heads to turn. In glided a Jaran lady, moving faster than seemed possible given her tight underskirt. Lenses worked into her mask swept the room, settling on Torisen.

"My lord, have you heard?"

"Just now, Matriarch. How did you..."

Trishien produced a tablet covered with a spiky script not her own. "Caldane has seized Mount Alban!"

"What about Valantir?" demanded Rowan. "The Jaran are closest, and the college's natural defenders."

"The fog is even worse to the north," said Trishien impatiently. "The keeps there are cut off from each other, and no one closer than Gothregor can far-write."

"We'll have to ride fast, then," Torisen said, belatedly grabbing his pants and struggling into them. "It's a good hundred miles to Mount Alban. With regular changes, post-horses can make it by tonight."

"There are only a dozen or so remounts standing ready at each station," Rowan warned.

"My vanguard will take them, leaving one or two for emergencies. The rest of the Knorth must follow as quickly as they can. They may be able to pick up fresh horses at Falkirr, Shadow Rock, and Tentir. Call up an armed hundred-command, Rowan."

"I'll find a divided skirt and come with you," said Trishien. "Don't leave without me." She was gone before anyone could protest.

Torisen finished dressing more slowly, thinking, as people rushed about him. How big a force had Caineron brought? What exactly did he mean to do, and how quickly could he do it? The heart of the Kencyrath lay at Mount Alban, encoded in a matrix of scrolls and songs. True enough, the last two had become confused during the flight to Rathillien, and the Lawful Lie hadn't helped, but to lose any one of them risked unraveling the very fabric of his world.

As he buckled his belt, he thought of something else.

"Burr, go back to my quarters and fetch Kin-Slayer. Yes," he added, seeing his servant's startled expression. "It's that serious."

IV

KIRIEN AND ASHE hurried down stairs that jinked precipitously through the wooden heart of Mount Alban. The cliff face had been carved out and replaced by a labyrinth of chambers, hallways, and steps all at different levels. Sometimes one could look up the stair well for several erratic stories. Other times, one had to duck under low beams, all the while watching one's feet on worn, moss-covered treads. There was a more direct stair, but they had chosen not to take it for fear of whom they might meet. Diffuse light filtered through from various outside windows, aided by candles set on banisters, weeping wax. Indistinct voices murmured about them, but the usual morning chatter of the college community was absent.

"You there. Halt."

The command came from above them on the last landing which they had passed. A big Kendar stood there, clad in Caineron hunting leathers.

"My lord wants to see you," he said, "and the scrollsman Index. Where is he?"

Ashe stepped in front of Kirien, her iron-shod staff raised.

"Don't be foolish," said the man, and drew his sword.

He had barely taken a step forward, however, when a stone crashed down on his head. As he collapsed, a ball of twine bounced on the boards beside him.

"You see?" said someone above. "The rock and the ball fell at the same speed."

"They did not!"

A tall, gangly scholar clattered down the stairs, followed by a short, squat colleague. Both wore the college's usual belted coats with many pockets in which to carry tools, notes, or perhaps lunch.

"The rock was clearly traveling faster than the lighter twine," said the short man, glowering.

The tall scholar looked down his long nose at him. "You just say so because that oaf's head got in the way."

Ashe inspected the fallen Kendar. "Only stunned," she muttered. "Good. Now...what's going on?"

"Besides experimentation?" The short scholar bent with a grunt to retrieve his rock, which required both hands to lift. The Caineron had been very lucky not to have suffered a smashed skull. "As you may have noticed, we've been invaded."

"By how many?"

"Ten around the main door. Some forty inside, hunting."

"I can see why Caldane wants Index," said Kirien, "but why Ashe and me?"

"You, Lordan, presumably as a hostage," said the taller scrollsman, rewinding his ball of twine. "Ashe...well, the rumor is that m'lord has a former priest with him who knows the pyrrhic rune."

Kirien ran distraught fingers through her close-cropped black hair, leaving some of it on end. "Madness! Does he want to start a war?"

The short scholar laughed. "When has Caldane ever thought through any of his grand schemes? My guess is that he talked some of this over with his uncle, then went off on his own. Corrudin would never support something so half-witted."

"Good hunting, then," said Ashe. "We go ... to find Index."

They continued down the stair. At its foot lay a great hall roughly hewn out of bedrock by Hathiri masons with Mount Alban's main gate at the far western end. Shapes with torches moved around before it, casting gigantic shadows. On the other side of the hall was the door that led down to Index's herb shed. It stood open. Kirien and Ashe paused by it, listening. Voices rose from below, and glass shattered.

"Who's mucking about in my shed?" demanded a shrill voice behind them, and there stood Index, gray beard abristle, eyes glaring with outrage. "No, I won't be quiet! Let go of me!"

They hustled him away from the door, still expostulating, and across the hall, but others had heard his sharp protests. Voices called from below and feet thundered up the stairs. The guards at the door came running, their shadows leaping before them.

"Quick," said Ashe.

She led them back up into the wooden maze, but soon left the twisting stair for a murky, narrow hallway. This ended at an iron-bound door set in the college's eastern wall, against the rock face. Ashe parted a slit in her robe. Underneath was a corresponding sword slice in her skin. The edges of the old wound were shriveled and bloodless. Under them, hard against a rib, was the outline of a key. This she fished out as if from an inner pocket.

"I am going ... to take Index ... out of Mount Alban ... for safekeeping," she said as she fitted the key into the rusty lock and turned it with effort. "You ... stay here."

"But, Ashe ..."

"No." Death-dulled eyes peered at Kirien from under the shadow of the singer's hood. "You ... will be safer ... with Caldane ... if he catches you."

She forced open the door. Beyond was a tunnel ending in dim light.

"I don't understand."

Voices called to each other behind her in the maze. The Caineron were casting about for traces of the fugitives. Ashe pushed a protesting Index through the door and followed him.

"If you really...want to help," she said through the crack as she pulled the door shut, "lead them away."

The lock reengaged with a clunk of gears behind her.

Kirien was left standing in the hallway, surrounded by Mount Alban's interior gloom. What in Perimal's name...?

A faint glimmer on the floor caught her eye. Ashe had tried to slip the key back into its hidden pouch of skin, but it had fallen through. Kirien picked it up and fingered its ornate wards. Should she? What would Jame do? She rarely found herself in the sort of situation that came so readily to the Knorth Lordan, except when Jame was present. That kind of thing was a bit too dramatic for her taste and, she thought, it called for different skills than those possessed by even a talented scrollswoman. But scholars were always curious, and so was she. At the very least, she should open the door since Ashe had just accidentally locked herself and Index out of the college.

Kirien inserted the key and carefully turned it. It worked more easily for her than it had for Ashe, perhaps because the singer had knocked off some of the rust. The door swung open with only a muffled protest. Beyond, at the end of a tunnel cut through living rock, was a wall of drifting mist, lit from above. Kirien had never considered what lay behind the college, assuming it would only be more stone. This seemed to be a cavity in the cliff, open at the top. She edged forward, stopping with a gasp as her foot came down half over the edge of an abyss. A pebble, kicked forward, fell and went on falling, it seemed, forever. Where had Ashe and Index gone? To the left, she heard their muffled voices. Index was still protesting.

Kirien felt along the wall with hand and foot. The latter detected a ledge, which became a narrow path. She edged out onto it. Once started, it seemed impossible to turn back, although the way sometimes slanted downward into emptiness and sometimes the stone wall bulged. More pebbles rolled underfoot, causing her to gasp and clutch at the rock face. The voices drew nearer.

"You've wrenched me away from my proper station," Index was saying. "For my own safety, eh? Well and good. Ancestors know, though, what damage those louts are doing in the meantime. So I'm calling in all my barter chips with you, haunt. For the answers to two questions."

Kirien's hand groped around the edge of an opening. A side cave, she thought, and pulled herself toward it.

Down three stone steps, Ashe and Index confronted each other in a small, stony chamber lit by a torch held by the singer. At the back of it was an iron door, scabrous with rust, toward which Index gestured.

"Now, where exactly are we, and what's behind that door?"

"That," said Ashe, "is no concern . . . of yours."

"I'm still asking. D'you want to be declared a cheat?"

For a scrollswoman, that was almost as bad as being called a liar. No one would ever barter information with Ashe again.

"You . . . are being unreasonable."

Kirien thought so too. The old scholar was acting like a petulant child; his will thwarted in one direction, he was striking out in another. She wondered, for the first time, if he was going soft with age.

"This . . . is a secret prison," said Ashe. "Bashtiri masons created it. Kendar builders found it. As for what it contains . . ."

The singer's bony fingers touched her side, then groped futilely at it.

Kirien stepped forward into the light. "This is what you lost," she said, extending the key.

"Ha!" Index snatched it from her. "Now we'll see!"

He scurried over to the door and thrust the key into the lock. As he turned it, Ashe dropped the torch and grabbed him around the waist. She wrestled him away, but he clung to the handle and pulled the door open on screeching hinges as he went.

Light flickered across the floor inside. With a chitinous rustle, its surface seemed to split open as a carpet of black beetles seethed back into the shadows. Index craned to look.

"There's a table in there," he said, "and something on it. A book and a knife, both white. Sort of."

He moved to investigate, but Ashe restrained him.

"You fool . . . stand still."

She placed herself between the other two scholars and the open door, facing it, gripping her staff.

Ahhhhh . . . breathed the darkness.

Kirien thought she saw a figure standing in the shadows, slightly bent under the low ceiling. It looked over its shoulder at her—the crescent of a face with a silver-gray eye, a high cheekbone, and thin lips that twitched into a smile.

Ahhhh . . . ha, ha, ha . . .

It turned and advanced. Its eyes reflected the flickering light of the fallen torch. Kirien retreated a pace, still staring. The thing looked like Torisen before he had grown a beard, but with an obscene twist to its features. The three upward leading steps were behind her. She tripped over them and fell, sprawling.

Ha...ha...ha...

It ducked its head under the lintel and stepped into the antechamber, drawing the darkness behind it in a train of seething shadows, as if the noisome room it had just left was turning inside out. It raised a pale face masked with the fluttering wings of moths. Its smile spread and split open the lower half of its face. White teeth writhed...no, maggots. A mouth full of them.

Ashe snatched up the guttering torch and thrust it into the creature's face. Moths ignited. Beetles popped in the heat and stank. It fell back a step as incandescent cracks opened across its face and chest. Then it surged forward again with a hiss.

"Run," said Ashe over her shoulder to Kirien.

Kirien scrambled to her feet and dived out the door. She had no conscious thought where she was going, even as her feet scrabbled on the sloping shelf of the trail. It seemed to go on forever. Stones rolled under her feet. The unseen abyss called.

Suddenly her hand began to twitch, almost making her lose her grip on the wall. Aunt Trishien was sending a message. Kirien fumbled for her tablet, and dropped it. When she awkwardly bent to retrieve it, a shuffling foot inadvertently kicked it off the ledge into the void.

Moments later, with a lunge, she found herself back at the mouth of the tunnel, gasping facedown on the stony floor.

Her hands still shook, but with nothing more than fatigue and strain. Whatever her aunt had tried to tell her was lost.

What had happened, though, back in the cave?

As her head had turned, she thought she had seen the thing crumble even as it had lurched forward, but instinct told her that it wasn't dead—well, no more so than it had already been. On the path, she had heard the door thud shut behind her and the rasp of the key in the lock. Ancestors, please, let Ashe and Index be safe. She should go back to check, but her nerve failed her.

Voices called to each other down the stone tunnel and the wooden hall, from within Mount Alban.

"If you really want to help," Ashe had said, *"lead them away."*

Kirien struggled to her feet.

At the outer door she paused a moment, then shut it, hearing the lock engage within. Now that Ashe had the key which apparently worked on both doors, on both sides, she needn't leave it open.

Where were the Caineron? The wooden maze that made up the college's core distorted sound. If she could reach the stair...

As she dashed forward, however, someone stepped into the corridor in front of her. Kirien skidded to a stop, turned, and ran into the arms of another tall Kendar.

"M'lady Kirien, isn't it?" he said, looking down at her. "M'lord Caldane would like a few words with you."

V

"WHAT TIME D'YOU THINK IT IS?" asked Rowan, gazing up into the fog-bound sky. The sun had to be up there somewhere.

"Late afternoon, I'd say," Grimly replied, reshaping his mouth for human speech. Otherwise, he was in his complete furs, trotting beside Torisen's post horse. "And my paws are getting sore."

"You should have accepted a mount at Falkirr," said Torisen, glancing down at him.

"Then my butt would ache."

The mist was denser than it had been at Gothregor. Now one could barely see more than a horse's length ahead. Their pace, accordingly, had been slower than expected, although they were still outpacing the main Knorth force which now, hopefully, had been augmented by the Brandan keep. Ten riders and two wolvers, with at least fifty miles yet to go. Bare branches dripped on their heads. The wet stones of the River Road were slippery underfoot. When the dark came—all too soon now—it would be hard to see anything.

Yce loped along at Torisen's other stirrup, making no comment. No one had thought about Yce in the rush to leave Gothregor, and by the time she had ghosted up level with them out of the fog, it had been too late to send her back.

"Lady?"

"I do well enough," answered Trishien, through gritted teeth. It was a long time since she had last ridden astride and her muscles burned, but be damned if she meant to hold anyone up. Her gloved fingers fluttered to the tablet that she carried thrust into her coat. Why had there been no word from Kirien since that last, terse message?

Kindrie saw her motion. "I'm sure your niece is all right," he said. "Caldane would never dare hurt her."

"As for what Caldane would or wouldn't do," she replied tartly, "Ancestors only know."

Grimly and Yce both pricked their ears.

"Someone is coming," said the former.

They must be approaching Wilden by now—near Shadow Rock too, for that matter, but the Danior keep was on the other side of the Silver from both them and the next post station, for which the Randir were responsible.

Torisen signaled a halt. Behind him, swords rasped free of their scabbards. His own hand dropped to the hilt of Kin-Slayer, but before he could draw it, a pale horse splashed with mud to its shoulders plunged down the slope to their right and into their midst. The rider set her mount back on its hocks to stop it, then dropped the reins and raised empty hands.

Rowan barked a challenge.

"Quiet," came a low, rasping response, "for Ancestors' sake."

The stranger drew up next to Torisen, ignoring the two wolvers although they made her mount dance nervously.

"Highlord, an ambush has been set for you at the Wilden post station," she said in a voice that grated on the nerves.

As far as Torisen could recall, he had never met this Kendar before, and he thought that he would have remembered her. She had a distinctive, square face, small eyes, and the clenched, blunt jaw of a Molocar. A scar across her throat explained the gravel in her voice.

"How did the Randir know that I was coming?" he asked.

"As I understand it, Lady Rawneth had prior knowledge of Lord Caineron's plans. She knew that the Jaran Lordan would communicate with her aunt—that's you, I assume, Matriarch—and that her aunt would tell you, lord. No one could doubt what would happen next. I can show you a way around the trap."

Rowan snorted. "In order to lead us into another one? Why should we trust you, Randir?"

"Look." The woman bent forward and lifted a heavy fall of hair off the back of her neck. The wavy lines of the rathorn sigil were branded into her flesh, the white scars decades old.

"An Oath-breaker," said Burr, and his eyes grew hard. As a rule, Knorth Kendar did not sympathize with those of their house who had failed to follow their lord Ganth into exile after the White Hills.

"I carried an unborn child at the time," said the woman in a flat voice. "It died anyway. After that, the Randir took me in. Follow if you will."

She turned her horse and plunged back up the slope.

Rowan reined about to regain Torisen's side. "Are you mad, Blackie? She betrayed your father. Why not his son?"

"Was it sensible for anyone to follow Ganth Grayling over the Ebonbane? Remember, he threw down his power like a petulant child with a broken toy and abandoned his followers, all but the ones who couldn't conceive of life without him. Those I pity and hope some day to reclaim."

He summoned one of his riders and sent him back to warn the main Knorth body about the ambush. Another rider peeled off to cross the Silver as best she could to alert the Danior keep to Mount Alban's plight.

The diminished vanguard left the road. The slope above was slick with last year's matted grass and cut across by streams that tumbled down from Wilden's moat higher up. The widest of these were bridged; the rest required fording. Their guide rode before them, barely visible. Then she disappeared.

"I warned you," said Rowan, keeping her voice low. "Now what?"

Grimly had trotted on ahead. Now he slipped back to rejoin them.

"She's met someone on a bridge," he reported. "Most likely a guard. They're talking."

Torisen edged forward, acutely aware of the muffled jingle of tack as the others followed him. Now he could see the bridge and two mounted figures on its crown, their horses standing head to tail. There was a grunt. One of the riders slumped and toppled. The other signaled the Knorth to advance and rode on. Crossing the bridge, Torisen looked down at the huddled figure of a Randir who appeared to have been knifed. His horse stood over him, whickering to his oncoming mates. Grimly offered him to Yce, then swung up into the saddle himself when she refused, much to the animal's distress: no horse wanted to have a wolver on its back.

Eventually they turned downhill again and regained the River Road to find their guide waiting for them.

"Why did you do this?" Torisen asked her.

For a moment she was silent, looking down at her hands as they gripped the reins.

"I had a son," she finally said. "My last child. A randon cadet. His name was..." Her normally expressionless face worked as she tried to remember. Then she rolled up a sleeve and read the name etched in deep, crude scars on her forearm. "Quirl. He tried to assassinate the Randir Heir at Tentir, and failed. Lady Rawneth took away his name, his soul. She did the same to all the cadets who failed to do her will. Their parents can't remember them, only that they have lost something precious. My bond to the Randir broke that night, but no one seemed to notice except me."

"To whom were you bound?"

"To a minor Randir Highborn, a Shanir confined to the Priests' College. Lady Rawneth only binds her favorites. As for Lord Kenan..." She shrugged. "Who knows?"

"What is your name?"

"They call me Corvine. I petitioned once to rejoin the Knorth."

Ah. Now Torisen remembered. He had received the request at the same time that Merry and Cron had asked permission to have a new child. At that point, he had only been able to grant one such appeal, having learned the danger of overextending himself. Since then, however, the Gnasher had killed several of his herdsmen, opening new vacancies. So had the sudden absence of Brier Iron-thorn.

"If you still wish it..."

Corvine raised her eyes. "I do," she said in a husky voice, and held out her hands.

Torisen cupped them in his slim, long fingers. His scars and the Kendar's seemed to run together, although her hands were nearly twice the size of his own.

"I confirm our bond and seal it with blood," he said, using the ancient formula that went back to the time when Highlords were often blood-binders. That latter foolishness, of course, was no longer needed.

"My lord," she said, and bowed her grizzled head.

KIRIEN WATCHED as Lord Caineron paced the library, back and forth, back and forth, as the floor creaked under him. The day was dwindling toward dusk, not that one could clearly see this through the continuing overcast of fog. Some time ago the Director had gone with a Caineron guard to check on the rest of the college. Neither had returned. Kirien suspected that Taur, ever the tactician, had only stayed in the library long enough to be sure that she stood in no immediate danger from their unwelcome guest. Now he would be plotting a counterstrike.

Caldane had been polite to her, but with a sarcastic edge that told her he didn't take her role as Jaran Lordan any more seriously than he did Jame's as her Knorth counterpart. Both of their houses were playing the fool, in his opinion, and would shortly realize their mistakes.

"M'lord," she said, "do you really think that destroying a particular manuscript will negate the Knorth mandate?"

"'Rise up, Highlord of the Kencyrath,' said the Arrin-ken to Glendar. 'Your brother has forfeited all. Flee, man, flee, and we will follow.'" Caldane snorted. "Talk about a song providing a legal precedent! Gerridon lost the Kencyrath through his treachery. Who can doubt that? So what if someone copied such foolishness down? A touch of fire, and where is our precious Highlord then?"

Kirien considered her words. She had long ago discovered that if she phrased things properly, people told her the truth, at least as they saw it.

"If Torisen loses power, who takes it up?"

"Why, the strongest, of course. Who but me?"

"Based on how many Kendar are bound to you, I suppose, but how many actually belong to your seven established sons?"

"Humph. They all still serve me. To whom can Torisen turn? I'd like to see that sister of his add to his numbers, not that he would ever let her. Even he isn't that stupid."

"And if you claim the Highlord's seat, will you also claim the Kenthiar?"

Caldane turned away with a petulant scowl. "That filthy old thing. It's already decapitated three legitimate Knorth highlords.

Did you know that? No one even knows where it came from. Torisen would never have risked wearing it if he had had his father's ring and sword to give him authority. Bloody show-off."

"In other words," murmured Kirien, "no Kenthiar."

Caldane shot a discontented look out the window at the gathering gloom. "Where *is* that wretched Index? Am I going to have to burn the entire library?"

"You wouldn't!"

"Ha. Try me. And I mean to incinerate that obscenity who calls herself Ashe, if I can lay hands on her."

Kirien caught her breath. The man was serious.

"Do you have any idea," she said carefully, "how much trouble you are in already? For that matter, what do you hope to gain by holding me hostage?"

He glowered at her. "Wait and see."

"If you hurt me, the Jaran will declare war on you, maybe the Knorth, Brandan, and Danior as well. They take my rank seriously, even if you don't, and they value the records held here at the college. Think. Where would we be without them?"

"Free to create our own destiny. Don't you see? The dead past shackles us. Our god abandoned us ages ago. What do we owe him? Even after all these years, this is still a new world, ours for the taking. That we haven't already is an indictment of Knorth leadership. As for you, what if I were to take you back to Restormir, eh? My eldest son Grondin needs a new consort. He crushed the last one."

"This is the man so fat that he has to be trundled about his own house in a wheelbarrow, isn't it? I don't think so."

"I wasn't asking for your consent, girl."

"D'you think that my uncle Jedrak would grant it?"

"If I have you, what choice does he have?"

Kirien regarded him curiously. She was used to academic discourse where contestants might disagree, but each side had a grasp of basic logic and of the shared concept of reality that bound the Kencyrath together. Caldane seemed to live in his own world, defined by his ambition and power. Thanks to his scrollsmen, he had half-glimpsed a possible shortcut to the Highlord's seat. Now, however, what had once seemed simple was putting forth as many barbs as a porcupine. She read this in his heavy, anxious pout and in the gathering sheen of sweat on his brow.

"I think," she said, not unkindly, "that you should consult with the Caineron Matriarch about such matters."

Caldane shivered. "I don't talk to my great-grandmother Cattila if I can help it. She only laughs at me."

Kirien's hand began to twitch. "Excuse me," she said, and groped inside her jacket for her tablet, only to remember that it had fallen into the abyss behind the college.

Caldane was watching her. "Now what?"

"Aunt Trishien is trying to contact me. I need something to write on."

He looked around impatiently. "This is a library, full of parchment."

"I do not intend to turn any of it into wastepaper, thank you."

But what else to use? There was an ink bottle on the table and a cup full of sharpened quills. Kirien snatched one of the latter, dipped it in the ink, and began to write on the tabletop. Caldane leaned over her shoulder, breathing heavily, trying to read the rough script. Trishien usually wrote with an elegant hand, but this time her letters jerked all over the tabletop. That and its wood grain almost defeated their transcription.

Kirien lay down the pen and regarded her efforts. "There was an ambush at Wilden," she deciphered. "Now, who could have arranged that? But Torisen escaped it. He should arrive here soon. With Kin-Slayer unsheathed."

VII

THE DAY DRAGGED ON for the Knorth vanguard. The River Road had been largely repaired since the earthquake that had shattered sections of it the previous year, but one still had to watch for rough patches. One would have supposed, Torisen thought sourly, that horses had more sense than to step into holes, but they still needed continual guidance.

Meanwhile, muscles ached, stomachs growled, and eyes grew weary of the perpetual, featureless, white shroud that enfolded them.

Corvine rode ahead.

Trishien fretted that she had had no new messages from Kirien. Torisen tried to ease his throbbing leg.

Yce finally tired of trotting beside him, assumed a nearly human shape, and jumped up onto his horse's back behind the saddle, almost making the animal bolt.

Now there were ten riders, counting the two wolvers, on eight mounts. Once or twice, Torisen thought he glimpsed a ninth horse and sometimes a tenth lagging behind them, downwind, but then the fog closed in again. He wondered how far back his one-hundred-command was and if they had roused the friendly keeps as they had passed.

The randon college at Tentir now lay behind them. It was growing dark, with the ghostly presence of a waxing crescent moon rising over the Snowthorns to the east. Torches were kindled and lit the way, but not very far. The fog was as dense as ever. Lightning glowered in its depths, followed moments later by sullen growls of thunder.

Torisen found himself simmering about Caldane. The Caineron lord had been his enemy ever since Torisen had joined the Southern Host as a fifteen-year-old, sometimes in person, sometimes in the form of his sons, especially Genjar and Nusair, both long since dead. Caldane's ambition had always been clear. To him, Honor's Paradox was a way to avoid responsibility while reaping its rewards. He would gladly break the Kencyrath to his liking, as long as enough of it remained for him to rule. It was that recklessness that Torisen found chilling. Caldane was capable of anything.

Corvine suddenly emerged from the fog.

"Mount Alban lies some five miles ahead," she reported. "There are lights in every window."

Sweet Trinity. Had Caldane set fire to the college?

...I propose to visit Mount Alban at winter's end to undertake some long overdue housecleaning. If I hear nothing from you before that time, I will assume that you agree with the measures that I intend to undertake...

It would be Torisen's fault as much as Caldane's if Mount Alban came to grief this night.

Torisen spurred forward, hearing the rest of his escort break into a rattling canter after him. He drew Kin-Slayer. To his left, Trishien gave a muffled cry. In grabbing for her tablet, she had nearly fallen off her mount. Burr seized her reins to lead her as she balanced the paper on her jolting pommel and scribbled a hasty, barely legible note on it to her niece.

After that long, long ride, they hadn't far to go, but it seemed to take forever. Finally, here was Mount Alban's outer wall rising precipitously to the right, and Corvine had been correct: some seventy-five feet up, where the college's windows began, rectangles of firelight bloomed in the murk.

Torisen swung down at the door, nearly falling as his weight came to bear on his sore leg.

Mount Alban's double front gate was big enough to accommodate a full company of riders, but it was shut. However, a smaller door set into its right leaf swung open as they approached. A tall Kendar stood on the threshold—the college's Director, Torisen saw, as he advanced at a hasty limp.

"Welcome, Highlord. We had word that you were coming."

A slim, neat figure slipped past the Director. "Aunt Trishien! Oh, Ancestors be praised! And Kindrie!"

"It pleases me to see you as well, Lordan," said Torisen dryly as Kirien flung herself into his cousin's arms. "Is the keep on fire?"

"No. We are trying to signal Valantir, now that Lord Caineron has left us."

"He's gone?"

"As soon as he heard that you were nearly upon him and he couldn't find any of his own men. Over the course of the afternoon, we ejected them all one by one from the college." The Director gave a smile warped by the scars that crossed his face. "He should have remembered that many of the scholars here are former randon. Some of the traps that they devised were quite ingenious."

"I'll go fetch Index and Ashe," said Kirien happily. "I may not have the key, but I can still shout through the keyhole. Someone, send to the kitchen to start dinner if they haven't already. I expect that soon we will have a considerable company to entertain. Will you enter, my lord?"

The lure of a hot meal and a place to sit that didn't bounce drew Torisen forward, but he checked himself short of the door. Kin-Slayer hung from fingers already grown numb from tightly gripping it. Tradition said that the war-blade couldn't be sheathed until it had killed.

"Go ahead," he told his followers. "I would like to...uh... stretch my legs first." Stepping back, he disappeared into the mist.

 **VIII**

TORISEN WALKED AWAY from Mount Alban, going downhill toward the Silver because that was the easiest path to follow. The college's lit windows faded behind him. The crescent moon above the cloud cover shone only brightly enough to distinguish up from down while the fog pressed against his face like a dank, dark hand. Thunder rumbled closer. Despite it all, however, part of him felt exultant: at the first word of his approach, Caldane had panicked and fled. He had never expected that, although perhaps he should have. While no coward, Lord Caineron didn't react well to surprises.

Had Torisen really meant to use Kin-Slayer, though? All too well, he knew what a threat the sword represented. However, the college had appeared to be in danger. He hadn't stopped to think.

For that matter, why had he brought the sword with him in the first place? Presumably, as an emblem of his power as Highlord, should Caldane choose to contest it. When he had first declared himself Ganth's son and heir, he had had nothing to prove such a claim except for his willingness to wear that potentially lethal silver collar known as the Kenthiar. Then Jame had brought him his father's emerald signet ring and fabled sword, both of which were said to perform miracles for their rightful owner.

"Wear the ring on the same hand that wields the sword," his sister had told him.

She had also said something about the shattered blade having been reforged in Perimal Darkling, unlikely as that sounded.

Fact or fantasy? Similar questions had brought Caldane to Mount Alban in the first place.

Torisen had once combined the sword and ring to hack through a mirror and the wall from which it had hung. He had been half out of his mind at the time and for many days thereafter. When he had finally tried to resheathe the sword, he had found that he couldn't even release it—that is, until he had pried its hilt loose from his grip by breaking three of his fingers. That had been nearly two years ago. He hadn't touched the damned thing since. Was it an accident that even now he carried the blade in his right hand and wore the ring on his left? Perhaps that meant they were both inert and no threat to anyone, at least at the moment. He could test that hypothesis by trying to sheathe the sword or by switching it to his ring hand, but he hesitated to do either.

Ganth jeered at him from behind the locked door in his soul-image. *Do you expect to claim my power when you refuse to accept the responsibility that comes with it? And you call yourself my son.*

"Shut up," Torisen muttered to himself. "Shut up, shut up."

Downhill, a glow appeared. Torisen thought at first that it was a pocket of weirding, but it pulsed strangely and an odd, two-noted sound came out of it. As he approached, he recognized the site of the hill fort ruins that lay between Mount Alban and the river. Stepping between fallen blocks, he found himself in a cave of sickly light cut out of the fog. The cavity took the internal shape of the hall it once had been, circular, some forty feet across. Someone sat on a rock on its far side, sharpening iron claws with a whetstone and humming to himself. It was from him that the light emanated. He glanced up at Torisen with feverish blue eyes from under a ragged thatch of white hair.

"Well, sit," the Gnasher said. "Neither of us wants to spring directly into battle, I suppose, although that will come soon enough."

Torisen lowered himself onto a block. Mindful that it would soon begin to stiffen but seeing no other recourse, he stretched out his sore leg. Kin-Slayer's pattern-woven blade rippled in the peculiar light as he grounded its point beside his sound foot.

The man he faced wore dirty homespun probably taken from one of the shepherds whom he had slain near Gothregor. One pant leg had been ripped off above the knee. Below, bent at an unnatural angle, was a wolf's hind leg, its shattered tibia lancing out through discolored, matted fur. The stench of gangrene emanated from it. Clearly, the wolver king of the Deep Weald could not have run all the way from Gothregor in such a condition.

"You were the rider I saw lagging behind us," said Torisen.

"Between your vanguard and your growing army, yes. How do you think the latter will feel about having come all this way for nothing? They will probably laugh at you, although to tell the truth I didn't think the fat man would run away like that. Oh, and there was someone else close on my heels. A genuine postrider, I think. Were you expecting one from Kothifir?"

Torisen was, of course, but he put that out of his mind for the time being.

"So, now what?" he asked.

The Gnasher thoughtfully drew a long, jagged nail across the whetstone.

Rasp, rasp, rasp...

"The easiest thing would be for you to give me my daughter— Yce, d'you call her? A pretty name, although it doesn't do to grow attached. Then we both can go home."

"No," said Torisen.

"Is that you speaking, or your father? When we last met, you almost turned to him for help. I could feel your hand on the latch to his prison. That's his sword, isn't it?"

Torisen's hand rested on the pommel. He gently twisted it back and forth so that the blade's point bit into the old keep's cracked paving.

"You don't want to face Kin-Slayer," he said, "whoever wields it. Nor do you want to confront my father. Remember how the mere sound of his foot on the stair turned you into a cringing pup."

"And you into a cowering boy." The Gnasher grinned. His teeth were very sharp. "I have grown since then. Have you? No one becomes a man until he has put his father into the ground or, in my case, into the stew pot. I told you, all those years ago, that you had to kill your sire. But you haven't. I smell the stink of his blood in you."

Torisen sensed Ganth's presence too, waiting, listening.

Scree... went Kin-Slayer's point, uprooting shards of pavement with a spray of dislodged soil. *Screee...*

"Then too," said the Gnasher meditatively, "I learned my lesson from King Kruin, better than he did himself. Name an heir and someday he will take your place. My offspring are all dead, except for this last one. Her death will give me the strength to heal and to live on."

"Forever?"

"Perhaps."

He put aside the stone, stretched, and yawned. Jaws gaped. Hinges cracked. Hands became huge paws as they stretched out to touch the ground. The shepherd's clothes ripped down the back and fell away. He was as big as ever, the size of a small horse, but gaunt with thickly matted fur, and the light his soul cast flared a sickly yellow.

"You see how an heir's very existence poisons me. Learn from it. They say that you have named your sister as your successor. That was foolish. She may seem hardly more than a mouthful, but she has unexpected qualities. How long can you keep a step ahead of her, eh? Oh, your father would laugh to see you now. Can't you hear him?"

What Torisen heard were distant voices calling his name. Would his people find him in this murk? Did he want them to?

The grass behind him rustled. Grimly slipped out of it to his right, Yce to his left, both in their complete furs.

"Ah," breathed the Gnasher.

"Grimly, take her away," Torisen said over his shoulder to his friend.

"No."

They all looked at Yce. None of them had ever heard her speak before.

"My father," she said, showing white teeth. "My fight."

"Ah," said the Gnasher again, with a breath of laughter. "Ah, ha, ha, ha..."

Torisen started to rise, but Grimly slipped forward to block him. "Wait."

The two wolvers of the Deep Weald circled each other within the ring of ancient stones. One was barely half the size of the other, but she moved with fluid grace while he dragged his shattered limb behind him. He lunged at her, jaws agape, and bowled her over. Pinning her with his weight, he snapped at her throat, but missed. She twisted under him. Her teeth closed on his ear and shredded it as he reared back.

"You little bitch!"

Yce grinned.

He came at her again, half-blinded by a mask of blood. She ducked under his charge and snapped sideways at his sound hind leg as he passed. Bones crunched. The Gnasher screamed and dragged himself around to face her with iron fingernails that gouged into the ancient pavement.

"All right," he panted, raising himself. "Meet your siblings."

Whorls of light gathered around him, tracing the patterns in his ragged coat. The line of an infant jaw, the curve of a muzzle, blue eyes barely open, small paws, scrabbling... How many pups he must have slain and devoured, litter upon litter. They covered him now like a moving coat, their edges limned with a purer light than his own. Milk teeth bared, and bit. The wolver king yelped with surprise and pain as red tears opened in his hide. He was bleeding from a dozen gashes, a hundred, and still those tiny teeth worried into his flesh, laying bare muscle, gnawing at bone.

Yce sat and watched. Once or twice, she licked her black-fringed lips.

The Gnasher writhed on the ground, snapping at himself, doing more harm. With a savage slash, he laid open his own guts, which spilled out onto the ground.

Torisen put his hand on Grimly's shoulder and levered himself to his feet.

"Enough," he said.

Thunder boomed closer. The phantom interior of the old hall faded and the mist within it became tinged with a foretaste of rain. Drops splattered into the growing pool of gore, thinning it until it ran deep into the circle's network of cracks. The Gnasher gathered up his steaming entrails and regarded them with disbelief. He raised what was left of his face.

"Am I going to die?"

"Yes. Hold still."

Torisen gripped Kin-Slayer with both hands and raised it. As the ring and the hilt touched, lightning raked the sky. Down came the blade, and the ancient circle split in two. Thunder rocked from side to side of the river valley. Almost unnoticed in that rolling cacophony, something bounced away down the slope into the shadows.

Yce stood opposite Torisen by a sundered, smoking stone, her slim, white figure ghostlike in the gloom. Crossing to his side, she slid her arms inside his coat, around his waist. He felt the warmth of her body, the firm pressure of her small breasts against his chest. With one hand, he gingerly held Kin-Slayer clear. With the other he returned her embrace.

"I will miss you," she breathed in his ear.

"And I, you."

When she disengaged and drew back, not hands but paws rested on his shoulders. The wolver girl bared white teeth in a grin and licked his cheek. Then, dropping to all fours, she loped off into the downpour.

"She's going to return to the Deep Weald to claim her father's place," said Grimly. "I'll escort her—not that she needs it—and return as soon as I can."

Then he too was gone.

Torisen became aware that the shattered ruins were surrounded by silent, watching Kencyr. His people had found him after all. Kin-Slayer tingled in his left hand, light rolling up and down its rain-washed length. He sheathed it, to a long sigh from the shadows.

"Has someone brought me a letter from the Southern Host?" he asked.

A bedraggled postrider approached, drawing a folder from her dripping leather pouch.

"Are you sure you want to read it here, now, my lord?"

Torisen wished no such thing, only that the long day be over at last, but that was impossible until he had finished every piece of business related to it.

He drew out Harn Grip-hard's missal and unfolded it. Judging by the familiar, crabbed script, the Commandant hadn't trusted his response to a clerk's fair copy, which was just as well. Torisen read the message three times, memorizing it, before the rain washed it away. Then he tore up the sodden paper and let it drop into the mud. Those watching could make little of his expression except, perhaps, that they had never seen him look more like his father.

"Get something to eat and rest while you can," he told the rider. "My answer will be ready by dawn at the latest."

The Kendar was startled. "What, all the way back south?"

"Yes. To Kothifir."

⚔ CHAPTER XXI ⚔
Before the Storm

Winter 120

A GHOSTLY GIBBOUS MOON had just risen above the eastern horizon, signaling midafternoon on the last day of winter. Most of the Southern Host was busy in the training fields south of the camp, as usual. Dust rose there, and steel glinted through it in mock battle.

So much practice, to what end? wondered Harn Grip-hard as he stood on his balcony, looking south over the inner ward and the red tiled roofs of the Host's camp. The Kencyrath had many foes, but at that moment, the war he feared most brewed within it, between brother and sister.

Blackie's latest message lay on his desk. It was written on a scrap of parchment with jerky, dark red letters that looked like dried blood. So, Harn expected, it was. The Ardeth cadet who had presented it to him three days ago with a bandaged hand had looked quite unwell.

"The Highlord asked Lady Kirien to send this to me to give to you, Ran," he had said. "Torisen wasn't previously aware that the Ardeth had a far-writer among the Southern Host."

Harn hadn't known that either. One tended to overlook the Shanir until they suddenly became indispensable. How much time might have been saved if he had known about this earlier—except it was a surprise that Blackie had stooped to using a Shanir at all. He must feel very strongly about this message.

Harn remembered when the first letter had arrived by the usual postrider fifteen days ago:

"Something is wrong with Brier Iron-thorn."

He had summoned the Kendar, of course, and there she had stood before his desk, dark red hair aglow, green eyes cautious in an immobile, sun-darkened face. He had known her since she was a stocky, inscrutable child, and her mother before her.

"Well, Iron-thorn. You've done something to upset the Highlord. What?"

"I suppose," she said slowly, "it's because the bond between us broke."

Harn was shocked. "Why? What did he do?"

"Nothing. It's just..." She floundered for words. "He's so gentle."

Harn sat back, absorbing this. He knew how gingerly Torisen dealt with those bound to him, as if they were all at his mercy—which, of course, they were. Raised by Kendar, he had never really understood the Highborns' sense of entitlement. Harn valued that freedom. Others, especially those like Brier raised under tight control, might mistake such care for weakness.

"Still," he said, "that's no reason to break from him."

"It wouldn't be, except..." She had paused, a frown gathering as she thought. "His sister... I don't really understand it, especially in one who seems so fragile and, well, peculiar, but there's an iron core to her. She can also be merciful. I was in great distress over the death of the seeker's baby. Torisen wasn't there. She was."

"So she bound you."

Brier raised somber eyes. "One might almost say that I bound her."

Now, *that* had been a tricky message to convey. Torisen's answer had come back virtually overnight. Harn wondered that the blood in which it was written didn't smolder.

Below in the ward he saw eight figures emerge from the streets of the camp, some walking together like the Brendan and the Jaran, others aloof like the Randir. They crossed the grass. Soon they would be at his door. It was, of course, only a regular meeting with the barracks' commanders.

"Huh," he muttered, under his breath.

Some fifteen minutes later they were seated about the round table in Harn's cramped conference room. Genjar had adopted the southern style of lounging on pillows. Harn and Torisen before him had preferred northern formality, although Harn frequently prowled around the room while the others sat, saying that it helped him to think.

"Where's Coman?" he asked.

"He's expecting a report from his outriders," said the Edirr, with a grin.

The others smiled indulgently. The young Coman commander was responsible for gathering information on Kothifir's external foes. Raids from Gemma aside, though, what enemies did the city possess? However, as one of the Kencyrath's smallest houses, the Coman always made a fuss about whatever they did to inflate their own self-importance. The Coman commander had been hinting since late summer that Gemma was up to something.

"All right," said Harn. "What news from the Overcliff?"

The Ardeth commander folded his thin, aristocratic hands, gathering his thoughts. "The Change hasn't yet resolved itself," he said. "Life goes on in the city, but in a bumpy fashion without the authority of king, guild lord, or grandmaster to steady it. More towers have fallen. Krothen remains in seclusion. Merchandy and Professionate are in hiding. Ruso, the former Lord Artifice, has taken up quarters with the former Master Iron Gauntlet, Gaudaric. Grandmasters like Needham are trying to gather followers . . . on what basis in his case I don't know, given that the silk trade seems to have ended forever. Prince Ton and his mother Princess Amantine are also looking for supporters. Politics aside, I don't know what natural laws are in operation here."

"I've always said that we don't adequately understand Rathillien religions," said the Jaran commander, leaning forward.

The Caineron snorted. "You and your scholar's obsession with native cultures. What is there to understand? We know the truth."

"As we see it, yes. Our Three-Faced God is behind everything. Has it ever occurred to you, though, that his power is in short supply on this world?"

"Blasphemy," growled the Caineron. "Our lords stand, do they not?"

"And our priests," murmured the Randir, Frost.

"Oh, leave them out of this," snapped the Danior. His home keep, after all, was across the river from the Priests' College at Wilden, too close for comfort. "What good do they do any of us?"

"Here in Kothifir, they seem to benefit the natives more than us," remarked the Jaran. "The current mess started when our temple disappeared. And if you can explain how *that* happened, you will have my full attention."

Harn raised his big hands to stop the wrangle. Religion was the last thing on his mind at present.

"What about the treasure towers?" he asked.

"We share guard duty there," said the Brandan. "Everyone knows that control of them equals control of the city. Needham and his followers are constantly threatening to storm them, while Prince Ton wants to distribute their wealth to buy himself support."

"And the Rose Tower?"

"Krothen prefers native guards, or so we hear," said the Brandan. "These days, nothing comes from him directly."

The others stirred uneasily. Krothen was the Host's paymaster, but he had paid no wages since the beginning of the Change. The Kencyr quartermaster had been reduced to buying rations on credit in the common market.

"I still say we should break into the towers and take what's owed us," grumbled the Caineron.

"If we do that," said the Brandan, "how can we justify keeping others out? We are sworn to protect Kothifir, not to loot it. Anyway, it would start a riot."

Harn waved away this troubling subject as he had that of Kothifiran religion. "What about the rumor of Karnids in the city?"

The Ardeth shrugged. "No question, they are there in the shadows, biding their time."

"Until what?"

"We don't know."

"How many of them?"

"We don't know that either."

The Caineron snorted.

There were other, more mundane subjects to discuss: class schedules involving the training fields, a clash between cadets and regular troops, thieves sneaking into the camp. Harn started to relax as the usual wrangles played themselves out.

"If that's all..." he began, rising to dismiss the council.

But the Randir Frost didn't move. "There is one other thing," she said, examining her nails. "What are we going to do about the Knorth Lordan, Jamethiel? She's been absent without leave for—what? Twenty days?"

"That is house business," Harn growled, and began to pace around the table. Here was the topic that he had feared most.

"Also remember: this isn't a meeting of the senior Randon Council. Our authority is limited to the Southern Host."

"Which is where she belongs," said the Randir. "What are you going to do about her?"

Ran Onyx-eyed, the Knorth commander, had barely spoken during the meeting, but that was her way. Now she looked up. "We've made inquiries, of course," she said mildly. "Our patrols have visited all the places in Kothifir she might be, without success. She does have a record of disappearing, though, as noted during her career at Tentir."

"Might she be dead?"

"No," said Harn. Brier would have told him if that were true. For that matter, he suspected that he himself would have known, given his link to the Knorth.

"With any other cadet, such behavior would merit being sent home in disgrace. Are we to judge lordan by a different standard?"

"We did your Randiroc," snapped the Danior. "Ancestors know, he was as peculiar a cadet as ever won his randon's collar."

Frost's smile turned brittle. "We won't discuss the so-called Randir Heir, thank you very much."

"There is also such a thing as detached duty," remarked the Jaran. "Your cadet Nightshade has been assigned to Ran Awl this entire year. And she's missing too, along with a dozen others of your house."

Harn continued to pace as they wrangled. From the beginning, he had sensed that Jameth, or Jamethiel as he supposed he must learn to call her, had other duties than most cadets, first with the Merikit hill tribe and now here in Kothifir. He was aware of her unique status as the only other Highborn besides Torisen to possess pure Knorth blood, discounting for the moment rumors about their cousin Kindrie. The Knorth had led the Kencyrath from the beginning. To disrupt their fragile hold now felt to him like the end of the world.

"You put great faith in your two remaining Highborn," said Frost, as if reading his mind. "Do they really merit it?"

Onyx-eyed stirred. "At Gothregor, Torisen opened a door that to all others was locked. In the camp, on her first day here, his sister did the same. I don't quarrel with such power. You should think twice before you do."

Hasty footsteps sounded on the stair, and the Coman commander burst into the room, red-faced, panting.

"I *told* you," he wheezed, hands on knees, pausing to regain his
breath. "I said Gemma was up to something. My scouts report
a Gemman army on its way to Kothifir."

"By what route?" snapped Harn.

"Along the Rim."

"How strong?"

"At a guess, twenty thousand, composed of Gemmans, raiders,
and any other opportunists they've been able to hire. Kothifir's
weakness draws them. Besides, I always said that Krothen shouldn't
have hung that assembly man's son. They will be here by dusk
with horses, chariots, and mounted war lizards."

Everyone had risen.

"The livestock is a challenge," said the Jaran, "but we should
be a match for the rest. We've got to get everyone on top of the
Escarpment and outside the city walls to meet them. There are
four lift cages, but only one of them is big enough to accommodate horses."

"So, no horses," said Harn.

He could see the battlefield laid out in his mind. The Gemmans
would lead with their thunder lizards, not as big as rhi-sars but
quite large enough to rout an unprepared foe. The Kencyrath, on
the other hand, had clashed with such beasts before. The rest,
discounting chariots, would be hand to hand. It could indeed
be done, if enough Kencyr could be conveyed to the battlefield
in time.

"We need to move," he said. "The cadets should stay in camp,
though. For one thing, we haven't time to get everyone Overcliff.
For another, someone has to watch our back door. Commanders,
see that your second-in-commands stay behind to monitor them."

Thus the Kencryath rose to war and streamed through the
city streets toward the wall, watched by many dark eyes. In their
wake, as the sun set, the shadows began to move.

ᘒᘂᔬ CHAPTER XXII ᘂᔬᘒ
The End of Many Things

The Feast of Fools

I

THE STEP-FORWARD TUNNEL snaked through the earth, one side of it plunging down into an abyss with a pulse of fire in its depths. Rising heat made the air dance. The lichen which had provided Jame with light before now crunched to powder underfoot. Everything trembled.

Shade went first, clutching the wall. Jorin followed her, and then Jame.

The path seemed very narrow, making Jame wonder how she had trod it before, in the near dark, without falling off. Underfoot, the way sloped toward the abyss, and stones dislodged by their boots rattled over the edge.

She also worried about the Randir. Shade seemed to have pulled herself together, but her face still twitched grotesquely as memories of those whom she had slain distorted it.

Jame wondered if she could have done the same, granting such dire mercy. True, people often died around her, but she seldom killed them, even in a berserker rage. It was more as if she created a climate in which death was prone to occur. How much worse would it be if she became That-Which-Destroys? Who would be safe from her then?

The earth belched and coughed up a fiery plume. The mass of molten rock was still far down, but rising, and the surrounding walls shook with its approach. Judging by the number of calderas within calderas at Urakarn, Jame guessed that such volcanic activity happened there relatively often. This, however, seemed like something special.

With a sharp crack, the path fragmented under her feet. She threw herself forward to claw at what remained, her frantic nails finding cracks, involuntarily widening them. Jorin squawked as Shade thrust him aside. Her hands closed over Jame's wrists. For a moment, Jame thought that all three of them would go over the edge—no, all four since Addy still clung to her neck. The serpent slithered up her arm onto Shade's, then higher still around the Randir's shoulders. Jame had the distinct impression that Addy didn't care if she fell or not, but Shade hung on. The changer's shape altered to that of a short, burly Kendar, spreading from her hands up. With a sudden jerk, she hauled Jame to safety.

"That's the first time..." she gasped, collapsing back into her own form, "that I've been able...to use...someone else's strength."

"Interesting."

Jame looked back the way they had come. The path had fallen into the abyss for more than a hundred feet. Let the Karnids try to scurry home now.

They kept going, leaving the glow below behind. The lichen regained enough of its fluorescence to light their way dimly, and there was no sign of feral trocks. How far did each step take them? A mile? Ten? A hundred? Perhaps an hour passed until at last they came to the spiral stair that led up toward the top of the Escarpment.

Light filtered down the steps. Was the lid off above? No. Here was a new hole in the wall at the level of the Undercliff. Jame peered out of it and gave a low whistle of surprise. An Overcliff tower had fallen through the roof into the Undercliff's largest cave causing landslides, fallen stalactites, and damage to the walls due to the concussion.

Obviously, things in Kothifir had gotten a lot worse.

From somewhere came the shrill cries of children.

Jame and Shade clambered down a rubble slide to the cave's floor. The fallen tower's debris reached nearly from wall to wall, on top of which perched its roofed upper story incongruously intact, like a hat. They edged around it.

On the far side, water spilled across the floor, running from the back of the cavern, where some branch of the Amar had been breached, to the front, where it spilled out of the cave's mouth. It seemed barely deep enough to wet boot leather, but Jame stopped Shade before she could step into it.

"Look."

One couldn't make out much due to the poor light, but in the middle of the flood a long, serrated line broke the surface, moving in a sinuous ripple that cut the flowing water. Something seemed to lurk beneath it, impossibly big for so shallow a depth.

"I've seen such a thing before," said Jame. "A leviathan in a puddle. Then, it was a dead god."

"That's not all that's dead."

Shade gestured downstream. Black-robed bodies sprawled in the shallow water, or at least parts of them did. Their blood darkened the flood.

"I think this is an Old Pantheon water god," Jame said, "probably the one that walks on baby feet. Listen."

They heard the children's voices again, coming from the other side of the water, echoing flatly as if within some close-set place.

"We've got to cross," said Jame. "No, not you, Jorin. Stay. Shade, you'd better go first. This is likely to rile it."

Shade gave her a sharp, sidelong look, then took a deep breath and backed up. The stream was about twenty feet wide, split down the middle by that shifting spine. She took a running start and jumped. Her foot came down on the monster's back between notches. She launched herself off of it and made the far shore.

WHOMP.

The creature's head jerked up in a spray of water, toothy jaws agape, baby hands flailing. Jame leaped to its back. Slimy scales shifted under her feet, nearly throwing her off, but she managed to lurch to the far side where Shade caught her.

THOMP.

It settled back into the water grumbling, only its nostrils above the surface, its tail atwitch.

The voices echoed out of the entrance to a maze of side caves. More luck than skill led them down the right branch into a cavern shaped like an amphitheater. Fang's urchins scuttled around its upper galleries, pelting a black-robed figure below with rocks. He in turn swung a long sword wildly, trying to bat the missiles away. Fang herself stood guard at the narrow mouth of a side cave. The man rushed at her. She ducked back as he swung his sword. It hit the stone lintel and almost jumped out of his hands with the shock. Before he could recover, Fang stepped in and knifed him under the ribs. He fell. The children cheered. Fang wiped her blade on his robe, then saw the newcomers.

"About time you showed up," she said to Jame. "This is the third we've killed in the Undercliff so far, not counting the ones that the Guardian of the Ford has claimed."

Jame prodded the fallen man, who was obviously a Karnid.

"What are they after?"

"Come and see."

She stepped back into the side cave. It was fairly comfortable as such things go, lit by glowing chunks of diamantine, its floor covered with rugs and furs. The former Lord Merchandy lay on a pallet by the far wall, unconscious, breathing with a harsh rattle. Dani, formerly Lady Professionate, sat beside him, holding his hand. She looked up, her eyes wide with fear.

"Are we safe?"

"For the moment," said Fang, sheathing her knife. "It would be better if we shifted you farther back into the caves, though."

"He can't be moved. I think he's dying. Oh, why did Mother Vedia have to go Overcliff?"

Then she saw Jame. "At last!"

Jame wondered why everyone was so glad to see her. What did they expect her to do? For that matter, what was going on?

"I told you," said Shade, reading her expression. "The city is infested with Karnids and has been for months. Come the rising, which I guess is tonight, their mission is to kill every former guild lord and grandmaster who doesn't support Prince Ton."

"Why would they do that for a Kothifiran?"

"Ton is a Karnid sympathizer, or so he tells them. If the Karnids can make him king, their prophet hopes to gain indirect control of the Southern Host."

Jame stared at her. "Now you tell me?"

Shade shrugged. "When has there been time?"

"But surely this means that King Krothen is in danger too, more so than anyone else."

"We hear," said Fang, "that Prince Ton is holding him prisoner at the top of his Rose Tower. All of his Kencyr guards are outside the city walls on the clifftop plain. Gemma has finally sent an army against us."

Jame remembered how raiders from that rival city had plagued Kothifir even before the Change had weakened it. Just the same...

"Why now?" she asked, helplessly.

Fang shrugged. "The rumor in the city is that Ton has promised Gemma the treasure towers if it attacks at the same time as his palace coup. More likely, though, that's a lie, and it's his mother Princess Amantine who's behind all this maneuvering."

Jame stood for a moment, fitting all of this together in her mind, deciding what to do next.

"I have business Overcliff," she said. "Will you be all right here?"

Fang grinned, her filed teeth flashing. "We'll manage."

Without the need for immediate action, Shade had sagged against a wall, hands over her face. Between her fingers, her features twitched and changed. "I'm no good to you like this," she said in a distorted voice. "Go on without me."

"Walk wary," Fang called after Jame. "All the Old Gods except for the Guardian went up into the city last night to protect it from the Karnids. You may meet some of them coming back."

II

JAME FOUND JORIN on the near side of the stream, anxiously waiting for her with pricked ears and wide, moon-opal eyes. He had apparently crossed by jumping from Karnid body to dismembered body, as she probably should have done herself rather than risk the Guardian's maw. They returned by this route to the west bank and climbed up the regular stair that debouched on a back street, the same shaft down which Hangnail had pushed Jame so long ago. Luckily its lid was still off, maybe permanently so in order to accommodate those who depended on this route to the Undercliff.

By the time they reached the Overcliff, the eastern sky was faintly aglow with the harbinger of dawn and the moon had set.

To the right, Jame could see the gaping hole through which the tower had fallen, surrounded by leaning buildings. Some swayed, creaking, and dropped stones into the pit. Others settled, crunching, on their broken foundations. The sooner Kothifir got back its god-king, the better.

They made their way toward the former site of the Kencyr temple. The towers Jame passed were dark and quiet, their windows shuttered. Threatened both by the army outside its gates and by the enemy within, the citizens were hiding. From somewhere in the distance, though, came shouts and an occasional crash. The Karnids wouldn't be so noisy, nor probably the Old Pantheon gods. Who else was abroad tonight?

Here was the place where she had last met Dorin, son of Denek, son of Dinnit Dun-eyed, next to the broken foundation of the tower that had contained the Kencyr temple. Rubble still loomed dark in the predawn light. However long she had been gone, no one had yet done anything about it.

Jorin pressed against her leg, growling. Three dark figures had emerged from the shadows and were silently approaching. Karnids, for certain. Jame might have run, but she had unfinished business here. She slid into fighting stance. Then someone stepped between her and the advancing men.

"Don't look," said the Earth Wife's red-haired Favorite to Jame over his shoulder. Then he spread wide his coat.

A blinding flood of light emerged, fiercer than it had been for his predecessor when he had appeared as the sun at the summer solstice. It painted the inside of Jame's eyelids crimson as she turned her face away and shielded it. She heard the Karnids cry out and smelled something burning. They stumbled away, their faces seared, their eyes, burst, streaming down into their beards.

The Favorite closed his coat and buckled it, although light still shone through the seams. He turned back to Jame. "What are you doing here?"

"I have something to return."

She drew the miniature temple out of her pocket, where its sharp edges had been bruising her hip all night, and carefully placed it on the road near the entrance to the step-forward tunnel. Tiny, outraged voices piped up inside it. It pulsed and grew, making Jame and the Favorite hastily retreat, but stopped when it was only three feet high. One side opened like a door and a crumpled figure forced its way out. The high priest straightened up and shook out his robes.

"Well?" he demanded, blind eyes fiercely aglare. "Are you quite done shaking us around like dice in a box? Answer me, whoever you are!"

"Will the temple keep growing?"

"In its own good time. I know your voice. You're that wretched girl who calls herself the Talisman. Where is my grandson Dorin?"

How best to answer that?

"I'm afraid," said Jame carefully, "that he died trying to save you from the Karnids."

"What, here? Oh, never mind. Somehow, you're to blame. Ishtier warned us that you were trouble, and he was right."

He reached out to grab her, but she dodged away. His clawlike hands flexed, trying to pull in the power with which to strike her, but the temple was still too small.

"Later," he panted. "Now, go away!"

"What an unpleasant old man," remarked the Favorite as they left, not quite at a run.

"You understood him?" The priest had been speaking in Kens.

"No, but ill will translates itself."

"What's going on in the city?"

"We are hunting, as you see."

They paused to let a swarm of frogs hop past in formation: "GEEP, *geep*, geep..."

"But there are fewer Karnids than we expected. Meanwhile, Master Needham and his followers are storming the treasure towers, but I think they will hold. Then there are Prince Ton's bully boys, defending the Rose Tower against the Armorers' Guild."

"King Krothen is still there?"

"At the top, with Prince Ton and Princess Amantine. Ton wants his uncle to abdicate. He's afraid, if he commits regicide, that the white won't come to him. They've been at Krothen all night. The king must be tougher than he looks."

He paused and gave her a sidelong glance. "I'm right, aren't I? You were once a Favorite."

"How d'you know that?"

"Odd thoughts come to me, since I won the red. So tell me: how did you manage all of those women? They line up outside my door every night. I hardly get any sleep at all."

⟨⟨⟨⟨ III ⟩⟩⟩⟩

AFTERWARD, trotting through the streets with Jorin at her side, Jame decided that the Favorite hadn't really believed her tale of the Four as worshipped by the Merikit. He seemed to think she had some as yet undisclosed secret that would make his own life more bearable. In that, she was sorry to disappoint him. It occurred to her that she had been lucky in her own experiences. That in turn made her wonder, yet again, how her growing family in the hills was doing.

She also thought about what the Favorite had said regarding the Karnids in Kothifir, that there were fewer of them than he had expected. When she had left Urakarn—Trinity, had that only been a few hours ago?—it had seemed to be deserted. If its residents hadn't used the step-forward tunnel to flood Kothifir, where were they?

To the northeast, firelight bloomed out of the streets accompanied by distant shouts. Master Needham was trying to breach the treasure towers with flame. Jame had seen them. They had no lower windows, iron doors, and granite walls. All in all, they hardly required guards. Needham's chances of sacking the treasuries without inside help didn't look good.

She stopped on the edge of the central plaza. There was the Rose Tower, twisting up into the sky like an inverted tornado. Its outer spiral stair swarmed. A handful of Prince Ton's militia held the top of the steps. Jame recognized the bully whose head she had set on fire before Paper Crown's tower. Half the Armorers' Guild assaulted from below, led by Gaudaric and Ruso. The militia had made a barrier of furniture at the level of Krothen's apartment that functioned like a cork. Despite superior arms, armor, and numbers, Krothen's would-be rescuers were making little progress.

Black-clad figures slipped out of the mouths of surrounding streets, intent on taking the attackers from behind. As Jame drew breath to shout a warning, however, a gray form materialized in front of the foremost Karnid. Smoke issued from its hooded cloak. It spread wide its arms and enveloped the oncoming man. The cloak momentarily bulged with its thrashing prey and then dissolved into a sooty cloud. A second later it rose again behind another Karnid who, in swerving to avoid the greasy spot on the paving where his mate had disappeared, ran full into its arms.

Poof, poof, poof...

Then it reared up before Jame.

There was no face within the hood, only churning ash, and it stank of charred flesh.

"Burnt Man..." she gasped.

But guilt and grief choked her. Never mind that she seldom killed; how many had died because of her? Faces swirled in the ashen flakes: Dally, Theocandi, Vant, Bane...

"Father!"

Child of Darkness, where is my sword? Where are my...

He had meant to say "my fingers," for they had broken off when she had pried Kin-Slayer out of them, and she had carried away one of them with his signet ring still on it—all for Tori, who hadn't known what to do with either.

Accept my judgment. That was the voice of the blind Arrinken who called himself the Dark Judge, whose precinct was the Riverland. *You know your guilt.*

...yes...

"No."

A hand grabbed her by the collar and jerked her back. Jame landed on her butt, shocked to feel real pain.

Brier Iron-thorn stood between her and the hooded figure who might or might not be the Burnt Man. It coughed in her face. The image swirled on its breath of a stern-faced woman who looked much like Brier herself.

...*my daughter*...

"No," said Brier. "I was a child when you died, not to blame for your death, nor would you want me to feel that I was. Go away."

The gray form writhed within its cloak as if trying to strike out, but the Kendar faced it down, glowering. With a groan, it melted into the pavement.

Brier turned to Jame.

"I had a feeling that you were back," she said gruffly. "D'you know that you've been gone twenty days?"

Jame got gingerly to her feet. "I thought as much, if not worse. For me, it was yesterday."

"Huh."

"Anyway, why aren't you with the Host outside the walls?"

"No cadet is." The Kendar glanced to the west. The growing glow of the eastern dawn tinged her red hair with smoldering accents. "Only so many could take the lifts Overcliff in time for the general engagement, which happened last night. As far as I can make out, the Gemmans arrived at dusk yesterday and settled into camp for a dawn offensive. They didn't reckon with our ability to see in the dark, which it wasn't anyway with a nearly full moon. The rest of us stayed in camp to defend it, don't ask me against what. The last I heard, the Host was still sweeping the last of the Gemmans back."

So much, then, for one foreign threat.

Jame looked across the plaza to the struggling figures on the stair, who had so conveniently been left to strive on their own, without Kencyr intervention.

"Krothen is in trouble," she said. "We need to help him."

"How?"

Jame paused to think. "Everyone is focused on the outer stair, but there must be a way up through the interior."

They circled the tower. At its foot stood a gleaming mechanical dog the size of a small pony. Ruso had been busy. Two apprentices were struggling to wind up the metallic beast with a thin iron rod thrust through the bow of a key set between its shoulder blades. With each jerk, its head rose a notch and flanges twitched lips back from iron teeth.

Beyond that, they found a side portal that opened into the servant quarters. These were deserted, everyone either apparently having run away or been driven out. There was indeed an internal stair, spiraling up the center of the tower's shaft. They climbed, all the time hearing the muffled shouts of battle outside the walls. Past guard rooms, kitchens, offices, the chambers of royal ladies....

Here was Krothen's apartment, once so elegant, now ransacked to provide material for the barrier raised on the landing outside its door where Ton's militia swarmed. The inner stair went no further.

Someone was sobbing. Jame circled the ruins of a massive bed and found Lady Cella crouched on the floor in the crimson pool of her skirts, cradling the body of her handsome boy toy. His head lolled over her arm, a swathe of golden hair hanging over his eyes. Someone had broken his neck.

"He tried to defend my cousin Krothen," she wailed. Tears had soaked her veil so that it clung unflatteringly to her nearly chinless, middle-aged face. "Oh, I should have taken him away before Prince Ton's bullies burst in! Ton never understood about us and, when he was dead, Princess Amantine only laughed. Gods damn her!"

"I'm sorry," said Jame. What else could one say? "How do I get to the top?"

Cella gulped, trying to compose herself. "Krothen's dais rises and falls. Right now, it's stuck in the throne room."

Outside, someone shouted a warning. Jame heard the scrabble of steel claws on the stair, circling the tower. Rotating, she followed the silver body as it surged up the steps. Gaudaric's men hastily made way for it. The mechanical hound slammed into the barricade raised by Ton's followers and shattered it. Debris hurtled into the room and out over the balustrade, likewise most of the militia. Cella screamed. Then someone caught the dog in midstride, off balance, and tipped it sideways. It hit the railing and bumped along it from baluster to baluster, legs churning, until stone gave way. The metal dog flew out into space and down, to a cry of protest from Ruso.

"No," said Brier, as if echoing him, but her attention was fixed on the one who had destroyed his creation. "Amberley."

She stepped out onto the stair to confront her former lover. "Why?" she asked.

Amberley tossed back honey-gold hair and smiled at her. "Sweet, sweet Brier Rose. You always have to be right, don't you?"

"Have I said that?"

"Not in so many words, but I watch rather than listen."

She began to circle the other Kendar, who stood rigid on the landing. Her fingers slid under Brier's hair to caress the nape of her neck. Auburn hair rippled at her touch. Brier shivered.

"Was it your fault, though? The Knorth tempted you, and you fell, like your mother before you."

"Rose Iron-thorn never swore to the Knorth."

"She might as well have, after what happened at Urakarn and in the Wastes." Amberley flicked Brier's hair and stepped away. "Lord Caineron never forgave her for that, or you, by extension. It was clear enough that he meant to break you to his service. That's why I didn't want you to go to Restormir to become a cadet. And I was right, wasn't I?"

"About Lord Caineron, yes."

"So you came back to me, until the Knorth lordling whistled you away. Well, what if I told you that there was a stronger lord than Torisen? And no, I don't mean Caldane. I met him, the Master of us all. He came to me in the mountains when I was on patrol. My horse spooked at his shadow and threw me among the rocks. When I looked up, there he was, and there was no gainsaying his power."

"You mean Gerridon," said Brier evenly.

Jame was surprised. Few Kencyr thought about the Master of Knorth anymore, as if he were lost in the mists that confused history and legend. That was one of his strengths.

"Who else?" Amberley's white teeth flashed again in her sun-darkened face. "The Karnids may call him their prophet, but we know who he is, and what he will become."

"And what is that?"

"Why, our Master again, as he was always meant to be."

"Have you encountered Torisen since he became Highlord?"

"No. Why?"

"Then you don't know his true strength."

Amberley's smile became a grimace. "As I said, you always have to be right, and now you are bound to that freak whom he has named his lordan. Oh, Brier, Brier."

The Southron took a step forward and Amberley, despite herself, took a step back. Her foot struck the first step of the final flight.

"What do you know of so ancient a bloodline and of its last descendents? It was you who told the Karnids the lordan would be on wide patrol the day she was nearly kidnapped, wasn't it? And I suppose you arranged for that note to be slipped under her door in the first place."

"Yes, of course."

"Will you stand aside?"

"What do you think?"

They drew back into fighting position, Amberley mounting the stair to gain the higher ground. Gaudaric's forces watched from below. Ton's above were too scattered and shaken to care.

Jame shook her attention away from the members of the militia lying groaning on the apartment floor. She crossed to the opposite eastern side of the tower, dodging through wreck-age, and leaned out a window. Above her was the ring of stone thorns from which the Gemman raiders had hung. She jumped and caught one. It began to give way. Hastily, she swung a leg up over it and scrambled onto the walk that circled the marble rose petals of the dome. Voices rose within.

"Abdicate," Prince Ton was pleading. He sounded exhausted and near tears, his adolescent voice cracking. "Even now, physicians may save you!"

Princess Amantine's deep voice answered him with a scornful snort: "Pull yourself together, boy. You know that there can be only one god-king."

Krothen laughed, choked, and laughed again. "That may not be you, cousin . . . whatever happens to me . . . especially if it be . . . at your hands." He paused, wheezing. "Only you and I . . . are left . . . among the male heirs of our house. Who comes next? Your mother?"

Jame slipped between the stone petals, emerging behind Krothen's massive bulk as it slumped on the dais. Bending to peer under his arm, she saw Amantine draw herself up to her full if negligible height, her court gown rising to reveal shoes with improbably high heels. Ton hovered at her elbow like an overstuffed bolster, in sweat-stained, premature white with bedraggled pink trim.

"Would it be such a disaster if I came to rule?" demanded the princess. "I have more courage and skill than either you or my son."

"Mother . . ."

"Face the truth, boy. Where would you be without me? Even if the white should truly come to you, you need my guidance."

"Your Magnificence," Jame whispered to Krothen under cover of the growing familial ruckus. "How can I help?"

He laughed again, ending with a wet, racking cough. "You see Life on my right hand . . . Death on my left."

In the filtered, predawn light, Jame made out Mother Vedia's plump form wreathed with restless snakes to one side of Krothen and the crone with a box to the other. The box was open. The crone raised a skinny finger to chapped lips.

"Only the god-touched can see us," whispered Mother Vedia.

Jame could hear the muffled sound of Brier and Amberley battling on the stair. At a guess, they were moving upward. She wondered briefly which form of combat, Kencyr or Kothifiran, they were using. Did one favor unequal ground over the other?

A sudden glow of light came through the stone petals behind her and began to climb Krothen's back. Sunrise. To the north of the chamber, it slanted in through the gap where a petal had broken off during the earthquake when Jame had last been here.

Krothen groaned.

Jame circled him. The princess was trying to shake the much heavier prince, only succeeding in shaking herself, but Jame ignored them both. Krothen exhaled with a rattle, and his eyes rolled up in their sockets. Then he was still.

The crone closed her box and faded away.

From outside at a distance came the crash of falling towers. Jame wondered if the treasuries had been taken, but the sound came from the wrong direction.

"That's your temple," said Mother Vedia. "It's coming to life again, knocking over its neighbors. Where did you place it, anyway?"

Jame thought that she could feel the return of power, when she extended her sixth sense. She certainly felt the high priest's rage; somehow, he had learned of his grandson's fate, if not necessarily of its circumstances.

"Quick now!" hissed Mother Vedia. "Help him!"

"Who?" Jame stared, helpless, at the edifice of inert flesh before her. "How?"

Krothen sat there with mouth agape and blank eyes. His exposed flesh had taken on the waxy translucence of marble. When she touched the folds of his robe, they were hard, and cold, and she could see the shadow of her fingers through them.

The chamber's doors burst open. Amberley skidded into the room, propelled backward by Brier's attack. Ton and Amantine scuttled out of the way, clinging to each other. Brier followed her lover's retreat.

"It doesn't have to be this way," she said.

Amberley laughed breathlessly and drew a hand across her mouth, smearing blood from a split lip. "I always said that you were good. Would I have settled for anything less?"

Gaudaric and Ruso appeared in the doorway. The latter's red hair and beard, which had hung limp during the Change, now bristled with energy and sparked at the tips. "I can't believe it," he was saying, excitedly waving his once-too-heavy axe as if it were made of balsa, making Gaudaric duck. "I'm Lord Artifice again!"

Amberley backed toward the gap in the stone petals, into the slanting stream of morning light. Her hair glowed like a golden crown. Bloody face notwithstanding, she looked magnificent.

"You have the advantage here," she said. "I see that. Another time, then."

"Amb—"

"No." She stepped over the broken marble stub onto the outer walk. "Where I am going, death cannot follow, nor can you. Good-bye, sweet Brier Rose."

With that, she took another step out into space and was gone.

Brier had taken a hasty stride after her but now halted, staring at the vacant slice of sky beyond the dome. Then she turned to Jame with a blank face and stricken eyes.

"What did she mean?"

"About death? The Karnids claim to have conquered it. From what I've seen, though, I doubt it."

She also wondered if Amberley had counted on landing some twenty feet below on the spiral stair, not realizing that on the north side of the Rose Tower, due to the twist in its construction, the drop was sheer.

"Brier." She tugged on the Kendar's sleeve, trying to reclaim her dazed attention. "I need your help. Gaudaric, M'lord Artifice, yours as well."

The latter two approached Krothen's motionless hulk.

"Is he dead?" asked Ruso, staring.

Gaudaric touched the marmoreal vestments and jerked his hand back, as if cold could burn.

A faint sound escaped from between those parted, rosebud lips: "...help..."

"Kroaky!" said Jame. "He's still inside! Mother Vedia, how do we save him?"

Gaudaric started, having apparently just seen the Old Pantheon goddess standing in Krothen's shadow. So his god-given status as guild master had also returned.

"I don't know!" wailed Vedia, wringing her hands in agitation while her snakes tried to wring each other's necks. "Just get him out!"

"This looks like a job for a mason," said Gaudaric. "What we need is a chisel and a mallet."

"No time for that." Jame looked around frantically for something to use. How much air did Kroaky have? "We've got to smash our way in."

Princess Amantine pushed past her to stand in the way. "Sacrilege!" she boomed. "This is my nephew's sepulcher. I forbid you to desecrate it!"

Ruso picked her up and put her, sputtering, aside. Prince Ton attacked him with a flurry of plump fists.

"How dare you lay hands on my mother!"

"Not now, sonny. King Krothen is dead, but the white hasn't come to you, has it? So stand aside."

He turned back to the petrified former monarch.

"A sculptor once told me that marble is softer when first quarried than later," he said, and tapped the figure's distended belly with his axe. The translucent marble robe covering it shattered like thin ice over a pond. Beneath was dimpled, marble skin apparently drawn over billows of former flesh.

"Go on," said Gaudaric, leaning in to watch.

Another harder blow near the deep navel cracked the surface. It gave way. They stared at the next layer, which resembled tightly packed pebbles.

"I think this was fat," said Jame, and poked it with a finger.

Her touch broke the surface tension. They jumped back as a landslide of stones crashed down to rattle and bounce on the floor. More and more fell, hundreds of pounds' worth. Was the entire abdomen emptying? No. As the dust cleared, inside they could see the petrified organs: loops of frozen intestines, an enlarged liver, but most of all the stomach, which filled most of the enormous cavity. From within this last came a faint scratching.

Ruso scrambled back through the sliding, shifting pile of pebbles. He took careful aim, but as he swung his axe, stones rolled under his feet and he nearly fell.

"Again, again!" said Mother Vedia, clasping her hands in an ecstasy of agitation.

Ruso grunted and regained his stance. This time he used the butt end of his weapon to rap on the distended organ, lightly at first, then harder and harder. Cracks laced its surface. Then it disintegrated and a body spilled out.

"Kroaky!" said Jame, and rushed to help.

Krothen's younger, thinner self sprawled on the pile of rocks, gasping for breath. He was coated with dust but otherwise naked. Also, he appeared to be choking.

Mother Vedia waded to his side and gave him a firm slap on the back. He exhaled a cloud of dust, then began to breathe more naturally. His eyes opened.

"Well," he said, gasping, "here I am...again."

Gaudaric regarded him dubiously. "So we see. And yes, I remember you from some fifteen years back. Where have you been?"

Kroaky laughed and drew a shaky hand across his face. Dirt and dust smeared. "Most recently, being introspective. Before that, having fun."

He looked back at the former shell of himself and sighed. "I suppose those days are over now. No more frolicking anonymously in the Undercliff. Well, I've had a good run."

Amantine and Ton had been edging closer, eyes round.

"I don't believe it," said the princess. "You can't be he. This is a trick to deprive my son of his rights."

"On the contrary," said Kroaky, not unkindly, "I hereby name him my heir apparent, unless I should have children of my own. What do you think?" he appealed to Jame. "Will Fang marry me?"

"Queen Fang." Jame tasted the words. "I like it."

"Well, I don't." Princess Amantine drew herself up, ruffled as a disturbed partridge. "I will fight this. No one will believe it anyway. Ton, come!"

She trotted to the door in her high heels, only noticing when she reached it that her son had not followed.

The prince looked at Kroaky askance, sheepishly. "Er...peace?"

"Ton-ton!" bellowed his mother.

"Mother, I'm sorry, but this has gone much too far already. Besides, I'm tired of fighting."

She opened her mouth, closed it, opened it again. Her eyes were bulging. "You...you little ingrate!"

With that, she turned and stormed down the stairs. They heard her startled exclamation when she reached the level of Krothen's apartment, then a scream, suddenly cut short. Gaudaric went to investigate.

"Lady Cella was waiting for her below," he reported back. "She tackled Princess Amantine and they both fell through the broken rail, off the tower."

Ton uttered an indistinct cry and plunged toward the door. There he got stuck before turning to edge through sideways. They heard him thunder down the steps.

"For what it's worth," said Jame, "the tower overhangs the stair at that point. Still, it's a significant drop."

CHAPTER XXIII
The Feast of Fools

I

AS IT HAPPENED, Princess Amantine survived the fall, if with sundry broken bones. The unhappy Lady Cella did not.

Jame, Brier, and Jorin left Kroaky thrashing out with Master Iron Gauntlet and Lord Artifice how he was to present his transformed self to the city. There would, Jame supposed, be problems. However, no one could deny in the end that, for all his pimples, the lanky young man was indeed Kothifir's god-king, reborn.

With dawn and the end of the Change, the city was astir. Doors and windows opened. People scurried about in the streets and gathered at corners, eager for the latest news. Who were the new grandmasters and the new guild lords? What was this about Krothen's dramatic return? Jame heard, in passing, that Mercer was again Lord Merchandy and Shandanielle, Lady Professionate. She wondered if Mercer was still deathly ill. Dani had said that immortality was a burden to him, but apparently he had again set aside his poor health to serve his city.

They met Needham's disgruntled troops filtering back from their failed siege of the treasure towers. Needham, it appeared, had not regained his position as Master Silk Purse. Some reported that they had left him hammering bloody fists against the treasury's iron door and sobbing.

There was no sign yet of the Southern Host's return to the city. Presumably it was still out on the plain, chasing Kothifir's would-be invaders back to Gemma.

In contrast to the noisy streets, Jame and Brier walked together in silence. The Kendar had barely spoken since Amberley's death. Jame glanced more than once at her emotionless face, but didn't know what to say. The bond between them told her nothing. As a Caineron, Brier had clearly learned to hide her feelings. Jame had supposed that she would go to find Amberley's body, but she hadn't. Someone else would have to retrieve it for the pyre.

As for Jame, she didn't quite know what to do with herself. Walking through the city with Jorin trotting at her side, she felt disconnected from the streets' excited bustle. She had had a role to play here, but now, with the king's return, it seemed to be over. It occurred to her that she should say something to someone about the possibility of mining diamantine from the deeper caves to replace the lost silk trade. The city didn't seem to realize that the stone was valuable. But that was a minor thing. Kothifir would go its own way now, into whatever the future brought.

Would her own people welcome her back, though, after so long an unauthorized absence? Before that, she had turned command of the barracks over to Ran Onyx-eyed and missed many days of lessons—not behavior expected of a leader-in-training.

Face it, she thought disconsolately. *You would rather act alone, and that's where events keep taking you. Were you ever meant to be a randon at all?*

"Leave and never return," the note shoved under her door had said during the season of challenges.

Others had no doubt that she didn't belong and never had.

Here was the Optomancers' Tower, a thin, crooked structure thrusting up into the growing clouds like a gnarled finger raised to stir the sky. On impulse, Jame climbed its outer stair, followed by Brier and Jorin. Near the top, she was almost bowled over by the gangly young man with the enormous glasses who had showed her and Byrne the Eye of Kothifir at the end of summer.

"Whoops," he said, grabbing the rail to steady himself. "I wasn't expecting visitors. Is it true what they say about King Krothen?"

"I expect so, depending on what they say."

His eyes, greatly magnified, blinked at her through thick lenses. "It's a great day, then, but life goes on. What can I do for you?"

"I'd like a glimpse of the city and its environs. To gain perspective."

"Come along, then."

He led them up to the Eye and threw open its door. When he closed it, complete darkness again fell within. They heard him stumble around the room, muttering to himself, then a shutter creaked open and blinding light fell in a circle on the floor. Jame blinked watering eyes and tried to focus. The image was of the upper plain. Perhaps the caretaker of the Eye had been keeping track of the battle there, of such concern to the entire city. As she had guessed, the Gemmans were in flight, with their war lizards mounting a rearguard defense. The Host, mostly on foot, surrounded each of these giant reptiles in turn and pulled it down, then moved on to the next. As Jame watched, the Gemman line broke and fled.

"So much for that," said the caretaker's voice from the shadows, with unmistakable relief. "Where next?"

"The Rose Tower."

The lens of the Eye rotated, groaning.

There stood King Kroaky, Lord Artifice, and Grandmaster Gaudaric on the lowest turn of the spiral stair, a sea of upturned faces beneath them. Mouths opened in unheard cheers, which grew as Mother Vedia descended to join the royal party. Perhaps now the Old Pantheon would be welcome Overcliff once more. Certainly, Kroaky owed this goddess for serving as midwife to his peculiar rebirth. Below, the crowd parted. Jame glimpsed Dani's blond head and Mercer's white one. The healer was supporting the merchant, who raised a weak hand to return the city's applause. Citizens lifted them up and carried them to join the company on the stair. All seemed to be well there.

"Where next?" asked the caretaker again.

"Show me the Host's camp."

The lens shifted to point, dizzyingly, down the Escarpment to the stone barracks at its foot. These seemed unusually quiet, even for so early an hour. Only the cadets were there, Jame remembered, as well as a skeleton staff of randon. How they must regret missing the fight above. Char and the other Knorth third-years were probably grinding their teeth, her own second-year ten-command as well. For herself, she had seen battle and its attendant horrors at the Cataracts, enough bloodshed to sate her for a lifetime.

She was about to turn away when the lens swung yet again, perhaps reverting to its set point.

"Wait. What was that?"

"What? Where?"

"Westward, up the valley."

"I didn't see...oh."

The Eye had caught a teeming blur moving down the Betwixt, filling the valley between the Escarpment and the Apollyne mountains. The lens tightened its focus. The mass became horsemen, headed toward the camp which lay some ten miles ahead of them.

Brier leaned in, staring. Her head cast a shadow over the scene and she withdrew with a frown.

"Has Gemma launched a second attack to the rear?"

Jame had thought so too at first. Then she had seen that all of these riders wore black, and the front rank rode black horses. Thorns?

She remembered Urakarn, apparently deserted. Where had its inhabitants gone, given that they couldn't take their mounts anywhere by the step-forward path? It would, on the other hand, have taken them about this long to arrive overland by the Betwixt Valley. It was potentially the Urakarn massacre in reverse. The Karnids were coming.

On the point of turning away, she glimpsed another rider out in front of the thorns. His mount, steel gray, fought against its bit. Even the thorns edged away from it.

Memory caught Jame by the throat: The stallion surged up over the hillcrest with nostrils flaring red. Its steel hooves nearly clipped her as it roared over her head. It landed and turned, torn grass shrieking underfoot. Its iron teeth were bared, its eyes rolled white and dead...

The changer Keral, jeering at her: *"We can always feed you to his new war-horse."*

It couldn't be...could it?

"What?" the caretaker demanded as she turned from the bright image and floundered through the darkness in search of the door.

Jorin squawked as she tripped over him. Glass shattered. Here at last was the way out, the door smashing open to admit a wash of early morning light across the floor.

Jame scrambled down the steps with the ounce on her heels, still protesting, and Brier Iron-thorn bringing up the rear. Here was the street, leading to other streets crowded with people celebrating the end of the Change and, incidentally, the Feast of Fools, that day between winter and spring that is recorded on no calendar. Usually, it was a festival of misrule, when powers secular and religious were set aside. How ironic that this year it marked the return of the king and the gods, both old and new. Whispers had grown to whoops and shouts, timorous groups to an excited mob.

"Dance with us!" cried a plump matron in a nightgown bedecked with fluttering ribbons.

She grabbed Jame's hand. Jame in turn grabbed Brier's. Thus they were pulled into one of many chains of celebrants that snaked back and forth down through the city's byways, between the legs of stilt walkers, around men wearing the giant heads of gods. Jorin wound about the pounding feet to keep up, chirping in agitation and occasionally squalling when someone stepped on his toes. This was not his idea of fun. The chain broke and re-formed. Now Jame was holding hands with a baker, whose every step raised clouds of flour from his clothing. She freed herself while maintaining her grip on Brier. They plunged into another group who were tossing one of their number in a blanket. Their victim flew free in a mill of limbs. Brier caught him.

"Wheee!" he said breathlessly, laughing, as she set him down. It was Byrne.

"Your father is at the Rose Tower," Jame told him.

"Let him find his own blanket!"

With that, he plunged back into the crowd.

Another turn brought Jame face-to-face with the spy Hangnail, who looked terrified at having been hauled out into the open.

"Who's your new grandmaster?" she asked him.

"That gray sneak again, gods damn it."

"See that you honor him, or I'll come back to haunt you."

Hangnail gave her a look compounded of incredulity and horror. Then the dance whirled him away.

They reached the main avenue where shopkeepers had set out their wares with the dawn. Cabbages and rutabagas now flew over the crowd, kicked from the sidelines. Jame ducked a flailing bunch of carrots. An onion hit Brier in the face. They broke away near the boulevard's end and headed across the paved forecourt toward the lift cages. Of these, only one was at the top. However, its attendants had left their post to join in the general rejoicing.

"Wonderful," said Jame. "How do we get down?"

"We could use the stairs, or you could take the lift. I can use the brake to regulate your descent—I think—and let gravity do the rest. It will be a bumpy ride, though."

"And you?"

"Someone has to warn Harn Grip-hard."

Jame looked at the cage and gulped. Three thousand feet down....

"All right," she said, and stepped into it, followed by the ounce.

Brier fumbled for a minute with the winch and crane, then used them to lift the cage up and out over the balustrade. She released the brake. The cage fell in a rush that left both girl and cat hovering in midair. Then the floor leaped up at them, nearly making their legs buckle. Down it plunged again, again stopping with a jerk as the brake reengaged. By such fits and starts they descended, falling the last ten feet for an abrupt and noisy arrival.

Jame staggered out of the cage.

"All right, kitten," she said to the distraught ounce, trying to catch her breath. "All right."

She stumbled through the north gate and the tunnel that led under the official offices, then across the inner ward. The Knorth barracks had a gate that opened onto the ward, but it was sealed for repairs. Jame plunged into the streets that separated the various houses. Early rising cadets turned to stare at her as she passed.

"Returned at last, have you?" Fash called from the Caineron's eastern door. "What makes you think that we want you back?"

Onyx-eyed's second-in-command, Ran Spare, met her as she entered the Knorth by its western gate.

"Where have you been?" he demanded.

"I had business elsewhere." Jame paused, trying not to pant. "Listen: the Karnids are coming!"

He stared at her. "What?"

"I saw them through the Eye of Kothifir, coming down the valley. It's all done by mirrors, you know."

"You aren't making sense."

Jame realized that he had never been exposed to the Eye. Really, Kencyr didn't know Kothifir as well as they should, given how long they had been here.

"They're coming," she said again. "My word of honor on it. Don't you believe me?"

"I have to, don't I? Either that or declare our lordan mad. How many?"

"More than I could count. Ten thousand? About ten miles out."

"We could match that, if we were all here," said Ran Spare,

thinking out loud. "As it is, there are fewer than two thousand cadets in camp. I'll sound the alarm."

He left at a run, and Jame pounded up the stairs to her apartment, where Rue met her at the door, almost limp with relief.

"Ten! Brier Iron-thorn said that you'd come back! What's going on?"

Jame told her.

"Truly?" Her eyes widened.

Then she started as the great horn outside Harn's apartment blared out over the drowsy camp. One by one, the waking compounds added their alerts, the Knorth's immediately above Jame's quarters, on the roof. Below, feet hit the floor and cadets scrambled into their clothes. Damson appeared at the door, barefoot with her shirt unlaced. Quill and Niall were behind her.

"What?" she asked, then registered Jame's presence. "I should have known."

"Just answer it," said Jame. "I'll catch up as soon as I can."

They turned and ran.

Now, where was . . . oh, there. Gaudaric had delivered the rhisar armor as he had promised, in bundles piled at the foot of her bed. Jame tore off the wrappings and arranged the pieces on her blanket over the mound formed by Jorin, who had crawled under the cover and was resolutely ignoring her.

"They're forming in the inner ward," Rue reported from the northern balcony, hanging over it to look down. "Here come the other randon in camp. Ran Spare is talking to them. Some are arguing with him—no wonder when, from what you say, we're outnumbered five to one. But as a Knorth he's senior to the others."

The horns stopped, little Coman piping to the very end and finishing with a discordant, excited bleat.

Rue turned back to the room. "What's that?"

Jame unwrapped a large, round parcel. It was, as she had suspected from its shape, a shield, made of braided rhi-sar leather laced back and forth over fire-hardened ironwood. Another package yielded up barding in the form of a quilted crupper to cover a horse's flanks. She hadn't forgotten Death's-head's last, unfortunate encounter with the fangs of the black Karnid mares. That left one bundle. Now, what was this?

"Oh," said Jame, and held up the rathorn ivory vest, which she had last seen on display in Gaudaric's showroom. Morning light glimmered off its intricate, overlapping plates, each barely two fingers wide, drilled at the top and laced to a sturdy, padded jacket. Its collar was high, its skirt long enough to cover the upper thighs and divided for riding. It shifted in her hands, its scales softly clinking. A note tumbled from its folds.

"*I could see that the gorget fretted you,*" Gaudaric had written. "*Please accept this as a gift from my family and a grateful city.*"

"It's beautiful," breathed Rue, touching it with a fingertip.

"Yes. It is. And now it has to be useful as well."

Jame regarded the armor laid out on her bed, trying to remember the arming sequence. One started at the feet.

Ran Spare's voice echoed below, distorted by stone walls. He was telling the cadets what they faced.

Jame fumbled with the hooks that secured the back- and front-plates of the greaves, then remembered that she hadn't buckled the heel plates onto the articulated boots. Quick, quick...

Next the belt, to which the thigh guards were attached.

"Now what?" Rue indicated the padded gambeson and the equally padded ivory vest.

Should she have put on the former first? Too late now.

"The vest."

Rue helped her on with it and laced it up the back. Then she dropped the breast- and backplates of the cuirass over Jame's head. Below, Spare was ordering the cadets to the armory, then to the stables.

...arm harnesses, spiked shoulder guards, gauntlets...

Jame started to pick up the helmet, then remembered that she needed a weapon. Gaudaric hadn't sent her a sword because he knew that she already had one. It hung from a hook in its leather sheath in the corner, a nicely balanced, sharp-edged piece of steel with the wavy patterns down its blade of many foldings. Her lack of skill with it was legendary. As the doggerel verse went:

> *Swords are flying, better duck.*
> *Lady Jameth's run amuck.*

She had never yet managed to hang on to a sword throughout an entire engagement.

Beside it were her scythe-arms, those elegant double-pointed blades that functioned as extensions of her claws. Of the two weapons, Jame much preferred the latter, but they weren't intended for mounted combat. Reluctantly, she took down the sword and strapped its belt around her waist.

"Here." She gave Rue the shield and barding to carry, herself taking Death's-head's high, heavy saddle and bitless bridle from their racks. "We need to get out the South Gate before the cadets catch up with us."

Horses neighed in excitement behind them in the ward as they hurried down the deserted street.

Creak, creak, creak went Jame's leather armor. It might not be as heavy as steel plate, but it certainly was noisy. And stiff. *I'm a dragon, not a tortoise,* she told herself, beginning to sweat and pant as the saddle's weight dragged her down and its dangling stirrups tripped her up.

Meanwhile, she called silently to the rathorn, but received only sullen silence in reply. She had visited Death's-head as often as she could over the past year, but had had little to ask of him even though she sensed that he was growing bored and resentful. Now he was sulking.

Bel-tairi met them beyond the gate, over the bridge. Jame slung the saddle onto the Whinno-hir's back and tightened the girth as far as it would go but, designed for a much larger barrel, it hung loose. Rue grabbed the right stirrup as Jame swung herself up, then handed her the shield, bridle, and folded crupper while she balanced precariously.

"I don't think she can carry me too," the cadet said, stepping back. "You go on."

Jame looked down at her, remembering how Rue had longed to prove herself to the rest of the Knorth barracks. "You're sure?"

"Yes. Go."

She rode across the training field, into the dips and hollows carved by the Amar's overflow. From ahead of her came the sound of swift water, and of something noisily churning in it. Splashing around a curve, Bel knee-deep in the early spring runoff, she saw the rathorn in the shallows, vigorously rolling in the mud. He regained his feet with a snort and shook himself. His white coat was streaked with muck, his mane and tail tangled. Jame regarded him in dismay.

"Oh, no. Not now."

She shifted to dismount, and felt the saddle slide sideways under her. There was barely time to kick free her feet before she hit the water. Trinity, but it was cold, even so far from the mountains that had given it birth. She surfaced sputtering to find both rathorn and Whinno-hir watching her. Death's-head snorted again, as if in scornful laughter. Jame pushed dripping black hair out of her eyes and scowled at him.

"Come here, you."

At first she thought he was going to sidle away from her, but she must have put more command into her voice than she had thought. He stood, blowing with impatience, as she sluiced water over his shoulders and raked her claws through his unkempt hair. Beyond the ravine, out of sight, horses thundered past, the cadets riding to war. Quick, quick...

Death's-head accepted the saddle, bridle, and crupper with an ill grace, but his ears had twitched at the sound of hooves. Something was afoot, something interesting.

Jame swung up into the high saddle, feeling water drain down inside her armor and run out of the gap at her heels. She had barely gathered the reins when the rathorn was in motion. He trotted up the creek bed with his horn-crowned head held high and his nostrils flaring red, then clambered up its steep bank to the valley floor. The other riders were a cloud of dust to the west. Death's-head started after them at a canter that quickly grew into a gallop. Jame resisted the urge to clutch his mane, instead tightening her legs around his barrel. At the touch of her heels, he went even faster.

Some two miles from the camp, a mountain spur cut into the valley from the south while a recent massive landslide from the Rim pinched it to the north, leaving only a hundred feet clear between them. The cadets were racing for this bottleneck, the only place along the Betwixt where their inferior number might hold off the far larger Karnid horde.

But for how long? Jame wondered.

By now, hopefully, Brier had alerted Harn Grip-hard. The bulk of the Southern Host would come as soon as it could, but it would take time for a significant number to descend the Escarpment, and then how many horses had the cadets left them to reach this new battlefield?

Two miles for the cadets to cover, eight for the Karnids, but the former had spent a good half hour getting ready. Who would reach the gap first?

The mountain spur loomed ahead, its steep sides bristling with stunted trees and shrubs. Opposite it was a slope of rocky debris, reaching from the valley floor halfway up to a giant bite taken out of the Escarpment's rim. Sunlight climbed both. Beyond, westward, the sky was still dark enough to show scattered stars, although building clouds soon obscured them.

Ah. The cadets were pulling up just short of the gap, with no Karnid yet in sight. They had won their race, for whatever good that might do them.

Jame hauled back on the reins, but the rathorn only tossed his head in irritation, almost unseating her, and plunged into the Kencyrs' back ranks. Horses squealed, fighting to escape his rank scent. Some threw their riders and bolted back toward Kothifir. Others collided with their mates and fell in tangles of thrashing limbs.

"Sorry," said Jame to startled faces as she bucketed past. "Sorry, sorry, sorry..."

She emerged through the broken front line to face a crescent of nine senior randon who had turned to observe her precipitous arrival.

"I don't believe it," said the Caineron, scowling. "Where did she spring from?"

None of them looked pleased to see her, Ran Spare least of all.

"You should turn back, Lordan," he said. "This is no exercise."

There was a jostling among the riders. Timmon emerged on her left riding a palomino, Gorbel to her right on a sturdy dark bay. The Ardeth wore hardened leather with rhi-sar inserts over gilded chain mail; the Caineron, a full suit of unornamented black rhi-sar. Most of the other cadets had donned less, down to mere padded jackets, depending on the wealth of their respective houses. Jame began to feel overdressed. She also felt rising anger.

"Why the Caineron and Ardeth Lordan, but not the Knorth?"

Death's-head fidgeted under her. He wanted to get past these blockheads and at the enemy, whoever that might be. The officers' horses stirred uneasily.

"For one thing," said Ran Spare, "you see what effect that monster of yours has on our mounts. Are we to sacrifice the entire cavalry for one rider?"

He rode toward her as he spoke, calming his nervous mare with the touch of his hand. Death's-head's nostrils flared with interest. Pray Ancestors that she wasn't in season.

"For another, have you ever fought in that armor? I thought not. For some reason, you're also dripping wet. Worse, where is your helmet?"

Jame touched her bare face, shocked by memory. The helm with its fearsome guard of ivory teeth still lay on her bed in camp, where in her haste she had forgotten it. She hadn't even missed it until now.

Fool, she thought. *What* am *I doing here?*

The randon was beside her now, their mounts head to tail. The rathorn sniffed. The mare stood her ground, although her withers darkened with nervous sweat. "Most important, though, there is this." Spare spoke too softly now for anyone else to hear. "In the next hour, we may all die. Your lord brother survived Urakarn, otherwise no one would have known what happened to him or to the troops under his command. Someone must survive here too, to tell our story. Please, lady."

Timmon rose in his stirrups and pointed. "Here they come!"

Beyond the gap, the valley widened and turned toward the southwest. Black-clad riders appeared around the bend, filling the Betwixt from side to side as their front line swung across it. They seemed to bring the wings of night with them, under whose shadow they rode in a many-legged mass. Likewise, their hoofbeats rolled together into a continuous rumble like distant thunder and dust rose like smoke in their wake. Through rents in the latter, one could see something looming behind them that was neither the Escarpment nor any Apollyne peak. Black it was, high and wide enough to dominate the sky, although its snowbound summit was broken. Columns of steam rose above it from its hidden interior and its flanks were fissured with cracks that glowed red in the dusk of its shadow.

"'Black rock on the dry sea's edge,'" Gorbel growled, quoting one of Ashe's songs to the surprise of those close enough to hear. "'How many your dungeons swallowed. How few came out again.' D'you mean to tell me that that hulk is..."

"Urakarn," breathed Timmon. "Or a counterfeit of it, like a mirage."

Snow tumbled down from the heights and a cloud of ash belched up over its ramparts. Jame remembered the boiling lake and the seam of rising fire within the earth. Some moments later, the ground shuddered slightly underfoot, but any sound it might have made was swallowed by the rumble of the oncoming horde.

Jame watched the gray stallion in the vanguard. It really was Iron-jaw, she decided, who had been her father's war-horse. She remembered Tori daring her to ride the brute, and that bone-jarring fall, and Tori dragging her back through the fence, out from under those deadly, steel-shod hooves. Iron-jaw had always had an evil temper. Then Ganth had ridden him to death in the Haunted Lands, searching for the Dream-weaver, his lost love. When the stallion had come back as a haunt, the changer Keral had claimed him for his master, Gerridon.

. . . we can always feed you to his new war-horse . . .

Was that who rode Iron-jaw now?

The figure on the haunt stallion's back wore silver-gilt mail and black steel plate of an ornate, antique design that predated the Kencyrath's experience on Rathillien with the rhi-sar. A horned helm obscured his features. It occurred to Jame that, despite growing up in his house, she had never seen the Master's face clearly. He had always stood in the shadows, or behind her, or behind something else, such as those red, bridal ribbons. Tori had met him at least twice in his youth with the Southern Host but never face-to-face, if her experience of his dreams was to be believed. Only the Randir Matriarch Rawneth had had that dubious honor in the Moon Garden, but it was the changer Keral with whom she had mated, not Gerridon as she still believed.

How had she known one face from another?

How was Jame supposed to now?

"M'lord Caineron," said Ran Spare, "take the rocky slope. We can't afford to be outflanked. M'lord Ardeth, can you fortify that hill?"

It required someone who knew him to see the strain in Timmon's answering smile, but it wasn't cowardice. He hadn't yet proved himself to his house. This might be his last chance.

"With pleasure," he said, and wheeled his horse back into the crowd, followed by the Ardeth cadets.

Spare turned back to Jame. "Lady . . ."

Death's-head snorted and pawed the ground. When he tossed his head, he nearly pulled Jame out of the saddle. Spare tried to grab his bridle, but Jame knocked his hand away before the rathorn could take off his arm.

It comes to this, she thought.

Ever since she had first seen the gray stallion and had guessed who might be riding him, this fight had become personal. The Master had betrayed the entire Kencyrath, but his own house first, including her own hapless father. And she owed him for a miserable childhood which she still only partly remembered.

Yet doubts arose: what could a single rider do, even on such a mount as Death's-head? To make a sacrifice was one thing; to make a fool of oneself while doing so was another, and to what end?

Moreover, despite her suspicions, what could have possessed the Master to risk his person after so long lurking in the shadows— not that he was really in the light now with night roiling over his head, slashed by distant lightning. If he was here, he must think that there was no real risk. He meant to smash through the cadets and seize the camp before the Host could arrive to defend it. Meanwhile, he must believe that his puppet Prince Ton had overthrown King Krothen to become the Host's paymaster. To whom did the Host belong then, if not to him?

Jame didn't think it would be that simple, but the Master of Knorth was arrogant enough to believe that it was.

Thus her thoughts and emotions churned, underlaid with an unspoken fear: was she simply afraid?

The Karnids had seen them. They came on at a gallop that made the earth shake, Iron-jaw thundering before them with sparks under his hooves where steel met rock. Thousands of swords cleared their scabbards and flashed back the dawn light from under the boiling clouds of night.

In the next hour, we may all die.

At the very least, she might buy them some time.

"I'm sorry," she said to Spare. "He was Lord Knorth before he betrayed us all. This is house business."

With that, she put her heels to the rathorn's sides and he bolted forward, almost leaving her in midair.

They passed through the gap, hearing the cries behind them as the cadets formed ranks. They would hold their position as long as they could, but not follow, nor did Jame expect them to. The rathorn's hooves devoured the ground. She felt his back arch with each stride while the wind tore at her loosened hair.

Her shield was slung across her back. She slipped it down onto her left arm, truly feeling its weight for the first time. The rhi-sar lashings might be light, but the ironwood backing was not.

Iron-jaw lunged toward her. Jame remembered meeting him

in the soulscape, how he had nearly run down the foal that had been Death's-head, how she had grabbed his thick neck, swung up, and plunged her nails into his eye. Sure enough, the right socket was a scarred cavity weeping thick, dark blood. Blind on that side...

The space between the two equines was closing rapidly. Trinity, were they going to crash head on? The haunt was larger and heavier than the young rathorn, his hooves the size of platters. He loomed over them like a gray cliff.

At the last moment, Death's-head swerved to the right. As they hurtled past each other, the rathorn slashed at the haunt and its rider hammered down with a battle axe on Jame's raised shield.

Jame thought for a moment that he had broken her arm, but he had only driven the shield back to her shoulder, momentarily numbing it.

Death's-head turned faster than the haunt could and surged up on his right side. Jame finally remembered to draw her sword, but how was she supposed to manage it, the shield, and the rathorn all at once?

Have you ever fought in that armor? Spare had asked. *I thought not.*

Ah, well. Death's-head would do as he wanted. As always, he was her primary weapon.

She took the reins in her fingertips behind the shield. The haunt's rider hammered down on it again, chipping its ironwood rim. She could see the glint of his eyes on either side of his nasal guard and hear the hollow boom of laughter within his helm.

Iron-jaw turned to the left. Death's-head, following him, almost ran into a wall of rearing, lunging thorns. Jame saw that the black mares surrounded them in a circle, around which the Karnids streamed to throw themselves against the front rank of cadets. To either side, they were dismounting and swarming up the rocky slope to the north and the mountain spur to the south, to be met above by Gorbel's and Timmon's forces respectively. She glimpsed the Caineron Lordan in his black armor methodically chopping at *cheche*-covered heads as they rose to his level. On the other side, the Ardeth fought in a shimmer of gold, backlit by the rising sun.

Jame reined in Death's-head who, surprisingly, obeyed. Iron-jaw plunged ahead of them. Coming up on the haunt's left from behind, Jame saw the gleam of white ribs where the rathorn's nasal tusk had ripped open his side but not noticeably slowed him. She slashed at his hindquarters. He screamed in pain and rage. Jame shot past, and again pulled hard to the left to avoid the mares. Their wicked black heads snaked out to snap at the rathorn's barded flanks as he passed.

Iron-jaw cut to the inside and drew up level where he rammed his shoulder into his lighter opponent, lifting the rathorn off his feet. Jame was thrown up onto Death's-head's neck and only kept her seat by clinging to it. The gray haunt rounded on them. His head shot over the rathorn's as he tried to pin the white equine to his chest, the better to kick him to death with his steel-shod fore hooves. Ropes of slaver swung from his mouth into Jame's face. His white eye rolled at her. She stabbed at it, and the haunt reared back with a squeal, letting the rathorn drop. No fool although dead, he had already lost half of his sight to her.

Somehow Jame stayed in the saddle and Death's-head regained his feet, stumbling but not falling.

Meanwhile, the haunt nearly toppled over backward into the ring of shrieking mares. His rider was still off balance when he thudded down. The other's shield had jerked up. Jame came in to the left and hacked at the exposed wrist. The rider's gauntlet flew off, taking the shield with it . . . and his hand too? Where the vambrace ended, there was nothing.

. . . a hand, reaching out between red ribbons to claim her, her knife chopping frantically at it . . .

I cost him that, Jame thought. *It is Gerridon after all.*

The reality of it almost took her breath away. Whatever she had suspected, to find herself actually at sword's point with the Master of Knorth seemed too fantastic to believe. Scrollsmen would sing about this encounter, however it ended, for he was a creature of legend. But then so was she. Jamethiel Priest's-bane, daughter of Ganth Gray Lord and the Dream-weaver, sister of Torisen Black Lord, Lordan of Ivory . . .

"Ha!" she said, and slashed at him again.

He turned in his saddle to meet her blade with the edge of his axe. With a flick of his wrist, he disarmed her.

Jame dropped her shield, kicked free from her stirrups, and threw herself at him. The axe's return stroke hissed over her head. She felt his strength as she grappled with him, but also his unsettled mass shifting. Then they were both in the air, falling, she on top, his hot breath roaring in her ear. Jame twisted to lead with the spike set on her left shoulder guard. She thought she heard a startled cry just before she crashed down on him. The rhi-sar tooth scraped against the nasal guard, then plunged into the helmet's eye slit. The next instant her weight slammed into the steel shell, and something snapped.

The impact took away both Jame's breath and, for a moment, her wits. She regained the latter to find herself lying on her back, staring up at the ragged sky. What had happened? Where was Gerridon? Silence spread about her, the clash of arms and more distant cries dying away one by one. Was she going deaf? What had broken? Sweet Trinity, not her neck...

Hooves scraped the ground close by, and she found herself looking up the length of two black, slender, equine legs. The thorn's head descended. It sniffed at her, stirring the lock of hair that had fallen into her eyes, and bared its fangs behind curling lips. Like Death's-head, it was a carnivore and had carrion breath. Would the rathorn ivory at her throat protect her? Then it sneezed in her face and stretched its neck to prod something that lay beside her with a nasal tusk. Metal rattled. The thorn snorted and withdrew.

Cautiously, Jame turned her head. There lay the Master's horned helmet, scored where the rhi-sar tooth had entered it. Its mangled eye slit seemed to stare back at her, dark and empty.

She started to rise, and gasped as pain lanced through her left shoulder. Finding that arm limp, she struggled up onto the other elbow. The rest of the black enameled armor sprawled on the ground nearby, also tenantless, held together by various buckles and straps.

Iron-jaw was gone too. Whether he had vanished like his master or simply walked away, she didn't know. Death's-head remained, looking about curiously with head high and ears pricked. The battle had stopped in its tracks. Jame had the impression that the Karnids had all turned to stare at what remained of their fallen prophet, but now their attention was fixed on something to the west. She craned to follow their gaze.

Urakarn still loomed behind the rags of night, but its face had changed. A massive column of ash billowed above it, stabbed through by lightning bolts, and fiery chasms had opened down its flanks. As Jame watched, the eastern face of the mountain bulged and slid. Another explosion belched clouds of steam near the summit, and another, and another. Everything was in motion, rising or falling, to a sound like that of distant thunder. The Betwixt appeared to be in the direct path of that vast, roiling collapse. Just when it seemed that a wall of debris would come rolling around the valley's western curve, the sun lifted over the mountain spur to the east and night rolled back, taking the shades of Urakarn with it.

The sky growled and the ground briefly trembled. A trickle of smoke rose on the far horizon from a mountain hidden by the curve of the earth.

The Karnids stirred and muttered. From where Jame lay, she could see mostly shifting black legs, of horses, of men. All seemed to reach the same conclusion at once. With that, they turned and trudged off westward, away from the battlefield, toward the ruins of their home.

Jame rose slowly, carefully, as if one joint at a time. Her left arm hung dead at her side and her left shoulder slumped forward within her shell of rhi-sar armor. All around her, Karnids were retreating, skirting the circle of combat as if the ground there were tainted. No one so much as looked at her.

"That's it?" she asked Death's-head.

The rathorn snorted and shook himself.

When she turned to the east, the sun blinded her. The two ridges and the gap between them appeared to be full of waving figures. Their voices seemed far away and faint, but she thought that they were cheering. Jame waited for them, holding her arm by the elbow close against her side, feeling cold and sick.

II

THE CAMP SURGEON told her that she had broken her collarbone.

"It's nothing serious," he said cheerfully. "A healer could set it right in a few days, but we don't have one. Say, two weeks in a sling with plenty of *dwar* sleep, four or five weeks without it."

Then he had given her a sleeping draft, which she had hardly needed. It seemed an age since she had last closed her eyes— twenty days, if one went by the calendar.

Toward dusk, she woke in her dimly lit quarters with Jorin curled up beside her. Rue had propped her upright with pillows to ease the pain in her shoulder. Sounds of celebration filtered through curtains drawn across the windows. She gathered that the rest of the Host had returned to camp during the day, following Harn Grip-hard who had ridden up on a donkey, the only mount he could find, as they had quitted the pass.

"I see that you've done it again," he had said to her. She still wasn't sure exactly what he had meant.

Her mouth was very dry, her lips chapped. "Water," she croaked, hoping that Rue was nearby. Instead, a dark figure loomed up beside her holding a cup of water.

"Here. Drink," said Harn. "I sent your servant off to enjoy the festivities. The Feast of Fools has been going on all day, Overcliff, Undercliff, and in the camp. You, however, got your foolery in early. What possessed you to take on the entire Karnid horde single-handed?"

Jame thought that she had had her reasons, but none of them sounded convincing now.

Harn drew up a chair and sat down beside her. Wood groaned under his weight while his knees peaked halfway up his chest.

"Never had a broken bone before, have you?" he said. "It's disheartening. Everything will seem worse than it is until you get used to the idea, and by then the bone will have knit."

Jame sipped the water, tasting the tang of pomegranate juice. "How many casualties?" she asked.

"In the Betwixt? A dozen wounded, but none killed. The cadets had too strong a position, and their line held. On the other hand, the Karnids must have lost several hundred. We'll never know for sure since they took their dead with them. Given the way the valley funnels there, most never got within striking distance."

Jame regarded him. *Everything will seem worse....* "You have something else to tell me, don't you?"

Harn looked away, then back at her. "While you were gone, I got a message from Blackie. He wanted to know what had happened to Brier Iron-thorn. As far as I knew, nothing had, until I asked her. She said that her bond to the Highlord had broken, and re-formed with you."

Jame sighed. She had known this was coming, but had hoped that, somehow, it would never arrive. "It was an accident," she said. "Brier was very upset when the seeker's baby died in her arms, and Tori was too far away to help her."

"Whereas you were right there. Yes, I understand. Hopefully Blackie will too, when he hears the full story."

A moment's silence fell between them. Both were thinking that Torisen's responses weren't always rational, and that this one had sprung from the heart of his deepest insecurities.

Harn clapped his big hands on his knees with an air of someone facing up to the worst. "There's more. He's ordered you to return to Gothregor. Immediately."

Jame stared at him. "But I still have sixty days, all of spring, left of my year at Kothifir!"

"The randon will understand a summons from your lord—I hope. You'll take Iron-thorn, of course. And your ten-command as an escort, on extended duty. Cheer up," he added, seeing her expression. "However mad your actions this morning, you aren't exactly leaving under a cloud."

Her eyes dropped to a little pile of paper scraps on the floor. She remembered waking earlier that day to find third-year cadet Char standing by her bed, glowering down at her.

"D'you still have that note I slipped under your door?" he had asked.

She had fished it out from under her pillow and mutely handed it to him. He had torn it up. Then he had left without another word. Just now, waking, she had thought that it had all been a dream. Apparently not.

Harn stood up, seeming to scrape the ceiling and fill the room. "For all Blackie's histrionics, you needn't leave until tomorrow. Go back to sleep."

In the doorway, he passed Brier. The Southron stepped into the apartment, glanced after him, then raised an eyebrow at Jame.

"Tell the others to pack," Jame said, leaning back against her pillows with a sigh. "We're going home."

⊰⊱ CHARACTERS ⊰⊱

Addy—Shade's gilded swamp adder, to whom she is bound

Adric—Lord Ardeth

Ahack—in the Wastes, the west wind

Amantine, Princess—Kruin's sister, Krothen's aunt

Amberley—a Kendar, Brier's former lover

Anooo—in the Wastes, the north wind

Apollynes—the mountain range parallel to the Rim

Arrin-ken—catlike third of the Three People

Ashe—a haunt singer

Awl—a Randir senior randon

Bane—Jame and Tori's half-brother, who may be alive or dead

Bear—Sheth's brain-damaged brother

Bel-tairi—a Whinno-hir

Blackie—the common name for Torisen

Brier Iron-thorn—a Kendar randon cadet, first bound to Torisen and then to Jame

Burnt Man, the—the one of the Four who represents fire

Burr—Torisen's Kendar servant

Byrne—Gaudaric's grandson

Caldane—Lord Caineron

Cella, Lady—cousin to King Krothen

Char—a third-year Knorth cadet

Corrudin—Caldane's uncle and advisor

Corvine—a Knorth oath-breaker, bound to the Randir

Cron—a Knorth Kendar

Cully—one of Torisen's first command

Damson—one of Jame's ten-command

Dani—Shandanielle, Lady Professionate

Dar—one of Jame's ten-command

Dari—Lord Ardeth's would-be heir

Death's-head—a rathorn

Dorin—grandson of the Kothifir high priest

Ean—Gaudaric's son-in-law

Eaten One, the—the one of the Four who represents water

Erim—one of Jame's ten-command

Evensong—Gaudaric's daughter, Ean's wife, Byrne's mother

Falling Man, the—the one of the Four who represents air

Fang—a Waster girl who has ended up in Kothifir

Fash—a Caineron cadet

Four, the—the elementals of Rathillien

Frost—the Randir barracks commander

Ganth Gray Lord—father of Jame and Torisen

Gaudaric—Master Iron Gauntlet

Genjar—Caldane's son, Commandant of the Host

Gerridon—Master of Knorth, arch-traitor of the Kencyrath

Gnasher—wolver king of the Deep Weald

Gorbel—Caldane's lordan

Graykin—Jame's servant, sometime Master Intelligencer

Greshan—Jame and Tori's uncle, Ganth's brother

Grimly, the wolver—a wolver of the Grimly Holt

Hangnail—a spy

Hull—Torisen's chief forester

Granny Sit-by-the-Fire—an Old Pantheon goddess of the Wastes

Harn Grip-hard—commandant of the South Host

Index—a scrollsman who knows where everything is

Iron-jaw—first Ganth's war-horse, then Gerridon's haunt war-horse

Ishtier—former high priest of Tai-tastigon

Jame—Jamethiel Priest's-bane, sister of Torisen Black Lord

Jamethiel Dream-weaver—consort of Gerridon, Master of Knorth;
      mother of Jame and Torisen

Jedrak—temporary lord of the Jaran

Jorin—Jame's ounce

Kalan—a Kothifiran seeker
Kells—herbalist at Gothregor
Kenan—Lord Randir
Keral—a fallen changer, servant of the Master
Killy—one of Jame's ten-command
Kindrie Soul-walker—a healer; cousin of Jame and Torisen
Kin-Slayer—Torisen's sword
Kirien—a scrollswoman; Lordan of Randir
Kroaky—young Krothen
Krothen—god-king of Kothifir
Kruin—former king of Kothifir; Krothen's father
Lady Professionate—Dani or Shandanielle; a guild lord
Lainoscopes—king of Langadine
Lanek—young son of Kalan
Lanielle—a Langadine seeker, granddaughter of Laurintine
Laurintine—a Langadine seeker
Lord Artifice—a Kothifiran guild lord
Lord Merchandy—a Kothifiran guild lord
Lurcher—Jame's moa
Marc—Marcarn, Jame's Kendar friend
Mercer—Lord Merchandy
Merry—one of Torisen's Kendar
Mint—one of Jame's ten-command
Mother Ragga—the Earth Wife; one of the Four
Near, Prince—Princess Amantine's husband
Needham—Master Silk Purse
Niall—one of Jame's ten-command
Onyx-eyed, Marigold—commander of the Knorth barracks
Pereden—Timmon's father; Adric's son
Prophet, the—leader of the Karnids
Quill—one of Jame's ten-command
Quirl—Corvine's son
Qrink—Master Paper Crown, Kalan's brother-in-law
rathorn—a carnivorous bi-corn
Rain—replacement for Storm

Rawneth—the Randir Matriarch

Rose Iron-thorn—a Caineron; Brier Iron-thorn's mother

Rowan—Torisen's steward

Rue—one of Jame's ten-command, her servant

Ruso—Lord Artifice

Shade—a Randir cadet

Shandanielle—Dani, Lady Professionate

Sheth Sharp-tongue—the Caineron war-leader; former
    commandant of Tentir

Shrike—a third-year Randir cadet

Shuu—in the Wastes, the south wind

Snow—replacement for Rain

Spare—second-in-command of the Knorth barracks

Storm—Torisen's war-horse

Talisman—Jame's identity as a Tastigon thief

Taur—director of Mount Alban, a former randon

Tenebrae—mountain range to the east of the Wastes

Timmon—the Ardeth Lordan

Tishooo—the Falling Man, the Old Man, the east wind

Ton—prince of Kothifir, son of Amantine

Torisen Black Lord—Tori, Blackie, Highlord of the Kencyrath

Trishien—Jaran Matriarch

Twizzle—Gorbel's pet pook

Uraks—mountain range to the west of the Wastes

Vedia—Kothifiran Old Pantheon goddess of healing

Whinno-hir—one of the equines who have followed the Kencyrath
    since the beginning

Yce—a wolver pup